HARD SLEEPER

JENNIFER SCHEEL BUSHMAN
&
JEAN ARTLEY SZYMANSKI

LOST
COAST
PRESS
Fort Bragg
California

Hard Sleeper
Copyright © 2003
by Jennifer Scheel Bushman
and Christopher John Szymanski

Lost Coast Press
155 Cypress Street
Fort Bragg, CA 95437
(800) 773-7782
www.hardsleeper.com
www.cypresshouse.com

Disclaimer
This novel is a work of fiction. Any references to real events, businesses, organizations and locales are intended only to give the fiction a sense of reality and authenticity. Except for well-known historical figures, any resemblance to actual persons, living or dead, is entirely coincidental.

Cover Design: Chuck Hathaway / Mendocino Graphics

Library of Congress Cataloging-in-Publication Data
Szymanski, Jean Artley, 1944-1998
  Hard sleeper / Jean Artley Szymanski
  and Jennifer Scheel Bushman.-- date
    1st ed.
    p. cm.
  ISBN 1-882897-73-0 (alk. paper)
  1. China--Fiction. I. Bushman, Jennifer Scheel, 1969 - II.
Title.
PS3619.Z96 H37 2003
813'.6--dc21   2002152541

2   4   6   8   10 9   7   5   3   1

Acknowledgements

My mother, Jean Artley Szymanski, and I wrote *Hard Sleeper* while she was battling breast cancer. We wrote with a shared passion and a desire to do something together. Sadly, my mother passed away shortly after we completed *Hard Sleeper,* but with the determination that she always taught me was the only way to see my dreams come true, *Hard Sleeper* was published five years after her death.

I want to thank my mother for always believing in me and encouraging my ideas, no matter how farfetched. I also want to thank her for being such a wonderful role model as she aspired to become and do what she loved. You will always be in my heart, Mom.

I want to thank my stepfather, Christopher Szymanski, who believed in this book and was with me every step of the way in getting *Hard Sleeper* published. It couldn't have happened without him. I am eternally grateful.

I want to thank my husband, Kevin, who was understanding and supportive throughout the long process of writing and publishing a novel. Thank you, too, for letting me cry on your shoulder night after night after my mother died, and for saying that you loved and missed her too.

I also want to thank all the many people in the United States, China, and elsewhere, who sacrificed valuable time to help us with this book. Your advice, assistance, and generosity are greatly appreciated.

Lastly, I want to thank my friends and relatives who continued to believe, throughout the years, that I would eventually become a published novelist. I love you all.

Jennifer Scheel Bushman

Publisher's Note

Hard Sleeper is a story of China old and new, a story of individuals caught up in an intense personal drama set against the backdrop of dramatic historical events that tore apart and reshaped modern China.

The book was co-authored by Jean Szymanski, a Foreign Service officer who spoke Chinese and served as a diplomat in the U.S. Embassy in Beijing, and her daughter, Jennifer Bushman. The two finished the book during the final year of Jean's life, as she battled advanced breast cancer.

While writing *Hard Sleeper,* Jean was undergoing intense chemotherapy and radiation treatment, and Jennifer was pregnant with her first child. Jean Szymanski never wavered from her commitment to finishing this book, even though writing and reading became very difficult. Jean and Jennifer's love of telling a good story, and their appreciation of the complexity of Chinese culture and history, show very clearly in this intriguing story.

Jean and Jennifer finished the book just two months before Jean died. *Hard Sleeper* became a lasting gift of love, time shared together, and a dream come true. We are proud to be able to present this fine work of fiction for your enjoyment. A portion of the proceeds will be donated to cancer-prevention research, in hopes of helping conquer an illness that has shortened the lives of so many talented individuals.

The lines quoted before the Prologue were written by Wang Wei, one of China's classical Tang Dynasty (A.D. 618–907) poets. The source of the translation is listed at the end of the book.

For our husbands,
Chris and Kevin, with love

HARD SLEEPER

All year I stay alone in my bedroom dreaming of
Mountain Pass, remembering our separation.
No swallow comes with letters in its claws.
I see only the new moon like the eyebrow of a moth.

— Wang Wei
Eighth century

PEKING, 1936

On the night of April 20, 1936, a grisly murder took place in Peking.

Near midnight, a neighbor heard shouts behind the walls of a compound belonging to an American missionary family. The neighbor, a Chinese merchant, remembered this only when questioned later. At the time, he hadn't thought it important. A noodle vendor, who had spent his entire day's earnings gambling and getting drunk, had paused at a street corner to sleep off the effects of the rice wine before going home. Later, learning of the murder, he told friends that he remembered hearing running footsteps and the sounds of a rickshaw on what was usually a nearly deserted lane so late at night.

The missionary home was not well guarded. The son, sixteen, was away with friends, spending the night in a temple in the Western Hills. The fifteen-year-old daughter was asleep in her room. The Number One Boy—a mainstay of even the smallest household—the cook, and the gatekeeper had slipped out to join the nightly gambling at a small market nearby, the same place the noodle vendor had lost his day's income. The children's elderly amah had retired to the servants' quarters and fallen asleep. The family's old dog had died the previous year.

The missionary couple, Cyrus and Della McPherson, sat up late, arguing. Their quarrel had not cleared the air, and so, still hoping to resolve their differences, they had postponed going to bed. Both tried to read, she with an occasional sniff and ragged breath and tears dried on her face, he with a scowl. Preoccupied with their thoughts, they didn't hear the muffled footsteps crossing the uneven cobblestones in the courtyard; they heard nothing until they looked up and saw someone in the doorway.

The house was old, a Chinese courtyard house in a secluded neighborhood east of the yellow-roofed Forbidden City—the old imperial palace. Previously, the McPherson house had belonged to a Chinese family of middling means who had passed it down through several generations. Thirty years earlier, this family had inherited money from a childless uncle and bought a better house. Careless with their newfound wealth, they sold the old house at a low price to a missionary board of trustees in far-off America.

Even the dim, forgiving light of two low-wattage bulbs in the main hall, now the McPhersons' sitting room, failed to hide the shabbiness of the missionaries' furnishings. American chairs shrouded in faded cretonne marked the outer perimeters of the room. A tattered, almost colorless patterned rug partially covered the scuffed wooden floor. Badly colored, framed reproductions of religious paintings and photographs of missionary groups hung halfway up the walls under high ceilings that had been designed for tall Chinese cabinets.

Besides the bare bones of the room itself, the only other Chinese item in the shabby room was a blue-and-white Ming Dynasty bowl from the fifteenth-century reign of Cheng Hua. It sat on a carved wooden table next to a stack of books, as if left carelessly one day and then forgotten. In the room's dim interior, the glaze on the bowl's porcelain surface glowed as if from an inner light. The design, stylized and repetitive, was floral, grayish-blue against a blue-white surface. A friend who collected Chinese art had given Della the bowl, but no one in the family fully understood its beauty, rarity, or value.

The house was quiet except for the ticking of a Seth Thomas clock and the occasional turning of a page. In her room at the opposite end of the compound, the young daughter stirred and mumbled in her sleep because a spray of blossoms from a flowering plum tree had brushed against the oiled paper lattice of her window. In the servants' quarters nearby, the old amah dozed sitting up on a bench. She had been waiting for the cook, the gatekeeper, and the Number One Boy to return and share whatever gossip they had picked up in the market.

A footstep creaking on the floorboards just outside the sitting room door made Cyrus look up. The lights in the room were so dim that they cast long shadows, one of which fell across the page Della was reading. Startled, she too looked up.

Amah later claimed to have dreamed of shouted oaths and dripping blood—a story no one believed. The young daughter woke suddenly, not knowing what had roused her. She lay for a long time in the dark, wondering if she had imagined the scream that seemed to linger in her ears. She felt frightened. The branch from the plum tree outside her window again brushed against the latticed wood, a familiar sound now somehow menacing. The girl pulled her padded quilt up tightly around her chin. After a while, she fell asleep again.

The next morning, the Number One Boy crossed the courtyard, stretching and yawning in the early sunlight. A dark red spot on the paving stones caught his eye. He stooped, peered more closely, and a line appeared between his eyebrows. He dabbed at the spot with his finger, sniffed at it, then scrambled to his feet, making a frightened sound. He glanced up, as if something had fallen from the sky, then wiped his hand on his pant leg. Frowning, he made his way down the passage to the sitting room, where, he had noted earlier, a light still burned.

Now he entered the room cautiously—not noisily, propping open the double doors and humming or singing as he usually did. He tiptoed forward, noticing that the lamp had burned so low that it gave barely a yellow glow. The sunlight sparkling in through the windows and the open door behind him was far stronger. It cast spots of light that reflected off the glass of the framed pictures, and created a bright oblong that slashed across the room, revealing an overturned chair and a smashed blue-and-white bowl.

He trod on Cyrus' body before he saw it, then looked down and gasped—the body was separated from its head. Della's body, also headless, lay alongside it. Dark blood pooled under both, and had congealed in the terrible wounds.

The Number One Boy felt something rising in his throat—a scream, vomit. Clapping a hand over his mouth, he lurched out into the courtyard and sank to his knees. It was several seconds before he realized that the sound he heard was his own voice. It was loud and frightened, and caused the other servants and the young daughter to come running.

CHAPTER 1

PRESENT-DAY CHINA

I first saw the two women, one middle-aged and Chinese, the other elderly and American, when they boarded the train in Chengdu. They stood close together, not quite touching, yet seeming to present a common face to the world. As I watched, they appeared briefly on the platform, then mounted the steps and disappeared inside, the younger one holding the elder woman's arm to help her up the stairs.

I watched them closely, not wanting to lose sight of them. Beside me, the train hissed sharply, making me jump. It jerked and clanged, stopped, and jerked again. I glanced at my watch. Oh, God, where was he? I thought, scanning the crowded platform, looking for one Chinese in a throng. My Chinese interpreter and guide had promised he could get me a last-minute ticket in a sleeping car, a nearly impossible task. He knew someone at the ticket office, he said. "Great," I'd told him, and followed blindly while he steered me past the barrier — saying something to the guards at the gate — planted me on the platform, and promised to come right back.

The train jerked forward again. I hopped from one foot to the other. This wasn't going to work after all, I thought. The two women had boarded the train and I was going to miss it. A piercing whistle made me whip around and caused a woman next to me to frown and put her hands over her ears. Only a few feet behind me, my Chinese interpreter pushed through the crowd, favoring everyone with a huge, excited grin. He waved a piece of paper at me.

"Oh, thank God," I cried, shoving myself between a man and woman to reach his side. "You miracle worker — you got the ticket." The train inched forward again. "Oh, hurry, hurry," I said.

The interpreter pulled me through the crowd, pushing people out of the way, chattering all the while about knowing this person and that person, and finally got me a seat.

"It's not only in the same car, but, listen to this… in the same row of bunks," he said. His grin couldn't have stretched any farther.

The train began to roll forward. I jumped at the nearest steps, scrambled aboard, and hung on. Clutching the ticket in one hand, I waved to the interpreter with the other as he trotted alongside, waving and calling out for me to keep in touch.

"I'll call you from Beijing. I promise!" I screeched, remembering that he had joined the ranks of many urban Chinese who had the latest model cell phone, the critically important status symbol of the New China. People standing on the platform waved to departing friends and relatives. The train passed the end of the platform. The interpreter stopped and waved, a receding figure in the crowd. I gave one last wave, then turned around, plunged through a doorway, and found myself in the narrow aisle of a compartmented sleeping car. Stopping a moment to catch my breath, I put out a hand to brace myself, and was immediately confronted by a uniformed female attendant.

I had never been on a Chinese train before. I didn't speak Chinese, and couldn't read my ticket. Clutching my backpack, trying to keep my balance against the train's convulsive movements, I held up the ticket so the attendant could see it. She gave it a quick, practiced glance, shouted at me in Chinese, and gestured roughly toward the back of the car, at the same time snapping her fingers, gesturing for me to give her the ticket.

I handed it over. "But I don't know what you're telling me," I said. "I don't understand Chinese."

Instead of replying, the attendant pocketed my ticket and handed me a piece of plastic.

"What's this?" I demanded. "Where's my ticket? How do I find my seat?"

She dismissed me with a hard stare and turned her back. I was sure she had never cared for foreigners, especially Americans.

Confused and annoyed, I pushed my way through a bevy of Chinese passengers crowded by the door, stepped out over the couplings, and entered the next car.

I realized I was blocking the way of several Chinese just behind me, and stood back to allow them through. As they surged around me, laden with suitcases and shopping bags, one young man separated himself from the mass and asked in perfect English, "May I help you, miss?"

Feeling relieved to have some help, I showed him my plastic chit and he said, "That's for hard sleeper class. Look, this is the number of your car, this is the number of your bunk, and this character means you have the middle bunk." He gave me a nice smile. "Lucky." He adjusted his shoulder bag and said, "Follow me."

He led me through a series of identical compartments with three-tiered bunk beds close together, which made me think of the hold of a crowded refugee ship. I hadn't yet learned that most Chinese regard hard sleeper class as relatively expensive and desirable, and soft sleeper—first-class sleeping compartments—an unobtainable luxury. Mostly, I was aware of the narrowness of the aisles and the cramped spaces between the bunks. The top bunks couldn't have been more than three feet below the ceiling.

The compartments buzzed with activity, as people heaved suitcases onto upper bunks or spread out their belongings on the lower ones. Some had already lit cigarettes and were chattering with neighbors. Others settled down at small tables under the windows, or peered into bright-patterned thermoses that contained hot water for tea.

A loudspeaker blared the theme to *Davy Crockett*, the 1950s American television series. Though I was too young to have watched the original show, I had seen pictures of actor Fess Parker in his coonskin cap, an incongruous image to conjure up on a train in the interior of China.

Holding my free hand over my ear as we passed the loudspeaker unit by the doorway, I followed the young man into the next compartment. "Here you are," he said, giving me another smile, and disappearing down the length of the car.

I saw the two women right away. They sat on a lower bunk. The elderly American rummaged through a burgundy-colored nylon bag. The

Chinese woman held a hand mirror and combed her hair. They looked up at me as I entered the compartment. At least I've found them, I thought. I mentally threw a kiss to the Chinese interpreter, and glanced down at the indecipherable mark on the plastic chit, which meant I had the middle bunk between the two women. Perfect, I thought.

Jane McPherson, the old American woman, gave her nylon bag a brisk pat and raised her head. Her faded blue eyes met mine and looked at me with puzzlement. I smiled and nodded, and Jane raised her chin in reply. At first glance, I thought she almost looked Chinese: she had the frail, chicken-bone thinness of an old Chinese woman. Her fine features trembled in an almost arrogant disregard of her surroundings. She wore a blue polyester pantsuit that might have come from a Chinese market. Then, peering closer, I could see clearly that she was wholly Caucasian. Her nose was slightly beaked, her chin sharp, her white hair slightly curly. The faintest of freckles from some long-ago sun were discernible under her eyes.

Di Meihua, the Chinese woman beside her, was pretty for her age. Her movements were graceful. Her skin was fair, as if she had lived a life of leisure and had always stayed out of the sun, belying her bad teeth and the roughened hands folded in her lap. Her hair was black without a touch of gray, and had a slight curl from a perm. Her face was without wrinkles, and her eyebrows were those of an ancient Chinese beauty—finely drawn and high. Her lips were thin, red lipstick her only make-up. She was neatly dressed in a buttoned-up red cardigan sweater and black slacks, ankle-length nylon stockings, and flat shoes. A triangular shard of blue-and-white porcelain ringed with silver and attached to a silver chain hung down the front of the red sweater, and trembled with her every movement.

Jane smiled, showing strong yellowing teeth. "Hullo," she said. When she smiled, her eyes creased into slits.

"Hi. I guess I'm sitting here," I said, patting the bunk above the women's heads.

"You an American?" Jane asked.

I nodded. "Yeah. Coincidence, huh?"

"Coincidence, nothing. I understand they tend to pile all us foreigners together." Jane peered up at me. I imagined I looked like a typical twenty-something American woman in designer jeans and a fashionable haircut, clutching rather than wearing a North Face Gortex backpack against a T-shirt that proclaimed I RACED FOR THE CURE to aid breast cancer research. "You're a tall young woman, aren't you?"

Jane gave Mei a tap on the arm and said something in rapid Chinese, and both women looked me over, making me feel self-conscious. Mei smiled at me, and I suddenly felt more at ease. Jane hitched herself over on the bunk and spoke to Mei, who also moved over.

"Please sit down here," Jane said, "at least until it's time to go to bed. You can't very well sit up there, legs dangling over the edge." She chuckled to herself. Her laugh was full and throaty, the laugh of a much younger woman. "You can help us guard the seat," she said. "I'm told others will come and sit here during the day even though it's my bed." She gestured toward Mei. "She has that bunk way up there. They put you in between us."

"Oh, I'm sorry. You want to trade?"

"It's not your fault."

"I'll take the top bunk. I don't mind."

"You're a dear," Jane said. "Come and sit down here with us."

This is a good start, I thought; I had been able to do them a favor, and was encouraged by their friendliness as I eyed the bunk that hugged the ceiling. I didn't mind scrambling up to the top, but wondered how much sleep I would get; there seemed to be too little room to turn over.

Oh well, I thought, slinging my backpack onto the upper bunk and sinking down beside the two women — the old American by the window, the Chinese woman in the middle, and me next to the aisle.

As the train picked up speed, I held on to the metal frame of the bunk and stared at the floor, wondering if it would be okay to put my feet up on the bunk and get more comfortable. The loudspeaker music stopped abruptly. A man's voice speaking rapid Chinese filled the car. An attendant entered the compartment and engaged in a spirited, high-pitched conversation with one of the other passengers. The women next to me began talking to each other in Chinese, but all I could understand was the word "Beijing." On the next set of bunks just behind us, a Chinese couple chatted away. To my untrained ear, their words blended with those of my seatmates and with the sounds from the loudspeaker. There were only sounds, no meaning. Feeling like a total alien, I began to think about the thirty-four-hour train ride, and wondered if I could convince these women to tell their story.

Two days earlier, I had stood on the grounds of Du Fu's cottage, a Chengdu tourist attraction honoring an eighth-century Tang Dynasty poet. A thatched cottage on the site was supposed to be where Du Fu had actually lived all those centuries ago. Now, the grounds were extensive and beautifully landscaped. I stood on the path, ignoring the Chinese and foreign tourists pushing past me, and clutched a book of Tang Dynasty poems that my colleague, Tim, had given me. I tried to remember how excited Tim and I had been, knowing that China was a "hot topic." I was a field producer for a small documentary film company based in Minneapolis. Tim and I were sent to China to check out possible story ideas. But the trip had thus far been unsuccessful, and Tim had decided to travel to Dali, the Burma-China border, and the foothills of the Himalayas, where drug trafficking was rampant. He wanted to do a story on how drugs were making a comeback into China after having been virtually wiped out by Mao, but I couldn't bring myself to like the idea. I thought the topic was too broad. I wanted to do something that dealt with China's history and personal struggle in recent times. Even after I told him this, Tim was determined to go, so we decided to split up.

"I'll meet you in Beijing in a week…" Tim consulted his watch, and we set a date and a place where we would meet, and then fly out of Beijing and back to the States together.

At Du Fu's cottage, where I thought I could find inspiration, I closed my eyes and tried to let the creative juices flow. I let the cool wind brush against my face, and strained my ears to hear in it a whisper to guide me in the right direction.

"Did you hear about the American lady who found her long-lost daughter? Pretty interesting."

"Huh?" I blinked into the sun and saw my Chinese interpreter and guide standing in front of me.

"No. What about it—are you saying there's a story there?" I shaded my eyes from the sun.

Trying to look cool and American, the young interpreter wedged his fingers into the band of his brand-new jeans and scuffled his foot around on the path. A star-struck kid with dreams of Hollywood, he loved the wages the Americans paid him, and saw me as the first rung on the ladder of his ambition. I was fond of him, thought him cute and likeable and an awful lot of help, but wondered if he also worked for the People's Republic and had been hired to keep an eye on us. I wasn't too concerned, though, as I felt I had nothing to hide.

He told me, "Maybe I have found a good story."

I took his arm and led him off the path to a garden seat. "Tell me."

"The American woman lost her baby daughter long ago. A half-American baby. It was during the Anti-Japanese War. Now she has found her. Here in Chengdu."

I squinted in the sun and thought about it. "How old's the daughter?" I asked.

"Somewhere around sixty," he guessed.

"Hmmm."

"Yes. It was in the paper, but it was in Chinese, so you couldn't read it." He sprawled on the bench next to me, sunlight glinting off the metal buttons on his jeans. He spoke English well and he knew it.

"How did she come to have a Chinese daughter? Was there a husband? A lover? Was this some kind of wartime romance?"

He smiled. "I don't know. You want me to find out more?"

I returned his smile. "I'll love you to death if you do."

He threw me a strange look. He was almost Americanized, but not quite.

Later, the Chinese interpreter tracked me down at my hotel. He waved a newspaper clipping and talked so excitedly he got his English mixed up.

"Tell me, tell me," I said, and pulled him into the hotel bar and ordered him a beer. "Slow down," I told him.

"The newspaper story is nothing." He read from the clipping, quickly translating it aloud. It said an American woman named Jane McPherson Cahill had searched for years to find a daughter she had lost when China was at war with Japan. The daughter had been born in Shanghai in 1938. Finally, the woman had enlisted the help of the Chinese embassy in Washington, and they in turn had contacted the Foreign Ministry. After that, according to the People's Republic, it was a snap. The Chinese government found the daughter and helped stage a family reunion.

He shoved the clipping into his breast pocket. "There is much more to come."

The waiter set our beers on the table. I pushed his glass toward him. "Drink up," I said. "What do you mean, 'more to come?'" He took a large gulp and wiped his mouth. Speaking choppily, he said, "In the nineteen-thirties," then something quick and hissing in Chinese, and then "murdered," he said in English. "Two missionaries butchered in their own house. Someone chopped off their heads." He drew his forefinger across his throat.

I made a face. "What in the world are you talking about?"

"Jane McPherson Cahill was their daughter. She was in the house the night these people were murdered. She was just a child at the time."

I drew in a breath as goose bumps rose on my legs.

He said, "In 1936 the police blamed it on the communists. Of course, the police were Kuomintang. There was a big fuss at the time."

"Wait, slow down. Explain, please."

He blinked at me. "Chiang Kai-shek's Kuomintang government was glad to blame such a terrible murder on the communists. They were rivals. Both sides wanted to rule China."

"Okay. Are you saying someone else was to blame?"

He leaned forward, grinning excitedly. "Nobody really believed the story about the communists. When somebody asked Jane McPherson Cahill the other day why she had a Chinese daughter, she said that tragedy led to blessing. Her parents died, and this led to her daughter being born."

"Did she explain?"

"No."

"How do you know all this?"

He grinned and leaned back. "Like American journalists say, I have my sources."

I grinned, too, and shook my head. "You're too smart for me. Can you help me find this woman?"

"You better hurry. She's on her way to Beijing."

I thought of Tim and felt a stinging regret that we couldn't work on this story together.

The train rolled through the outskirts of Chengdu. The day was over-cast, and the seemingly endless rows of nondescript one-story buildings were depressing. Inside our compartment, a young man and woman sat at a small table under the windows, pouring hot water from a thermos, drinking tea, and cracking sunflower seeds between their teeth. The young man smoked, and the ashtray was already full. A sullen-faced train attendant moved down the aisle, listlessly pushing a broom. She pounced on the ashtray and emptied it.

I held my handbag between my knees. I opened it, took out the translated book of Tang poetry, and laid the bag on the floor at my feet, hoping the book might serve as a conversation opener. I opened the book and read a poem. I was developing a taste for the vivid and concise language.

Jane leaned across the bunk and held out her hand. "What is your name, dear? You can just call me Jane, if you want." She nodded at the Chinese woman. "This is my daughter, Di Meihua, but we just call her Mei." Jane's voice softened on the sounds of the Chinese words, which dipped, then sustained a high tone for the last syllable.

"I'm Pippa James." I grasped Jane's warm, dry palm, feeling awkward at clasping hands across the Chinese woman's lap. I let go of Jane's hand. "I'm from Minneapolis," I said, glancing at Mei to include her in the conversation.

"A Midwesterner, huh?" Jane said.

"Yep." I stared at the two women to see if there was any resemblance between them. It wasn't just that one was Asian and one was Caucasian.

There seemed no point of resemblance; I would have never known they were mother and daughter.

The two women consulted rapidly in Chinese. At one point, Jane interrupted herself and told me she would interpret for both Mei and me. "Mei doesn't speak much English, but she understands some."

Mei leaned toward me and studied my face. I felt self-conscious and tried to smile. Mei smiled back, close-mouthed, revealing dimples, and glanced over her shoulder at Jane. "Pretty girl," she said to both of us. She turned back to me and said something in Chinese.

"What did she say?" I asked Jane.

"She wants to know how old you are." Jane threw Mei a quick, somewhat baffled glance.

"I'm twenty-eight," I said.

Mei reached out and touched my hand—a feather touch, swiftly withdrawn. The gesture set her ceramic pendant swinging. She clutched it to stop the movement and smiled. "How lucky your parents are to have such a young, beautiful daughter," Jane interpreted for her.

"Do you have a daughter?" I asked Mei, speaking slowly so she could understand my English.

Jane, eyes bright as she peered at me over Mei's shoulder, answered for her, "No, she has one son. He's an engineer. Smart and good looking, my grandson is."

"You speak no Chinese?" Mei struggled again with the English words.

"No. It's too bad. I've learned a few Chinese words the last week or so, though. 'Mei' means beautiful, doesn't it?"

Mei didn't understand my question, but Jane said, "Mei sometimes means beautiful. Mei's name, Meihua, means plum blossom. I was told long ago that the plum blossom stood for good Chinese qualities—fortitude and the art of survival. Things were terrible when Mei was born; I knew the right name would be important."

Jane gestured toward the book of poems on my lap. "So, you read these too?" she asked. I handed her the book and she flipped it open. There was a silence while she read one of the poems to herself, her lips moving. Then she slapped the book shut and gave it back to me. "What I've always noticed," she said, "was how these poems pointed out our common humanity with the Chinese. So long ago, and they felt just the same as we do about so many things."

She fell to musing then, and I searched my mind for questions to make her talk. So many older women I had known liked to talk about their pasts—my own mother, for instance. I remembered the last time she told me about her family history and childhood years. It was in my mother's home, on a cold winter's day in Minneapolis. The two of us were on the living room sofa, wrapped up in the same blanket, the wind howling against the windows, the cold coming in through the cracks. Fresh snow had blanketed the city in white. I could feel my mother's warm body, and the smell of her Joy perfume, and the sound of her voice as she told me about her past and how much she loved the city in winter.

"So, there was some kind of terrible time going on when your daughter was born?" I prompted.

Jane threw me a strange look. "World War Two," she said, her voice heavy with sarcasm.

I ignored her tone. "Mei was born during World War Two?"

"We didn't call it that, then. In China, we called it the Anti-Japanese War. The Japanese were swarming all over the place by that time. Just like cockroaches." She chortled.

When she didn't go on, I said, "I have to admit I heard about you from a newspaper article."

"Oh, that." Jane made a face, then shot me a sharp look. "How'd you know it was us?"

I hesitated. "It's sort of complicated..."

Another pointed look. "That newspaper article told you a lot, didn't it?"

"Well—"

"Typical government blather. I'm surprised it didn't say they bore the baby themselves. Patting themselves on the back like that." Jane shook her head. "They didn't find Mei for me. Nosiree bob." She gave Mei a grim little smile.

"Then how did you find her?"

Jane looked at Mei again. "I could tell you about it," she said, "but I'm not so sure I want to."

"But it was in the paper."

"Not the whole story—the real story."

"I'd be happy to listen."

"Well… we might visit a little, then. See where it gets us." She narrowed her eyes at me. "You sure you want to hear about all this?"

"We've got hours on this train. I'm sure it's interesting."

"I'd want this to be a three-way conversation. I wouldn't think of leaving Mei out of it."

"No, of course not." There was a short silence, then I added, "But… before we go any further, I have to explain something; I have to tell you who I am."

Jane gave me a concerned look. "Well, young lady, who are you?"

As I explained what I did for a living, I clutched the side of the bunk so hard that I wore a deep groove into my hand, aware they could simply refuse to talk.

"When I heard about your story," I said, "I thought, that's it—the story I've been looking for!"

"You think so?" Jane ran a hand over her thin, wrinkled lips. "It's so dry in Peking," she said. "I better get out my ChapStick." It was the first time I'd heard anyone refer to the Chinese capital by the old name Westerners had given it. She dragged her handbag onto her lap, opened it, and began to rummage. "I was born in Peking, you know," she said. "My parents were missionaries." She gave me another sharp look. "You probably know that already, don't you? You must have heard what happened to my parents. This business about Mei seems to have raked up that old story again."

I admitted having heard something about the death of her parents.

Jane rubbed the ChapStick over her lips and put the tube back in her handbag. She kept the bag open and continued rummaging through it, all the while darting glances at me. Finally, she said, "Funny, your sitting right next to us the way you are."

I felt myself blush. "I arranged that, too," I admitted. Jane looked at Mei and said something in Chinese. They had a rapid exchange; I couldn't tell whether they were arguing. At the end of it, Mei gave me a sweet smile.

"She wants to know if she's going to be on American television," Jane said, her tone grudging, as if she hadn't wanted to tell me this.

"Maybe. It depends on what it looks like when it's finished. I can't promise anything."

Mei asked another question and Jane squinted. "She wants to know would we get paid anything?"

"No, I'm sorry. We don't pay for this sort of thing."

Jane spoke again to Mei, who looked disappointed. Then she said something to Jane, who interpreted. "She says not getting paid is okay as long as we can learn a little bit about you, too."

I shrugged, wondering why Mei wanted to know about me.

Jane leaned back after that last statement, seemingly in deep thought. She took her time getting back to me, and then suddenly looked down and shut her handbag with a snap.

"How much do you need to know?" she asked.

"How much do you want to tell me?"

"My parents' death has to be in your film too, does it?"

"Probably. It would depend on how it plays into the main story—you and Mei."

"Oh, they're linked together, all right." There was a long silence. Then Jane said, "You talking about putting me in front of a camera and all? Mei and me?"

"I'm afraid that's part of it."

She didn't say anything right away, and I knew it would be a mistake to push her. While I waited for her response, I glanced out the window, trying to make out something of the darkening countryside. I knew we would go through the mountains that separated Sichuan Province from Northern China, and wondered when we would begin to feel the climb. I remembered a college roommate, who now worked in Beijing, telling me that the Chinese called trains "fire wagons" and the railway line the "iron road," both highly descriptive and appropriate, I thought. I had read that most of the rail lines in the vast country were built after the communist revolution, though main lines between major cities were built in the early part of the century. I had also read that peasants who'd seen the lights and heard the shrieking of the trains on dark nights thought dragons were racing across the land.

Jane cleared her throat. She glanced at Mei as if wanting to reach out to her, but looked at me instead and gave a long sigh. "All right," she said, her voice cracking a little. "I don't mind telling you a few things about my past. I'm not sure you'll want to make a film out of it, though."

"Let me be the judge of that. Why don't you start by telling me a few things about being the daughter of missionaries?" I asked, hoping that if Jane talked about her parents at all, she'd end up telling me what happened to them.

"You just hold off," Jane said. "I'll tell you a little bit, but I don't know about your using it. Can we wait and see?"

"I won't do anything you don't want," I said without hesitation.

"Good. Where shall I begin?" She thought about this a moment, then said, "I had a happy childhood. I suppose I was a typical "mishkid"—missionary kid, you know. Church and Sunday school, lessons, and wonderful times—picnics at the Forbidden City. The emperor had left by then. You could just go in and wander around. There was a place behind the walls where my parents used to take us—big, old ancient trees and the most wondrous peonies." She looked at me. "But you don't want to hear about all this."

"Yes, I do," I said.

Jane closed her eyes. "Peking. I was in love with a city." She opened her eyes and peered at me. "Ever been there?"

I nodded, afraid to break the flow of her story.

She shut her eyes again. "But you want to hear about the bad times. Naturally. Well, those came soon enough." She paused for so long I was afraid she'd fallen asleep, lulled by the movement of the train.

When she spoke again, it was seemingly on a different subject. "I had a friend who was a communist. His name was Li Han, the son of Li Wutang—Li was their family name, you know. Han's father worked with my father at the mission since the day our family stepped inside the walls of Peking. My father thought he knew Li Wutang inside and out, but he didn't. He thought he understood the Chinese too, but of course he didn't."

Jane cleared her throat again. "As it turned out, Wutang's son, Li Han, was the most influential person of my childhood, more than my mother or father or my brother Will. But this was at that time when China, and Chinese families, and everything else was falling apart, and people were going separate ways. China was unraveling at the seams, and the Japanese were knocking at the door." Jane paused, then corrected herself. "No, not knocking. They wanted to stomp all over the Chinese with their bloody boots. And I mean bloody."

She paused, caught up in the emotion of her last statement. After a moment, she went on. "When things started to crumble, they crumbled very fast. A small thing led to tragedy and ultimately to…" She blinked several times, then smiled, and reached out and patted Mei's hand. Jane leaned over to peer at me as if to make sure I understood what she would say next. When she spoke, it was to paraphrase what my Chinese interpreter had told me earlier. "The tragedy and the horror brought me the greatest blessing of my life." She patted Mei's hand again. "Life comes round in cycles, doesn't it?" She gave Mei another glance, unsmiling this time, as if sizing her up. Mei didn't see this; instead, she watched me.

The train rocked beneath us. From time to time, it shrieked as it rushed at something or someone in the growing darkness. The movement kept knocking me against the metal frame of the bunk, wearing a sore spot on my hip. Nonetheless, I sat still.

"When all these things started happening, I was only a girl of fifteen," Jane said. "Innocent as the day is long by today's standards. Yet, in other ways, I must have known far more about life than the little girls of today. Let me tell you… I knew enough to sense the danger that was building up all around us. When Han began to hide things from me, I became frightened."

"His being Chinese didn't create a barrier between you?"

"Not to me—I was too young to know about such barriers. But looking back, I can see of course that Han knew about the barriers, as I know now. Nevertheless, there was a strong bond between us. More than friendship." She looked at Mei and then at the book of poems in my lap. "And maybe our common humanity?"

Her voice took on a faraway quality as she began her story. "I was only a girl, but I knew my own mind."

Chapter 2

Peking, January 1936

J ane tried to hide in her room, because the McPherson house was in an uproar. Della, her mother, had raised her voice that morning, crying out in tones Jane had seldom heard from her calm, dispassionate parent. Her father, Cyrus, had paced the sitting room. Jane could hear his footsteps on the scuffed wooden boards, back and forth, back and forth. The footsteps were accompanied by his voice, speaking rapidly in words Jane could only partially make out. Della's higher tones cut in sharply at intervals.

The servants too were upset. Amah, always scolding and shrill voiced, now went at the cook in harsh staccato notes, hammering away at the poor man, who, as far as Jane knew, had done nothing wrong. The cook said nothing, but pounded his meat cleaver with more force than necessary. The Number One Boy lingered in the passageway, afraid equally of Amah's rough tongue and Della's anger. The garden boy and the gatekeeper huddled together outside in a patch of sunshine by the gate, not wanting to venture into the kitchen for bits of food and gossip as they usually did.

Amah finally came and found her, clomping down the passageway on her bound feet, coming nearer and nearer, so Jane knew there was no escape. Amah's sharp voice outside Jane's door, calling her Chinese name, was not to be denied. Jane grabbed her padded jacket and stepped out into the courtyard, blinking in the thin winter sunshine. "What?" she asked in Chinese, knowing perfectly well Amah wanted mainly to probe for information and to vent her spleen.

"What are you doing?" Amah demanded.

"Nothing." Jane moved out of the shadow of the eaves so Amah could see her better.

"Your mama is too angry."

"I know. It's a terrible day." Although Amah understood English well enough, having worked for the McPhersons for years, she and Jane never spoke to each other in that language. Jane was fluent in Mandarin, the elegant northern language used in Peking.

"Aiyah," said Amah. She lowered herself onto a concrete bench. She never seemed to feel the cold; Jane thought this was because Amah was plump. Jane, slender as a Chinese girl, shivered and rocked from one foot to the other.

Amah grunted and pulled herself to her feet again. "Come inside. We will light the coal brazier and keep you warm. We cannot have you catching cold on top of everything else."

That morning, Della had followed her son Will, Jane's brother — tall and handsome, a model student, star athlete, and his mother's pride and joy — around the house, demanding to know why she had overheard the servants snickering about a trip to a brothel. Will, red-faced and secretive, hounded by his mother's relentless questions, finally broke down and confessed. Della, outraged, had called Cyrus into the room so he too could hear what the boy had to say: Cyrus' closest friend, an American businessman in Shanghai, had taken Will to a brothel, and Will had bragged about it to the Number One Boy.

No one was as upset as Della was. Jane's first reaction was that, for once, perfect Will was the one causing problems, not Jane, who was rebellious and didn't do as well in school. Amah told Jane the servants were upset because Della was so angry. Amah sighed and grumbled about what Will had done, but Della had made it clear that morning that there was a lot more snickering than praying going on in the kitchen, even though all the servants attended Christian church services regularly. "They think it's funny," she spat at Will and Cyrus. This was one of the exchanges Jane heard clearly, simply by standing in the passage outside the sitting room door. Cyrus had replied in thundering tones, saying something about Will being sorry now, but what could he have been thinking about at the time?

"It's your friends I blame," Della had hissed.

That was when Jane had whirled around and sought the privacy of her room. She didn't want to hear her mother say harsh things to her father or abuse his friends, the Baumans, whom Jane liked and admired so much.

Amah, sighing and muttering to herself, steered Jane back into the girl's room, and checked on the amount of coal in the brazier. Although some foreigners' houses in Peking now had central heating, the McPhersons' shabby, old-fashioned home was heated as the Chinese had done for centuries to keep off the chill and the icy winds of Peking winters. Jane's room, like the rest of the house, had changed little from when a Chinese family had lived in it. Latticed paper windows overlooked the courtyard. Their frames, now faded, had once been painted red and green. The overhanging eaves were decorated with painted animals and flowers. There was a plum tree just outside the window. It was ancient, but it still bloomed every spring.

Jane loved the McPhersons' shabby old Chinese house, which was a cluster of rooms arranged around a courtyard. Her family had moved into the house when Jane was only eighteen months old, so she had known it virtually all her life. At that time, the nearby mission compound had become overcrowded, and Cyrus had agreed to move his family to the Chinese house the mission board had bought some years before. Jane had often heard her mother say how thankful she was for the privacy of the secluded old house. Jane herself was sure she felt even more thankful that she had a room of her own, with its sheltering old tree in the courtyard outside.

Amah turned from the coal brazier and said, "Young Miss, there is far worse trouble in this household than what your brother did."

Jane, who had been staring out the window, turned around, startled. "What are you talking about?" she asked.

"This terrible trouble with the Li family," Amah said.

Jane crossed the room to Amah's side, and laid her hand on her nurse's plump arm. "What terrible trouble? Tell me, quickly." She had just seen her friend Li Han the day before, and there had been no indication of a quarrel between their families.

Amah sighed. "Yesterday, your father dismissed Little Gao from his job. He did not first consult with Li Wutang." Little Gao was a Li family cousin.

"But why? What did Little Gao do?"

"That other missionary's wife, Mrs. Appleton, caught him stealing money out of the box meant for the poor people."

Jane's hand went to her mouth. The mission kept a box for contributions for feeding poor women and children and anyone else they could manage to help from Peking's teeming, dirty streets. The missionaries feared it was a small effort, a mere drop in the bucket, but coins from the mission box had filled many empty stomachs, and had even saved a few lives.

"Your father was red-faced and angry and shouting. But he should have talked to Li Wutang first. Now the Li family has lost much face and Li Wutang is torn. Should he be loyal to his family or to the mission?"

"But he's a Christian," said Jane.

Both Amah and Jane knew it was more complicated than that.

Cyrus called Little Gao's uncle, Li Wutang, his "right-hand man." In fact, Cyrus was patronizing Wutang when he said this. Wutang held equal status to Cyrus; both were ordained ministers. In those years, many Protestant-American missionaries in China were making an effort to "Sinisize" their missions, so their Chinese counterparts could eventually replace them at the helm. However, out of long habit and ingrained relationships between Caucasian and Oriental, Wutang still deferred to Cyrus and Cyrus let him do it.

There was an unusually close tie between their two families. Cyrus and Wutang had worked closely together since 1912, when Cyrus and Della had come to China for the first time. Not only was Wutang smart, helpful, and a dedicated Christian, but also his presence had given the young American couple a reassuring sense of continuity. Wutang's uncle had converted to Christianity under Cyrus' father's tutelage. The uncle had died, along with Cyrus' father, in the Boxer Rebellion at the turn of the century, when an "army" of Chinese with mystical beliefs had incited an uprising against foreigners. Subsequently, Wutang had been baptized a Christian, as had his uncle's son, Little Gao.

Everyone in the McPherson household, including the servants, liked Little Gao. All made allowances for him because he was mentally slow, especially now that he was over thirty. As he had never married or managed to retain more than a few characters and so couldn't read, everyone still called him by his milk name, which meant "Little Cake." Lately, some young men in the Li family jokingly called him "Little Telephone," because Cyrus employed Little Gao as messenger boy. Proud of his job, Little Gao had done it well, running and panting through the streets of Peking, clutching notes and letters in his sweaty hands—nobody would have trusted him with a verbal message. Although people laughed at Little Gao, and he, having an excellent sense of humor, laughed with them, no one who knew him made the mistake of underestimating him. He was capable of fierce family loyalty, and he had a temper. Cyrus and Della often said he was more intelligent than his relatives believed.

As soon as Amah left her room, Jane pulled her padded jacket back on. She knew Han had gone out that morning and she knew where he was. He had gone to the house of an American named Ambrose Varley, who had agreed to allow Han and some of his classmates to meet secretly there to discuss politics. Jane thought that if she were the first to tell him about the trouble with Little Gao, Han would appreciate her act of friendship, and know that her father's insensitivity to his family could not poison their close friendship. She was afraid that if Han went home before she found him, and learned about Little Gao from someone in his household, it might affect his feelings toward her.

She stepped out once more into the icy air, tiptoed down the steps, and crossed the courtyard. When the gatekeeper and the garden boy, hunkering down in their patch of sunlight, saw her coming, the gatekeeper jumped up and pulled open one side of the double-door gate to let Jane slip out into the quiet lane, or *hutong*. The gate creaked shut behind her, its faded red-painted surface cracked and peeling from long exposure to the sun on the earthen south wall of the compound.

Jane half-walked, half-ran down the narrow hutong alley to the corner market, and negotiated the price of a ride with one of the emaciated rickshaw coolies, wrapped in torn blue jackets, who crowded around her. She climbed into the rickshaw, which as always rocked unsteadily on its spring seat, and told the man to take her to Dong An market. "I will tell you where to go from there," she said. "Hurry. I am late."

"Young Miss, I can only run as fast as my feet can carry me." The coolie shifted the poles in his hands and began to jog, jolting the rickshaw over the uneven ground. Jane clung to the sides and willed the man to hurry. There was little traffic on this quiet back street, and she could hear the flip-flop of his straw sandals and his ragged breathing. She could also see his breath on the frosty air. They rolled and bumped through splashes of alternating sunshine and shadow, following the line of the old wattle-and-daub walls.

The coolie stopped suddenly, lowered the poles—nearly dumping Jane out of the rickshaw—and began to cough. He spit on the sidewalk, picked up the poles again, and waited a second or two to catch his breath before pulling the rickshaw forward again. Jane looked away. The man was sick. She was in a hurry. What should she do? She prayed silently: Please God, don't let me be too late to see Han, and I promise to put money in the mission box the next chance I get. Thinking about the mission box reminded her again of what first Little Gao and then her father had done. Their actions now threatened the foundation of her tranquil life in Peking. She felt a surge of anger, then fear. Oh, hurry, hurry, hurry, she said again to herself.

The coolie pulled her out onto wide, macadamized Hatamen Street. Here, the rickshaw rolled smoothly, passing others with people also bundled up against the cold. For a few minutes, Jane's rickshaw raced evenly beside a rickshaw containing a Chinese girl who didn't look much older than Jane. Jane glanced at her curiously and saw flour-like, pasty make-up and finely drawn, cherry-red lips. Jane sucked in her breath. A prostitute, she thought. Maybe like the one Will went to. The thought filled Jane with awe, rather than repulsion. By this act, Will was now a grown man, remote and set apart from her.

The coolie dropped the poles at the entrance to Dong An market. "It is too difficult to go through here," he said. His eyes looked stubborn.

"All right. I'll walk," Jane said. She was in too much of a hurry to argue. Besides, the coolie was right. The market was packed. If she cut directly through and came out the other side, she could easily walk the rest of the way. It would be easier than arguing with the coolie or going around the long way. She climbed down over the shafts and paid the man, then turned and plunged into the crowd.

The noise was deafening. People crowded over the frozen, rutted ground, chattering and shouting. Vendors bawled out their wares. Two men argued furiously. Someone pushed on an automobile horn, over and over.

Jane cautiously made her way around a camel that stood placidly chewing its cud in the sunshine, its coat roughened and shaggy because of its winter growth. A sharp stench of camel dung hit Jane's nostrils, mingling with the smells of meat and garlic being cooked on braziers nearby. She could also smell roasting chestnuts. All these smells overlaid the constant odor of bad sanitation, to which Jane was so accustomed that she rarely even noticed it.

She climbed up on a rise of ground to get her bearings. Across the low-lying buildings, she could see the yellow roof tiles of the Forbidden City, just two blocks away, peeking over its thick, reddish walls. She half-ran, half-slid down the sloping ground, and pushed her way past a tangle of horse-drawn carts, whose the drivers, with shocks of black hair and wearing dirt-encrusted rags, cursed at each other and pulled at the horses' reins.

The market gave way to an open street. A legless beggar followed her for a while, expertly steering a wheeled platform that supported his body, and whispering a litany of pleas. Jane knew she dared not give him anything; she was on foot and there were many other beggars around. A signal from one would alert the rest and she would be mobbed. She had been warned countless times that Peking's beggars were a well-organized, hierarchical group, and that most of what she gave a beggar would be divvied up among the leaders of the organization. Cyrus defied this conventional wisdom and gave freely, but Jane was afraid to.

She heard the deep, rhythmic boom of a drum and the high wail of musical instruments. Shading her eyes with her hand, Jane peered down the street. A mass of wailing, white-robed people was making its way toward her. Oh, no, she thought, a funeral. If it was large enough, it could block her way.

A large catafalque with embroidered curtains swung into view. Jane lost count at forty men straining under the weight of its red-lacquered poles. A large number of men on foot and dressed in white—all official mourners—plodded wearily before the coffin. Female mourners brought up the rear. The drummers and musicians came closer. Now she could hear the wailing of the paid mourners. The natural noise of the street intensified.

"Eh, a very rich man has died," a ragged old woman said in Jane's ear. "Just look at the size of the procession." She smiled with delight, showing toothless gums.

A man next to her grinned and marched in place. "Maybe, if I'm lucky, I'll be so rich before I die." Both he and the woman broke into laughter.

The procession paused to give the bearers a rest. Jane ran alongside the line of mourners, looking for an opening so she could break through the crowd and be on her way. She had seen funeral processions before, and noted only that this one was unusually large in its number of mourners and in the fineness of the coffin that dipped and swayed above the crowd.

Jane's father had once pointed out that the desperately poor Chinese seemed to enjoy watching such displays of wealth. They were eager for amusement and full of curiosity. "The Old One Hundred Names," he had said, using the colloquial term for the masses, "have a vivid sense of fun. We in the West could envy their gift for life."

Jane enjoyed the street life too, but as Han grew older he scorned such sentiments. He brought to Jane's attention the emaciated rickshaw coolies and filthy children. "I am ashamed," he said. "China is neglecting her people. They are hungry, dirty, and sick. Things must change."

Hurrying down the street, Jane nearly stumbled over an exhausted young mother in filthy rags, nursing a half-naked baby, and jealously guarding a scrap of paper weighted down with stones, which detailed the sad circumstances of her life. The woman grabbed at Jane's skirt with a filthy hand. "Give money so I can eat. My baby will starve." She tugged at Jane's skirt to draw her closer. When she moved, the infant's head lolled unsteadily, making Jane wonder if it was even alive.

Jane jerked away from the woman's grasp. Everyone, including Han, told her people such as this woman also were professional beggars. She ignored the stabs of pity she felt. There was nothing she could do for this woman.

Several rickshaw coolies vied for her attention. "Young Miss, Young Miss, you must not walk. You must ride. Take my rickshaw. It is best."

Jane shook her head and pressed on. Swerving to avoid a man bent double by the bundle on his back, she crossed the street. The rich man's funeral procession started forward once again. Someone threw paper money into the air to appease the spirits. Later, the dead man's relatives would burn paper money, so he would be as rich in heaven as he had been on earth.

By contrast with the market, Ambrose Varley's compound—Jane's destination—was an oasis of serenity. Varley was a peculiar, quiet American, who, like the McPhersons, lived in a Chinese-style house. Unlike them, he wore Chinese dress, the ankle-length robes and brim-less hats strangely suiting him. Varley's house was filled with treasures he had collected since he had come to China years earlier. Unlike other Americans in Peking, he kept mainly to himself, refusing to attend lega-tion parties, though he was often invited. He spoke excellent Chinese, and was criticized by many of his compatriots, as well as by the British expatriates, for "going native."

Varley's number-one servant, an old eunuch, was named Chen Lifu. Chen had been driven out of the Forbidden City when the last Qing emperor, the young Pu Yi, had dismissed all the eunuchs, because they were stealing too much from the imperial storehouses. Although most of these eunuchs had managed to enrich themselves at the emperor's expense, Varley's old Chen had managed his own money badly and lost it all. His present life apparently suited him, however. Together, Chen and his American master combed the antique markets for treasures. Han had told Jane that he had met the two several times returning from their forays among the curio stalls. Han thought the eunuch very odd and frightening, and insisted the old man had the eyes of a devil.

Jane had heard darker stories about Varley: he was said to frequent opium dens and brothels. Once, he had acquired a long-term Chinese mistress, but then Cyrus had stepped in and somehow convinced the young woman of the error of her ways. Some said Ambrose Varley had despised her newly Christian views and had thrown her out on the street, where she had fallen to her knees at the gate, begging to be let back in. No one knew what had become of her. Someone in the American community said it was the first time a missionary had stolen a whore away from the man who kept her, and this was widely quoted, to Cyrus' discomfort.

In spite of Han's repugnance toward old Chen, the boy was fond of Ambrose Varley, who loaned him books and listened to him struggle to understand the world around him. Inexplicably, Varley had now taken to allowing student activists to meet in his house. Han had told Jane the day before that an ex-student who had since joined the communists would be at Varley's house to meet with Han and some of his classmates from Yenching University, a school established by American missionaries. The students from Yenching, outraged at what they perceived as the Chinese government's cowardice in the face of Japanese aggression, had become progressively more politically active. Several weeks before, they had taken part in massive demonstrations on the streets of Peking, and a number of them had been beaten by policemen.

Jane had visited Varley on a number of occasions, always in the company of Han or Will, or both. The children never told Della when they went to Varley's house. Although Varley knew the McPhersons quite well, was usually on friendly enough terms with them, and had even once given them a valuable gift—an antique Chinese bowl—Jane and Will sensed Della would have strongly opposed their visits to his house.

Now, for the first time, Jane was going to Varley's home by herself. She felt worldly and adventurous as she hurried up to the gate and pounded, announcing her name, and saying that she wanted to come in to see Mr. Varley.

Always eager for a glimpse of the eunuch, Jane was rewarded that day when the gatekeeper summoned the evil-looking old man instead of Varley. The eunuch came at a half-run. He greeted Jane politely, addressing her as "Missy," and asked after her father and mother.

Trying to restrain her impatience, Jane replied as politely, and then burst out, "Are there visitors here?" She hardly dared breathe until the old eunuch nodded.

"Yes, yes," he said, and motioning for her to come inside. Jane scurried through the gate.

"Is Li Han here?" she asked.

"He is here."

"Ah, good." Jane relaxed and breathed in the fragrant air of Varley's courtyard. Her mad dash through the streets had been worth it. She followed Chen to the main court, where wooden beams, darkened by time, held up the sloping tiled roof. An ancient pine cast its shadow across the door, blocking most of the light from the dim recesses of the inner hall. Inside, a pair of oversized cabinets stood on either side of the room, and carved chairs and several tables were pushed back to its edges. Jane knew from past visits that some of the tables were used for meals, some for playing Chinese games. Scrolls hung on the walls, and several pieces of porcelain gleamed from a fretwork cabinet in the corner.

The eunuch waited while Jane stepped over the high threshold into the room. She stole glances at him. It was difficult to tell his age, though she knew he had arrived at the palace during the time of the next to last emperor, the one most people thought had been poisoned by the dowager empress in 1908. Perhaps because Chen had been castrated as a boy, he seemed curiously unfinished, his face unlined, his body soft looking, his voice high-pitched. Han had told Jane and Will that the eunuch's father had castrated the boy himself, as sometimes happened in those days, to assure his service to the emperor and consequently to improve the family's fortunes. Every time Jane saw him, she couldn't help thinking about what had been done to him so long ago.

"I will tell the master you are here," Chen said.

"Can't you just slip in and tell Li Han I'm here? I don't need to disturb Mr. Varley."

The eunuch bowed and disappeared. Jane lowered herself down on one of the massive carved chairs and waited. She shifted her weight on the broad, hard, wooden seat, propped her feet on a wooden footstool, and looked around her. The room was very still, the silence seeming to press against her ears. She concentrated on the characters on a scroll across the room, trying to decipher their meaning. She finally gave it up. The unknown scholar's calligraphy was remarkable, even to her untutored eyes, but impossible for her to read, as she had never been taught to decipher this kind of classical Chinese.

A white-robed servant with black felt shoes brought her fragrant jasmine tea in a translucent cup with no handle. Jane remembered Varley once telling her mother that he prepared his tea by tossing fresh, not dried, jasmine buds into the tea leaves. She sniffed at the steaming liquid; its scent was strong.

After about five minutes, she heard soft footsteps on the wooden floorboards. She jumped up out of her chair, ready to greet Han, but it was Ambrose Varley who stepped into the room. "Jane?" he said. "I was surprised when Chen told me you were here."

As always, the sight of Varley warmed and reassured her. She had known him since she was small and had always liked him. She knew her parents disapproved of his lifestyle, but they seemed to like him anyway, as if in spite of themselves. He was particularly partial to Della, and had once told Jane that her mother represented all that was best about the United States: simplicity; forthrightness; integrity; and idealism. His words had made Jane squirm—his tones were always ironic, as if he meant much more than he said—but she had nodded in agreement that her mother was admirable.

Jane now said to Varley, "I asked to see Li Han. I didn't want to bother you."

"I came out to see you for myself. You've given me a surprise."

Jane looked up at the tall American. In spite of his brown hair and light eyes, Varley never looked out of place in a Chinese setting. As usual, he wore Chinese dress, an ankle-length robe with narrow sleeves, and Chinese cloth shoes. "Please, Mr. Varley. I need to speak to Li Han," she said.

"He's here. Is something wrong?"

"People are upset at home. Someone caught Little Gao stealing, and Pa fired him." Jane had made up her mind to be frank with Varley.

He gestured for her to sit, then settled himself in a chair next to hers and, in his unhurried way, turned to face her. "How does Li Wutang feel about that? Little Gao is his cousin." He folded his large, shapely, and beautifully groomed hands in his lap and kept them still. He was one of the few Americans Jane knew who did not gesture when he talked.

Jane wasn't surprised that Varley went straight to the heart of the problem. Since she could remember, he had been interested in the minutiae of her household and Han's. He seemed to like gossip and had a good memory for names and relationships.

She said, "I'm afraid Li Wutang must be very upset. Pa should have consulted him first."

Varley sighed. "Li Wutang might think this an affront to his whole family." He peered at her more closely. "Why do you have to talk to Han about this now? Why not wait until later?"

Jane lowered her eyes. "I'm afraid to have him hear it from anyone except me. It's between our two families, you see."

"Do you think he'd want to see you here?"

Jane hunched in the chair, feeling dangerously close to tears. "I don't know."

"I hope you're not in love with him. That wouldn't do at all, you know."

Jane swallowed and kept her eyes on the floor. "I'm not in love with him. But I love him."

Varley thought about this a moment, then nodded. "Yes, I see there's a difference." He narrowed his eyes. "I take it your mother doesn't know you're here."

Jane knew this comment required no answer. She raised her eyes to Varley's face. "May I see Han? I won't look at the others. I don't need to know who's here."

A line appeared between Varley's dark, well-shaped brows. "What do you know about who's here in my house today?"

"Someone told me you were having one of your meetings today, and that the students would talk with a communist."

His eyes glinted. "Someone's been talking? That's dangerous. Who told you?"

Jane bit her lip. "Please... I don't think — "

"All right, you don't have to tell. I assume it was Han."

"It wasn't!" Jane lied.

He flicked her a sharp look. "I hope it was someone who could be trusted. Aside from the very real danger to the students, I certainly don't want to be kicked out of China, which I suppose is what would happen to me should this little indiscretion be found out."

Varley raised his head and called out softly for Chen. The servant must have been waiting just outside the door, because he appeared immediately. "What does my master require?" he asked, somewhat breathless.

"Fetch Li Han from the meeting."

Chen padded out of the room and Jane said, "Mr. Varley?"

He looked up and waited for her to speak. "Mr. Varley, may I ask a question?"

He smiled. "You arrive unannounced and now you ask permission to ask a question?"

"I'm sorry."

He watched her from beneath his heavy lidded eyes. "What do you want to know?"

"Why do you help the communists with these meetings? Do you believe the communists are right?" Jane's father was virulently anti-communist and made no secret of it. Han, on the other hand, praised the communist movement.

Varley said, "I let the students meet here because they're very young and sincere and they need a place to vent their frustrations."

"But do you believe they're right?"

Varley stared down at his hands for a second, and then, raising his eyes to look at her, said, "I don't know. Do you understand anything about Marxist theory?"

"Not much." She tried to remember Han's excited, often incoherent, descriptions of what the communists stood for.

"The communists want to change this country from the bottom up," Varley said.

"Is that good?"

"I don't know. The problems seem so deep-seated, there may not be any other way."

"How can we know for sure?"

"We can't. Of course, you hear the things your father has to say about the communists, don't you?" It wasn't really a question, and Jane waited for him to go on. "Marxist theory is the basis for the kinds of changes the students and others want to make. People like your parents see the same problems in China that the communists do, but they don't approve of the Marxist solution."

"Many people don't approve of it. I—I think I'm afraid of it."

"You should be. It would require a clean break with the past. That's what's so hard to accept." He stared across the room. "Do you see that table over there, directly under the scroll?"

Jane looked. "Yes." The table was of a reddish wood, polished to a warm glow. Its lines were simple, almost austere.

"Look at the shape, the lines from top to bottom. Do you see the resemblance to the Qian Gate near the Forbidden City?" The Qian Gate was one of the main gates of the city of Peking.

Jane nodded and raised her hands. She let them drop, sketching a shape that was wider at the bottom than at the top. "They're Ming, aren't they, the table and the gate?"

"Good girl. Yes, they're Ming. The Ming dynasty ended in 1644, yet no one since has come up with anything more perfect than the shape of that table. This is the past that the communists are denying. They must be very sure of what they want to do." He stood up with a sudden graceful movement. "Han must be reluctant to leave the meeting."

But then they heard the plopping sound of Western leather shoes on the polished boards, and in a few seconds Han stepped into the room. Like his classmates, he wore a traditional Chinese robe—to show he was patriotic, he had told her—and Western shoes. Han did not have a distinguished face; his features were rounded and his smile brought out a dimple, but in Jane's eyes the robe gave him height and distinction. Now, he looked at her and paled. "What are you doing here?" he asked.

Jane slid off the chair and stood to face him. It felt so good and right just to stand there looking at him again that she wanted to prolong the moment. "Please don't be angry. I'm worried about you." She stole a look at Ambrose Varley, then turned back to Han. "There's trouble in both our households. Did you know about this?"

Han shook his head. "No. What is it?"

Varley walked over to the doorway. "I'll leave you to speak in private. I'm going back to my study. There are all sorts of intrigues in my house today." He turned at the doorway and smiled. "You two aren't nearly as dangerous as those others." He stepped over the threshold and padded away in his soft Chinese shoes, barely making a sound.

Han turned to Jane. "Tell me."

She told him about Little Gao. "And my father didn't say anything to your father first," she said. "Everyone is very upset."

Han shut his eyes with exasperation. "Always family. Why do they have so many problems?"

"So you don't blame my father?"

"I blame all our fathers. They're all clinging to the past, to the old ways." He ran his hand through his hair, making it stand on end. "I feel desperate sometimes."

Jane took his hand as she had when they were children. He stiffened but didn't pull away. "Come and sit down," she said. "I hurried over here because I was afraid that if you heard about Little Gao from your family, you would hate both me and my father."

He shook his head. "Oh, little sister." He always called her that; it meant younger sister. "That is so silly. We're a different generation from our parents."

"Don't you feel sorry for Little Gao? Or for your father?"

"Of course I feel sorry for them, especially for Little Gao, but he did steal the money, didn't he?"

"Your grandfather is going to fuss about this, isn't he? Won't that make things difficult for you?"

The Li family was already being tugged in two directions. Recently, Han's old grandfather had decreed that Han must marry the grand-daughter of an old friend, the fourth daughter of the Ding family. Han had complained privately about this to Jane and Will, and told them he feared that the family meant to force him to go through with the marriage. He said he knew his modern thinking and interest in politics were driving his grandfather's determination to marry him off at only eighteen. Also, he told them his father, Wutang, didn't object to the grandfather's plans. Han had expressed sympathy with the communists. This was not only dangerous, but it went against the Li family beliefs.

Like other Chinese of his generation, Han's father, Li Wutang, was a confused mixture of modern and traditional thought—in his case, Christian and Confucian. Han said he suspected that his father par-tially sympathized with his desire to be up to date, but part of Wutang understood and agreed with the grandfather's conservatism. Han's grandfather was a frail but stubborn old man who clung to Confucian tradition. Although his son and one of his brothers had converted to Christianity, the elder had refused to follow suit. He despised most things Western, and made no secret of his dislike and distrust of foreigners.

In turn, Jane loathed and feared Han's grandfather, whom she privately called "the old spider." Everyone knew that things were changing in China, and that the old customs were slipping away. How could Han's old grandfather, who stuck stubbornly to tradition, make his forward-thinking, modern grandson marry a girl he didn't want to marry? Han was a good student and far too young to think of marriage. In Jane's eyes, the old man had been selfish in sealing an agreement with old Mr. Ding when Han was born. The girl had been two years older, and the two men had agreed their families should unite. In the world in which they had grown up, this was not only the preferable way to choose mates for the young people in their families, it was the only way.

"What more can Grandfather do?" Han said. "He's already convinced father to go ahead with my marriage. He thinks that if I'm married I won't have time for politics. Huh! What does he know?"

They sat side by side on the carved chairs and remained silent for a moment. Han, who was taller than Jane, was able to plant his feet squarely on the floor. Now, he looked down and tugged up the edge of his robe so he could admire his leather shoes. "They're so shiny," Jane said. She and Han had discussed his proposed marriage so many times that it seemed pointless to talk about it anymore.

"I polished them this morning," Han said. "I like to polish them."

"Old-style scholars would have made their servants polish their shoes."

"Old-style scholars wouldn't have worn leather shoes. We're different now. We stride around a lot. We exercise body and mind. We don't just sit in our studies. That's what was wrong with the old China, you know. Scholars refused to labor. Laborers could not read or write."

"They still can't."

"That's what they're talking about in there." Han jerked his head in the direction of Varley's study.

"Talking about communism?"

He looked at her out of the corner of his eye.

"What are you going to do?" she asked.

He looked away and bit his lip. "I don't know, but whatever I do, I'll follow my own convictions."

"Are you a communist?"

He threw her a stern look. "We shouldn't be talking about these things." His eyes softened. "I'm trying to protect you, little sister. It's better you don't know."

Footsteps sounded outside, and a round face with an unruly shock of hair peered around the edge of the door. "Han? We wondered where you were."

Han flushed. "Liang Chu, please come in. This is Jane McPherson, whose father works at the mission where my father works."

Liang Chu stiffened. "How do you do," he said to Jane in English. She replied in Chinese. He gave her a stiff little bow and turned to Han. "I must talk to you." He glanced at a wristwatch that looked too big for his thin wrist. "I haven't much time."

"Will you excuse us, Jane?" Han's eyes pleaded for understanding.

Jane nodded, not trusting herself to speak. In Liang Chu's presence, Han seemed almost a stranger.

"Don't worry about Little Gao," Han said. "That problem will sort itself out."

As it turned out, he couldn't have been more wrong, but of course she didn't know that then. She stood there in Varley's Chinese room and watched the two young men disappear through the doorway.

She didn't wait for Varley or the old eunuch. Although she knew it was discourteous, she slipped out the door and let herself out the gate without saying goodbye.

CHAPTER 3

PRESENT-DAY CHINA

J ane, the elderly woman, stared at the train window, eyeing her reflection as if trying to see something of her young self. I felt a tinge of guilt making her relive her past, as if she hadn't already been consumed by it her whole life. I couldn't imagine what it would be like to be separated from your child for so many years. I wasn't a mother, but I knew there was nothing more powerful than the bond between mother and child. My mother and I were very close, and I couldn't imagine my life without her, and I couldn't conceive of my mother ever separating from me for any reason during such a turbulent time. I wondered how Mei felt about all this. Maybe Jane herself was trying to figure it all out.

Jane combed her curly white flyaway hair behind her ears, giving her a curiously vulnerable look, then turned and pierced me with a sharp glance—at odds with her soft vulnerability. "You find all this interesting?" she asked.

"So far," I said.

"You said you've been to Peking?" Jane asked.

"Yes. Have you been there recently?"

"Not for quite awhile. All the times I came back to China, I knew Mei was probably in Southern China, so I concentrated on the south coast and worked inland. I was in Peking once in the seventies."

"Well, I was in Beijing for about a week," I said, refusing, for some reason, to use the old name.

"What'd you think of it?" Her expression became more vulnerable, yet expectant. She blinked rapidly, not sure whether she wanted to hear what I was going to say. "I'm told it's changed beyond recognition," she prompted.

"I wouldn't know about that; I was only there once."

During our one week in Beijing, when we weren't wrangling with minor Chinese officials about what we could and couldn't film, Tim and I sneaked off to see the Great Wall, the Forbidden City, the Temple of Heaven, and other famous tourist spots. We were disappointed. All these sites hummed with tourists. The Chinese had commercialized the most popular site at the Great Wall to the point of making it a parody of the crassest American theme park. The city itself was congested and crowded, with rampant construction and the constant noise of jackhammers.

We didn't get much sense of the old China we were looking for, until we rented bikes and steered them inexpertly through Beijing's remaining *hutongs* — narrow lanes lined with ancient earthen walls, where faded red gates and broken-tiled roofs offered a glimpse of ruined courtyard houses and China's past. One afternoon, we passed a large cleared area where, we had been told, an old neighborhood had fallen victim to the wrecker's ball. Bulldozers were pushing away the debris. Tim and I stared at them awhile, then bicycled away, feeling that if we didn't pedal fast enough, the old city would disappear before our eyes.

I had mixed feelings about Beijing, which someone had explained to me meant "northern capital" in Mandarin. I had read about "old Peking," as the Westerners used to call it, the beautiful "city of lingering splendor." Foreign visitors, beginning with Marco Polo, had described a city with ancient walls, lakes and palaces, tiled roofs, courtyard mansions, and fairy-tale gardens tucked away in a network of broad avenues and dusty alleys, all set against azure skies and the purple, temple-crowned Western Hills in the distance. All this had been laid out on a geometric grid.

Not much of this city existed anymore. Communist leader Mao Zedong had ordered the outer walls torn down to use the materials for air raid shelters. Now, twenty-five years after Mao's death, and well into the Deng Xiaoping/Jiang Zemin era of reform and opening to the West, the city's once graceful low skyline was transformed by ugly, tall modern buildings, its peace disturbed by the dirt and constant noise of construction, its wide avenues snarled by traffic. The lines of the geometric grid were barely visible.

"This is progress?" I asked a Chinese acquaintance—a sophisticated, English-speaking businessman.

He had replied quietly, "China's past has had much disturbance. Now, people happier. Make money. Live in modern buildings."

There were unexpected moments when old China came to life. Tim and I had wandered through a market near the Temple of Heaven. People stopped their bikes to push at each other and squint in the morning sunshine at a man selling pet crickets. The greenery of the park was half obscured by morning mist—caused as much by pollution from the booming new economy as by the more traditional cooking fires and coal stoves. Here, old men, their cherished caged pet birds beside them, sat on park benches, watching a column of elderly people sway-ing in unison in the stately motions of traditional Tai Chi exercise, to the recorded strains of ancient music. These were the moments when I thought to myself that China and the Chinese were irrepressible and indestructible: despite all the horrors of the past, so many of the old ways seemed to have survived.

Mei joined the conversation, seeming much more interested in me than in Beijing. She spoke to Jane, but looked at me with a bright glance.

"How long have you worked for that film company?" Jane and Mei wanted to know.

I forced myself to smile and answer. "I've worked there a little over two years."

Mei watched me intently.

"Was it difficult, dear, to get a job like you have now?" Jane asked.

"You bet." I closed my eyes a moment, thinking back to all the plan-ning and networking that had culminated in what seemed like the job of my dreams.

"You're still so young. Don't you have plenty of time?"

"It's when you're young that you need to move ahead in this field." I had dreams of someday winning an Oscar, but I didn't want to tell them that.

"Mei wants to know if you're married," Jane said, "if you have a child."

"No, on both counts."

There was a rapid exchange. "She wants to know why not," Jane said.

I felt a surge of irritation while the two women waited, watching me. Finally, I mumbled, "I have a very special friend." I was thinking of Tim. We were really good friends, but nothing romantic had ever happened between us. Except for one brief moment when we were in Chengdu together, in a taxi on our way back to our hotel. Tim reached over and placed his hand on my leg. He did it almost as if by accident as we both stared out the window and pointed at things of common interest. Tim had casually touched me before, of course, but this seemed more intimate. I could barely concentrate on the sights we passed as I felt the warmth of his hand. Tim looked over at me and smiled, which gave me the urge to grab him and kiss him passionately. But I didn't.

I thought too about the last night that Tim and I were together. He had given me the book of Tang poetry. He was unable to meet my eyes as he told me he'd seen it in one of the stores in the Hong Kong airport on our way to the Mainland. I took the book, and when I flipped through it and read some of the poems, I fell in love with them immediately.

Jane spoke again: "Mei says it isn't too late. Women marry later these days." Mei's eyes lit up when she said this.

"Maybe I won't marry at all."

There was another rapid exchange. "She says that's all right too. Chinese girls also have careers these days. Some of them make lots of money. Like the young men. Still, she would like to see you happy and married to a nice man. She wants me to tell you that her late husband was a good man. He worked at a government-owned factory. She says she misses him very much. She hopes your friend is a good man too."

"He is," I said, and smiled despite myself. But I wanted to change the subject. "I'm fascinated by this Ambrose Varley," I told Jane, to get back on the topic of her past. "He's mysterious. Was he handsome? Sexy? After all, we are speaking of men." The women chuckled.

Jane opened her handbag, pulled out a tissue, and wiped her mouth.

She narrowed her eyes, pondering my question. Finally, she said, "I wasn't old enough to be able to tell if he was attractive or not—he seemed old to me."

"It's that touch of wickedness," I said. "The opium dens, the nasty old eunuch."

"He gave my mother a very valuable Ming bowl," Jane said. "Later, it was broken."

"Because of war?"

She gave me another of her funny looks. "Something worse than that."

Jane didn't elaborate, and I was afraid to push her. Instead, I decided it was a good time to get some background. This would also enable me to pull out my notebook and use it in front of Jane and Mei. I opened the notebook to a clean page and spread it out on the table. I uncapped my pen. "Just wanted to go over a few historical points with you," I said.

Before coming to China, Tim and I had boned up on Chinese history. We checked out books from the library, and bought books, and read everything about China that we could get our hands on. Yet, our knowledge was superficial, though I now knew the general outlines of China's recent past, and was able to see the framework in which Jane's story unfolded.

It was a complicated period in Chinese history. The Revolution of 1911 had put an end to the decaying Manchu Dynasty, or Qing Dynasty, as it was more formally known. After several false starts at setting up a republic, powerful warlords staked out claims in various parts of the country and fought among themselves, resulting in fear and bloodshed throughout the land. In the late twenties, Chiang Kai-shek seized the nation's helm. He fought the warlords or made deals with them, and brutally cleansed his Nationalist Party, known as the Kuomintang, of the communists who had been his former allies. In 1927, he moved the capital from Beijing—or Peking—to Nanking, in the south. The communists, in scattered remnants after Chiang's betrayal, were now on the run, but began to regroup in the countryside, building support among the peasantry.

I asked Jane if her family and friends in 1936 had fully appreciated the threat to China that Japan represented. At that time, the Japanese had taken over Manchuria, swarmed into parts of Shanghai, and were moving ever closer to Beijing—they had set up a demilitarized zone between Beijing and the Great Wall. "Everyone had to have been aware of Japan's desire to rule Asia and walk over China to get there."

"Of course we knew. China was in pieces, already torn apart by the West, the warlords, the infighting between Chiang Kai-shek and the communists. Now Japan was greedy for her share. The Chinese understandably were very upset. Students protested in the streets of Peking, demanding their government do something about Japan. They thought Chiang Kai-shek seemed more interested in stopping communism than in fighting the Japanese."

"We foreigners were nervous, of course, but I don't think it seemed quite real. To be frank, we felt invulnerable. In those days, to be white in Asia was to be above the ordinary. No matter what threatened China, we thought we were safe."

"And yet," I asked, "the Japanese didn't make that distinction at all, did they, when they finally did come in?"

"No. After Pearl Harbor, they treated white people, especially the British, as brutally as they treated everybody else. But it was poor China and the Chinese who suffered the brunt of their cruelty." Jane moved restlessly and stretched out her legs.

Mei got up and pulled one of the train company's hot water thermoses from under a table. She opened it and peered into it, then asked, in English, "Want tea?"

Jane and I both nodded.

Mei pulled her bag over to her, opened it, and found a box of tea bags. She showed me the box, which was blue-green and had a dragon design. Mei's work-worn hands brushed over one of the Chinese characters on the box. "Green tea," she said.

I stared at the character—stylistic, like a motif. "I wish I could read Chinese."

Deftly, Mei poured water from the thermos over tea bags she had put in three white cups supplied by the train company. I reached for one and she stopped me. "Wait. Too hot." Mei sat down beside me again, picked up the tea box, and showed me some more characters. "This mean China," she said. "Easy." She traced the characters in her palm.

I stared at the characters on the box. The first looked like a flattened circle with a line through it. "I've seen this one!" I said. I rummaged around in my pocket and drew out the plastic chit the train attendant had given me in exchange for my ticket. "There," I said, triumphantly holding up the piece of plastic. There was a flattened circle with a line drawn through it.

Jane and Mei both laughed. Mei took my plastic chit and held it next to the box of tea. "Zhong," she said.

Jane explained. "That character, Zhong, means middle—middle bunk, Middle Kingdom; China is the Middle Kingdom."

I couldn't help smiling. "Hey! I've learned a Chinese character." I felt absurdly proud. Mei laughed gently, as proud of me as if I were her daughter. After that, it was easier for me to ask if I could pull out my little video camera and ask them a few more questions. "I just want to see how a train interview would look on camera," I explained.

I trained the camera on Jane and decided I liked the idea of close-up shots with the train in the background. I knew I could take these now and a camera crew could work them into a finished product—if it ever came to that. I shot a few seconds, then played them back. Although Jane had agreed I could use the camera, I could tell she wasn't sure she liked the idea. Mei, on the other hand, wasn't at all bothered by it. She settled herself comfortably, sipping the tea. On camera, Jane looked exasperated; Mei's smooth features filmed better. I wondered how Jane would react when I told her our cameramen would want to film her all over again, maybe take her back to Chengdu and shoot scenes of a family reunion in Mei's house. But I'd never get these train shots again, or the freshness of her tale told to me for the first time.

Again, I reminded myself that I really didn't know what kind of story I had evolving here. The elements sounded promising: unsolved murder; war; and a lost child—the last, at least, with a happy ending. Well, I thought, glancing at my watch, I still had thirty-plus hours.

I laid the camera aside and picked up my notebook. "So. Tell me about how you found Mei. You said it took years." This, after all, was the heart of the story. "So you just now found her?"

"That's right. That's why I flew straight from Hong Kong to Chengdu. She'd been living there all her life."

"Tell me about it."

She hesitated, a play of emotions flickering over her features. "The whole experience has been so surreal. Even now I look at Mei and..." Jane paused a moment, then said, "Do you have any idea how hard it would be to find a child in China? I searched for her in nineteen forty-six, forty-seven, but I got so sick I had to leave. I came back in forty-eight, then was forced out when the communists marched in. Then China closed down."

I felt a chill on the back of my neck at Jane's last words. I remembered talking to someone my father knew, in preparation for this trip: a ninety-year-old former diplomat who had served in China. He told me how awful it had been all those years when most people couldn't get into China, and he had no idea what had happened to so many friends left behind.

Jane went on. "I've always had Chinese friends — those who escaped the communists and those who stayed. I always knew someone in the Chinese embassy in Washington, and I made sure to keep in touch with our embassy in Peking after we reopened relations with China. I came back as soon as Americans could travel to China again. I came back again in the early eighties. Then I got sick again, real sick. Then, like a sign from God, I went home one day and found a letter shoved into my mailbox. Mei doesn't write English, you know, so someone had obviously addressed it for her. It had been so long since I had read Chinese characters, I had to ask a Chinese friend to help me read it." Jane stopped to clear her throat. "I was so weary, I had almost given up. Then there was that letter, covered with bright Chinese stamps."

I got my camera up just in time. I got it all, the comments about the Chinese stamps, the pain in Jane's face. She blinked into the camera and looked away.

That's fantastic, I thought. I was getting excited about how this documentary was going to look.

Jane looked out the window again. "I don't know if I want to do this."

Three other people — two women and a man — shared our compartment, and a steady stream of people made their way down the aisle, moving from car to car. Once, a man came in and stopped to talk to the man in our compartment. They sat on a lower bunk and pulled out cigarettes and smoked, speaking intensely and rapidly in low tones.

An attendant banged her way into the compartment and glared at the interloper with small, piggy eyes. Leaning over the bunk, she berated him loudly, her voice harsh.

"What's she saying?" I asked Jane.

"He can't come in here; he's in first class — soft sleeper."

The man stood. He kept smiling and talking to the other man over his shoulder as he left the compartment. Staring at him, the attendant stood her ground.

"What's her problem?" I asked.

Mei said something and Jane interpreted: the man from soft sleeper obviously had some money. The attendant worked for the government-run railroad. The work was boring, but the other rewards were worth it. She got to coast along, but was never going to get rich, and she resented these newly wealthy people. There were rules about passengers sticking to the compartments they had paid for, and the attendant must have enjoyed enforcing them.

Once the attendant left, the young couple who shared our compartment got up from one of the tables by the window and settled themselves opposite me. Smiling shyly, they told me they wanted to practice speaking English. They spoke for several minutes about mundane things; their English was stilted. After a while, the other woman in the compartment, a young Chinese, joined us.

I thought she was the most interesting of the three. She told me she worked in a cafe in Chengdu, frequented by foreigners, where she earned more than her father, who had been a teacher for many years. Her father felt this turned the generations upside-down, but the young woman was pleased to be earning so much.

She had other plans, she said. "I try to find rich foreign lover, maybe Hong Kong businessman. My friends also find. These rich men take care of us." She was very pretty and she knew it. She had been leaning forward to confide in me, her long hair falling across her face. Now she straightened up, her triumphant eyes meeting mine. I was startled at how her plan sounded like the old concubinage system.

The Chinese man, sticking to English for my benefit, asked, "You mean a real foreigner or a Hong Kong Chinese?"

"I mean outside-country Chinese businessman. Hong Kong. Singapore. They have more money than Mainland businessmen."

The young man said, "Soon, they are same. Mainland businessmen get rich fast. You see." His wife was much plainer than the ambitious little beauty. The couple inched closer together and glared at the would-be concubine. My fingers itched to pick up my video camera, but I didn't dare.

At this point, Mei joined the conversation. Having been able to follow some of the English, she now said in Chinese, which both Jane and the good-looking young woman interpreted for me, "In Chengdu, more people than ever are 'jumping into the sea.'" This meant leaving the cozy certainty of government work for the private sector and a chance to take advantage of the economic boom.

"What about your family, Mei?" I asked. "Do your people work in the private sector or in the government?"

Mei held her head up and said, in Chinese, "My foster parents were very poor, and I didn't have much of an education. But now, my son is an engineer. He too works for the government." She raised her chin even further when she told the other Chinese in the compartment that her son earned enough to take care of her — a widow — and his wife and child. "He doesn't gamble on private business," she said. "It's better this way. Now, I am an old woman and I should live quietly."

I caught her glancing at the budding concubine. Was she jealous? I wondered. There was uncertainty in government jobs too, because there are fewer government jobs than there used to be. The private sector was growing, and the cumbersome machinery of the old state enterprise system was, in many instances, grinding to a halt. It had provided food and shelter, what the Chinese had referred to as "the iron rice bowl" — iron, because they had thought it couldn't be broken.

After a while, the others wandered off, and Jane began to tell me some more of her story. "You can even use that... thingamabob." She waved her hand impatiently at my video camera. "If you want, that is."

I put my hand on the camera. "Just keep talking," I said. "Let me worry about the technical stuff."

CHAPTER 4
PEKING, FEBRUARY 1936

Unable to sleep, Jane lay in her room. She stared at a scroll Li Han had given her, and, in the darkness, found it frighteningly unfamiliar. The expertly brushed characters seemed to take on new shapes and dance around on the paper. Jane blinked. Were the characters on the scroll slipping into the pools of shadow on the wall? She rolled over, turning her back to the scroll and forcing her mind back to the recent events that roiled in her head—the events that threatened to pick up her happy home and turn it flat on its back.

Although she was angry with everyone involved, she found herself worried about her father, who looked increasingly unhappy as the days passed. He had lost weight, become irritable, and developed dark circles under his eyes. Sometimes she heard her parents arguing—something she had seldom heard in the past. From the little she was able to overhear, she concluded that Della had not recovered one iota from her fierce anger about Cyrus' friend Donald Bauman taking Will to a brothel.

Donald and Electra Bauman had invited Will to Shanghai several times each year since he had turned twelve. The Baumans had no children of their own, though they had two Jack Russell terriers they doted on. They had always been particularly fond of Will. Donald made no secret of his desire to bring the bright young man into his network of businesses. From time to time, Cyrus protested that Will would first go to college in the United States, and then either become a missionary like his parents, or use his knowledge of China and the

Chinese language to join the American Foreign Service. When Cyrus told Donald he couldn't see a son of his going into business, Donald said he recalled a youthful Cyrus from thirty years before—another bright young McPherson who had almost gone into business with his friend Donald before deciding to follow in his father's missionary footsteps.

Electra especially seemed to like having Will around. A pretty, fashionable woman, she hosted large dinner parties at the impressive Bauman house in Shanghai's International Settlement, and liked to invite Will to meet their friends and acquaintances. Will confided in Jane that some of his classmates thought he spent time with the Baumans because they were wealthy and had no heir for their considerable fortune. One of his friends had winked at him and said the McPherson parents were being very clever. Somewhat ashamed of his unworldly parents and at the same time enormously protective of them, especially of his mother, Will had laughed and pretended Cyrus and Della were fully aware of the implications of the Baumans' wealth and their fondness for him.

"Mater and Pater realize people will think this sort of thing," he told his friends—he had taken to calling his parents Mater and Pater in emulation of some of his British friends—"but they're missionaries, you know. They've forsworn worldly goods. I kind of admire the old folks, myself." Because Will was so popular, his friends had second thoughts about the issue and finally admitted they admired the McPhersons' integrity. A few of the diplomats and businessmen's sons who looked up to the handsome, athletic Will found themselves wishing their parents were missionaries.

Although Cyrus and Donald had been friends since boyhood, Jane and Will were aware of tension between Della and Electra, and knew it was the friendship between the husbands that kept the families in close touch. Unlike her mother, Jane admired Donald and Electra, especially Electra, who was the most stylish woman Jane had ever seen: Jane had overheard a Peking matron say to another that Electra's clothes were "bang up to the minute."

"I wished she fussed over me the way she does over you," Jane had once told Will.

Will wriggled uncomfortably. "Oh, she doesn't really fuss so much."

"She's my ideal," Jane said when she was sure Della wasn't listening.

A number of foreigners in both Peking and Shanghai had remarked on the odd friendship between the McPhersons and the Baumans, who appeared to have nothing in common. When Donald first came to Shanghai, he worked for Jardine-Matheson in what people said was one of the wickedest, most exciting cities on earth. Less than twenty years earlier, he had gone into business for himself, played his cards right, sent for his new bride, Electra, and now, like a circus juggler, kept a series of balls in the air. Some of his business interests were rumored to be less than savory; he was said to have good connections with an old triad—or Chinese Mafia—family, which in turn had connections with Chiang Kai-shek's nationalist government. Sometimes described as "sleek," Donald looked it. He combed his hair straight back in the style of the 'teens and early twenties—Electra couldn't get him to update it—and wore showy tailored suits.

When they visited Peking, Donald and Electra always stayed with English friends who lived in a former high official's palace filled with antiques and bustling with a large staff of servants. The English couple was considered a part of Peking "society," and when Donald and Electra were in town they hobnobbed with heads of legations and famous authors. They played tennis on Saturdays at the Peking Club, and brought their two terriers, Lizzie and Pearl, up to Peking for the annual dog show.

Cyrus and Della seemed the Baumans' opposites. Cyrus was unworldly and naive, and Della staunchly maintained she was a homebody. Short of time and money, she neglected her natural good looks. Her sparse wardrobe was cheap and unfashionable and, unlike Electra, she did not watch her figure and had allowed her once slender waist to thicken. The McPhersons were occasionally invited to large semiannual receptions at which the head of the American legation included all Americans in Peking, but, as missionaries, they did not mingle with the glittering crowd of diplomats and literati that flocked to the Chinese capital during the 1920s and '30s.

Yet the McPhersons and the Baumans retained close ties; Cyrus had even asked the Baumans to take care of Jane and Will should anything happen to Della and him. Cyrus and Donald had been roommates at

Yale, and had planned to go into business together after graduation. They had had much in common, as service in China ran like a thread through their respective family trees. Donald's grandfather had barely escaped death in the Chinese countryside during the Taiping Rebellion more than a half-century before. Cyrus' father had died at the hands of the Boxers in 1900.

Donald had been bitterly disappointed when Cyrus told him Jesus Christ spoke louder than dollar signs, and that he was being called to plow the fields of the Lord, as he put it, as had his father and grandfather before him. Donald thought there were better ways to modernize China than by being a missionary.

Jane tossed again on her narrow bed, tangling her feet in the quilt and impatiently kicking free. A sound from outside rose and fell in the darkness — the faint sound of men laughing. Oh, the Chinese, she thought, and sighed. However harsh their lives, they were still able to forget their troubles, if only for a moment, and laugh with their friends. Why can't we forget and go on with our lives? And why was Ma being so stubborn about the Baumans? Didn't it teach in the Bible that one should forgive? Shouldn't one also forget, as if the bad things hadn't happened? Why couldn't they go back to that sparkling September day, the last time the Baumans had come to the McPherson home for tea?

The day had been warm, but with a crispness in the air, the first hint of the sparkling autumn that would follow — the season most foreigners believed was Peking's loveliest. As usual, Cyrus had been delighted to hear that his old friend was going to be in Peking again and had invited the Baumans for tea, making the same joke he always did, that nobody was anybody in Peking society who hadn't been to the McPhersons' for tea. As far as Jane knew, Della never objected to Cyrus' impulsive invitations. She compressed her lips and didn't say much, but she always asked the cook to serve a lavish spread of home-baked rolls and cake, or anything else she happened to have on hand.

Hearing a commotion at the gate that day, Jane rushed into the courtyard. The gatekeeper had swung the gate wide. Two rickshaw coolies, glistening with sweat, dropped their poles and rubbed their hands as Electra climbed out and strolled through the gate, laughing, while Donald hung back to pay the men. As always, the Baumans looked out of place in the shabby mission home. Donald wore a light tweed suit, with a crisp handkerchief in his breast pocket, and Electra was dressed in a long, pencil-slim skirt, a fawn-colored belted cardigan, and a little hat perched over one eye. Lizzie and Pearl, the Jack Russell terriers, trotted back and forth around their ankles; the dogs had ridden in the rickshaws.

"Hi, Lizzie. Hi, Pearl." Jane greeted the dogs, while grinning broadly at Donald and Electra.

Donald answered for the dogs in a falsetto tone, the corners of his small mouth twisted down with the effort, making Jane laugh, until Electra said, "I bet you still miss your sweet old Raleigh."

Raleigh, the McPhersons' old spaniel, had died the previous winter. Jane nodded and tried not to think about when Raleigh used to greet Donald and Electra, before Cyrus had found Raleigh stiff and cold one morning. The last time the Baumans had seen the old dog, Raleigh had dragged his tired body to the gate to snuffle at Electra and Donald and to warn passersby that he was still in charge of the compound. He had waddled out through the gate, as he always did, and sniffed the packed dirt of the *hutong* to see who had lately passed by. Electra had knelt in the dust—never mind her dress—and hugged the dog, telling him he was getting too old. When she looked up, there were tears in her eyes.

Jane tossed her head to put Raleigh out of her mind just as Della emerged from the house to see what the commotion was all about. Jane glanced anxiously at her mother, who had twisted an apron around her thick waist. The apron made her look even bulkier than she was. Jane's sharp, critical eyes also noticed that Della had bundled her brown hair into a clumsy knot at the back of her neck and that it didn't suit her.

Della seemed unaware of her shortcomings. She wiped her hands on her apron and called, "Come in, come in."

Donald raised his hand in greeting. "I hope you've been baking those wonderful rolls I've been hankering for."

Della smiled, not widely, but with a slight tightening at the corners of her mouth. "I made the rolls, and other things besides." She stood aside as they came up the steps. As usual, she and Electra did not meet each other's eyes. "Aren't the streets dusty?" Della addressed the question to Donald. "You must miss your wonderful big automobile." Donald and Electra kept a 1933 Packard in Shanghai. The state of the roads and the danger from bandits and tag ends of warlords' armies did not permit them to bring it to Peking; they always took the train, instead.

Electra put up a hand to shield her eyes from the late afternoon sun. She laughed. "This is fun. I love Peking. So different from naughty old Shanghai. One lives at a different pace here. A dreaming pace, a world of the mind, rather than of the pocketbook and too many thoughts of war."

"Never knew you objected to the pocketbook, old girl," Donald said. He sometimes liked to affect English mannerisms and ways of speech.

Holding on to her hat with one hand, Electra took Donald's arm. "You know what I mean, darling. I don't express myself very well."

They mounted the steps into the sitting room.

"You express yourself very well, Electra," said Della, in her quiet voice. "And you're right about Peking. It does have a dreamy quality."

"Pei-ping, not Peking," said Donald. "Why do we never learn to say Peiping?" The nationalist leader Chiang Kai-shek had changed the city's name from "northern capital" to "northern peace" in 1927 when he had established his capital in Nanking.

Donald stepped over the high threshold and helped Della, then Electra, into the room. The dogs followed, hopping lightly over the smooth, worn threshold into the room. As everyone—people and dogs—moved out of the sunshine into the dimness under the old rafters, Electra laughed again. "Because, darling Donald, it's silly to keep changing the names of these places. I know you have to use it because you always have to talk to those dreary old men around Chiang Kai-shek. But none of the rest of us have to use it, do we, Della?"

"The name's been changed for several years now," Donald said.

"Well, people don't change as readily as the leaders would like them to," Della said. She nudged Jane. "Go and tell your father Donald and Electra are here, would you?"

Jane ran to Cyrus' study, stealing a backward glance at Electra's fashionable clothes.

Over English tea, which the Number One Boy served in sturdy Western-style cups with handles, along with sugar and milk, the four adults discussed the current political situation, while Will and Jane sat silently, listening and eating sandwiches and cake. Both children were bored, because their father had seized on the issue of communism, which he did at every opportunity; the whole family had heard his opinions all too often. Will, trying to divert attention from his father's anticommunist diatribe, made what he thought were amusing remarks, which were rewarded by sparkling glances from Electra.

Della had been polite, but distant. Jane knew her mother also hated it when Cyrus got carried away with his anticommunist talk. She didn't interrupt him though, just kept pressing more tea on the guests and asking Jane and Will to pass the sandwiches and the cake around.

When the visit began, Electra had been vivacious, even chatty, but as the afternoon wore on, she became restless. She began to trace patterns with her foot. Her fist clenched and unclenched. Cyrus seemed to notice none of this. He was too engrossed in expressing his opinion of the communists. Donald agreed with Cyrus that the communists spelled trouble. Donald worked closely with the officials of Chiang Kai-shek's Nationalist Party, or Kuomintang, as it was called, and had no time for what he described as "the so-called idealism" of the communists and many of their youthful followers.

As usual, Cyrus got carried away. He saw the communist versus nationalist struggle from an angle somewhat different from that of a Shanghai businessman like Donald. Cyrus believed the rumors that communists were harassing missionaries, particularly American missionaries, throughout China. Though it hadn't happened in their community so far, Cyrus had heard that some communists accused missionaries of killing Chinese babies and gouging out their eyes to make medicine. Cyrus was certain this kind of irresponsible rumormongering would eventually result in mob action somewhere, sometime, against the missionaries.

"He's brought this up in some of his sermons," Della said quietly.

Cyrus raised his voice and tried to ignore Della's comment, which was her way of reminding him that he himself was guilty of propagating the vicious rumors. "These rumors have an unfortunate effect on so many of the young people today, especially the students, who want to believe everything the communists say," he said. He grimaced as if he couldn't understand what there possibly could be to admire about the communists.

The others looked uncomfortable, and Della said, "Not all the missionaries feel this way, you know. Some understand that there's a genuine need for reform and that the communists are trying to address it."

Donald spoke up again, his small mouth twisting in his ironical way, making his words seem friendlier and less serious than they might have been. "You know, Cyrus, the missionaries are responsible for all this free thinking in the first place. Who else taught the Chinese to love the masses and think for themselves?"

Electra laughed, making the others turn and look at her. "Donald's not very happy about this, are you, darling?"

"You missionaries could have been a little less zealous," Donald said. Again, the corners of his mouth twisted down, but his eyes were flinty.

Cyrus flushed and Della said quickly, "You ask us to do less than our best?"

Donald shrugged. "In the long run, it doesn't matter," he said. "China's bound to change, whether we like it or not. The trick is to change with her."

"Han admires the communists," Jane said suddenly. Everyone looked at her. "You know Han," she said to the Baumans.

"Li Wutang's son," Della murmured.

"The kids' Chinese friend," Cyrus said.

"Of course," said Donald.

Electra said nothing, but stole an appraising look at Jane.

There was an uncomfortable silence. Jane was sorry she'd spoken. She suspected Donald didn't like Chinese people very much. She had once heard him defend the practice in Shanghai of restricting the Chinese to certain parts of their own city.

"Un-Christian," Cyrus had pronounced sternly, opposed to the practice as always.

"But practical and necessary," said Donald, his small mouth tightening. Della had told Jane that Donald had never completely gotten over his anger with Cyrus for abandoning their plan to go into business together. Donald laughed and made light of Cyrus' pronouncements, but all the McPhersons could sense his impatience with Cyrus' beliefs. Donald told people he often didn't agree with Cyrus, but would defend his old friend "to the death."

Electra laughed. "On top of everything else, Donald feels he has to be nice to these dreadful Japanese that are swarming all over the place." She made a face at Cyrus. "Can you imagine? They're so arrogant. I refuse to speak to them." She crossed her legs and swung her foot back and forth. "If Donald has to go someplace where there're Japanese, I won't go. I hate them. I really, really hate them."

Donald looked troubled. "I'm afraid their arrogance is justified, my dear. They are swallowing up China, and no one seems inclined to stop them. So, I feel I have to be practical and deal with them."

"Poor China," said Electra. She sighed heavily.

"These are terrible times," said Della. The two women stole a look at each other, in agreement for once.

Jane stopped listening. It was not a subject she liked to talk about; Japan's aggression troubled her deeply, and disturbed her peaceful dreams and her plans for the future. The city gates she used to think invincible would not keep out the Japanese.

Electra apparently didn't want to listen either. Still restless, she shifted around in her chair, glancing swiftly at each of the others in turn. The blue-and-white Ming Dynasty bowl caught her eye. She frowned, narrowed her eyes, then turned to Della and asked in a low voice if the bowl was new. "I haven't seen it here before. It looks real, but surely..." She paused, waiting for Della to answer.

Della glanced at the bowl and said, "Ambrose Varley gave it to me. It was a surprise for my birthday."

Electra stared at the bowl. "Then it is real," she whispered. She looked at Della, her eyes wide. "Do you have any idea what that's worth?"

Della lifted her shoulders. "I think it's real pretty, don't you? It was fine of Ambrose to think of me that way."

"Cyrus doesn't mind another man giving you gifts?" As always when she talked to Della, Electra's voice sounded unnatural. Even to Jane, who admired Electra, the older woman's tone seemed strained and silly.

Della snorted. "My, no. Cyrus was pleased as punch that I got such a pretty thing. I haven't had that many pretty objects in my life."

Electra stared at her again, then got up and asked where her little dogs were, keeping her voice low so the men could go on talking. Della got up too, and said Little Gao was playing with them in the kitchen.

As Cyrus and Donald continued their heated discussion about the Japanese, Jane could hear the two women's voices behind her. Della said, "I hear the dogs now."

Electra said, "They're calling Mommy. Naughty babies." She laughed again.

Della, her voice flat—which Jane knew meant disapproving—said, "Jane, take Mrs. Bauman to the kitchen. Then come right back. There's another plate of rolls out there. Bring it back with you."

Jane scrambled out of her chair and led Electra out of the room and into the kitchen, where Cook, now that the McPhersons' tea was out of the way, prepared a meal for the servants. He chopped a stalk of green onion on a wooden table, wielding the cleaver rapidly in staccato taps over the wooden surface. Nearby, smoke rose from a blackened wok perched aslant on the stove. The cook tossed the handful of onion into the oil, making it sizzle. He grabbed a piece of meat and chopped it in smooth, quick motions. He tossed the meat into the wok with the onions, and an appetizing aroma rose to greet Jane and Electra.

A grinning Little Gao sat on the floor, making faces at Electra's dogs and feeding them scraps of meat. When Little Gao inched too close to the stove, forcing Cook to step around him, the cook merely smiled. Everyone made allowances for Little Gao.

When the dogs saw Electra, they abandoned Little Gao to hurl themselves on their mistress. She knelt down and gathered them both into her arms. Little Gao rocked back on his haunches, his face contorted with disappointment. "It's all right," Electra said to him, dodging her face this way and that because the terriers frantically licked at it. "Yes, Lizzie. Yes, Pearl," she said to the dogs. Then to Little Gao, "You love my little darlings, don't you?"

Little Gao grinned and nodded. Despite his limitations, he understood rudimentary English. Electra pulled herself to her feet and spoke to the prancing dogs. "We'll go to the garden, my darlings. You'll get your walk." She crossed the kitchen and the dogs followed. "Come," Electra said to Little Gao. "You may come with us." He ran after her and scooped up one of the dogs. It was Lizzie, always his favorite.

Picking up the plate of rolls her mother had wanted, Jane watched Electra, Little Gao, and the two dogs disappear into the bright sunshine of the courtyard. Cook asked her if she was hungry and she nodded absently. With a pair of chopsticks, he handed her a piece of meat, which she chewed on while she watched a square of sunlight on the paving stones just outside the kitchen door. She heard Electra's voice say, "My little darlings love their mommy, don't they? No one else loves me."

Jane had wondered what Donald, deep in conversation with Cyrus in the darkened sitting room, would have thought about this kind of complaint from his wife.

Little Gao was surely a problem. Jane pulled the padded quilt tighter up to her chin as she continued to ponder these relationships. There was nothing she could do about her mother's anger at the Baumans, but the Little Gao incident affected the very heart of her life in Peking.

Cyrus too seemed mostly haunted by Little Gao. He couldn't stop talking about it, even in front of Jane and Will, continuously castigating himself for acting too hastily, for not being sensitive to Li Wutang and the rest of the Li family. Jane remembered overhearing her mother, obviously exasperated beyond bearing, cry out, "What's done is done!"

How happy Little Gao had seemed that day last September, following Electra and the dogs into the courtyard. Jane wondered what he was doing now, and what he thought about everything that had happened. Did he hate her family? Since Electra was a friend of the McPhersons, would he ever again look at her with those same admiring eyes, or even hold his favorite dog, Lizzie, close to his chest?

Jane knew from Han that Cyrus had apologized to Li Wutang for summarily dismissing a member of the Li family. While Han remained unconcerned about the Little Gao incident and seemed increasingly wrapped up in politics, Jane thought she could read between the lines of what Han said: Cyrus' action had stung Wutang; Old Grandfather was furious.

Li Wutang had been courteous and graceful in accepting Cyrus' apologies. He told Cyrus he understood perfectly and that they were not to talk of it anymore. When Cyrus offered to rehire Little Gao, Wutang protested, saying he had given the scamp a few cuffs on the side of the head himself. No, if the boy was unreliable, don't hire him, Wutang said. At the same time, he managed to let Cyrus know how upset Old Grandfather was, and how the entire family had had to placate the old man, which also meant moving up the date of Han's wedding, which would now be in March, the following month, Wutang said.

Cyrus came home and smote his forehead with the palm of his hand. "What have I done to that boy?" he asked.

Jane wondered if he meant Little Gao or Han.

The McPherson family was at the supper table when Cyrus had said this. While they ate, the servants gossiped in the kitchen and sometimes moved in and out of the dining room, frankly listening to what the family had to say. Cyrus and Della had learned long ago that they had no secrets from the servants, and had decided not to waste time trying to shut them out.

"I was thinking, Mother." Cyrus addressed his remarks to Della. "We should offer to hold the wedding here in our home. That might help make up for some of this. It would give Wutang enormous face, wouldn't it? He said it would be proper to have a Christian wedding, although Old Grandfather insists it must also be Chinese."

"Like the Li family—Christian and Chinese," Will said, reaching for more bread. The McPhersons seldom ate Chinese food at home, though all of them were familiar with and liked many Chinese delicacies.

"A wedding in our home?" Della asked. "Oh, Cyrus, I don't know. How would we be able to put on such a hybrid Christian-Chinese wedding? Besides, I'm not certain we could afford it." Out of necessity, Della was a frugal housekeeper. She kept hard-to-get staples such as vanilla extract and white sugar in a padlocked storeroom, and doled out supplies to the servants a day at a time. She and the cook

canned fruits and vegetables grown on the compound or purchased
at the local market, and made apple cider in a homemade press. The
McPhersons' meat came from the local market, their milk from goats
raised by other missionaries.

"It would seem such a mongrel event, wouldn't it?" Della said. "Besides, you know as well as I do that Han isn't a good Christian. He's
fought it every step of the way and would probably fight this too. He's
rebellious, like so many young Chinese these days. And his sisters
married non-Christian men."

"The sisters don't matter, they now belong to other families," Sometimes Cyrus didn't realize how Chinese he had become. "Wutang and
Ailian will know what to do about the ceremony. We merely provide
the space and offer food and drink."

"They're making Han go through with this just because that nasty
old grandfather insists on it? If you tried to do that to me, I'd run off
to America," Will said.

Della put more food on Will's plate. "You sound as if we were Chinese, Will."

"Well, we are, practically."

"Will, finish eating. You don't know what you're talking about. The
Li family is under tremendous pressures," Cyrus said.

"I know that, Pa. But, gee whiz, Han's a modern man."

"He's still a boy, my dear," said Della.

"Then he's too young to marry!" Will shot his mother a triumphant
look.

"We all believe he's too young," she said quietly. "But we can hardly
interfere in their private family matters."

"It's not fair," said Will.

Jane saw no point in arguing with Cyrus and Della. To divert her
brother, who was capable of debating for hours, she asked, "Would the
bride come to our house in a red chair?" They all had seen traditional
Chinese brides being carried through the streets of the city, shut inside
a covered sedan chair, their faces hidden by red veils. They were accompanied by prancing, capering men playing horns, drums, and cymbals.

"Will they have the traditional bride teasing?" Will wanted to know.
"You know, where they—"

"That's enough, Will," said Cyrus, stealing a look at Jane.

"I just wondered," Will mumbled. Jane smiled to herself to see how quickly Will had backed down this time. He had been greatly chastened over the brothel incident, as well he should be, thought Jane, still shocked at her brother's behavior.

A dull flush swept across Cyrus' face. Even at fifty, tall, ungainly Cyrus was easily embarrassed and blushed like a boy. He was more emotional than his calm, analytical wife, and it seemed every passing thought announced itself in his face.

Will shrugged and stretched in a sudden, graceful movement. He had his father's height, but none of his awkwardness.

Jane knew exactly what the bride teasing at a Chinese wedding was all about. The more rowdy of the groom's friends made jokes with sexual innuendoes, and tried to confuse and embarrass the bride. They would go on all night if encouraged, and often someone had to intervene to get them to leave.

Jane had a fairly good idea of what took place in a bridal bed, though she lived a sheltered existence, and had been taught nothing about the facts of life beyond her mother's self-conscious explanation of menstruation, which, Della said, meant that young girls could have unwanted babies, causing great shame and ruining their lives. Sensing there was a lot she wasn't being told, Jane listened carefully to the things the servants and other Chinese said, and the Chinese — an earthy people — said a great deal about sex. Jane learned these things in the most graphic and colorful terms, none of which she could or would have expressed in English.

She realized she didn't want to think about Han in bed with his bride. She lowered her eyes and, as soon as she was allowed, slipped away from the table.

Jane had heard from the servants that the Ding girl Han's grandfather wanted him to marry was ambivalent about marrying Han. She too was modern, but not in the same way as Han. To her, being modern meant wearing lipstick and dancing to American music. Jane had heard one of the missionaries describe her as a listless, not-too-bright girl who told people she supposed Han would make a good husband. She wanted badly to get married, and he seemed as good a catch as any. However, she pouted with boredom when anyone mentioned politics, and Jane wondered what in the world the couple would find to talk about.

Jane's face burned as she remembered telling Han only six months ago that they could marry each other. He had come to the McPhersons' house with his father, who had wanted to confer privately with Cyrus on some business concerning the mission. Cyrus and Wutang had gone into the study, leaving the two young people in the sitting room.

Han had talked to her about politics until they heard Amah's voice rising, shrill and scolding, from the courtyard, as she harangued one of the rickshaw men who had brought Wutang and Han to the McPherson home. Amah often railed at laborers or rickshaw coolies who lingered at the gate after finishing their business with the household. They usually wanted someone on the compound to give them a sip of tea or water, so they would have the strength to be on their way. Jane's parents had decreed that no one should be turned away, so Amah or the Number One Boy almost always gave them something. But Amah thought they were dirty, and unworthy to enter the gate, so she made them pay for their refreshment with her harsh words.

Jane knew Amah would be coming in to scold her next, because she was alone in the sitting room with Han. Della, as a modern American mother, saw no harm in Jane talking alone with the nice young son of the Li family. After all, Han and her children had been childhood friends. Amah thought it a scandal, however. She had warned Jane that she was a young woman now and could not meet alone with young men. Jane had laughed at her, and said that even Chinese young people did not follow those rules any longer, which had angered Amah.

Speaking quickly, afraid Amah would come in and embarrass her in front of Han, Jane lost her head and embarrassed herself by blurting out they shared so many of the same interests and ideas, and so should remain together for the rest of their lives.

Han laughed and wouldn't meet her eyes. "You're still a child. You don't know about these things."

"I was only trying to explain how things are," she whispered. She could feel her cheeks burn. "But I'm not a child. Not any longer."

Han stopped laughing. "I cannot marry my little sister, who just happens to have fair hair and round blue eyes."

"But your family is like ours. Your father is Christian too and works with the missionaries."

"It is not the same," Han said gently. "We are Chinese."

"I'm Chinese too. I was born here. I don't feel like an American."

"I think that in your soul you are partly Chinese. But I cannot marry my little sister. That would be against both Christian and Chinese teachings."

This, like so many of their conversations, was in Chinese. Sometimes they spoke in English, because Han wanted to practice his English, which was not nearly as good as Jane's Chinese.

After that day, Jane's feelings about Han underwent a subtle transformation. She became aware that he was almost a grown man: his body had filled out; he was taller. His quick, excited glance—seeming always to burn with intensity at his interests—now slid away when their eyes met. For the first time, she realized what it would mean for Han to make a Chinese marriage. He would grow away from her and would be intimate only with his wife.

Li Han had been a strong force in her life ever since she could remember. She knew her parents probably didn't realize the extent to which Han taught the McPherson children about the city and about Chinese culture and history. It was not unusual for the three to sneak away to the crowded markets, to gobble street foods, which Della had forbidden her children to eat: in winter, fragrant roasted sweet potatoes that warmed first your hands and then your stomach; and sticks of bright-red candied crab apples all year round. Once, Han had even taken Jane and Will outside the walls to see an execution. Both children had come home sickened by what they saw, but had not dared tell their parents why, for several nights following this experience, they had had nightmares of bodies pitching forward and blood pooling on the dusty ground.

When Will became too busy with his studies and his sports—both he and Jane went to the Peking American School—to continue running around the city with his sister and his Chinese friend, Han continued his excursions with Jane. She frequently taunted Will that Han had found time for her though he was just as busy as Will with his university studies. "Maybe more so," said Jane, "because he has political meetings, too."

"Things that'll get him in trouble," Will said.

But Jane and Han kept up their outings around Peking, all the while chatting in a mixture of Chinese and English about their current studies and passions, and about the political situation in China. Several times, the two had raced in rickshaws to the city wall, which was crowned with battlements, like the parapets of medieval fortresses. Han and Jane would scramble up onto the wall and walk side by side along the top, where armored horsemen once galloped two abreast, bearing the banners of the empire. But the two young people encountered nothing more than an occasional goat or donkey that wandered unfettered along the top and tugged at the weeds that had sprouted up between the ancient bricks. Before the sun sank over the distant Western Hills, the two would lean on the parapets and watch the present-day soldiers who stood guard below. As in the old days, the city gates would be closed at night, though no one any longer believed this would keep out the enemy.

Thoughts of the city walls and sunsets finally lulled Jane to sleep.

She dreamed that she and Han clung tightly to each other's hands as they leaned over the battlemented wall. In her dream, she knew both Han and she were afraid of falling and had only each other for support.

The next morning, a tap on her window awakened her. She gazed at the scroll, which looked as it always had, and laughed at her nighttime fears. The tap sounded again, and she got out of bed, padded over to the door, and opened it. Will stood shivering and hugging himself in the open passageway facing the courtyard. His face was scarlet.

"What is it?" Jane asked.

"I'm supposed to tell you the Baumans are coming over for tea and you're to go out there right away."

"The Baumans? But they haven't been here since..." Jane stopped. She hadn't thought it was possible for Will to blush any harder, but he did. "Does Ma know they're coming?" she asked.

Will nodded, jumping up and down in the cold. "Ma's on the warpath." He grabbed at the wooden balustrade. "Damn!" he said.

"Will! You're not supposed to swear."

"I don't care." Will looked around anyway. "I like the Baumans. They've always treated me all right..." He stopped, and blushed again.

"I've never seen Ma so upset." He glanced away, looking miserable. Will loved his mother dearly; the two formed an alliance within the family, often going off to corners of the house or garden so they could talk and laugh together. Father and daughter were left out. Cyrus sometimes seemed in awe of his handsome, athletic son, and Jane, watching her mother's eyes follow Will about the house, felt she had nothing to say that would hold her mother's interest.

"Ma said you can't ever go to see the Baumans again," Jane told Will.

"I know. Pa's going to try to talk her out of it."

"Pa's forgiven you?" It was the first time Jane had ever spoken directly to Will about Donald Bauman taking her brother to a brothel.

"Sure. Donald is Pa's best friend."

"But why are the Baumans coming now? Who invited them?"

"Pa did, a couple weeks ago. They wrote and said they were coming to Peking, and Pa said they must come to tea, like always. I guess he and Donald set a date."

Jane shook her head.

"Jane, I'm cold," Will said. "Just come to the sitting room, will you?"

"Did Ma ask for me to come?"

"No, Pa did. I think he needs all the support he can get."

"We're not going to be rude, are we?" Jane asked.

"I'm not."

"Me neither." Jane could not remember a time when Della had failed to greet a guest with hospitality.

Jane quickly dressed and followed Will back along the passageway and into the sitting room at the front of the house. Della was nowhere in sight, but they found their father pacing in the outer courtyard. Jane noticed Will's subdued manner. Normally, he would have been joking with Cyrus and the gatekeeper, keeping everybody chuckling, and drawing admiring glances from his parents and the servants. Today, he hardly said a word. Still cold, he hugged himself and tried to take shelter out of the wind.

It was Jane who approached their father. "Pa?" she asked. "If Ma's so angry at the Baumans, why are they coming over?"

"We invited them." Cyrus flushed dark red and wouldn't look at Jane. She remembered that she wasn't supposed to know why Della no longer wanted to see Electra and Donald.

Jane tried again. "Where's Ma?"

Cyrus glanced around as if expecting to see Della pop out from behind a tree. "Oh, she's here somewhere," he said, and went on pacing.

"Are we serving tea?" Jane asked.

He whirled around, his eyes angry. "Of course. Don't we always serve our guests?"

A moment later, Jane heard the sounds of the rickshaws outside the gate. This time, Jane and Will stood back, silent, while the gatekeeper hobbled out to swing open the red-painted doors. Cyrus stepped forward, frowning, his shoulders hunched, to greet his friends.

Electra's dancing eyes appeared around the gate. She lifted her hand in greeting. "Darlings," she said, "why the long faces?"

Chapter 5

Present-day China

Jane excused herself to find the washroom. Mei and I watched her make her way down the aisle, grabbing at bunks and tables along the way to keep her balance.

I glanced out the window. It was quite dark. There were no pinpoints of light as you might expect to find in an American landscape, though I had always heard that China was one of the most densely populated countries in the world. I asked Mei if I could sit next to the window. She moved over, and I pressed my nose against the glass.

I was sorry it was dark. We were moving through the interior of China, and I wanted to see what it looked like. Earlier, Tim and I had flown from Beijing to Chengdu, and had seen it only from the air.

While I stared out the window, we shot past a cluster of lights. A farm, a village? I didn't know. Surely we had gained some altitude, I thought. I remembered the mountains I had seen in the distance as we left Chengdu, faintly etched against the horizon, almost invisible because of the polluted air.

I remembered a few lines from my book of Tang Dynasty poetry, something about mountains in China where no one is seen but human voices are heard. The words haunted me, running over and over in my mind, in time with the clacking of the train wheels. The poem echoed what I had been thinking: the people were out there; more than a billion of them, but I couldn't see them.

I felt Mei touch my shoulder and turned around.

"Have picture of boyfriend?" she asked.

I shook my head, "No, not with me." I thought about the picture of Tim and me that hung on the refrigerator in my apartment. It was taken on the day we went to the lake; we had asked someone to snap it for us. We sat on a towel in the sand, bodies leaning toward each other, our faces close, and our smiles wide.

Mei reached into her bag and pulled out a fistful of photographs. "Mother give me," she said. "You want see?"

"Sure." I took the black-and-white photos, all old, and dog-eared at the edges. I stared down at the first one. A tall, well-formed young man with thick hair worn in a side part stretched himself nonchalantly on a grassy lawn. He was almost movie-star handsome, with light-colored eyes and a fine, narrow nose. He wore some kind of athletic sweater. "Who is this?" I asked Mei.

"Mo-ther's bro-ther," Mei said, drawing the words out.

I peered at the picture again. "Is this Will?"

She nodded. "Will."

I slid the picture under the stack I held, and looked at the next one. It too was of Will, in formal dress, with two girls and another boy. "My God, he was good looking," I said. I stared at the picture. It was funny to think such a hunk had gotten old—if he had lived. I looked up and saw Jane coming toward us.

I wondered briefly if Mei should have been showing me the pictures, but Jane didn't seem bothered. Instead, she sat down beside us, took out her glasses, and put them on, prepared to take an active interest in the photos.

"Look," she said, "These are Will too." The next two shots were of Will seated in the front rows of what looked like athletic teams. Jane said something to Mei, and Mei dug out some more pictures. Jane passed me another, which depicted three people on the steps of what looked like a mansion.

"That's Donald and Electra Bauman in front of their house in Shang-hai." Jane said. "With Will, of course."

"Lots of pictures of Will," I said as I took the photograph.

"He was fun to photograph. He liked the camera."

"And the camera liked him."

I studied the picture in my hand. Donald and Electra Bauman stood on either side of Will, who was the tallest of the three. Donald was well dressed, thickset, and had a small mouth set in a quirky half-smile. Electra's face had a blurry look, as if she had moved just as the picture was taken, but I could see she was very stylish, in one of those elegant, impossibly formal outfits they used to wear back in the thirties. Her posture was excellent, causing me instinctively to pull back my shoulders. Two fat, little spotted dogs crouched at her feet.

I looked up at Jane. "I wish I could see Electra's face better."

Jane grimaced. "By the time that picture was snapped, she had taken to wearing too much make-up. Middle age was staring her in the face." She passed me another photo. "Here, look at this."

It was a family portrait of the McPhersons. Jane told me it had been taken in 1931. The parents were seated, the two children on either side. Although Jane, who would have been about eleven in this photo, had been a pretty girl, her brother's vivid good looks made her seem almost plain. Her features were delicate, her forehead broad, her eyebrows high and pencil thin, like those of a Chinese beauty in an old scroll painting. Cyrus was tall, like Will, though his features seemed blurred and heavy next to his handsome son. Oddly enough, my eyes were drawn to Della, who had an arresting face. Although not slender like Jane, she resembled her daughter—fine features and those same high, delicate eyebrows. But it was her expression that made me look at her more than once. Her chin was high, and her mouth was well shaped and firm. Her eyes looked directly at the camera. She didn't smile. She looked different from the others. I puzzled over this for a few seconds, then realized that Della had a contemporary face; the others belonged to the 1930s, but she would have looked equally at home in the present day. Aside from her old-fashioned hairstyle, I could easily have run into her on the streets of Minneapolis.

The next picture was of Della alone. She wore the same clothes as in the family portrait, which had obviously been taken at the same time. Both pictures were marked with the name of a Peking photographic studio embossed in gold across a lower corner.

Jane stared at her mother's face for a second or two without saying anything, then handed me another picture, again an informal black-and-white snapshot. "Electra gave me this one," Jane said, peering at me over the top of her glasses. "After my mother died."

I held it up to the light. This was a young, slim Della. She resembled the young picture of Jane. This time, she grinned into the sunshine. There seemed to be some kind of parade and people in uniforms behind her. I turned the picture over. Someone had written, "The Glorious Fourth. San Francisco, 1919."

"San Francisco?" I asked.

Jane nodded. "It was taken shortly before she left for China the second time. They had gone back on furlough."

Jane passed me the next photograph. "That's home," she said. "Those are the servants. See?"

Both pictures were somewhat blurred, but clear enough to see the lines of the courtyard Jane had told me about. The servants, a middle-aged woman and three men, were dressed in Chinese clothes. Their faces were difficult to make out.

"That's Amah," said Jane, moving her index finger across the snapshots I held in each hand. "She had bound feet, you know."

"Did Han's mother have bound feet?"

"No. Her family must have been more enlightened. When Han's mother, Ailian, was born—it must have been about the turn of the century—people were starting to question those old customs."

I glanced at my own size nines. "Did your amah walk funny?"

"She could go at a pretty good clip, but she sort of tottered. And her feet ached. She used to rub them." Jane moved her finger across the picture again. "That's the Number One Boy—he was in charge of the others—and the cook and the gatekeeper. And then this one…" She held up the next photo, then brushed her fingers across it. When she looked up, her face had softened. She held out the picture so I could see it. "The Li family," she said.

It was a formal family portrait. Han's parents, Li Wutang and Li Ailian, stood on either side of an elderly gentleman, who sat, hands on his knees, in a carved Chinese chair. He wore a long robe with long sleeves and a high collar, soft shoes, and a small cap. A tuft of white beard sprouted from his chin. "Old Grandfather, right?" I asked.

Jane nodded. I studied the picture some more. Wutang wore a dark Western-style suit, and stood with shoulders relaxed, his hands folded in front of him, eyes narrowed in the sun, lips folded into a scowl, probably because of the sun shining directly into his eyes. Ailian was considerably shorter than her husband. Her cheeks were plump, her hair pulled back into a knot and cut in curled bangs over her forehead. Her short-sleeved, high-collared, ankle-length dress was too tight; her belly protruded slightly. Several other people stood behind the couple, dressed in old-fashioned long-sleeved gowns.

I deliberately saved the boy for last. He too wore a traditional gown, but his hair was cut in a style similar to Will's, and looked as if it had been slicked down with oil or water. I stabbed at the picture with my finger and asked, "Is this Li Han?"

Jane smiled. "Yes, that's my friend Han."

Like Della in the other picture, Han gazed directly into the camera. Unlike Della, he smiled. His smile brought out a dimple on one side of his rather large mouth.

"He's appealing," I said. "When was this taken? How old was he?"

"In thirty-four or -five? He would have been about seventeen. See the way he dressed? Many students dressed like that. It was national pride."

I handed the photo to Mei. She put down the others and held the one of the Li family at arm's length, squinting at it.

"So Han became a communist," I said.

"He felt he had no choice. It was the times."

"But he must have believed in it."

"Oh, fervently. Sometimes, that was all we ever talked about."

"What about his family?"

"His father was crushed. I tremble to think what the old grandfather said or did."

"So everybody was against Han. Except you, of course."

"I didn't count. I was only a young girl."

Speaking of the communists reminded me of Ambrose Varley, and I asked Jane if she had a picture of him. She shook her head.

"Better yet," I said, "how about the eunuch?"

She chuckled and said, "No picture of him, either. Too bad. Whenever I saw him, I used to wonder so! About his anatomy, I mean, because he was a eunuch."

When I grimaced, Jane said, "It didn't seem so strange to the Chinese of the time."

"Well, it seems barbaric to me." I looked pointedly at the photograph remaining in Jane's hand. "There's one more. What's that one?"

She handed it to me. "Guess who this is." She held it up so both Mei and I could see it. Mei smiled and said, "Beautiful girl." She touched the photo lightly with a graceful movement.

I took the photo and looked at it. A lovely, wide-eyed and pensive young girl leaned back against a tree. Light-brown hair curled under to her shoulders, and she had light eyes with high, delicate brows. I looked up into Jane's wrinkled face—the same delicate eyebrows, now almost transparent. "That's you, isn't it? You were so pretty."

She smiled and said nothing.

"How old were you?"

"Nearly sixteen."

I held the photo up next to Mei's face. Did she have those same light, high eyebrows because she had inherited them from Jane or because she was Chinese? I wondered. Mei grinned and stuck her own face down close to the picture. She looked sideways at Jane, and suddenly I thought I could see a resemblance. Maybe it was the eyebrows, or maybe I was only imagining it.

"You look worried here," I told Jane.

"Things were building up when that was taken: Han's problems, the demonstrations, politics in general. The clouds were gathering over China. It was affecting all of us. You could feel it." Jane stared at the photo. "Right after this picture was taken, everything changed." She handed the photographs back to Mei, who stacked them neatly and returned them to her handbag.

"So you brought these to show Mei her family," I said.

"Of course. I also brought her a few other things from the family. Nothing valuable—we didn't have anything valuable left."

"What did you bring?"

"Some old children's books. They were Will's. They're in English, of course, but they have pictures and they belonged to our family. All lovingly inscribed by our mother," said Jane. "He had other books, of course, but these are the ones he kept. None of mine survived."

"How come his books survived and yours didn't?"

Jane sighed. "It's all part of a long story. The short answer is that he sent a trunk of these things to the States with a friend before the war started. We lost everything else."

"If we do this film, could we use some of those photos?" I asked.

Jane shrugged. "I don't see why not, but you'll have to ask Mei. They belong to her now."

I didn't know if Mei understood my question, but I decided we could discuss it when the time came. I opened my mouth to ask Jane where she and Will had been when the war started, but she forestalled me: "Mei showed me pictures too. Of her husband and son, her little granddaughter." She lowered her voice. "Mei's a widow, you know."

I nodded. "Yes, that's what she said. I get the impression she's had a rough life."

"I imagine so," Jane said. "But to tell you the truth, Mei hasn't told me much. I know the last fifteen years have been all right. But earlier…" Jane shook her head. "Mei's aging foster parents died just as things started to improve in China. Mei felt terrible when they died, of course. She mourned them like any good daughter, but in her case, it was even worse. She knew they weren't her real parents, and yet they died having told her all they knew. And it wasn't enough." Jane told me about Mei at her foster mother's funeral—which she had heard from Mei's son—knocking her head on the ground and wailing that the good woman had suffered so in life.

Jane looked at Mei and said something in Chinese; Jane interpreted her reply. "When I was growing up, there were times when I wondered how different my life would have been if my own mother had taken me to America. But that didn't happen, and one shouldn't dwell on what could have been. Still, so many forces were against me in China, and being different caused me the greatest pain." Mei took a deep breath. "I often asked my foster mother to describe my American mother to me, and with tears in her eyes she would tell me how much my American mother loved me. She said that my American mother would come and find me someday, but that she hoped it wouldn't be too soon. She loved me, you see. As a child I often dreamed of my American mother, and I could almost feel her caressing my hair, as if her spirit was with me.

I wanted so badly to know what she looked like. I had no photographs, only this pendant, this porcelain shard."

I gazed at the pendant. I had seen similar ones for sale in Beijing, but I could also see how protective Mei was of this one, how, at times, she clenched it in her fists. I glanced at the smooth porcelain surface: the glaze on the blue-and-white leaf pattern glowed as if with an inner light. The sharp edges of the shard had been ringed in silver. Up close, it looked nothing like the souvenir items I had seen in Beijing shops.

"I do have an early childhood memory that has always sustained me and given me warmth of the heart," Mei continued. "It is of two people hovering over me. I was on a woman's lap, being rocked in what seemed a rocking chair. The woman kissed my head, and sang a song over and over." Mei began to hum quietly, and then sang in a voice so soft Jane and I could barely hear it. "He gone a get a bon-nee skin a put a ba-bee bunting in..." Mei looked down and then said, "Somehow, I've always understood that it connected with my past."

Jane spoke suddenly; it was one of the few times I heard her address Mei in English. "I had no idea you remembered that song. I used to sing it to you every night. Did you know that? I, your mama, sang it to you, long, long ago. I rocked you as I sang." Jane's voice broke, and she shut her mouth with a sudden snap. Then her face crumpled, and she put up her hand as if to ward off whatever it was that was making her cry. She sobbed, "When you find your child after more than fifty years, you can't be certain. They told me she was my child, they showed me proof, but how could I have known for sure, even with the shard? How could I remember from all those years ago what it really looked like? Now... now I know. She really is my little Meihua, my little plum blossom."

Mei reached out her hand to her mother. Jane took it and squeezed her eyes shut. After a while, she regained control of herself, opened her eyes, and said to me in a normal voice, "It was a song my own mother sang to me when I was very small. It always made me feel so safe."

CHAPTER 6

PEKING, FEBRUARY-MARCH 1936

"Darlings, why the long faces?"

Jane saw Electra's eyes first as she poked her head around the gate—lovely, blue eyes, fringed with black lashes—and then Donald peered over her shoulder. Electra giggled, then the gate opened farther and they stepped into the courtyard.

As usual, they were stylishly dressed, despite the cold. Electra wore a fur coat that flashed open to reveal a black-and-white-checked suit, and she had wrapped a white scarf around her neck and up around her head. Donald too was bundled up, but in a fur-trimmed long coat and scarf, not a Chinese padded jacket such as the McPhersons wore. He carried his pipe, which meant he had been smoking it in the rickshaw. For once, the dogs, Lizzie and Pearl, were not with them. Jane was glad of this. As awful as she felt about the coming confrontation with Della, it would have been worse somehow had the dogs been present.

Electra was in an excited and chatty mood. She came forward, laughing, holding out her gloved hands to Cyrus, obviously expecting him to catch both her hands in his own. Cyrus had always treated Electra with deference—after all, she was his old friend's wife—but he blushed easily and often when he was around her. When she tried to embrace him or called him "darling," as she did so many people, he was visibly uncomfortable.

Donald noticed Cyrus' expression before Electra did. He wiped his smile off his face and said, "What's wrong, old man?"

Cyrus glanced uneasily at Jane and Will, then said in a low voice to Donald, "Why don't the three of us go off to my study. We need to talk."

Jane glanced at Will. He stared at the ground, not looking at either Donald or Electra.

It hadn't yet registered with Electra that anything was wrong. After aiming an air kiss in Cyrus' direction, she enfolded Jane in a tickly embrace, all perfume and warm fur, then turned to Will and did the same with him. "My darlings," she said. She backed up and looked around the courtyard. "Where's your mother?"

"Electra," said Donald, reaching out an arm as if to encircle her; it was a gesture to come with him and Cyrus. Electra yanked her scarf down from her chin, winked at Jane and Will, giggled, and followed the two men across the paving stones, tottering on her high heels.

Jane stared after her. "Do you think she might be drunk?" Jane whispered to Will.

"Nah. She acts like that a lot. She just gets excited."

"Do you think Ma's going to talk to them?"

Will shrugged his shoulders, trying to look as if he didn't care. Jane couldn't imagine what he must be feeling. This break with the Baumans—if that's what it should come to—was all his fault. She felt a sudden surge of sympathy for her brother, but didn't know how to express it without embarrassing him further.

Jane went into the sitting room and sat by the coal brazier, holding her hands out to the warmth and rubbing them together. A shaft of sunlight hit the scuffed floorboards, and Jane moved into its warmth. She could hear the Seth Thomas clock ticking, and distant voices—she recognized her father's deep rumble. She pictured Donald's and Electra's faces falling in dismay as Cyrus told them what was wrong, all that friendly brightness wiped out of Electra's eyes. Jane wondered where Della was. Had she joined the others in the study or had she remained hidden? Would she ever agree to see the Baumans again?

After about a half-hour, she heard light footsteps tapping on the wooden passageway outside. She scrambled to her feet and ran to the door. Electra came up the passageway from Cyrus' study. She had wrapped her scarf closely around her head and stared down as she tapped her way over the floorboards in her high heels. Jane stepped over the threshold.

Electra looked up. In spite of the cold, her face was shiny with perspiration.

"Are you all right?" Jane asked. "Do you want to come inside?"

Electra stared at her a moment, then said, "If I could just sit down. I feel a little wobbly." Her voice had lost its earlier lilt; she spoke almost in a monotone.

Jane took her arm, thick and soft because of its fur sleeve, and led her over the threshold and to a chair. Electra sank down and closed her eyes. "Can I get you anything? Maybe tea?" Jane asked.

"What? No, thank you." She flashed Jane a quick smile. "You're a darling," she told Jane. "I've always thought so."

They sat together in silence for several minutes, then Jane asked, "Have you seen my mother?"

Electra jerked up her head. She shuddered. "Your mother" was all she said.

Jane heard footsteps and voices outside. A moment later, her father and Donald came into the room. Both men's faces were flushed and their expressions were solemn.

Jane heard a great deal about the encounter over the course of the next several days. She filled in the little that Cyrus and Della told her with a great deal that Amah passed along. The meeting in the study had been unpleasant and embarrassing. Cyrus had tried gently to prepare the Baumans for Della's wrath, but had failed. "You have to understand her complete devotion to the boy…" he had begun, when Della burst into the room and swept them all with an icy glance.

"Your mama did not say much," Amah told Jane, "but they understood her meaning."

Della kept her voice low, even gentle. It was her eyes that conveyed her message: the Baumans must never, ever try to see Will again. They had corrupted a child. It was unforgivable. Maybe God forgave such sins. She, Della, didn't, couldn't.

Donald tried to interrupt Della several times, protesting the evening had not been planned, others had suggested the brothel — "a high-class joint," Donald had said — but Della had talked him down. When she asked Donald, "How could you do such a thing?" Electra had fled the room, saying she was going to be sick.

"Let her go," Donald said, his face paper white. "It's not her fault, anyway. She didn't know where I was taking Will. She knew nothing about it." He turned to Cyrus. "Don't you know how these evenings are? When the men get together?" Cyrus had averted his eyes.

Della left them then, and the two men had talked quietly, trying to mend the rift for the sake of their old friendship. Cyrus even had put his hand on Donald's shoulder and said, "We're all sinners. I'm not judging you. I want you to know that."

Donald had apologized again, and Cyrus patted his shoulder. Donald asked, "Della will cool off, won't she?" Cyrus shook his head. "I've never seen her like this," he said.

The next day, Della announced that Will was leaving China as soon as he graduated, and would return to the United States to go to college. No more dilly-dallying and talking about going into business. He would live with a distant cousin of Della's and try to get a scholarship to a good university. Since it was late in the year, he probably would have to work for a while first, but that would be all right. He could earn much-needed money. "Even a scholarship won't take care of it all," Della said.

Will had exploded, going red in the face and yelling at his mother for the first time in his life. He vowed he wouldn't go. He would run away first. He didn't know anything about the United States. He wanted to stay in China.

He only quieted down when Cyrus thundered at him, "You will never, ever again speak to your mother that way. What's the matter with you? Have you lost your mind? Every other boy around here goes to college. They brave the unknown."

Will had run out of the room, and Jane had sadly wandered out into the courtyard. Never had she felt so alone. She wanted badly to talk to Han, but knew he had troubles enough of his own. His marriage was fast approaching—and he was not happy about it.

Han was married on a cold, sunny day only a few weeks later. Wutang and his wife, Ailian, had accepted the McPhersons' offer to hold the wedding in their home. Wutang had seemed pleased at the idea, and Jane had heard her mother say it gave the Li family "face." For their part, the McPhersons were glad to put the Bauman incident out of their minds and concentrate on planning Han's wedding, however much they disapproved of arranged marriages.

At one point, Jane asked her parents how they could so readily help out with a ceremony they thought was a mistake. Della's answer was curt; she was busy with all the arrangements, and Jane had interrupted her. "Han must learn to put up with what can't be helped," she said, "just like the rest of us."

Cyrus had averted his eyes and said something about it being all for the good.

Jane, disgusted with both parents' answers, had flounced off to her room. There, she stared at the calligraphy scroll Han had given her, and rolled back and forth on her bed, feeling real suffering at the thought of Han being absorbed into China's ancient ways, becoming one with a people Jane was just beginning to realize would never fully accept her.

As it turned out, the "Christian-Chinese" wedding was confusing to most of the guests, who managed to enjoy themselves anyway. Cyrus officiated over the young couple's Christian vows. Miss Ding had approached the house in the traditional red chair; the banging and clashing of musical instruments—faint, in the distance, then louder, closer—signaling her approach. To add to the commotion, several of the Li cousins had lit a long string of firecrackers on the outer courtyard paving stones. As the bridal procession came into sight, the firecrackers jumped and popped. People grinned broadly or laughed out loud. Some held their ears. Small children giggled and danced and shrieked. A smoky mist from the firecrackers drifted across the courtyard.

The servants spread a piece of carpeting on the ground for the bride to walk on as she stepped out of her chair. She looked lovely in a white Western-style gown and veil that seemed to rise in a cloud around her, contrasting with her dark hair and eyes. Jane would have thought the bride intimidated by the noise and attention, stepping out of the

seclusion of the chair to see so many strange faces, some of them foreign. But Miss Ding wore bright-red lipstick like a banner—she had
obviously been victorious after a long battle with her mother—and
her black eyes danced with mischief and triumph through the almost
transparent veil.

There was another burst of music and a clash of cymbals. The guests
crowded into the main room, pushing each other in their eagerness
to see the bride. Even Little Gao was there as a cousin of the Li family. Jane saw him hurry by, joking noisily with a friend, his expression
giving no indication that he was embarrassed or angry over losing
his job.

Jane watched Han's mother, Ailian, hurry forward through the crowd,
a pleased smile splitting her plump features. Her modern-style silk
dress, with short sleeves and a high collar, was too tight, but otherwise
she looked pretty. For several weeks, Ailian had been telling people
her new daughter-in-law was modest and dutiful. Jane wondered what
people thought now that they had seen the bride with her lipstick and
her mischievous eyes. Maybe Ailian was merely putting the best face
on the situation, Jane thought. Wutang also was grinning today, but then
why shouldn't he? He had honored his old father's wishes. He kept
darting glances at elderly Mr. Ding—his father's contemporary—as
if to say, "You see? My family has kept its promise."

Old Grandfather sat inside, impassively accepting greetings and
congratulations from the steady stream of guests who approached
him; he was not happy that the wedding was part Christian. He wore
a plum-colored robe with side fastenings, a cap, and soft Chinese shoes.
Della had taken Jane up to greet him when he first entered the house,
supported by Wutang and one of Wutang's brothers. Jane had bowed
to the old man, trying to keep her anger and dislike from showing on
her face. She knew she would never forgive him for forcing Han to go
through with this marriage and possibly ruining his life. She also knew
her opinion on any subject was worth nothing to Old Grandfather, who
saw her merely as a female "foreign devil."

Most of the wedding guests were Chinese, though Ambrose Varley
was there because he was a special friend of Han's. Jane's friend Frances
Appleton also was a guest at the wedding, along with her missionary

parents. As soon as the Appletons entered the room, Frances spotted Jane and grinned excitedly. Both girls had both been part of the mission since they could remember, and, because they were the same age, had practically grown up together.

Frances slipped from her parents' side and hurried over to Jane. "Don't you just love weddings? Even Chinese ones? I cannot wait until it's my turn."

"You're only fifteen, like me." Jane was scornful.

"That's all right. I already know whom I'm going to marry."

"I suppose it's Will." Frances didn't make any secret of her admiration for Jane's handsome brother. Jane knew that Will barely noticed the plain-featured Frances.

Frances' face fell. "Shh. Don't say anything." She glanced around. "I'd have a real American wedding, though. I'd wear a white gown like Miss Ding, only much finer. And I'd be married in a church, coming down an aisle."

Jane said nothing, but knew that if she married, she would prefer a partially Chinese wedding like the one today. The ceremony would be Christian, too, of course, but Jane also approved of the Chinese traditions. She rather liked the notion of riding bumpily through the streets in the sedan chair, her face covered by a red veil. The world would be a reddish haze when seen through such a veil, Jane decided. According to custom, she wouldn't take the veil off, but would allow her bridegroom to remove it in the privacy of their room. In her mind, the unknown bridegroom had Han's features, and she pushed these out of her mind and determinedly gave the man the face of a stranger. As in traditional China, he wouldn't have set eyes on her before. Full of unbearable curiosity and nervousness, he would slowly lift her veil—

"What are you smiling at?" Frances wanted to know.

Jane couldn't explain how funny she found the idea of the poor Chinese bridegroom lifting the veil and discovering his bride was a foreign devil. To avoid answering Frances' question, Jane said, "Do you understand this ceremony?"

"No. I think it's boring." Frances stood on tiptoe and strained to see through the crowd.

Now Jane could catch a glimpse of Han's face through the crowd.

Unlike everyone around him, he wasn't smiling. Well, he hadn't wanted to marry, Jane thought. She felt another surge of anger at Wutang and Ailian, who were grinning so broadly.

Earlier in the day, Jane had cornered Han in the courtyard and said, "I wish you happiness." She stood still, waiting for his response and had been taken aback when he had not replied nor even met her eyes.

Finally, he said, "I am not concerned with happiness."

Jane felt sad. "What do you mean?"

Han raised his eyes and stared over her head. A gust of wind swept into the courtyard, touching Jane's cheek, then rattling the dried leaves of the past season. The wind went on to ruffle Han's hair. Jane shivered. It was as if the breeze were somehow bringing them together. She glanced up at his eyes, but he still refused to look directly at her. She thought about the bridal bed at the Li home, and imagined Han and Miss Ding in it together. No, she thought, pushing away the image. This is all wrong. She felt a surge of hatred for silly Miss Ding, and shivered again at the thought of Han stretched out in the traditional Chinese bed. A great, carved Chinese bed, she knew, was a private world where you could keep your most necessary possessions and draw the curtains against everyone else. When Han climbed into the bed that first night with Miss Ding, Jane would be among all those stranded outside.

Above their heads, a bird darted from the tiled rooftop to the paving stones, then back to the rooftop. Han kept his eyes on the bird while he said, "Today, I will do my duty to my family."

Jane opened her mouth to speak, but Han forestalled her. "Soon, I will do my duty to my country."

Jane looked up again and this time he looked directly into her eyes. "Your eyes are very blue," he said.

"But that doesn't mean—"

"Shhh. You are still my little sister."

He might have said more but they were interrupted by Little Gao and another, more distant, Li cousin, who leaned together against the house, out of the wind, and lit cigarettes.

Jane turned back to Han, wanting to ask him what he meant, but he signaled to her to be quiet and moved swiftly back to the house.

Now the ceremony was almost over. Han and Miss Ding had signed the scrolls. Cyrus was saying some words over their bowed heads. Someone moved and blocked Jane's view of Han's face. The murmur of voices rose. People crowded closer.

A burst of music. A clashing of cymbals. Han was married.

Chapter 7

Present-day China

The Chinese passengers in their compartment began to prepare for bed. They queued up for the washroom; some put on pajamas, plumped pillows, and climbed up onto their bunks. I stood up, stretched, and looked up at my bed. It was narrow, and the three-inch-thick foam covering didn't look very comfortable. I pulled down the pillow and looked at it. There were several smudges on it, so I pulled a sweater out of my backpack and draped it over the head of the bed.

"I guess we just do what they do," I said, gesturing to the other people in the car. "They're Chinese. They know the drill."

"Mei's Chinese," Jane said, her mouth pulled tight in amusement. She said something quickly to Mei and they both laughed. I felt my face grow hot.

"You know what I mean," I said, not sure I knew myself.

There was no way I was going to put on what passed for pajamas in my wardrobe, I thought—a long T-shirt. I had slept in jeans before and I could do it again. I figured I could go into the bathroom in the morning, use deodorant copiously, and change my shirt. I rummaged around in my bag, found my toothbrush and a bottle of clean water I had brought along for this purpose, and jostled my way to a communal sink where I brushed and spat. My spit, running down the drain, mingled with that of a Chinese girl next to me. Unlike me, with my bottled water, the Chinese girl held her toothbrush directly under the tap. Our eyes met in the mirror. She smiled at me, still brushing vigorously, and I recognized her as one of the women I had talked to earlier.

I offered the bottled water to Jane and Mei, who thanked me but declined. Jane said she had already used the clean water in the thermos, and Mei just smiled. After all, I thought, she was brought up in provincial China. I put away my washcloth and toothbrush, and steeled myself to visit the bathroom. The first time I'd made my way to the head of the car, waited my turn, and pulled open the door, I almost slammed it shut again. I had seen some filthy sights during my travel in China, but this bathroom—clumps of feces on the floor and unbearable stench—was beyond description.

I said something to Jane after that first trip to the bathroom: "Why? You grew up here. Why did they go on the floor?"

Jane, looking troubled, shook her head. "I guess they're not used to Western toilets?"

"Have you asked Mei about it?"

She made a dismissive gesture, then said, "Most of them don't have the kind of bathrooms we have, you know. Sitting up high on a kind of throne wouldn't make much sense if you've been squatting all your life. In fact, it might nigh be impossible."

Jane told me about a widely traveled Chinese who said that the United States impressed him in so many ways, but he couldn't understand why Americans went to such trouble to keep their bathrooms clean. They were, by nature, dirty places. This was a natural thing, and Westerners tended to fight it.

"Well, I'm going to keep on fighting it," I said. Just then, Mei came back from a walk through the car, and I looked away. I had been thinking of her as an American who just happened not to understand much English. Now, I realized how stupid I had been to think that way. Mei had been raised entirely in an alien culture and so was completely foreign. I wondered how Jane felt about this.

I climbed up on my upper bunk and sneaked my video camera out of my backpack. From where I lay, I had a bird's-eye view of the entire compartment. The woman who had brushed her teeth next to me had returned to her bunk, wearing what looked like her husband's coat as a bathrobe. He lay on the upper bunk and she climbed into the middle one and grinned up at him. They reached out their hands and touched briefly and laughed. I wondered if they had joked about being separated for the night and how they'd prefer to be someplace where they could make love. She slipped off his coat and drew a cover up around her. The other woman, the beauty who wanted to be a concubine, wore her T-shirt and tight slacks to bed. She stretched out on top of the bedcovers, laid her beautifully manicured hands on her chest, and closed her eyes. Earlier, I had seen her applying some kind of cream to her face, and I could see it shining now across her cheeks and on her chin. I wondered if she had access to good cosmetics. I had seen American cosmetics for sale in the stores in Beijing, but they had been horribly expensive. I would have bought them only if I were desperate, and even most urban Chinese salaries were far, far below mine.

I raised the camera and panned the compartment. I let it run for a few minutes to get the sense of the cramped quarters, the moving train, and the feeling of pitching forward through the dark night to the northern capital.

Before long, someone turned off the lights, and I lay in the dark, staring at the ceiling. I remembered watching the scene between Jane and Mei as they discovered their common memory. It hadn't dawned on me that Jane would have wondered if Mei were really her daughter. I tried to imagine what it would feel like to see someone you love after such a long time. As wonderful as it might be, I was sure there would still be some resentment, feelings of abandonment and regret.

Now that I was stretched out flat and free to sleep, I found I was wide awake. The car was stuffy and still reeking of cigarette smoke. As I had feared, the bed was uncomfortable. With the ceiling only inches above my face, I felt an unaccustomed claustrophobia. I tried to turn over, shaking the whole bunk.

Below me, I heard Jane whisper, "Pippa, can't you sleep, either?" On the middle bunk between us, Mei stirred.

I leaned over to look down at Jane. "Mei's doing fine," I whispered.

"She's used to this. You're not. I'm just old—I can't sleep anywhere."

"We're not the only ones," I said. The couple was still awake, now sitting up, talking and smoking. I could see the red tips of several lighted cigarettes bobbing in the darkness. To me, who couldn't understand a word of Chinese, the rapid rising and falling tones of their conversation sounded harsh, almost angry, yet I doubted they were arguing.

"You want to talk some more?" I asked.

Jane waited a while before she answered. "I guess so."

We rocked with the train for a moment or two, then I whispered, "Does it seem funny to you that that's your daughter sleeping on the bunk between us, that Chinese woman? She doesn't seem strange and alien?" In the dark, I felt able to ask that kind of question.

Jane's whisper came back immediately, harsh and slightly irritated. "Of course it seems strange. It took me so long to find her, I'd begun to doubt her existence."

"How did you feel when you first saw her?"

This time she took a while to answer, and I wondered if I had pressed too hard. The deepest part of night had descended. The train vibrated beneath us as it sped along the rails. The other people had gone to bed, all but one man who sat alone on his bunk and smoked. We passed through a sleeping town, barely slowing. Da-da da-dum. Da-da da-dum. We danced over the rail switches.

Finally, Jane said, "I'd left behind a small child, practically a baby. This was a woman, not only grown, but aged." She chuckled. "I felt old!" We laughed together for a moment, then Jane said, "I couldn't keep my eyes off her. Still can't. I see my mother in her face. When I arrived at her house in Chengdu, my grandson walked into the room, and my great-granddaughter—a little girl of three. I suddenly realized I was rich in family."

"You've had no other children? In the States?"

"No. I was married for a little while, but it didn't last. Looking back, I supposed it hadn't worked because I couldn't focus on it. My life was consumed with finding Mei, my lingering feelings for Han, and the tragedy that befell my parents."

Again, we were silent. Then I asked, "What do you do in the States? Where do you live?"

"I'm retired now. I live in Oakland, California. I've lived in the San Francisco area ever since I came back from China. What did I do? Well, I worked for the navy for a while, as a sort of secretary. I hadn't trained for much, you know, and only got that job because it was during the war and they needed people. They found out I spoke Chinese, and I got sent out to China after the war to help out with assistance efforts. 'Course, I would have gone anyway. I'd have done anything to get back to China and find Mei. Anything. I kept going back as long as I could."

"And your brother?"

"Will died some time ago."

"What about Li Han?"

There was another silence, then she said, "He's in Peking."

I shot up and banged my head on the ceiling. "He is? What's he doing?"

"He's an old man now. He was a Party official, and once was some mucky-muck in the Foreign Ministry."

I thought about the old men I had seen in the Beijing parks. The ones who dressed shabbily and met with their friends in the morning mists, bird cages by their sides. "Have you been in touch with him?" I asked.

"Not directly. Not for a long time. There was a period of years when it wouldn't have helped him at all to know someone like me."

"But indirectly?"

"He knows I'm in China. He's knows I'm coming to Peking."

I dozed off after that, braced uncomfortably against the hard edges of the bunk, though I didn't remember falling asleep. I woke once, feeling pressure on my ears, and realized we were gaining altitude. I looked out the window and could see the dark shapes of mountains. I remembered reading that earlier in this century Sichuan had been a remote province, sealed off by its mountains, its people made proud and independent by its inaccessibility to the capital. That was before they laid the first railroad tracks in the province. Someone had told me that missionaries and other foreigners making their way to Sichuan in the first decades of the twentieth century had to brave the strong currents and dangerous rapids of the Yangtze, as well as river pirates, while traveling in junks pulled upstream by crews on the riverbanks using plaited bamboo ropes.

I fell asleep again, and when I next opened my eyes, faint morning light had seeped into the car. The loudspeaker blared with some kind of announcement. An angry train attendant peered at me, scolding me in sharp, incomprehensible tones. I could see some of the other passengers rooting busily among their belongings, standing in the doorway and smoking, or sitting next to the windows, drinking tea.

"She wants your bedding," Jane said, gesturing to the attendant. Jane had cleared off her bunk and was standing in the narrow aisle. Mei was nowhere in sight.

I pulled the sheet out from under me and handed it to the attendant. "So early," I mumbled. I still felt half-asleep.

I looked around the car. "Where's Mei?"

"She's gone to find some breakfast. I had some tea, but didn't want anything else." Jane straightened her shoulders and smiled.

Jane seemed more relaxed this morning. She exchanged smiling glances with a middle-aged Chinese woman sitting on the next bunk. She had come in from another car. The two conversed rapidly in Chinese, and then Jane told me the woman, like others the night before, believed she was my mother or grandmother. The woman pulled out a package of wafer-like cookies and offered us some. I took one and munched on it; it was surprisingly good. While I watched, Jane made cups of tea from Mei's tea bags and the thermos of hot water the train attendant had supplied. Bracing herself against the movement of the train, she handed the cups to the Chinese woman and me.

"What does she do?" I asked.

"She works for the city government in Chengdu. She's going to Beijing for a conference."

I sat on the edge of the bunk, leaning forward, teacup in hand, both feet planted firmly on the floor. I turned to Jane. "Ask her what she did during the Cultural Revolution." The woman was fifty-one, the right age to have been a teenager in 1966, when the Cultural Revolution began.

Jane interpreted her answer, which had been given matter-of-factly: "She and her husband were Red Guards. She realizes now that the old people suffered terribly. Her father, who was a party official, died of his shame. Now all she wants is peace and quiet."

"You were a Red Guard?" I stared at the respectable-looking woman, who wore a yellow cardigan sweater, smartly creased slacks, and a pair of loafers. Her hair was cut and permed, and she carried a largish black handbag. The Red Guards, on the other hand, had been armies of howling, fanatical teenagers, set loose on the general population during

Mao's Cultural Revolution, which had been encouraged by his harpy of a fourth wife and her "Gang of Four." The Red Guards had cut a swathe of death and destruction across the land as they tried to grind China's past under their heels, victimized their elders, and blindly worshipped Mao, their "Red Sun." Many formerly respected officials and dedicated, self-sacrificing communists were killed or shamed during this agonizing period. In my conversations throughout my China trip, I learned that people didn't mind admitting the Cultural Revolution had been a rough time. On the other hand, I never heard a word against Mao.

"She says most of her generation were Red Guards," Jane said. The woman smiled suddenly, said something to Jane in Chinese, and giggled, a hand over her mouth.

"What did she say?" I asked Jane.

"She said there are now several Cultural Revolution theme restaurants in Beijing, where they sell the kind of peasant food glorified during the Cultural Revolution, and where former Red Guards post their business cards on bulletin boards so they can keep in touch with each other." Jane consulted the woman again, then said, "Most of these people are now very respectable—in business or government."

"Then why—"

"Aren't we all nostalgic for the period of our youth? You're still young. You may not know this yet."

I sat for a moment or two, unable to think of a thing to say. Nostalgic for a nightmare period in history, I thought? Something in me struggled and almost understood, but still it was mind-boggling.

The attendant came stomping down the aisle again, carrying a large load of sheets. The three of us watched her go by, united in our dislike. Jane's Chinese friend whispered something to Jane and giggled. She nudged Jane and nodded at me. Jane said, "She wants to tell you they don't wash the sheets very often. They give the passengers dirty ones all over again. She wants to know what you think about this."

I remembered the dirty pillowcase from the night before. "I don't think much of it. Why do they bother to strip the beds?"

Jane consulted with the Chinese woman. "She says they have been told to strip the beds, so they do it, but they don't do any more than they have to. She wants to know if we have government trains in America. I told her bureaucrats are bureaucrats the world over."

"I get it. Since the trains are still run by the government, the attendants are still part of the old party system."

Jane glanced at the woman, then nodded. "Some things seem to be changing rather radically; other things remain the same. It must be confusing, poor dears."

After a while, the woman got up and wandered off out of our compartment. I finished my tea and turned again to Jane. I had a question I wanted to ask before Mei got back. "Jane," I said, "What happened to Mei during the Cultural Revolution?"

"She doesn't talk much about it. From the little I know, she went through agonies because she was half-foreign. But I think she was mainly left alone because she was so poor and unimportant."

I chewed on the end of my ballpoint pen. "What about Li Han?" I asked. "What happened to him during that time?"

"He suffered. Like so many others."

"How did you hear this? I thought you hadn't been in touch."

Her smile faded. "There were people to tell me about him."

"What did they say?"

Jane cleared her throat. "He was called a 'capitalist roader,' you see." She cleared her throat again. "Because of his missionary background. I suppose he was paraded around, and had to wear the dunce cap while the Red Guards spit on him."

"When did he actually join the Communist Party?"

"I'll never know for sure, but I suppose it was back in thirty-six or shortly thereafter."

"He didn't tell you?"

"It was more complicated than that."

CHAPTER 8 - PEKING

APRIL 1936

On a Sunday evening in late April, Jane and Will went with their parents to the mission chapel where Cyrus was to preach the sermon. On Sunday evenings the mission chapel filled up quickly. Most of the congregants were poor, and probably "rice Christians"—people who cheerfully swore allegiance to a religion that gave out free food, warm clothes, and sometimes a place to stay. Such converts were good natured and attended services willingly. The building was warm, the foreign ceremony piqued their curiosity, and the occasion provided time for socializing. The Chinese relished Old Testament tales of bloody battles, supernatural beings, and the rise and fall of kings. One old man told Della that the story of Deborah reminded him of the legendary Chinese heroine Mu Lan, who disguised herself as a man and went off to battle to save her father.

The Chinese were baffled, on the other hand, by the teachings of Jesus, whom, they agreed, was a good man, but impractical in his philosophy. People listened politely to Cyrus' exhortations to turn the other cheek, then, puzzled, went to Wutang for explanations. Sometimes Wutang was hard pressed to explain the Scriptures himself, but he had the gift of gab, and usually was able to come up with an answer that satisfied his own conservative soul, as well as that of the listener.

Della had wanted to incorporate Chinese legends, such as Mu Lan, into her Sunday School teachings, but Cyrus had been adamantly opposed. "It might help the women put the Bible stories in contexts they can understand," Della had protested. "Some of them went to Ailian the other day, because what we were saying didn't make any sense to them. You should have heard what she said: she told them Jesus would throw stones at them if they did not stay in their houses and behave like traditional Chinese wives."

"What? Ailian knows better than that."

"It suits her own purposes. She's upset about her daughter-in-law." Della tried not to smile.

But Cyrus rolled his eyes. "I'd better talk to her. She understands the Scriptures very well. Throwing stones indeed."

On this particular Sunday evening, Della, Will, and Jane sat in their usual spot in the front row of chairs while people wandered into the chapel and settled themselves, laughing and chatting noisily, and staring at the foreigners with intense, friendly interest. Jane could see her father flitting in and out of the room, conferring with several others, sweeping the congregation with a wide glance. She kept looking at the empty chairs where Han's family usually sat, and wondered why they were late. Behind her, people shifted in their seats. Babies fussed and occasionally let out angry yells. Women, intent on chattering with their neighbors, shushed their babies by shoving the infants' heads under their jackets and nursing them; from where she sat, Jane could hear contented suckling noises from two just behind her.

The missionaries often complained about the smells in the closely packed room. Few poor Chinese possessed enough clothing to wash or change it, and especially during the cold months, the smell mixed with the pungent odor of garlic. Even in the spring the nights were still cool, and many still wore the padded jackets they had worn all winter. These smelled ripe, as did the unwashed bodies.

Jane was uncomfortably warm. She had felt cold at home and had selected a wool, long-sleeved dress. Now she felt overheated and itchy in the crowded room. She stared at the crudely made pulpit, with its embroidered cloth reading "God is Love" in English and Chinese, and tried to will her father to start the services. A few seats away, her friend, Frances Appleton, leaned forward and grinned at Jane, trying to catch her eye. Jane, who in the past few months had tired of Frances, shot her a small smile and quickly looked away.

Jane glanced at her mother, who sat serenely unconcerned at the smells and noise around her. Della had pulled a ball of yarn, knitting needles, and a half-finished sweater from a large bag she carried, and now calmly clicked the needles, keeping her eyes on the knitted form that lay across her lap. Jane knew her father strongly disapproved of Della knitting in chapel, and knew too that Della refused to obey him, though she always put the knitting away when the services started. "My busy fingers help control my thoughts," Jane had heard Della tell Cyrus. "Now I understand why the Catholics like their rosary beads."

Will sat next to Jane, overly large on the rickety chair, shifting and crossing and re-crossing his legs. He had not wanted to come. He was leaving the next day with friends from school for an outing in the Western Hills, and had protested to his parents that he had to pack. He gave in quickly, however, knowing he had lost much of his persuasiveness with both Cyrus and Della since his visit to the brothel. Where once they had stood in some awe of their handsome, accomplished son, they now apparently felt he had been cut down to size, and kept a strict eye on him. He had only been allowed the trip to the Western Hills because of assurances it would be well chaperoned.

There was a stir in the back of the room as Wutang, Ailian, Han, and his new wife came in. They settled in chairs in the row behind the McPhersons. Will turned, making his chair creak even more, and grinned at Han, who nodded, not smiling. Han looked like a child forced to do something he didn't want to do, his brow lowered, his mouth curled downward. Beside him, his wife ran her tongue over bright-red lipstick and glanced from side to side. She stole a few glances at Han, but he didn't look at her.

Jane looked again at Han and their eyes met briefly. She smiled, but, as he had done with Will, he refused to smile back and quickly looked away.

How unhappy he looks tonight, Jane thought. She knew why. The day before, Han's mother, Ailian, had arrived puffing and agitated, demanding that the gatekeeper find Della. The gate man bawled out for Amah, who hurried out to the courtyard on her bound feet, eyes bright with curiosity. Amah went back inside to get Della, while the Number One Boy had helped the plump and trembling Ailian into an overstuffed green plush chair in the sitting room, and gone off to fetch her some tea.

While Jane had hesitated, not sure whether to enter the sitting room, Della appeared, retying her apron and smoothing back her hair. "Yes, Ailian," she said, "whatever is the matter?" She had been in the kitchen, baking bread from an old recipe of her mother's. The cook had never mastered the recipe, and Della preferred to tackle it herself. She was always irritated when someone or something interrupted her in the midst of her baking. Her face was flushed and her hair had partly escaped its usually neat knot. She went on into the room, not noticing Jane, who had backed up into the shadows just outside the door.

Ailian burst into tears. "It is my ungrateful daughter-in-law," she wailed. She was too upset to use English, so Della had to strain to understand the Chinese. "She is a terrible wife to my poor son. This morning..." Ailian sobbed harder and could not go on.

Outside, Jane inched closer to the doorway in order to hear better. It was a fine April afternoon, sunny but cool. A dust storm had threatened the day before, but the wind had died down in the night. Sunlight sparkled off the tiled rooftops, and a bird sang repeatedly from the top of a cassia tree in a corner of the garden. While Jane strained to listen, the Seth Thomas clock in the living room sounded two rapid strokes.

Della had assigned Jane more tasks around the household than usual that Saturday. She had asked Jane to look through the Bible for a text for Della's Sunday-school class, and then to go search through her clothes for garments that needed mending. After that, she had to write letters to distant relatives in the United States, people Jane neither knew nor cared about, but with whom she had dutifully corresponded since she was a small child. Jane had done all these tasks quickly and Della then had sent her to her room to do her schoolwork.

Jane suspected all this was Della's way of ensuring that her daughter stay inside. Both Della and Jane knew that trouble had been brewing on the streets for the past several days. There was talk of planned student demonstrations similar to the marches the previous December, which had ended in bloodshed. The Yenching University campus buzzed with talk of revolution and students joining the communists.

Ailian's wails also had attracted the household staff. Each of the servants found a reason to wander into the sitting room, or at least linger nearby. Even the gatekeeper limped back and forth, with various pretexts, across the paving stones. They ignored Jane, who stood back where Della couldn't see her.

Ailian said, "My daughter-in-law refuses to obey us. Old Grandfather is very angry. Our household is in an uproar."

Remembering Miss Ding's mischievous eyes, Jane felt like snickering. How could Ailian have thought she was getting a traditional daughter-in-law? Jane inched closer to the doorway and peered over the gatekeeper's shoulder.

Della took Ailian's hand and murmured something Jane couldn't hear. Ailian grasped a handkerchief and wiped the sweat from her neck and the tears from her red, swollen eyes. She cried out again: "I blame my daughter-in-law. She sits around doing nothing. She only wants the modern life. There is so much unhappiness in our home!"

Della said, "Please explain to me, Ailian, what it is you expect this young girl to do?"

Ailian sat up straighter and stared at Della. "Respect and obey her elders."

"But your home is not Confucian. You practice the teachings of Christ."

"I don't understand. A home is a home. A family is a family. Respect is respect. Where does it say in the gospels that young people must be disrespectful?"

"You mean she is disrespectful to you?"

"To me and to Old Grandfather."

"But what does she do?"

"Do? She does nothing to help in the house. She wears lipstick and goes with friends to see films."

"This is not a country town, Ailian. Peking is a modern city. You cannot expect young people nowadays to stick to the old ways."

"Some things should never change."

"What about Han?" Della asked. "What does he say?"

Ailian sobbed harder.

"I think there is something you are not telling me, Ailian."

Ailian lowered her voice, and Jane and the servants had to strain to hear. Ailian spoke rapidly. "When I scolded her for her disobedience, she was defiant; she said no one had to obey their mother-in-laws anymore."

"This is not surprising, Ailian," said Della. "Things are changing. I don't think you can change it back."

"I slapped her," said Ailian, "and said she had better get busy and give me some grandchildren." Ailian burst into fresh sobbing.

Della clucked her tongue. "Oh, dear. You shouldn't have slapped her. And what did she do then?"

Ailian made an effort to control herself. She swiped at her eyes with the handkerchief and whispered, "She cried. And then she told me…"

"Told you what?"

Ailian buried her face in her hands. "She told me Han had not touched her. Not once. He will not go near her. All he is interested in is his books and the university and his politics. He cares nothing for our family! She said she will divorce him. She kept saying, 'it is not my fault, it is not my fault.' When I asked Han later, 'Is this true?' he told me he would not sleep with a stranger. A stranger! This is his wife."

"Oh, Ailian," said Della. "I am so sorry."

Amah stepped forward and poured more tea for Ailian, urging her to drink it. "Madam is right," she told Ailian. "As bad as this is, it is now happening all over China. Young people no longer care about the family."

"Tell me something, Ailian," Della said. "Would you and Wutang have insisted on this marriage if it hadn't been for Old Grandfather?"

Ailian gave Della a weary look and swiped at her eyes again. "It has caused so much unhappiness. But what could we do?"

Amah said, "I blame the young people. The old man should be allowed to die happy."

The gatekeeper nodded in agreement. The cook clucked his tongue and said nothing. At this point, the Number One Boy decided to interject himself into the conversation. "Han is not strict with his wife," he cried. "I have heard this. He asks her to do something, but when she refuses, he only shrugs and walks away."

"You see?" said Ailian. "They do not care for each other. Han dislikes his wife so much that he stays out until all hours. Sometimes he's out all night. When his father asks him where he has been, he refuses to answer." Ailian buried her face in her hands again. "Oh, why did this curse come into our house, when every day I pray to God for a good life? We did not deserve this. And I will have no grandchildren!" Ailian collapsed against Della.

The Number One Boy cleared his throat, about to say something else, and Della looked up and shook her head. Jane ducked back out of sight. Afraid to press her luck any further—if Della spotted her she would send her to her room again for more studying—Jane tiptoed back along the passage and sat down on the wooden steps overlooking the outer courtyard and the compound wall.

Next to the wall was a cherry tree; it, along with the plum outside Jane's room, flowered in the spring, and was now a mass of blossoms. Their scent wafted toward Jane, temporarily masking the stronger, more pervasive odors of the streets outside. A rusty tin bowl lay half submerged in blossoms at the foot of the tree. Looking at it made Jane sad. It was Raleigh's old bowl. They used to tie him to the tree at night, so he was near the gate and could warn them of late visitors, or even intruders. I suppose we'll have to get another dog, Jane thought, but Raleigh had been her special pet and she still missed him terribly. It was one of the reasons why she made such a fuss over the Baumans' terriers, Lizzie and Pearl, on their forays to Peking.

Jane buried her face in her skirt, unable to push Ailian's words out of her mind: "He will not go near her." Jane covered her eyes to hide the fierce, singing gladness she had felt ever since Ailian had spoken. She thought of Miss Ding with scorn. The bright-red, pouting mouth. The half-lowered eyes that kept darting glances up in what to Jane seemed like pretended modesty.

Now in the mission chapel, Jane heard Miss Ding giggle and whisper something. Out of the corner of her eye she saw Han make an impatient movement with his shoulders. She remembered hearing that there were strong, intelligent girls among the communists, and wondered if, left to himself, Han would have married one of them. She knew these strong Chinese girls existed, just as she knew that prostitutes existed—she remembered the pretty, painted girl she had seen in the rickshaw next to hers, face half buried in a white woolen scarf—but the only Chinese women she knew well were either servants or Christians, ranging from matrons such as Han's mother, to several plain and shy spinsters who helped Della teach Sunday school. Young as she was, Jane understood that she had no comprehension of the lives or inner thoughts of the many poor women who sometimes came to the mission for help. There had been a young Chinese nurse at the mission the previous year. Jane had admired her from a distance. But she hadn't stayed long. Once Jane had heard Cyrus complaining to Della that he thought the young woman was a communist.

Jane smoothed her skirt down over her knees; the muscles of her legs felt strong, and she knew that she too had the strength to march in protest. She found herself feeling glad that Han had married a silly girl whom he couldn't love, then felt guilty because she was rejoicing over her friend's unhappiness.

There was another stir in the room as Cyrus walked up to the podium, flipped open his Bible, and began reading a psalm in Chinese: "Lord, how they have increased who trouble me! Many are they who rise up against me. Many are they who say of me, 'there is no help for him in God.'" As usual, he read haltingly, sometimes stumbling and repeating words. As he read, he occasionally ran his hand through his hair in a nervous gesture. As always, Jane felt embarrassed at her father's obvious anxiety. She couldn't help comparing his performance with Wutang's smooth reading of the Bible. Although Cyrus spoke and understood Chinese well, he had never gained the sort of confidence in the language that would allow him to be a good preacher.

Jane stole another glance at Han. He stared straight before him, apparently not listening to Cyrus. His black eyes were like burning holes in his pale face. He kept fingering his chin, a nervous habit he had had since boyhood.

Cyrus looked at the ceiling as if he were speaking directly to God and spoke apparently from memory. His voice deepened and gained confidence. "But You, O Lord, are a shield for me, my glory and the One who lifts up my head. I cried to the Lord with my voice, and He heard me from His holy hill…" He looked down at the Bible again. "I lay down and slept. I awoke, for the Lord sustained me. I will not be afraid of ten thousand of people who have set themselves against me all around..."

Jane had spoken to Han only once since his wedding. He had come with his father to call on Cyrus two weeks earlier. Instead of sending him off to visit with Will and Jane as in the past, Wutang had said, "Han is a man now. He must stay in here and talk with the men."

Han had nodded gravely to Jane and said hello and asked how she was, but kept darting his eyes around the room and wouldn't look directly at her.

Wutang's words about Han being a man had made Jane feel unbearably young. She had looked down at her plain, short dress, and thought, I still look like a child! Han had turned then and followed the men into Cyrus' study. Jane watched the back of his head. He seemed remote and stern, no longer her closest friend.

Careful to avoid her mother and Amah, Jane had gone out through the neglected garden to a spot under the compound wall, where she would be able to see Han and Wutang when they emerged from the study. In this corner there was a stone bench, chilly to the touch and surrounded by the skeletons of last season's weeds and flowers. Jane sank down on the bench and waited.

It was still early enough in the day that the sun's rays had not yet reached over the wall. There was a haze over the city: the wind had strengthened in the night, and now the air was full of dust particles. Jane shivered and pulled her sweater about her chilled shoulders.

She hadn't long to wait. She heard quick footsteps, then almost immediately Han appeared. He spotted Jane and hurried across the hard, bare ground and the uneven paving stones.

"Where is your father?" Jane called out.

He came up next to her, but didn't sit. "They're still talking." He smiled, bringing out the dimple in his cheek. "Father says I'm a man, but he tells me to go outside when he and your father want to speak about really private things."

"What are they talking about?"

Han raised his shoulders. "Mission things. They wouldn't let me listen."

"Didn't you try?" Jane was referring to the many times when she,

Will, and Han had eavesdropped on their parents and shared their pool of information.

"Couldn't hear, but it doesn't matter." He glanced around. "Where is your mother right now?" From the time he was little, Han had been able to shake off Amah's wrath. She had reminded him of his mother and his own amah, both women he had been able to cajole into letting him have his way. Della's displeasure, on the other hand, made him uneasy. She always spoke quietly, but with firm, clear tones, and her light eyes could be icy. He knew she would not tolerate any misbehavior.

"She's teaching a class," Jane said.

"Where's Will?"

"With his friends. He's always with friends these days. Why don't you sit down?" Jane scooted over on the bench to make room for him.

"No, thanks." He paced up and down in front of her.

"What is it? Why are you so excited?" Jane thought, if he's not going to mention his marriage, I'm not going to, either.

Han sat down suddenly beside her, almost touching her, so that she was acutely aware of his physical presence. "It's Liang Chu," he said. "You met him at Mr. Varley's, remember?"

Jane thought back to that day the previous winter when she had gone to warn Han about the trouble over Little Gao and the possible rift between their families. She racked her brain and vaguely remembered a round boyish face and an unruly shock of hair. "I think I remember him," she said. "What about him?"

Han lowered his voice. "Now, you mustn't tell. Not anyone. Swear?"

Jane nodded vigorously and touched her breast. It was their old gesture of fealty. Will and Jane had taught Han the English saying, "Cross my heart and hope to die."

"He's a communist," Han hissed. "He's not much older than I am, and yet he's done so much!"

Jane couldn't speak. She was overwhelmed that Han had confided this in her, and just when she had thought he had grown away from her.

"You know how I feel about the communists," he whispered. "They're the only ones who have answers to China's deepest problems; they're trying to do something about them." Han waved his arm toward the compound wall and the city outside. "And here am I, merely going to school."

"Don't you help China by being a good scholar? Won't this help your country someday? This is what you told me before." Jane rubbed her hands together, agonizing over her inarticulateness, wanting to be responsive. He was so obviously in the throes of a deep passion, and she wanted him to believe it was right that he had confided in her.

"Yes, yes," he said, "but now things are happening too fast. Look at Liang Chu, how brave he is."

Jane thought the boyish-looking young man she barely remembered seemed no match against the Kuomintang. "I guess my father doesn't know what real communists are like," she said.

"I guess he doesn't!" Han straightened his back and gazed at the compound wall. He leaned forward again, muscles tensing, and again lowered his voice. "Liang Chu took part in the Long March."

"No! That thin young man?" Jane knew from Han that the communists, to escape Chiang Kai-shek, had trudged 6,000 miles through incredible hardship to the far northwest. "He went the whole way?"

Han nodded. "That is how dedicated he is. When you believe in something, you can do anything."

"And now he's risking his life coming back here to talk to the students?"

"That's what I'm telling you. It's very dangerous. He cannot stay anywhere for more than three or four days for fear of discovery." Han shrugged. "He may be killed, but others will take his place. He said this himself. Such dedication cannot be stopped."

"And what about you?" Jane looked down at the ground and began kicking at a pebble that lay near the bench. She kicked it too hard and it rolled out of her reach.

Han shrugged again and stared at the ground.

"Where does Liang Chu live?"

"I don't know. He doesn't tell. I do know that he can't trust anyone except a chosen few… and his grandmother. She gives him money."

A crow darted down from the tiled roof and began pecking at the ground near their feet. Han ignored it, but Jane hardly dared breathe for fear of frightening it away. Keeping her eyes on the bird, she asked,

"Has he ever been caught?"

"Once. A few years back, before the Long March, he was arrested. He was supposed to be executed."

Jane watched the crow as it hopped around a dying rosebush in a corner of the flowerbed. No one took care of the roses. It always seemed to be someone else's responsibility, and now the bush was dying. "How... how did Liang Chu escape execution?" she asked.

"He has relatives with connections. The relatives convinced the authorities to release him."

Jane looked up. If Han were arrested, probably nobody would intervene. The Li family was not important. Wutang probably did not have the right connections.

When Wutang came out of the house and signaled to Han that it was time to go, Han whispered to Jane, "Stay off the streets if there are demonstrations, little sister."

"Oh, Han, can't I come and see?"

His eyes flashed, then softened. "This is serious business, not something you can just come and watch. It's time to grow up, little sister. Stop daydreaming."

He stood up then and plopped his hat on his head. It was a Western-style man's felt fedora, and it looked odd with his Chinese gown. He grinned at her over his shoulder as he strode off to where his father stood waiting, Cyrus by his side. Jane stayed where she was, glad to have seen him, but feeling a chill from his last words. In one stroke, he seemed to have excluded her from what mattered most in his life. She was too young to articulate it, even to herself. She only knew that she felt left out and very lonely.

Now, in the mission chapel, Han's face was downcast and sulky, when earlier he had gazed over Jane's head as if he were looking into distances. He slouched down in his chair, feet crossed at the ankles, hands restless.

"Arise, O Lord; Save me, O my God," Cyrus read. "For you have struck all my enemies on the cheekbone; you have broken the teeth of the ungodly… They have increased who trouble me." He waited a beat, then said in a lower tone, no longer reading Scripture, "Great crowds of students in rural parts of China have paraded in front of missionary compounds and churches, such as this one, shouting anti-American and anti-missionary slogans and spitting in contempt."

Han shifted in his seat and sat up straighter. Why, Jane thought, can't Pa and Han be on the same side? They both hate injustice. They both are resolved to fight evil. Why can't they work together? Oh, don't say anything more, Pa!

Will dug his elbow into Jane's ribs. She lowered her head in embarrassment and watched Cyrus' face turn red. Beside her, Della kept her eyes on Cyrus, outwardly serene. Jane didn't dare look at Han now.

Cyrus hesitated, misspoke, corrected himself, and went on. He looked up in some distress, as if he were unable to stop talking. "The communists are igniting a flame of hate," he said, leaning forward, "which is making some Chinese anti-American and anti-missionary. If they are allowed to continue…" Here, he stammered, almost unable to get the words out. He mastered it and went on, "They will have to answer for the consequences." He almost shouted the last sentence.

There was a movement behind Jane. Someone tittered. The buzz of voices, always present in a Chinese audience, increased. Jane turned swiftly and saw Han stand up. Cyrus broke off his speech abruptly. Ailian tugged at her son's clothing and whispered furiously for him to sit down. Jane stole a glance at Wutang and saw his face had gone suddenly haggard.

There was a long silence, then Cyrus, not taking his eyes from Han's face, said, "There are Chinese Christians who are being so terrorized that church worship in some places has had to go underground. This is the work of the communists. There are other Chinese Christians who have been beaten and tortured. Is this also the work of the communists?"

Han's face, no longer pale, had turned bright red. He shook off his mother's hand and moved sideways out of the row of chairs. He gave Cyrus one more brief, angry look, then turned and stalked out.

The room erupted in rising voices, chairs creaking as people turned to watch Han walk out. They then turned and looked at Cyrus, waiting to see what he would do. Both Wutang and Ailian sat with heads bowed. Ailian's shoulders heaved and she dabbed at her face with a handkerchief. Han's wife looked bewildered.

Della shot an anguished look at Ailian, then an angry look at her husband. He kept his eyes on the podium in front of him. His voice low, seemingly not caring if anyone still listened, Cyrus hurried through the rest of his sermon, stumbling more than usual, then, mercifully, ending it.

As people surged toward the door afterward, Frances Appleton pushed through to Jane and started to say something. Jane cut her off by turning her back. Frances' mother, Dorothy, put a hand on Della's arm, leaned close, and said, "Something is terribly wrong with the Li family. They're all going mad."

Della looked at her and didn't reply.

Dorothy persisted. "Wutang has lost considerable face."

"So have we," said Della. She briefly touched Dorothy's shoulder, as if to make up for her harsh words, and hurried out.

Chapter 9

Present-day China

The engineer applied the brakes, beginning the train's long, slow slide into a station. Except for the dead of night, every time we stopped, vendors on the station platform crowded around the train calling out their wares. Now, Mei turned to me and said, "You hungry? I get food."

"I'll help you," I said.

Mei and I worked together at the open window, spotting a likely vendor and pointing to him, silently agreeing to buy. "Noodles," Mei said to me. She held up three fingers to the vendor, and they shouted back and forth before they came to an agreement about the price. When he handed Mei three white Styrofoam containers, standing on tiptoe to reach her, I counted out the money and thrust my arm through the open window. The man grabbed the bills, waved, grinned, and disappeared into the crowd.

Mei and I bore our trophies back to Jane. We spoke together: "Noodles," I told Jane, while at the same time Mei said something in Chinese. We laughed and set the boxes down on the fold-out table, opened them, and passed out chopsticks—disposable ones in paper envelopes.

Like Jane and Mei, I held the Styrofoam container close under my chin and shoved the glistening noodles into my mouth. "This is good," I said, my mouth full. Jane and Mei laughed at my surprise. Mei held up a thumb to show her approval.

While we ate, we watched new passengers make their way through the car, laden with bags, some balancing white Styrofoam food containers on piles of luggage. A young woman in an abbreviated miniskirt and leather jacket pushed her way past several older passengers. She turned a bold mascaraed eye on me, then looked away.

"I'd swear that was a prostitute," I said. "But aren't they illegal here?"

Jane turned to Mei and asked a question. "She says they're a problem here, like anywhere else," Jane told me. "But that girl could be just a modern girl."

I pushed more noodles into my mouth and stared after the young woman. "Boy, that's quite a change from the Mao suits," I said.

"If she is a prostitute, all I can say is the sing-song girls in old China had more taste," Jane said. "We used to see them out on the streets."

"You mean like the one Donald took Will to? Did your mother ever forgive the Baumans?"

"Events intervened," Jane said quietly.

We were interrupted by a Chinese couple, a thirty-something man and woman who, like so many others, wanted to practice their English. Both were plain looking; the woman had a fat, round face and a snub nose, and the man's broad, constant smile revealed a severe overbite.

The couple ignored Jane and directed their questions at me: Why was I in China? Did I like China? I gave them my standard answers, all the while wondering why so few Chinese I talked to asked questions about the United States. They asked about me, but most seemed uninterested in knowing about my country. Could it be, I wondered, that keeping up with all the changes in their own country sapped their intellectual energy? Or were the Chinese just naturally egocentric? I made a mental note to ask Jane what she thought, but suspected she would tell me Americans were just as egocentric, if not more so.

No matter, the Chinese couple was eager to talk about themselves, and I, looking for background for my potential film, was willing to listen. The woman was a high school science teacher, and her husband worked in a factory. He told me over and over what kind of factory it was, but the words never made sense to me, and Jane told me there didn't seem any way to translate it into English. Finally, I gave it up.

I asked if they had any questions about the United States. The woman told me she already knew a lot about my country. She watched American television on Hong Kong-based Star TV, which, like several million other people, they were able to pull in with the use of an illegal satellite dish, which was called a "little ear" in Chinese. I asked her what shows she watched and she said "The Bold and the Beautiful" and "Baywatch" were her favorites. "America is very different from China," she said.

I felt like saying, "No kidding," but refrained, knowing they wouldn't have understood my sarcasm. Instead, I said, "You must know that shows like that don't depict the real America."

They both beamed at me, and I had no idea whether they understood what I meant.

Then I asked them about China's recent past. "My parents died in the 1960s," the woman said. She didn't elaborate, but added, "They suffered because people called them 'rightists.'" She shifted herself forward and leaned toward me as if to make sure I really understood what she was saying. "It was wrong to call them rightists," she said. "They believed in the Party. They were sent away for 'reform through labor.' I too was called a rightist, because of my parents, even though I was just a child. I had to disown my parents so I could be accepted."

"And no one cares if you talk about all this now?" I asked.

The woman had opened her mouth to say something else. At my question, she stopped, obviously confused.

"Many people talk about the past," her husband said. He sounded slightly irritated. "But China is different now," he added. "Now we have reform and opening up. Now we can all get rich."

"But can you talk about politics?" I asked.

They looked puzzled.

"What about Tiananmen?" I asked, changing the subject. I was referring to the Tiananmen Square incident of 1989. The husband made his lips into a firm line and said that that had happened twelve years ago and no one wanted to think about it any more. They just wanted to make money.

"I know," I said feeling prickly and contrary, "But not everyone in China is making money. I've seen beggars on the streets of Beijing."

A flash of irritation crossed the man's face. "You have beggars in

America, too," he said.

"You're right. We do. It's a real problem. But what about these poor people? Hasn't the government, the Party, I mean, let them down?"

The man admitted there was a growing gap between rich and poor in China, but he didn't directly answer my question about the Party.

After they got up and left, I said to Jane, "It's amazing they talk as freely as they do."

"I think it's very recent, dear," she said.

"But they didn't answer some of my questions," I said.

I then asked Jane if she minded interpreting while I asked Mei a few questions.

Jane spoke to Mei, who nodded. "Tell her, her English is very good," I said, "only I need to be sure of what she's telling me. Tell her it's for my film idea."

Again, they conferred and Mei agreed.

"Go ahead and finish eating," I said, gesturing with my chopstick.

"I have enough," she said and put her chopsticks down.

I thought about my conversation with the Chinese couple and how they watch "Bold and the Beautiful" and "Bay Watch," and wondered if they thought Americans really acted or looked that way. I found it amusing. "Do you have a television?" I asked Mei.

She did, she said. She and her son and his wife had purchased it together. They all enjoyed it.

"Does your son live with you?" I asked, and she said he did. They shared an apartment in Chengdu.

My next question was about her early childhood. Mei put her hands in her lap and paused for a moment.

She remembered being taken by boat on a wide river. Or maybe it wasn't so wide, maybe it was just that she was so small. She was frightened and she cried, but she doesn't remember why she cried. She knows now that she was with her amah and Amah's husband, who became her foster parents. Her foster mother had told her that the three of them had made their way to freedom from Shanghai, where the Japanese were invading. She was told they went down the waterways, using bribes for spaces on the boat, then setting out by foot into China's vast interior. They eventually ended up in Chengdu, in

Sichuan Province. After that she remembers a little more, but still it is very vague. She was living in the countryside in her foster father's home village. They lived there with his mother, whom Mei called grandmother, and his unmarried brother, whom Mei called uncle. They were poor, but farmed a little land to grow vegetables and raise chickens. Her foster father and uncle worked in the fields, while she and her foster mother stayed home and took care of the aging grandmother. Grandmother didn't like Mei, who knew it even then. Grandmother saw that Mei was different and hated her for it. Mei's foster mother did her best to keep her out of grandmother's way, trying not to upset her mother-in-law.

Life was especially hard then because there was a war going on, and the Japanese were beginning to swallow up the country. What Mei remembers most about that time was having hovered in the kitchen while planes flew overhead, and hearing the sounds of bombs exploding, and gunfire all around them. At the time, Chengdu was being ruled by the Kuomintang, so they were somewhat protected by them. But the Kuomintang army still had trouble fighting off the Japanese. Mei could see in her foster parents' eyes how terrified they were at the prospect of the Japanese taking over.

She recalls bits and pieces of conversation about the war, the Kuomintang, the communists, and the horrible things the Japanese did. Once, while Grandmother was talking about the horror stories she heard about the Japanese and what they did to the Chinese people—torture, and rape, and injecting them with horrible diseases—Mei's foster mother got upset and told grandmother not to talk of such things in front of a small child. Mei had never heard her foster mother talk to grandmother that way, and it frightened her more than the stories.

Mei glanced at me, smiled, and then looked away. "Basically, that's all I remember about my early childhood," she told Jane in Chinese.

CHAPTER 10

PEKING, APRIL 1936

W hen they had come home from the mission chapel, and once Jane was sure her mother had gone to bed, she went to look for her father. Her feelings were in turmoil. She ached for Han, because he had acted impulsively, and probably was sorry now that he had embarrassed his parents. At the same time, she was proud of him for having the courage of his convictions. There was also a nagging ache of guilt over the shame she had felt at her father's awkward behavior. For the moment at least, she couldn't do anything about Han, but she could seek out her father.

She found him in his study. The dim light from the single lamp should have softened his features, but on this night it only accentuated the lines in his face. He held a book open on his lap, but seemed to be staring at it, rather than reading it.

Jane couldn't bear for Cyrus to look so sad and lonely. "Pa?" she said, pausing in the doorway.

Cyrus snapped the book shut and motioned for her to come in. She went to him, put her arm across his shoulders, and leaned against him; she used to stand like this when she was small. Cyrus stretched out a long arm and pulled her down onto his lap. Even sitting down, her legs touched the floor, and she felt too heavy for his thin frame. Keeping her arms around his neck, she glanced at the papers strewn across his desk, and thought some must have been the notes for his sermon that evening. There were also several letters stacked neatly to one side. An empty envelope lay beside them, and what looked like two pages of a handwritten letter lay on the floor by his feet.

"Pa," Jane whispered. "There's a letter on the floor. Do you want me to pick it up for you? I'll tidy up your desk if you like." She hunched her shoulders to slip out of Cyrus' grasp, so she could bend down and pick up the letter.

He kept his arm tightly around her. "I'll get it, honey," he said. Not letting go of her, he leaned down and swooped up the letter in one movement. Still using only one hand, he dropped it onto the desk.

Jane leaned closer to her father. She tried not to think about the terrible evening at the mission, and concentrated instead on the room's peace and the evidence of prayer and scholarship. The room was so quiet she could hear Cyrus' breathing. When he turned to look again at the desk, she noticed for the first time a small circle of bare scalp at the crown of his head.

Cyrus smiled at her. "How's my girl?" he said. He often asked her this, but tonight he seemed absentminded.

"I'm fine, Pa, but I'm a little worried about you. You seem so tired."

"I'm all right." He glanced out of the corner of his eye at the letter he had just picked up.

Jane followed his glance. "Pa, what's that letter? The one that was on the floor."

"A note from Donald." He said it dismissively, as if he didn't want to discuss it further.

But Jane pressed on. "A note? It's very long for just a note. I didn't know he wrote to you."

"He doesn't, normally."

Jane was beginning to feel a cramp in her side. She pushed herself gently away and stood up. "Let me rub your shoulders," she said, so he wouldn't feel hurt that she now was too big for his lap. She came around behind him and dug her fingers into his tense shoulders.

"Ahh, that feels good." Cyrus took off his glasses and rubbed his eyes.

"Pa, will Ma forgive the Baumans?"

The small bald spot on Cyrus' head turned red. "Jane, you don't know about such things." He twisted around so he could see her face. "Yes, of course she will. Well, we're a little upset with Will right now," he said.

"Young men get rebellious when they're growing up." He wriggled his shoulders to make her stop rubbing him. "There, that was nice. You can sit down now."

Jane came around and sat on a low stool near his feet. "Were you writing to Donald about this?"

He sighed noisily. "I had to. Your mother said some things she didn't mean."

Jane bit her lips. Della never said anything she didn't mean. "What did Donald say in his letter?" Jane asked. She longed to ask to read it, but was certain her father would refuse to let her.

"It was a very handsome apology."

Jane studied her father's face. "Donald's your old friend, isn't he?"

"Yes, I think he's the oldest friend I have. We go back a long ways."

"Even before Yale..." she prompted. She was familiar with Cyrus' stories about his friend.

"We were schoolboys together."

"I bet you got in trouble, too." Jane was amused to see the dull flush spreading once again over Cyrus' face and neck. "Never you mind that," he mumbled, trying to make a joke of it.

Voices sounded. Cyrus looked over Jane's shoulder and scrambled to his feet. Jane whirled around and saw Wutang and Han in the pool of darkness just outside the doorway. The Number One Boy moved up behind them, holding a lantern. Wutang pushed Han into the room. Han stared at the ground, and, like a much younger boy, refused to make eye contact with either Cyrus or Jane. Wutang stepped forward, bowing and apologizing for calling on them so late. Cyrus said it wasn't late at all and motioned for them to sit down.

Wutang refused to sit and Han remained standing by the doorway. Wutang said, "We have come to beg your forgiveness for the way my stupid son acted tonight. He is ungrateful and unworthy, and I am ashamed of him." Wutang turned to Han and lightly cuffed him. "Speak up, boy."

Han didn't say anything.

Wutang turned back to Cyrus. "He will speak to you in a moment. He is trying to think of the correct thing to say. He was unwell tonight. He—"

"I'll speak for myself, father." Han turned to Cyrus and this time looked him directly in the eyes. "What you said tonight was not true, Mr. McPherson."

Wutang's face reddened. "Please pay no heed," he begged Cyrus. "He is not well and does not mean what he says. You have been a second father to him since his babyhood. He means no disrespect."

Cyrus ignored Wutang. "Just what do you mean, Han? Why did you challenge me tonight and embarrass all of us?"

"I'm trying not to be disrespectful, but you won't listen to me."

Cyrus said, "I always listen to people. It's important to hear what people say. You can't accuse me of not listening." He started stammering again as he had in the chapel.

"Then why are you repeating lies?" Han asked.

"Lies?" Cyrus' voice rose. "You're accusing me of lying?"

Jane covered her mouth with her hand to keep from crying out. Wutang shook his son's shoulder. "Apologize, I say."

"I refuse to apologize. I am not ill. I know exactly what I'm doing."

"Show some respect!" Wutang's voice was anguished.

Han again looked directly into Cyrus' eyes. "You speak only of rumors, of what you have heard. You have no facts."

"I have facts," Cyrus said. He strode over to the desk, picked up some letters, and waved them at Han. "There are facts in these letters, my boy. They are from our brethren in the countryside."

"Those letters are repeating rumors, too. Everybody's confusing rumor for fact. So many people do this. Do you know how much harm it causes? You're playing into the hands of the Kuomintang."

"The Kuomintang is the government."

"They are murderers and worse. They are the ones who have made up these rumors. They want to discredit the communists."

Wutang staggered, and put his hand against the bookcase to steady himself. Cyrus moved swiftly to his side. "Old friend, are you all right?" He helped Wutang into a chair, while Han watched, looking stricken.

Cyrus looked up at Han. "Don't just stand there, help your father."

Han knelt by Wutang's chair. "Are you all right, father?"

Wutang closed his eyes. "You have shamed me this night. You have put the family and yourself in danger. Your mother is beside herself.

She cannot stop weeping. What have we done to deserve this from our son?"

Han rose to his feet and confronted Cyrus. "Why don't you see what harm you are doing? Young people are being hunted down; young people who only want to help their country. I don't mean disrespect to you or to my parents. I'm sorry my mother is home weeping on my behalf." His voice broke on the last words.

Cyrus spoke softly: "Han, your father is right. You have been like a son to me. Please think hard about what you do. Don't put your family in danger, I beg of you."

"Will you stop repeating these rumors?"

"I have a duty to warn people of the dangers that surround them. You cannot tell me what I can say or cannot say."

"Then I too have a duty. A duty to my country."

"What about your family? What about your father?" Cyrus gestured toward Wutang, who still leaned back in the chair, his face ashen.

Tears rolled down Han's cheeks. "I must do what I think is right. I can promise you I will not embarrass you by attending any more church services. You will not see me in the mission in the future."

His black eyes met Jane's. Then he turned and left the room. Jane, her father, and Wutang said nothing. The young boy they thought they knew was gone.

The McPhersons learned that Han slipped out of his house before dawn the next morning to meet a friend of the communist Liang Chu, who had agreed to guide him to the mountains so he could join the communists there. The servants woke Han's parents to tell them their son was gone; he had taken nothing with him, but someone down the street had seen him leave. Wutang and Ailian ran to his room, where they found a note telling them where he was going and what he planned to do.

The Li servants told the McPherson servants that Wutang behaved at first as if his only son had died. He sat alone for a long time, tears streaming down his face, refusing food and comfort. Ailian refused to get out of bed the entire day. Late in the evening, when she finally did get up, she made her way to her husband, carrying a bowl of congee and begging him to eat. He asked if the old grandfather had been told, and she said no one had yet dared tell the old man. After a while, she began to argue that Han could be found. They must not treat him as dead. They must not forget him. Even if war separated him from them, as they supposed was going to happen, he would come home eventually.

Ailian pleaded and argued. Finally, Wutang sighed, and agreed to treat his son's absence as temporary. Satisfied, Ailian pulled herself to her feet with some difficulty, and padded off to find her daughter-in-law, to tell her they all expected that her husband would eventually come home. Then she went to bathe her swollen eyes.

Jane heard all this from Amah.

There was a deserted tower near the southern wall of the city. Its crumbling bricks overlooked a small cemetery where some of the foreign victims of the Boxer Rebellion in 1900 were buried. The cemetery was neglected; the headstones leaning this way and that, weeds tangled over what once had been a path. Few people came this way — the foreigners because they wanted to put the blood and terror of 1900 behind them, and the Chinese because they believed the tower was haunted.

Whoever or whatever had lived in the tower had long since been supplanted by bats and foxes. The Chinese believed that foxes, which they regarded as werefoxes, were the spirits of women who had been mistreated in life and were now out to get revenge upon the living. Chinese lore abounded with tales of fox spirits and the grisly deaths of those who wandered into their realm.

For years, Cyrus had been fascinated by the Fox Tower, as people called it, and by the adjacent cemetery. His family assumed his interest in the cemetery lay in the fact that his father had died in the Boxer Rebellion. Although his father had died in Shanxi Province, southwest of Peking, and no one knew where he was interred, Cyrus liked to brood over the graves of the victims who lay buried there. Ghosts and foxes held no terrors for him; he lacked that kind of superstition. But several times he had brought his children to the cemetery and told them the story of their grandfather, cut down in the prime of life by Chinese swords.

Jane and Will had been a captive audience, spooked both by the bloody tale of their grandfather's death and by the Fox Tower and the lonely cemetery. China-born, they shared some of the Chinese superstitions and were not at all sure that the foxes posed no danger. They were also uncomfortable with the tales of Chinese killing foreigners. This was unsettling to think about, and Han had told them several times about the Western countries taking advantage of China's weak and dying Qing Dynasty to encroach on Chinese territory for their own financial gain. Such strong anti-foreign sentiment had led to the so-called Boxer Rebellion and the slaughter of a number of missionaries, among other foreigners.

"Why were they called Boxers?" Will had asked Han, flailing his arms in boxing motions. All three children were much younger then.

"That's right. They boxed, just like that." Han made boxing motions too. "It was mystical. They believed the foreigners' bullets wouldn't touch them."

"They were wrong, weren't they?" Will shouted.

"Yes, they were wrong," Han said. "They were just simple, country folk."

"And the old empress dowager," said Jane, picking up the story, "sympathized with the Boxers."

"But after the siege of the foreign legations in Peking, Americans, British, French—all the foreigners—swooped down on Peking—" Will began.

"And avenged their dead by killing Chinese—" Han hated this part of the story.

Jane finished the tale: "And by destroying the Imperial Summer Palace. That beautiful old place. And the empress built a new one, the one we can see today."

As Han grew older, he didn't want to talk about Chinese defeats at the hands of foreigners. Jane and Will had discussed the Boxer Rebellion between themselves and agreed that both sides shared the blame for that violent time. They did not, however, say this either to Cyrus or to Han.

The next afternoon, after the confrontation with Han in Cyrus' study and the day of Han's flight to the mountains, Cyrus, restless and depressed, decided he wanted to visit the cemetery. "It's my father," he told Della. "With China so close to chaos, and danger again stalking the land, I feel close to my father. I am aware of his fear."

Della patted his arm and told him, as she had many times, that it was now an entirely different situation than it had been in 1900. "We foreigners were the targets of the Boxers. The old empress encouraged them to kill us, until our governments came in and put a stop to it. Now it's China itself that's in danger. The Japanese want China, not us."

"It's not just the Japanese. Those stories about the communists... those anti-missionary tales." Cyrus shook his head, unable to go on.

"We'll go to the cemetery," Della said, "if that will make you feel better."

Jane agreed reluctantly to accompany her mother and father. Will wasn't able to come and told Jane he was thankful for it. He was leaving that evening to stay with friends at the American legation. They would start early in the morning on their trek to a temple in the Western Hills. Staying in the old temples scattered among the pine-covered hills was a favorite pastime of the foreigners in Peking, and Jane envied her brother. She thought about the undisturbed night sky and the silence so deep you could hear only the wind in the pines.

Della helped Will pack. Jane watched Della's face as she came away from Will's room. She had been frowning, and now the line between her eyes had seemed to deepen. "Do we have to go to the cemetery, Ma?" Jane asked.

Della looked at her a moment, her mind obviously somewhere else. Finally, she said, "Your father needs us."

Jane lacked the energy to protest further. She was saddened by Han's departure, though she secretly envied him for having the courage to act independently. She felt she would never see him again and realized that an era in her life had come to an end.

Jane also did not want to go to the Fox Tower because she was afraid. Although she was almost grown up and now knew better than to believe in fox spirits, the quiet, eerie spot still made her uneasy. "Please come with us," said Cyrus, and Jane, remembering her disloyal shame of her father in the church and her searing feelings of love in his study afterward, agreed to go.

No one said much as they rode in rickshaws through the busy city. It was late in the day, and the setting sun slanted across the city wall. Jane watched her mother and father in the rickshaws just ahead of hers. The rickshaw coolies called out to one another, voices sharp in the evening air, but even they fell silent as they approached the Fox Tower.

All three rickshaws stopped; the men dropped the poles and glanced uneasily at each other. Jane's coolie said, "Young Miss, you don't want to go there." Cyrus called back to Jane that they must get out here and walk the rest of the way.

"The Chinese are too superstitious," Cyrus said, his voice drawn thin and sharp with irritation. He paid all three men while Jane scrambled out of her rickshaw and hurried to catch up with her parents. She turned and watched the three coolies trot back in the direction from which they had come. One of them looked over his shoulder at her, his mouth open, probably with exertion, but it was as if he were trying to say something to her. Reluctantly, she turned and followed her parents, scraping her feet on the hard dirt path adjacent to the city wall.

The tower loomed above them, empty and desolate. Although she no longer believed the superstition that you would die if you looked at a werefox, Jane had no desire to see a fox and kept her eyes averted from the tower. She watched her father move toward the cemetery, and wondered why he seemed fearless now. She thought, I know I saw fear in his eyes yesterday evening when he talked about the communists. Can it be that he's afraid of all Chinese, as his father was? She shivered. She was only just old enough to sense what a tragedy it would be if this were so.

Up ahead of her, Cyrus sank to his knees by one of the foreign graves. Jane caught up with her mother and slipped an arm around her waist. "I wish he wouldn't do this," she whispered.

Della patted her hand and nodded, her face troubled. "You're shivering," she said.

"It'll be dark soon. I'm cold. I want to go home."

Jane stared at the graves and thought about her grandfather and the other missionaries who had died during the Boxer Rebellion. It had been thirty-six years ago. Ma and Pa were children then, she thought.

Both Cyrus and Della had been in the United States in 1900 when the

Boxers struck. Della had first come to China when she married Cyrus in 1912. Cyrus had been born in China, but had gone to the United States as a boy when his mother was diagnosed with tuberculosis. Her own parents had insisted she return to their home to rest and recover. This action had saved her and her son's lives. After learning of her husband's death by Chinese swords, she had vowed never to set foot on Chinese soil again. But Cyrus, drawn by his childhood memories and his sense of vocation, had come back.

The story about Cyrus' father's death was not so simple. Their grandfather had not died an unstained martyr, as family members in the United States believed. Shameful stories of his end had filtered out of China and eventually reached the McPherson family. Few people knew the family secret. Cyrus had told Will and Jane only a few years earlier, because he felt they had a right to know, but he made them swear they would never tell anyone.

"But Pa, the Chinese must know," Will said.

"I'm talking about people like us. I've never heard a hint from the other missionaries. I never want to."

The truth was this: sick with fear at the reports of missionaries and their families being hacked to pieces, and the growing certainty that the same fate would come to him, Cyrus' father had lost his reason. He had become fearful of all Chinese, even his faithful, long-time servants, including his Number One Boy. He ordered them out of his house, though they begged to stay.

But the faithful Number One Boy had crept back to the house after being ordered to leave with the rest of the servants. He was a Christian convert, and old Mr. McPherson had been kind to him and to his wife and the large family of children, whose ages ranged from two to twenty-five. Although he was called "boy," he was over fifty, and was grateful to the mission for providing food and shelter at this advanced age.

So he had sneaked back into the house, full of good intentions. He could not know that Mr. McPherson had loaded his rifle and was sitting alone in the dark, his mind full of the stories he had heard of missionary men, women, and children dragged one by one to a waiting swordsman, their heads cut off, and their bodies carried to unmarked graves. When he heard footsteps in the house, he waited until he saw a figure in the darkness, and then squeezed the trigger. Completely unhinged by the loud blast, he sat alone in the darkness, the sound of the shot gradually clearing from his ears. Other missionaries had come into the house and lit a lamp. After stumbling over the body of the Number One Boy, they had had to pry the rifle from Mr. McPherson's fingers. They had buried the faithful servant, then taken their raving colleague to sit with them until death caught up with all of them.

Jane shivered again and hugged herself. Della let go of her arm and stepped forward across the weed-strewn ground. "Cyrus?" she called out softly. He waved a hand to shush her, not looking at her. Della tiptoed back to Jane's side. "He's praying," she whispered. She put her arm around Jane, who leaned close to her mother's side, trying to absorb some of her warmth and strength. She thought she could feel Della shivering a little too, and this frightened her.

Through the growing dusk, they saw Cyrus sink down onto the grass and put his hands over his eyes. "Has he stopped praying?" Jane whispered. "What's he doing now?"

"I don't know."

"I want to go home." Jane whimpered, feeling like a small child, all her desolation of recent days coming to a head — Han's flight, her sense of Cyrus' fear and vulnerability.

Della squeezed her shoulder. "Shhh. You go ahead, run out to the main road and find rickshaws. Make them wait, and I'll get him out of here."

"He's afraid," said Jane. Della stared at her, and Jane was sorry she had spoken. She wanted Della to tell her she was mistaken, but Della said nothing.

Jane ran lightly over the packed earth and tangled weeds. The sun had slipped below the city walls, and it was growing dark. As she hurried past the tower, she glanced back at her parents. Della stood back, hands clenched on her breast, watching Cyrus, who knelt, head bowed.

Ma is worried too. She knows this isn't right, Jane thought. Fear shot through her and she hurried to the road to find the rickshaws.

When they reached home that evening, Will had already left. Lucky Will, Jane thought. She told Amah she didn't want any supper that night, she was tired and was going to go to bed early. She started toward the sitting room to say goodnight to her parents, but stopped when she heard their raised voices. Della cried out, "It shouldn't be like this. It wasn't meant to be like this." Jane heard Cyrus' deep rumble in reply, but couldn't make out his words.

Jane crept away from the sitting room door, longing for the privacy of her room. For the first time since she could remember, she failed to seek out at least one of her parents before retiring for the night. It had been a family custom to kiss her parents good night and say her evening prayers in their company. That night, she didn't want to see them. For the first time, she sensed vulnerability in her parents and it frightened her. She didn't want to see the worry in Della's eyes, or, even worse, the fear in Cyrus'. She hurried down the passage to her room, wishing old Raleigh were still alive so she could take him with her, as she used to do, and bury her face in his fur for comfort. Let Ma and Pa work it all out tonight, She thought; it would only disturb them for me to come in and say goodnight.

This lapse would haunt her for the rest of her life. She never saw them alive again.

Chapter 11

Present-day China

"That was the night my parents were murdered." Jane spoke quietly, almost dispassionately, as the normal daytime life of the train went on around us. "Someone came in very late, while they sat in the sitting room."

No one said anything for a moment or two. Mei apparently understood at least some of the English words; she took Jane's hand and patted it. A Chinese man and woman I hadn't seen before made their way up the aisle. The man had iron-gray hair and wore a smart-looking Western shirt and slacks. The woman had permed hair and wore a blue, one-piece dress of a kind I could have bought in Minneapolis. She carried one of those designer bags—maybe fake, maybe not—covered with initials. Two men across the aisle chewed on sunflower seeds and spit the hulls into an overflowing ashtray. A woman sat down with them and poked among the seeds they offered her. Somehow, the bustle and the chatter and the eating going on around us made Jane's words all the more horrible.

Jane spoke at last. "This is one of the central facts of my story."

"Did they catch who did it?"

"You remember my mentioning Little Gao?"

"Little Gao? The one with his hand in the money box? He killed your parents? But you liked him. He was Han's cousin. He was supposed to be harmless."

"Nonetheless, he at least was involved. There also seems to have been another person with him."

"Who?"

"That was a lot harder to figure out."

I waited. Finally, Jane asked, "You're probably wondering just why anyone would have done this?"

"And you're going to tell me?"

She opened her mouth, then shut it again. "If I told you who right now, you wouldn't understand why it happened. It's very complicated."

"And you want to tell it in your own way."

She nodded.

I shrugged. "How can I quarrel with that?"

Jane's voice rose a little. "Remember how violent those times were? My grandfather had been murdered thirty-six years before by the Boxers. Civil war and bloodshed had been going on for years. Young Chinese were being hunted down by their own government. The Japanese were about to commit some of the biggest atrocities of World War Two. People were living and dying in misery right outside our doorstep." She stopped suddenly and gave a short humorless laugh. "Looking back now, my parents, especially my father, were living in some kind of dream—a dream of idealistic expectations. Look at Pa, preaching those things from his pulpit. As if he could have stopped the tide of Chinese history."

I dragged her back to specifics. "Why are you so sure Little Gao was there?"

"He confessed."

"He did? What did he say?"

"Very little. Then he killed himself."

I made a face, and jotted it down in my notebook. Jane watched me write, then said, "I explained about the murder to Mei. Didn't I, Mei? It was at her house in Chengdu. After all, it was her family too, so I told her everything. Everything. And she made sure I ate something, and gave me the best chair to sit in, and talked comfortably about my parents' lives—her grandparents, you realize—and said it was all so long ago. And then the neighbors came in to meet me, and we all talked and laughed and ate some more and drank a toast to my return." Jane sighed. She looked at Mei with puzzlement. I tried to picture the reunion in my head. Jane made it sound nice, but, I figured, at the same time, it must have been very uncomfortable for everyone, not knowing how to treat one another after being separated for such a long time.

I drew my legs up under me and opened to a fresh page of my notebook.

"Little Gao," said Jane, drawing his name out. "The last time I saw him he was smoking a cigarette at Han's wedding. How very long ago." Her eyes took on a faraway look.

About half an hour later, I left Jane sleeping. She had leaned back and closed her eyes and fallen almost immediately asleep. Mei had lifted Jane's legs up onto the bunk and then settled herself back down. Then, Mei and I struggled to communicate. Without Jane, it was rough going, but I felt strangely comforted in Mei's presence, and at times I caught her looking at me tenderly, as if I were a little girl. Normally, that would have bothered me, but instead it made me want to be closer to her.

Needing to stretch my legs, I stood up. I looked across the aisle at Jane. Her mouth was slightly open and her glasses had slipped down her nose, reminding me of my grandmother when she would doze off while watching television. I used to wonder how she could sleep in such uncomfortable positions. When I asked her, my Grandma had said, "When you're young, you can sleep whenever you want. When you're old, like me, your mind, so full of memories, will not let you sleep, so sleep becomes your friend. You accept it gratefully whenever it comes to you."

When I looked up, I saw Mei watching me. I opened my mouth to say something, but Mei smiled and put her finger to her lips. I gestured toward the back of the car and made walking motions with my fingers. Mei nodded. She lifted her teacup—a thick, white ceramic—to her lips and smiled at me over the rim. I slipped my bag over my shoulder and made my way down the narrow aisle, through several mirror images of our compartment, before reaching the end of the car. I braced myself against the door and listened to the couplings rattle and shake.

I thought about what Jane had told me—I had taken careful notes—that the night her parents were murdered the house was half-empty. Will was away with friends, visiting a temple in the Western Hills. Most of the servants had gone out. The gatekeeper was there, but people later said they thought he'd fallen asleep, or had slipped out to join the gambling that took place by lamplight in a nearby market. From Jane's description, I could picture people squatting on the ground, faces avid in the dim light, someone tossing dice or whatever Chinese gamblers tossed, cries of victory, and groans from the losers.

Amah had been in the house, but she'd fallen asleep. Jane was asleep. I wondered what would have happened had they been awake. Would Jane and Amah have been murdered too?

Jane, of course, knew nothing of the murder until the next morning. The Number One Boy, no doubt bleary-eyed from his night of gambling, went into the sitting room and found the bodies lying side by side. It was only too easy to imagine that scene. The manservant, rubbing sleep out of his eyes, opening wide the door to let in the light and fresh air, then seeing the carnage. There was blood everywhere and signs of a struggle. A chair was pushed back, another overturned. The Ming bowl — the prize from Ambrose Varley that had been the only valuable item in the house — lay in pieces.

The Number One Boy told people later that he'd trodden on Cyrus' body before realizing what had happened. Even then, it took him a moment to realize Cyrus and Della were not only dead, but had been beheaded.

Jane was in her room, dressing, when she heard the Number One Boy scream. At first, she thought the servants were fighting. She put down her hairbrush and listened more carefully. The noise went on and on. She heard running footsteps and something banging. She had just had time to begin to feel afraid, when Amah rushed in and told her to come quickly. Amah thought someone had been hurt.

Jane's memories of the sitting room were not so clear. She remembered that someone had come in from the street. She stepped over the high threshold to go into the room, but Amah pulled her back. Jane stared at Amah, because there were tears rolling down the old woman's face. Jane said she hadn't yet caught on to what had happened. All she could think was, why is Amah crying? Then she saw that the Number One Boy was crying too.

Jane started screaming when she saw the blood. There was so much of it, and it was splashed all over the room, she said. Cook, a big, strong man, picked her up and carried her to the kitchen. Amah came, too, hobbling on her bound feet, fussing and wailing behind them. Jane cried out for her mother. She remembered Cook's warm, deep voice saying the same words over and over in Chinese: "Mama coming, Mama coming." She wasn't coming, of course. She would never come again.

Almost immediately, Jane learned that her parents had been beheaded. The servants, scared and white-faced, had gossiped about it in the kitchen, where Cook and Amah gave Jane cups of tea. "But that's like the Boxers," Jane had cried out. The tea, instead of calming her, had made her nauseous and she had hastily put the cup aside. "The Boxers beheaded people," she said, though nobody had seemed to listen to her. She remembered that her grandfather had been killed by the Boxers. "Pa was afraid of them," she said to no one in particular, then wondered exactly whom Cyrus had feared.

"Still, no one listened. The police came and went, and questioned the servants, and everyone bustled around with worried faces. Later, Will came home. Jane didn't even know who had told him. She heard him shouting at someone. Later, he came and found Jane. He was angry and pallid, and wouldn't let anybody touch him.

"Did the police blame Little Gao right away?" I had asked.

The immediate suspect had been the gatekeeper, but just as they were about to haul him off, one of the policemen yelled out from the courtyard, and everybody went rushing outside. The policeman knelt there, staring at some blood smeared on the paving stones. The one who had been questioning the gatekeeper dropped down beside him, and there was an awful silence while everyone waited to see what the two policemen would make of this latest development. It was obvious the murderer had tracked the blood out of the sitting room and then out of the compound. The police followed the trail of blood—it was pathetically easy—and found Little Gao curled up in his bed. Before they had a chance to question him, he screamed that he couldn't have done such a thing alone. Then he burst into tears and refused to say any more.

I wandered on through the train, thinking about this, and came to the "hard seat" section, which I hadn't seen before. People—mostly Chinese, though there were a few foreigners—squeezed together on uncomfortable-looking benches, their luggage and other belongings piled around them. In contrast to the people in first class and hard sleeper, these people weren't well dressed. They looked like country people; some wore head cloths, one or two wore high-necked blue "Mao suits." Some older people looked dazed and tired; one old man leaned forward, elbows on knees, looking very ill. However, most were chattering noisily. Many ate, holding bowls beneath their chins and pushing food into their mouths while they talked. Children cried or laughed, and ran up and down the aisles. I wondered why all these people were traveling. Where were they going? How could they afford it? Were they visiting relatives, or were they part of the "floating population" of migrant workers I had heard about—masses of people moving about the coastal and urban areas, to cash in on the economic boom. If so, they didn't look as if they were prospering.

"How did Little Gao kill himself?" I had asked.

When the policemen were still at his home, they left the room for a few minutes and when they came back he was hanging above the bed.

Jane explained that some of the other missionaries had a favorite theory: it was a communist plot, her father having been so outspokenly anticommunist. There were a lot of propaganda wars at that time, the communists blaming the nationalists for all manner of things, the nationalists, or Kuomintang, pointing fingers at the communists. The police liked this theory, so they said the communists must have paid Little Gao to do it. Everyone said Little Gao was very angry, because Jane's father had been unjust. Little Gao may have been dim, but he was capable of passion. He had a strong temper and a sense of injustice. He felt he'd been unfairly charged and dismissed from his job. It didn't really matter whether Little Gao actually stole the money, he had lost his livelihood and considerable face. Besides, Little Gao had grown up on stories about the Boxers beheading missionaries during the Boxer Rebellion.

Nobody bothered to investigate it further, because even the missionaries preferred to think the communists had murdered Jane's parents. The communists were Chinese too, but at least this was a new kind of nightmare. From the police point of view, they had far more important things to worry about. The murder of a couple of Americans in Peking was no more than a serious embarrassment. Japan was about to gobble up China. Chiang Kai-shek was trying to get the American government interested in helping China, but he was even more concerned about the communists taking over.

After the murders, the Appletons had invited Jane and Will to stay with them to finish out the school term at the Peking American School, after which, they said, they probably would have to return to the United States. Jane's main emotions during that time had been intense anger and loneliness. Frances Appleton didn't, and couldn't be expected to, understand what Jane was going through. The one person who did understand, Will, had changed: he became withdrawn, even unfriendly, shrugging off people's attempts to show sympathy or any kind of affection. Jane sometimes found him with reddened eyes, but never actually saw him crying.

One day, Amah had brought some of Jane's belongings to the Appleton house. Amah held Jane, and let her cry, and told her she mustn't grieve too much. After Amah left, Mrs. Appleton told Jane she thought all the McPherson servants had been in on the murder. At this, Jane lost her temper, and told Mrs. Appleton she was a mean, narrow woman who hated the Chinese and had no business living in China. Jane had walked out of the Appleton house — not even waiting for Will to come home — and hailed a rickshaw. The person she went to was Ambrose Varley.

When Jane, hot and disheveled from her ride through the streets, had shown up at Varley's gate, Mr. Chen, the eunuch, had marched her through the house to Varley's study. Varley had looked up, taken off his glasses, and asked her to sit down. He was upset about the death of Jane's parents and said so. He let her talk, listening quietly while she told the things she hadn't been able to talk about when she saw him at the funeral — for instance, what she had seen when she first entered the room where the murder had taken place.

In the end, Mr. Varley said to Jane what Amah and the other Chinese had said to Jane: she mustn't grieve. Her parents were good people and devout Christians. They were no doubt in their Christian heaven and were happy to be there. "I found him very comforting," Jane said, "just as I found Amah comforting. Nobody else eased my pain the way those two did."

Varley also asked her about the Li family. Wutang and Ailian had been at the funeral, heads down, faces averted. "They've lost so much," Varley told Jane. Han had publicly defied Cyrus. Now their relative, Little Gao, had committed an unspeakable act. Varley was concerned about them. A servant told him there had been screams and crying in the Li household the whole night after the murder was discovered. The old grandfather had taken to his bed and, some said, refused to eat.

"This is a terrible thing," Varley said.

Jane stayed in Varley's house only a few days. During that time, Will came twice, to bring her fresh clothes and to try to convince her to come back to the Appletons' and back to school. Each time, Jane refused. "At that time, Will was more rational than I was," she said. Reverend Appleton came too, and Jane refused to see him. "I regretted that later," she said. "He was a good man. He wasn't like his wife."

She said her stay in Varley's house had a dreamlike quality. She spent her time wandering through the old courtyards, examining his Chinese treasures, and was served meals by Mr. Chen, who hardly ever spoke to her. This, too, she found comforting.

"There was one very significant thing that happened during that time," she told me.

Varley had called Jane to his study one afternoon. She found him at his Chinese desk—a marble slab over twin rosewood pedestals lined with drawers. "Come and look at this," he said.

Jane came close and saw a pile of blue-and-white ceramic shards on the desk in front of Varley. He poked among them with his long, slender fingers, trying to fit them together. Jane reached out and touched one of the pieces. About three inches long, with sharp edges, it was a blue-and-white leafy tendril, a part of it missing.

Jane recoiled when she recognized it. "My mother's bowl," she whispered. "How did you get it?"

"I asked the police if I could take it home. After all, it once belonged to me. I loved it once."

Jane looked up into Varley's eyes. "It was in that room," she said. "I saw it."

Varley told her he wanted to fit the bowl back together. There was a man he knew who could repair broken porcelain so well you would never know it had been broken. There was only one problem, he told Jane.

She had moved closer to see what the problem was, still not wanting to touch the shards.

There was a piece missing, Varley told her. It was a small, triangle-shaped piece. Someone must have swept it up and thrown it away, he said. Either that or he had somehow neglected to collect all the pieces. He said he even had gone back to check the corners of the sitting room—it had been easy to bribe the police guard—but the piece was gone.

Then he told her that when the bowl was fixed, even though one piece was missing, he would give it to her. "If you want it, that is," he said.

Jane put her hands behind her back and shook her head. "I don't want it," she said. "You can keep it."

Three days later, Donald Bauman came to the gate along with Reverend Appleton and Will. Donald told Jane that her father had drawn up a paper a long time ago, naming him and Electra as Will's and Jane's guardians should anything happen to their parents. Donald was very kind and friendly. He told Jane he wanted to take Will and her to Shanghai, to live in the big house there and go to the Shanghai American School. There were no relatives in the United States, it seemed, close enough to willingly take in two unknown adolescents.

Jane was surprised, but had gone with Donald willingly enough. She had known she couldn't stay much longer with Varley and Mr. Chen. She needed to be with her brother, and she needed to get out of Peking. Her parents were gone, Han was gone, and she couldn't find the servants.

She didn't want to say goodbye to Ambrose Varley. She had turned back to look at him, as she climbed into her rickshaw to ride away from the quiet courtyard. Varley stood in the shadows, but she could see his face. "And you must remember I had always liked him," Jane said. She was silent for a moment, then added, "It was almost unbearable, leaving Peking. I felt like I'd lost everything. I soaked my pillow for many a night, I can tell you. But I managed."

"Did you hear anything more about Han after your parents were murdered?" I had gone back to our bunks to find Jane awake. Mei was looking out the window but smiled when she saw me coming.

"Not then. People were whispering about him, but I had to keep quiet. It was very dangerous to be a communist in those days. Because of what Han did, Wutang and Ailian were in some danger themselves. They were watched."

"He should have thought more about his parents."

"Knowing Han, he probably agonized over his decision, but went off in the end, because he could no longer bear leading such a false life."

"You really do understand how the Chinese think, don't you?" I stared at Jane, my admiration sincere.

"You think so?" Jane gave a short laugh and shook her head. "It's amazing how little I understand." She glanced at Mei when she said this.

"So you went to Shanghai—"

"My, yes. And what a different world that was."

CHAPTER 12
SHANGHAI, SUMMER 1936

The train ran along Peking's city walls, and picked up speed, aiming south to Shanghai and the coast. Sitting in a first-class compartment, Jane clutched a paper-wrapped packet in her lap, and stared blindly ahead of her.

She ran her hands over the parcel. It was crumpled and torn. Something hard and lacquered black showed through a tear in the paper. She ripped it further and peeked inside. It was a box, its lid painted with a repetitive bat motif—a sign of good fortune. She stuck her hand through the hole in the paper and lifted the lid. The inside too was lacquered black, shiny and smooth. She lifted it to her nose and sniffed; it smelled like new lacquer, a hot, slightly acrid odor. She thought the box looked large enough to contain the notebook and pen Mr. Varley had given her. "Keep track of what you see around you," he had said. "Things are changing very fast."

The box was a farewell gift from Wutang and Ailian. Jane had gone to their house to say goodbye shortly before leaving for the train station with Will and Donald. The Li house, dark and gloomy at the best of times, now oppressed her even more with its air of sadness. As usual, the windows were clouded with soot and cooking smoke; the heavy beams were darkened with age. The furniture—ornate European-style from two decades earlier, the early years of the Republic—was of dark, almost black, wood.

Wutang and Ailian had received her in their main room; there was no suggestion that Jane see the old grandfather. The two sat together on an uncomfortable-looking settee with a horsehair-covered seat and carved wooden back and arms. They invited Jane to sit in a matching settee opposite, a little too far away for comfortable conversation. The three sat quietly, making the necessary small talk and, from time to time, uttering deep sighs. Jane knew that Wutang and Ailian were deeply abashed that a member of the Li family had been accused of harming her parents. Amah had told her that, had the Li family not been Christian and so imbued with foreign ways, they would not have received her, because the loss of face had been so great.

Wutang looked noticeably older; his shoulders sloped more than ever, as if weighed down by some unseen force. His eyes were downcast, and the lines from nose to chin had deepened. Where once he used to smile a lot, now he barely made the effort. Ailian's eyes were red and puffy, as if she had spent hours crying. The puffiness swelled her already plump face and made her eyes seem smaller.

Ailian had insisted Jane eat and drink something. Although Jane wasn't the least bit hungry, she managed to taste each dish Ailian handed her, and to sip a little tea. After a servant cleared away the dishes, Ailian sat down beside Jane and took both her hands.

"Your parents were good people and are surely in Heaven," Ailian said.

"Yes," said Wutang, who still sat on the settee across the room. "Your mother and father deserve a place by Jesus Christ's side in Heaven."

"Thank you," Jane murmured. Inside, she was rebellious. They deserved to live here on earth until they were old, she thought.

She pressed down on Ailian's hands, returning her sympathetic pressure. "Have you heard from Han?" she asked.

Ailian made a choking sound and shook her head. Behind her, Jane heard Wutang grunt. She stopped, confused, and looked at them. "I'm sorry—" she began.

"It's all right," Wutang said. He bowed his head. "We are quite certain he is safe," he said.

Jane looked up quickly. "How do you know?"

Wutang and Ailian exchanged a glance. "There was a message," Wutang said. "He is in the mountains by now."

"With the communists?"

"Shhh! We must not talk of it." Wutang put a finger to his lips. He glanced again at Ailian and she said, "Han's wife is still here with us."

Jane was surprised. "Does she plan to stay here?"

Ailian looked down. "No," she said. "She wants to go home to her parents."

"Who can blame her?" Wutang said.

"If only she had been with child," Ailian said.

Wutang cleared his throat. "That marriage should never have taken place. I know that now. She'll probably divorce him. Perhaps he'll marry some girl in the place where he has gone…" His voice broke off, and he gave Jane a weak smile instead of finishing the sentence.

After that, they had presented her with the wrapped parcel, saying it was nothing, merely a little token so she would remember them. Clutching the package to her, Jane hugged them both, her vision blurred by the tears she was determined not to shed. "I am now your father," Wutang said. "Your Chinese father—Will's, too. You children must come to me, if ever you need me, for whatever reason, no matter how much time has passed. You must promise me this."

"I promise," said Jane.

No one had mentioned Little Gao.

Will and Donald were on the train with Jane. Donald had spotted a business acquaintance just as they were boarding, and excused himself, saying he had been trying to get in touch with that gentleman for some time. He asked Will if he would like to come along, and meet one of Shanghai's influential businessmen. Will had agreed and they left Jane settled in the compartment, promising to come back for her soon. She told them it didn't matter, she planned to fall asleep. The truth was, she was irritated and baffled by Will's continuing behavior since their parents' deaths. He now wore a kind of mask, grave, attentive, even sometimes friendly, but he reacted angrily if anyone tried to express sympathy or force a confidence. He still refused to let people hug him, and pulled away almost rudely every time a kind missionary or mother of a school friend had tried to embrace him to show her sympathy. He wouldn't let Jane get close either. It was as if the bereavement were his alone; at any rate, he refused to share.

Jane twisted around to stare out the window back at Peking's city walls, now barely visible in the distance as the train made its way across the North China plain. They had passed through the Qian Gate earlier that day on their way to the train station. It had been a warm, sunny day, and there had been those few moments of cooling shadow as the open car Donald had borrowed moved into the massive arched opening at the southern edge of the city. There had been a sense of adventure, then a piercing sense of loss.

Now she noticed a smell in the compartment, one that shouldn't have been there. She wriggled her nose, then smiled to herself. Of course, she thought. The smell was a combination of old leather, mildew, human sweat, bad sanitation—Peking's distinctive odor—let in when they had opened the compartment doors. She realized why the smell was unfamiliar: always before, when the McPhersons had traveled by train in China, either Della or Cyrus had boarded first and washed down the compartment with disinfectant. Now the smell was missing. Her parents were no longer there to protect her, even from the all-pervasive germs that were a fact of Chinese life. Jane felt her face convulse and she bent forward and covered her eyes. After taking a few deep breaths, she leaned back, closed her eyes, and tried to sleep.

Jane's first impressions of Shanghai were the sunny, jam-packed streets, where the light glinted off a thousand reflected surfaces, and the noise. Donald's driver met them at the train station and guided them into the Packard. Jane sat between Will and Donald in the roomy backseat and turned her head from side to side, looking out the windows. She had seldom seen so many automobiles and foreigners. Her one memory of Shanghai—at the age of four—was as distant as her memories of the United States. The imposing line of multistory buildings along the Bund, Shanghai's park-like waterfront, also resembled her hazy memories of the United States; there was a clock tower, and a policeman directing traffic from a raised platform, only the policeman was an Indian Sikh and wore a turban.

Beside her, Will leaned back against the leather seat, his hands in his pockets, his eyes half-closed. He had been in Shanghai many times and had seen it all before.

There were more crowded streets, huge department stores, and billboards advertising American movies. The constant roar on the street was interspersed by piercing whistles from the traffic police. When the whistle sounded, huge masses of people swarmed forward, milling around the Packard—all shapes, all sizes, all nationalities.

As the Packard rolled on down Nanking Road, the noise gradually lessened. There were more trees, fewer people. They turned off the main road and turned yet again. Here, Jane glimpsed large houses, half-hidden by greenery—upper stories with sunlight flashing off the windowpanes. The Packard turned into the drive of one of these and gravel crunched under the wheels.

The Bauman house was more imposing than Jane remembered from her one, long ago trip to Shanghai. She had retained no memory of the outside—its half-timbered walls, tall, rounded windows, and red-tiled roof—and little of the interior, beyond vast spaces that had bewildered and frightened her. Now, the driver tooted the horn and pulled up to the front steps. Large double doors popped open, a white-robed servant emerged, then stood aside to let Electra come out on the steps.

She was out on the gravel next to the car door almost before the driver could get out. With a grace that must have come from long practice, both the driver and the servant opened the Packard's back doors simultaneously. Donald got out, then Jane slid across the seat and somehow ended up in Electra's arms.

Jane was enveloped in black-and-white checked sateen and a wonderful smell of powder and perfume. Electra squeezed her, then let go and held her out to look at her. "You are prettier than ever," she told Jane. There were tears in her already reddened eyes, and her face was overly made-up. She gently pushed Jane to one side and held out her arms to Will. He leaned away from her and stiffened his shoulders. At the same time, Donald said, "Electra..." Electra dropped her arms to her sides. "Well," she said, blinking rapidly and looking around at them all, "let's go inside and get you settled." She opened her fist to reveal a wadded-up handkerchief and dabbed at her face. She smiled when she caught Donald's eye.

Electra led the way into the house. More servants in long white Chinese robes and black felt slippers slipped out of the house and carried the luggage in behind them. Other servants met them in the wide, high-ceilinged hall. Electra told Jane their names, but Jane was too tired and confused to remember.

The little dogs, Lizzie and Pearl, wriggled out of servants' arms and ran to Jane and Will, sniffing at their feet. They followed Jane and Electra up the polished, wood-paneled staircase to Jane's room. The dogs seemed to remember Jane from their visits to Peking, and trotted and leaped up beside her and tried to lick her hands. Jane knelt down and hugged each dog in turn.

Her room was beautiful—large with a four poster bed and a huge blue-and-yellow Chinese carpet. Yellow curtains at the four large windows picked up the color in the rug. Jane had her own bathroom, as big as her little bedroom in Peking, with white tiles, a claw-footed tub, and a toilet on a platform, with the tank high up by the ceiling. You had to flush by pulling a chain. The bathroom, too, had a window; Jane looked out and caught a glimpse of another large house through the trees.

Dinner was served late in the Bauman household. Used to informal family suppers in Peking, Jane's stomach was growling long before the gong sounded at eight o'clock. "We dine like the English," Electra told them, as she guided them into the dining room. She seemed more like her old Peking self, chatty, almost febrile. "But we won't always be this formal when it's just us. This is your welcome dinner."

The Baumans dressed for dinner, and Jane had had to put on her only good dress, which she also had worn to her parents' funeral—a dark blue, long-sleeved taffeta that looked too young and was painfully unfashionable. As Donald held out Jane's chair for her to sit down, Jane smoothed down the skirt of her dress and made a face. She looked up and caught Electra's eye. Electra said, "You and I are going to go shopping together sometime in the next day or two."

Jane threw her a stricken look and Electra seemed to read her mind. "You don't need money for this shopping trip." She laughed. "This is magical, you see. No money needed." She reached across the table and took Jane's hand and squeezed it. "I've never had a daughter to buy dresses for, so you'll have to put up with me. I hope that's okay with you."

Jane remembered the department stores Donald had pointed out on Nanking Road—Sincere's and Wing On—and his assurances that they could get anything they needed in Shanghai. For the first time since the death of her parents, she felt a twinge of hope and excitement. No one had ever taken her shopping for clothes—a Chinese seamstress had made her clothes ever since she could remember.

The dining room was huge, and lit from above by a crystal chandelier and lamps in the shapes of candles at intervals along the paneled walls. The four of them sat at one end of a long table, which was covered with a white damask cloth and set with delicately flowered dinnerware, heavy, ornate silver, and paper-thin crystal goblets. Four servants lined up just inside the door, holding steaming dishes of food. Once the four were seated—the dogs at Electra's feet—the servants moved forward and served each in turn, starting with Jane, appearing suddenly on her left and inviting her to help herself to the food—roast beef, mashed potatoes, small new peas, biscuits, and gravy.

After Jane had put a generous helping of each on her plate, she glanced at Will and then at Donald and Electra, wondering who was going to say grace. When there was no mention of it, she said a quick, silent prayer to herself and waited for Electra to pick up her fork so she too could begin eating. Will also watched Electra for a sign that he could start. Both children dug in as soon as Electra lifted her fork.

Electra beamed at them across the shining table.

"You children have such good manners," she said.

Jane smiled, but Will stared at his plate.

The food was delicious. Jane realized that it was the first time since her parents had died that she had really wanted to eat. She took a bite of mashed potatoes and gravy and closed her eyes, savoring the taste. She opened them when a servant appeared with a bottle and started to fill her wineglass.

"Oh," said Jane, glancing first at Will and then at Electra. "I don't drink alcohol."

Will was impatient: "Come on, Jane. You're in Shanghai now."

"You don't have to take it if you don't want it," Electra said. Donald sipped his wine and said nothing. He smiled slightly and seemed amused by the scene.

Jane was embarrassed. She looked at the wine, sparkly and deep red in the goblet. It looked like the currant jelly that her mother used to make in the summers, and Jane wondered if it had the same sugary taste. Pushing the thought of Della out of her mind, she reached out and grabbed the delicate stem of the glass, almost tipping it over. She raised it to her lips—trying not to notice that the rest of them were watching her—and took a sip. She couldn't help making a face: it didn't taste at all the way it looked; it was bitter and rough on her tongue. She put the glass down and tried to smile at the others.

Will looked amused. "Your first time?"

"You know Ma and Pa didn't drink."

Electra looked at Donald, "Donald, I wonder if we're doing the right thing, allowing these two to do things their parents wouldn't have approved of." Before Donald could answer, Electra said to Jane and Will, "You see, I've always believed in training children to appreciate good wine, which, after all, is one of the finer things of life. But if your parents didn't approve…" She broke off and looked at them, widening her eyes.

Jane picked up her glass and took another sip. This time, it didn't seem so bad.

"She likes it," said Donald. He raised his glass and smiled at her.

"You're supposed to raise your glass in return," Will told Jane. He briefly held up his own glass.

Jane lifted the frail glass of the deep red wine and smiled at Donald over the rim.

Electra laughed. "She's a fast learner, the little darling. Oh, I can't wait to take you shopping and to meet my friends."

Near the end of dinner, Will spoiled the mood by announcing that he was thinking about living at the school, which took boarding students, when he and Jane enrolled in the fall.

"But why?" Electra asked. Her face, beautiful in the soft light, suddenly looked haggard. "You have a home right here. It's not as if you live in the wilds of China somewhere, like some of those missionary children."

"Jane and I *are* missionary kids," Will said.

"Of course you are." Electra spoke quickly. "I didn't mean anything, Will. I only want to make you happy here."

"Maybe I'd be happier doing what Ma and Pa would have wanted," he mumbled.

Jane stared at him, feeling stricken. The warm feeling from the wine had worn off, and the house seemed huge, dark, and unfamiliar.

Donald cleared his throat. "We've got all summer to talk about this," he said. He glanced at Electra. "People change their minds."

"Please, Will," Jane whispered. She felt suddenly exhausted, and wondered if it had to do with the wine, as well as the long train journey. She regretted drinking the wine, feeling it had been disloyal to Cyrus and Della. Her first night in Shanghai, she thought, and already she was forgetting what her parents had taught her.

Another thought rose unbidden: Ma had been angry with the Baumans when she died, angrier than Jane had ever seen her. Della had been shocked and horrified when she learned Donald had taken Will to a brothel. Yet, there had been an earlier arrangement for Jane and Will to go to the Baumans' if anything happened to their parents. Where else would we have gone if not here, Jane thought, some distant relative in the United States? Thinking this, Jane suddenly realized how thankful she was to stay in China, how thankful she had been ever since the day Donald had shown up at Varley's house to take her away. If Shanghai and the Bauman house were unfamiliar, think how much more unfamiliar the United States and unknown relatives would have been. Besides, the Baumans seemed to want them. Jane doubted that any of their distant relatives would have welcomed two China-raised adolescents into their households.

Will tilted his chair back, his feet out in front of him, his hands in his pockets, the light shining off his auburn hair. Jane wished he would at least smile. There was a long moment when no one seemed able to think of anything to say. Then Electra turned to Donald and said, "You probably have some work to do. I'll entertain the kids. We can listen to the radio or we can play cards…" Again she broke off. She looked at Jane and Will in turn, as if asking for their help. Jane felt like crying, and Will stubbornly kept his face averted. Neither was prepared to be much help.

Later, at bedtime, Jane stood in the hall and gazed up at the staircase. Suddenly desolate, she felt as if she were going to cry and wanted to get upstairs before the tears started. She turned quickly to Electra. "May I take Lizzie and Pearl up with me? Just for tonight?"

Someone had unpacked her suitcase while she had been downstairs. Her few dresses hung in the closet, her shabby brush and comb set was neatly arranged on the dressing table. Her books, the parting gifts from Wutang, Ailian, Ambrose Varley, Frances Appleton, and others in Peking had been laid out on a long shelf that ran beneath two of the windows. She remembered several of the missionaries saying they would pack and send Cyrus and Della's belongings to Shanghai. Some of those things would look nice in this room, Jane thought. She would, of course, have to share their parents' belongings with Will.

Jane dropped the dogs, which ran off to sniff at various places around the room, and picked up the box Wutang and Ailian had given her. She smiled to herself and ran her hand over the box. I must thank them right away, she thought. I must ask Electra to help me buy some writing paper. I must have some pin money, too, she thought. I can't ask the Baumans for every little thing. She wondered if they planned to give her an allowance or would allow her to earn money in some small way. What might a fifteen-year-old girl do to earn money?" she thought.

Jane picked up her brand-new pen and notebook that Varley had given her, and carried them over to a small desk — partly Chinese and partly Western in style. It had curved legs, and the top was inlaid with different colored woods. Jane wished it had a blotter; she was afraid she might spoil the surface of the desk.

She pulled out the chair of lightweight bamboo, sat down, and opened the notebook. It had never been used, and she had to hold it down flat with her palm to keep it open. She kicked out her foot to shake off Lizzie, who wanted to play-fight. "Not just now, Liz. I'll play in a little bit." The dog made growling noises and ran in a circle, wagging her tail.

Jane picked up her pen and began to write on the blank white page.

Dear Han,

I don't know where you are tonight, and I'm sure you don't know that I'm in Shanghai. Mr. Varley gave me this notebook and pen as a parting present, and so I decided to use them to write to you. I know I can't mail these letters. Where would I send them? How would they get through? Still, I feel that, in a way, I'm talking to you. You are the only person in my life untouched by my parents' tragedy, since you left Peking before it happened. Writing to you is like revisiting the past.

I know I must live in the present. Have you ever been to Shanghai? It's so big and modern. We drove by the prettiest parks on the way from the station. I can't wait to take walks in them. I wish you were here to walk with me, although the Whites and the Chinese seem more separated here than in Peking, judging by some of the talk at dinner tonight.

Anyway, I have no friends yet and I don't know when I'll meet anybody. It's too late to start school here this year. Will and I will go to the Shanghai American School next fall. I hear there are a lot of other missionary kids there. (Will tells me we're called "mishkids.") Speaking of Will, he's acting strange. I think he's being selfish and unappreciative of how kind everyone has been. He acts as if he's the only one grieving for Ma and Pa.

If you were here, you would understand. You always do.

I wonder if I'll ever hear from you. I mustn't hope too much. Things seem very upset and we're very far apart. Even so, the thought of you is one of the good things of my life right now and it makes me feel grand.

Your friend always,

Jane

Writing the letter made Jane feel better. She put the cap back on her pen, changed into her nightgown, and climbed between the cool, scented sheets of the luxurious bed. Surprised to find her eyelids heavy, she fell asleep almost immediately.

As promised, Electra took Jane shopping the next day. She offered to take Will, too, but he refused, preferring instead to accept Donald's invitation to visit his offices downtown and later go to the race track with Donald and some of his friends. Donald told Will he would arrange for a temporary job for him if he liked. It would give him spending money and some independence, things Donald had appreciated when he was a boy. Donald had given Will a sizing-up look when he said this—they were all at the breakfast table—narrowing his eyes and pursing his small mouth. He nodded to himself and said to Will, "You should do very well." When Donald and Will got up from the table to go into town, Donald had joked about "men's work" and looked proud and happy when Will said he wanted to learn about doing business in Shanghai. Donald and Electra had blown kisses to each other, and then Donald and Will left the room. Not long after, Jane heard the front door open and shut, and the sound of the Packard idling outside. A few minutes later, she heard it drive away.

Electra, sleepy-eyed and tousle-haired, wrapped in a green silk bathrobe, told Jane, "The driver will come back for us. We have all the time in the world, darling." She rang the bell for more coffee and, while the Number Two Boy poured it, told Jane she never got up this early. She had dragged herself out of her bed that morning in honor of Jane and Will. "That's why Donald was looking at me so funny," she said, sipping her coffee and making a face, because it was so hot.

About an hour later, Jane came downstairs and waited for Electra in the front hall. She had put on the same dress she had worn to dinner the night before, as she had been unsure what was appropriate to wear in a grand shop in Shanghai. Jane sat down on a fragile-looking gilt chair in the hall and tried to talk to the Baumans' Number One Boy, who waited by the front door—it was open, the Packard had returned and was waiting outside. Jane spoke to the boy first in Mandarin, saying she didn't know Shanghainese. He eyed her curiously, but replied in Pidgin English, "Missee wantchee go buy plenty new clothes. You likee?"

Jane nodded, hating not being able to communicate in Chinese. She already felt distant from the Baumans' servants; they all dressed alike, and she hadn't yet learned their names. She wasn't even sure how many there were.

They heard the quick tap-tap of Electra's high heels in the upper hall. "Come quick, quick," the boy said. Jane stood up and watched Electra come into view, dressed in a slim, dark-colored suit and a small hat with a veil. She pulled on white gloves as she came down the last few steps. "All ready to go, darling? Lovely." She flicked a glance over Jane. Jane knew her clothes surely didn't meet Electra's standards, and she felt her face burn at the thought. But kind Electra didn't say a word. She shooed Jane in front of her as they went out the door to get into the car.

It was as sunny as the day before. The Packard rolled through residential streets dappled with sunshine and shadow, then turned onto what Electra told Jane was Bubbling Well Road. "So wicked at night, darling," Electra said, glancing out the window. "Lots of lights and clubs and things like that."

Jane darted her head this way and that to see it all. Like the day before, the streets were packed and noisy. The driver constantly had to bring the Packard to a stop, then start forward again. Jane, perched beside Electra on the backseat, felt encased in a kind of protective cage. Although the street sounds and a slight breeze came in through the windows—it was a warm, almost hot, day—she, Jane, remained clean and protected from the blur of faces outside. She was used to open rickshaws on wide avenues. It felt odd to sit for such a long time in a closed automobile, feeling hemmed in by the crowds and the multistory buildings.

The driver let them out in front of the Wing On department store, where, Electra said, they could buy a few essentials such as handkerchiefs and underwear. "After that, we'll try Lane Crawford. Someone told me they had nice girls' things."

There were no stores like this in Peking—vast, high-ceilinged, lined with cases of goods, and fragrant with perfumed smells. Jane saw a line of Chinese women in front of a turnstile. "They have to pay to come in," Electra told her. "Otherwise, the Chinese would crowd in here just to look around and we'd never get near the counters. It would be like an outdoor market."

"But we didn't pay."

"No, the man could tell we were going to buy something."

"Do they have to pay very much?"

"No, not much. Come, let's go upstairs." Jane followed Electra's slim figure, feeling in a daze from it all. "Is this like America?" she asked.

Electra threw her a smile over her shoulder. "You don't remember America?"

"Not much. I was so little when we went there."

"Well, it is, a little. It's not much like Peking, is it?"

It's not much like China, Jane thought. She tugged at the waistline of her homemade dress and felt like an awful country bumpkin.

In all, they bought cotton vests, panties, socks, and Jane's first pair of silk stockings. They also bought four dresses, a pleated skirt, a cashmere twin sweater set, slacks, and three crisp white blouses. At a counter in Lane Crawford, Electra bought Jane a lipstick—a pale pink color, which the woman behind the counter said was suitable for young girls. When Electra paid for the lipstick and the clerk put it in a bag and, smiling, handed the bag to Jane, Jane almost grabbed the bag out of the clerk's hand, she was so excited. The last thing they bought that day was a pair of shoes, black pumps with slightly raised heels. "Do you want these? They'll do for when you dress up," Electra had said when they first spotted the shoes. She had picked one up and held it out to Jane. Jane, who had not even considered buying high-heeled pumps, gazed at Electra. Electra laughed. "I guess that luminous look means yes, doesn't it, darling?"

Afterward, they left their packages with the driver and had tea on the roof garden at the Shanghai Hotel. While Jane stuffed herself with frosted cakes, Electra lit a cigarette, crossed her legs, and asked Jane questions about Peking and the Peking American School. She didn't once mention Cyrus or Della, for which Jane was grateful, but did ask a lot of questions about Will. Was he popular? Did he have a girlfriend? What were his favorite studies, his favorite sports and books? Jane answered all of Electra's questions as well as she could. Throughout the conversation, she kept thinking about the heap of packages on the backseat of the Packard, under the driver's watchful eyes, and felt a warm glow. She thought, it does feel good to have nice things.

Back home, Jane and Electra trooped up to Electra's bedroom, where they spread the new clothes on the bed and admired them again. Then Jane sat at Electra's dressing table, while Electra showed her how to apply her new lipstick and a little powder. "Not too much," she cautioned, leaning over Jane to get it exactly right, so close that Jane could smell her perfume. "You want to look like the daughters of the best English families, not like the Russian tarts on Fuchow Road."

Jane stared at herself in the mirror. She had changed from the shapeless cotton dress her mother's dressmaker had fashioned for her in Peking, to the oh-so-soft, butter-colored cashmere twin set and gray pleated skirt. A little earlier, Electra had combed out Jane's shoulder-length hair and pulled it back at each side. She wound the ends around her fingers and secured them with bobby pins. After she finished putting on Jane's make-up, she unwound the bobby pins, and the strands of hair cascaded onto Jane's shoulders in soft waves.

"It won't stay curly like this. We'll set it again before you go to bed," Electra said.

Jane didn't, couldn't, answer. She could only stare at the newly pretty, sophisticated girl in the mirror. Her eyes met Electra's in the mirror and Electra smiled delightedly. "How pretty. Now the boys will surely look at you."

Jane glanced down from the mirror. "I don't know much about boys," she mumbled.

"You have a handsome brother. He can introduce you after he makes a few friends himself. But didn't you know any boys in Peking?"

"I knew Han."

Electra gave Jane's hair a last pat and straightened up. She studied the comb and didn't look Jane in the eyes as she said, "You mean the Chinese boy?"

"You met him, Mr. Li's son. He was my best friend."

Electra pulled up a small gilt chair next to the dressing table, a twin to the one in the front hall, and sat down next to Jane. She crossed one silk-stockinged leg over the other and arranged her perfectly manicured hands in her lap. Addressing Jane's reflection in the mirror, Electra said, very clearly and carefully, "Shanghai is different than the way you lived in Peking, dear. You lived in a sort of dream world there. You didn't have much to do with the foreign legations and the others. This is the real world, here. This is the way it is. I liked your friend Han, what little I saw of him. I have nothing against the Chinese. In fact, I admire them. There are a few I even love. But when people ask about boyfriends, you cannot, must not, mention Han. It's all right to say it to me. I understand, but no one else will." She put her arm around Jane's shoulders. Jane caught another waft of her perfume and remembered that Della had never worn perfume. "Your dream world in Peking is gone, my dear," Electra said, "and you must live in the present." She squeezed Jane's shoulders and straightened up.

In the mirror's reflection, Jane saw tears run down her own cheeks. She saw rather than felt her head bow forward as she nodded in agreement with what Electra was saying. Electra tightened her grip on Jane's shoulders and the two of them sat still for a while, heads bowed, not saying anything.

Jane woke up that night, wondering for a moment where she was. The room was dark and very still. She remembered that her room was at the back of the house and that it overlooked only lawn, trees, and, through the trees, a neighbor's house. She remembered suddenly the quiet serenity of the inner court of the McPhersons' modest home in Peking. A sudden spasm of grief shook her, and she rolled over and buried her face in the pillow and sobbed. "Ma, Ma," she whispered, clutching the wet pillow. She remembered Cyrus that last night in his study, when she had leaned against him and rubbed his shoulders because he had seemed so tired and discouraged. The pain was so bad she wanted to scream, to rend the silence with her grief. She burrowed deeper into the pillow and stuffed part of the pillowcase in her mouth. Her nose and mouth and eyes dripped, dampening the pillow and the bed.

At last, exhausted, Jane sat up. Unable to breathe through her nose, but otherwise feeling better, she climbed out of bed and stumbled over to her bureau to find a handkerchief. As she pulled open the top drawer, trying not to yank it suddenly and make too much noise, she heard faint strains of music.

She stopped and listened, but this time heard nothing. She found a hanky, unfolded it, and gently blew her nose. She thought she heard the music again and stood still to listen. After a moment, she tiptoed to the door and put her ear against it.

The music, instrumental and with a slow tempo, seemed far away. Jane carefully pulled open the door and crept out into the hall. Now she could hear the music more clearly. She thought it came from the direction of Electra's room, so she moved silently, carefully down the hall. A light shone under Electra's door.

Now, Jane recognized the tune she was hearing. The day before, Electra had played some of her favorite records on the Victrola in her room, telling Jane that some of the songs were from her youth and brought back both happy and sad memories. Jane stepped closer to the door and put her ear against it. There were other sounds in the room. Someone was moving around, and it sounded as if Electra were talking. The music stopped suddenly. Jane stepped back from the door, prepared to take flight.

She decided Donald must be visiting Electra's room. Unlike her parents, Donald and Electra did not share a bedroom, and Electra had told Jane that Donald "visited" her in the night, "when the spirit moved him." She had winked, and peered at Jane to see if the girl understood. Jane, believing she understood, had felt herself blush. She knew Donald and Electra were not too old to sleep together, but they seemed old to her, even though Electra was so beautiful.

She was about to tiptoe back to her own room when she heard Electra sob. There was no reply, no answering and comforting deep male voice. Jane hesitated, uncertain what to do. There was a thudding sound as if Electra had fallen or bumped into something. For a moment, there was a complete silence.

Jane made a sudden decision and tapped lightly on the door. "Are you all right, Electra?" she called out, as quietly as she could.

There was no answer, so she tapped again.

The music started again. Jane hopped from one bare foot to the other, uncertain what to do. From down the hall, she heard the flushing of a toilet, and a deep rumble as the water made its way through the pipes. The sound had come from the direction of Donald's room. Did that mean Donald was in his own room and not Electra's?

Electra's voice, shaken with sobs, began again, this time over the music. She heard light steps, then the voice—words Jane couldn't make out.

Jane seized the door handle, turned it, and pushed it in.

A single, soft electric light lit the room, throwing a romantic glow on the richly cushioned bed with its tousled covers, the deeply tufted carpet, and the woman who moved gracefully in circles, hands raised as if she were dancing with someone.

Electra was completely naked. Her body, accentuated by light and shadow, looked mysterious and young. Any lines and sagging of middle age had been erased by the soft lamplight. Her short auburn hair—looking longer because she leaned her head back to gaze up at her imaginary partner—looked dark, with a reddish glow where the lamp shone behind it. Her face, turned up, was wet with tears.

Jane stared, afraid to move.

Electra acted as if no one had come into the room. She clasped her raised hands together, as if around her unseen partner's neck, and smiled through her tears. "You worry too much, my dear," she said, her voice breaking with a sob. "Our child is alive and fine." Electra closed her eyes and a spasm crossed her face. "We'll all be happy again, you'll see," she whispered to her invisible partner.

The imagined reply must have been soothing, because she smiled wearily and leaned her head forward, as if on a man's supporting chest. "You must never tell Donald," she whispered. "He has been so good to me."

Jane slowly backed out the door and shut it silently behind her. Shocked and moved, she tiptoed back to her room, climbed into bed and lay awake for a long time. She remembered Della telling her that Electra had had a miscarriage years ago and had been unable to have any more children. Now she talked about a child as if it were alive. Jane shivered. This, then, was Electra's tragedy, the explanation for her sometimes-strange behavior.

Exhausted, Jane drifted off to sleep, and dreamed of soft music and a man whose face she couldn't see, but who was warm and comforting, nonetheless.

CHAPTER 13

PRESENT-DAY CHINA

"Look at this." I tapped the open notebook on my knee. "This is a taxi driver in Chengdu—born there. He graduated from high school in 1966, just as the Cultural Revolution was getting up a good head of steam."

I was sharing with Jane and Mei some notes I'd taken earlier, hoping to find ideas for documentaries. "The taxi driver was a Red Guard," I told them. I consulted the notebook again, straining to read my own shorthand. "He was sent into the Sichuan countryside for two years, then joined the army. Afterward, he got married and had one son. Now he works in a state factory during the day and drives a taxi at night." I turned a page. "Listen to this. He and his wife own their own taxi. He drives at night, she drives during the day. They hardly ever see each other." I looked up at Jane and Mei. "What kind of life is that?"

Jane asked, "Did he seem satisfied with his lot?"

I thought about it for a moment, then said, "Yeah, I think he did. He seemed proud when he told me about owning the taxi. He said that in China people work very hard. He said it as if it was a good thing to work so hard."

Jane spoke to Mei in Chinese. Mei then said to me in her halting English, "Before, people suffer. Now, they like work. They choose work. They have money."

"Money, money, money," I said. I shut the notebook. "That's all the Chinese talk about."

Mei chuckled and shook her head. She then spoke to Jane, who translated.

Mei remembered there was a time when she detested people with money, and thought that no one should have more or less than anyone else. Her foster father in particular thought everyone should endure hardship, and he resented people who had many comforts.

There was a wealthy family down the road who owned the land her family farmed, and she vaguely remembered the house, but she knew that the man of the house was a Kuomintang official of some sort. From what she could remember, the landlord had treated them well, but her foster father despised him nonetheless. He hated the Kuomintang, and spoke very openly about it to their family. He talked of how the communists cared for the peasants, and the cities in which the communists had taken over from the Kuomintang, and how the communists had greatly improved the conditions of the peasants by providing land and restoring order and the economy. The Kuomintang, he said, had no concern for the ordinary worker, and only catered to the rich.

Once the communists seized Chengdu, the peasants in the area rose up against the wealthy. Mei's foster father took part in many of these "settling accounts sessions" where the communists would incite the peasants to confront the landlords in the village square. The peasants in one area of Sichuan even dug up a notorious landlord, Liu Wencai, who had died before the communists had come to the area, so he could "attend" the settling accounts meeting. Often, the peasants would ransack the landlords' homes, destroying or stealing valuables and food. Many times, the family would be dragged to the center of town, where they would be publicly executed. Mei's foster father took her to the public execution of the wealthy Kuomintang official who was their landlord. Mei covered her eyes through most of it, afraid she would have nightmares of the dead man's face. She was sure he would come back to haunt her.

The train stopped in Xi'an, the walled city in dusty Shaanxi Province, where almost thirty years earlier a farmer had unearthed a larger-than-life-size terra cotta statue of a warrior, with finely detailed battle dress and strangely life-like features. The discovery had led to extensive excavations on the loess plain outside China's ancient former capital.

Warrior after warrior had emerged from the earth. Experts had come from all over the world. Photographs appeared in *National Geographic* and other major publications. Now, tourists jammed the excavation site to stare at the Qin emperor's vast terra cotta army. It was generally believed that legions more remained to be excavated.

I promised myself I would visit Xi'an on my next trip to China. It was maddening to have to stay on the train, while tourists — Chinese and foreign — swarmed around me, getting on and off at the Xi'an station.

Jane reminded me Xi'an had also been the site of a bizarre kidnapping in December 1936: Zhang Xueliang, a warlord known popularly as the "Young Marshall," had held Chiang Kai-shek in an isolated room not far from what was now the present day excavations. Mao's right-hand man, Zhou Enlai, negotiated Chiang's release. The result: both communists and nationalists agreed to unite in their common struggle against the Japanese.

"And you remember this?" I said.

"I remember it being talked about."

"Where? In Shanghai, you mean?"

Jane nodded. "During dinners with the Baumans' friends, or when we'd go to the club or the racetrack."

"Sounds like a pretty fancy way of life."

Jane sighed and didn't answer. I said, "I suppose your mom would have thrown a fit if she'd known you and Will were living there."

Jane shrugged. "Well, there was this agreement. Pa and Donald cooked it up between them, I guess, years and years earlier."

"It's a wonder your mom didn't cancel it when she was so mad at the Baumans."

"She hardly expected to be murdered," Jane said, sounding touchy.

I looked away. Sometimes Jane seemed so eager to tell her story, I thought, and other times I felt as if I was only irritating her. I thought of Tim, running into excitement and maybe skirting danger down on the Burma border, while I dealt with this prickly old missionary.

I pictured Tim in the heat of the day, sweat dripping down his face, but insisting on continuing, his blue eyes sparkling in the sun. Had he been able to interview some of the drug traffickers there? I remembered how he seemed so confident. This made me feel discouraged about my idea. Sometimes I had to force the story out of Jane, and I resented that. I stood up and swung my arms. "Can't get any exercise around here," I complained.

"Walk up and down the train," Jane suggested. She took up a paperback book and began reading. I wondered if I was ever going to get her attention back. I saw my interview falling apart, my once creative idea coming to nothing, while Tim triumphed. He's really going to think I'm a loser, I thought.

"Hell and damnation!" I said, not caring if Jane found my swearing offensive. I certainly could have said a lot worse.

Jane looked up from her book. "You really do need to take a walk, dear," she said, and went back to reading.

I looked at Jane through narrowed eyelids and then stomped off in a terrible temper.

I didn't approve of missionaries anyway. Where did they get off telling the Chinese their ways were heathen? I was beginning to sense that the Chinese were traditionally an unusually tolerant people — ill suited to puritanical American notions of right and wrong.

This led me to think about the whole human rights issue. Now I felt uncomfortable. If the missionaries shouldn't have been in China, should the Americans be preaching at them today? I truly believed people in Tibet were oppressed, and that the Chinese Government had acted barbarously at Tiananmen Square. So, I wondered, where was the answer? Where did I get off condemning the missionaries, when I went "rah-rah" every time someone in America stood up and told the Chinese leaders they were the butchers of Beijing? Didn't I now feel some sneaking sympathy for the Chinese, because they were sick and tired of having foreigners tell them what to do?

Tim and I had gotten onto the subject of human rights when we were in Chengdu.

"Look at what we Westerners have pushed on China since the early nineteenth century," Tim had told me. He laughed. "What a range of values: opium and Jesus Christ, venereal disease and John the Baptist, Western science and extraterritoriality, rampant capitalism and human rights. Their heads must be whirling."

"What's wrong with human rights?" I had asked.

"Nothing, of course, but why would they want to hear this stuff from us? Why should they trust us? We conk them over the head every chance we get."

"If we don't tell them, who will?" I asked.

Tim shrugged. "That's a good question," he said. "Who indeed?"

When I came back to our compartment, I put on the sweetest voice I could and asked Jane about when she had left China. Was it because of the war?

"It was the Japanese," she said.

"But you came back as soon as you could."

"I always came back whenever possible. I had left the most precious thing in the world behind." Prompted by my questions, she said that she was forced out in early 1950, for that long hiatus while the United States and China worked out their complicated relationship. "They kicked me out," she said, still looking surprised and unhappy about it. "The communists objected to my missionary background." An official of the newly formed People's Republic of China, someone she knew fairly well, had paid a call on her and conveyed the government's insistence that she leave. "I told them I was trying to find my daughter," she said, "but they told me—quite politely—that they were kicking me out."

"What about Li Han? Where was he then? Couldn't he help you?"

"He had gone off to the west. By that time, he was a party cadre. I asked about him, thinking I would get him to intervene, but I ran right up against a stone wall. I came to know I wouldn't do him any good by insisting."

"I understand that a number of foreigners got to stay," I said.

"Tell that to the officials that kicked me out." She spoke sharply.

"So what did you do?"

Jane put her book down on her lap. She said she had returned to San Francisco, where she had worked for the navy during the war, and married the naval officer who had helped her get back to China in 1946. The marriage had lasted only five years—in the telling, Jane quickly skipped over this part—and she had landed a job with a non-profit organization that promoted study about China at first, and later the reestablishment of relations between the United States and the People's Republic. She made one last comment before returning to her book. "And I never stopped pushing for ways to get back here," she said. Jane looked over at Mei, who gave her a slight smile. I wondered if Mei really understood how important she was to Jane.

It was late afternoon during the second day on the train. I sat next to the window, going over my notes, adding things I remembered and making corrections. The slanting rays of the sun poured into the car, dazzling my eyes and forcing me to move. I climbed up onto the middle bunk—Mei's bunk—and stretched out to continue my work. Below, Jane still read her book, and Mei had struck up a conversation with a woman who had wandered in from another car. Their voices went on and on, rising and falling with the tones. Mei seemed wholly Chinese then, totally unrelated to the elderly American woman who sat reading next to the window.

From the bunk, I had a good view of the rest of the car. As the sun sank, a party-like atmosphere began to spread through our car. The noise level, never low, rose even higher. People—obviously some from other compartments—there might have been a group traveling together—gathered at the little tables next to the windows, snacking and drinking tea and soft drinks. There was a lot of laughter and the crackling sound of cellophane packages of nuts and candies being opened. A group at a table near us passed an open bag of sunflower seeds first to Jane and Mei, then up to me. I grabbed a handful and thanked them in my very bad Chinese; I had found the Mandarin word for "thank you" one of the most difficult to pronounce.

One of the young men at the table pulled out a portable tape recorder, a sort of boom box. He rummaged through a bag at his feet and brought up a fistful of tapes. I couldn't understand what he said to his friends, of course, but I caught the word for America: *Meiguo,* beautiful country.

"American music?" I called down from my bunk.

The young man grinned and nodded and held up his thumb in approval. He stuck a tape into the machine and pushed the play button. At the same time, he turned up the volume.

A familiar boom, boom blared out above the noise of the train. I raised my head from the notebook because I recognized the tune. It was "Centerfold" by the J. Geils band. I had listened to it when I was in high school. I remembered moving to this beat with my friends, driving around in my shabby old station wagon, singing out the words at the top of my lungs.

I leaned down over the edge of the bunk. "That's 'Centerfold!'" I called out over the music. Heads whirled to look up at me, including Jane and Mei, both of whom looked puzzled. The young man with the tape recorder grinned widely and started clapping his hands to the beat. The others at the table joined in. When the young man turned up the volume, they clapped even louder, laughing out loud.

I scrambled forward—there wasn't enough space to sit up—and leaned down even farther. The familiar tune, the clapping, the laughing, it all made me suddenly homesick. I started to sing—loud, not much in tune: "My blood runs cold... my memories have just been sold..."

Several young Chinese joined in, like me, shouting more than staying in tune. "My angel is a centerfold." A young man and woman—the solemn young couple I had interviewed earlier—now scrambled to their feet and tried to dance in the narrow aisle. They snapped their fingers and turned in circles, then danced in place. The others yelled, egging them on. Another woman started giggling. The young man who was dancing let go of his partner and tried to grab the woman who had been giggling. She squealed and hid her face and made all of them laugh.

Over the noise, I imagined for an instant the parents of these young people, the ones who had been Red Guards, parading in the streets and forcing their humiliated elders to wear dunce caps. Did things change at such dizzying speeds in China? Westerners had pried open Pandora's box, and look what had emerged. Or did the West have anything to do with it? Were the Chinese at last masters of their own fate, or were they not? Were they really happy about all this, or did they feel they had no choice but to join the modern world?

These dancing young people at any rate enjoyed the present.

I glanced again at Jane and Mei. Jane looked bemused. She caught my eye and grinned. Mei looked happy and interested—too old to join in the fun, but not too old to appreciate it. Was there a secret here, I thought, an ability to seize the moment that we would do well to learn? Or was I only imagining, even romanticizing, present-day China? Was a policeman going to charge into our compartment and stop the party?

But no one stopped us. I stuck my head and shoulders through the narrow space between the bunks and waved my hands in time to the music, singing louder than ever. At this, Jane actually laughed out loud in a nice kind of way, pleased to see me having a good time. Finally, in time to the tape, I slowed down the music of my arms, as if bringing their impromptu chorus to the grand finale. "My angel is a centerfold," we shouted in unison and brought the song to a close.

Chapter 14
Shanghai, January 1937

It was a Saturday, and Lizzie the dog had gone missing just that morning. After Donald had left to go downtown earlier, taking Will with him as usual, Jane had found Pearl skulking under the altar table in the entrance hall and Lizzie nowhere in sight. She heard loud sobs upstairs and recognized Electra's voice. She was surprised Electra was up so early, as she had begun sleeping until almost noon.

"What's the matter?" Jane asked the Number One Boy.

"Too muchee trouble. Little dog not here."

"Lizzie? Where is Lizzie?"

"Velly bad," said the Number One Boy. "I look evelly-where top side."

"Did you look downstairs, out in the garden?" Despite her distaste for the sound of Pidgin English, Jane now understood it without difficulty.

"Evelly-where," he said. He spread his hands, as if wanting Jane to see he wasn't hiding the missing dog.

Upset, Jane stormed up the stairs and entered Electra's room without knocking. Electra lay face down on the bed, sobbing loudly. Clothes were strewn about the room, open medicine bottles had spilled onto the floor, and wadded up bits of paper lay on the carpet, as if Electra had started a letter and then torn it up. Jane sat down on the bed beside Electra, and smoothed her hair, which was wet and disheveled. "Electra? Electra, what happened to Lizzie? Tell me quickly and I'll go find her."

Electra raised a red and swollen face to look into Jane's eyes. "You won't be able to find her," she whispered. "He's come back to get her."

"Who? What are you talking about?"

"Little Gao. He loved Lizzie, remember? Now he's taken her away." She burst into fresh sobbing, and Jane jumped off the bed and went over to the lavatory in the corner of the room. She found a fresh washcloth and held it under the cool flowing water. Wringing it out, she called out to Electra, trying to keep her voice normal, "Just tell me about it. We can solve it." She went back to the bed and dabbed at Electra's face with the cloth. "There, doesn't that feel better?"

Electra sighed and closed her eyes. Her sobs subsided into a steady hiccup. She murmured something Jane couldn't understand. "What did you say?" she asked Electra.

"…the worst mommy in the world…" Electra mumbled, her eyes still shut.

"What? No, no you're not. You can't help it if Lizzie got lost."

"…hates me…"

"Nobody hates you. Just tell me where Lizzie might be. I'll find her for you." Jane knew she shouldn't hurry Electra, who was more upset than she'd ever seen her, but she was beginning to worry increasingly about the little dog.

Electra sighed once more, then turned her wet, mottled cheek into the bed cover and lay still.

"Electra," Jane urged. "Turn over and let me wash your face."

Electra didn't reply. She began to snore, a gentle yet rasping sound.

"Electra? Come, please. You must tell me what's happened to Lizzie." Jane shook the woman's shoulder, but Electra didn't stir. Jane climbed down off the bed and stared at the sleeping woman. She put her hands on her hips. "All right, if you don't tell me, I'll have to go ask the servants. I bet they can't tell me anything." She felt tears rising to her eyes. "You need to help me find Lizzie." Electra still didn't move and Jane said, a sob catching in her voice, "You're being selfish, you hear that? Very selfish."

She turned, ran out of the room, and thundered down the stairs. She pushed open the kitchen door and found the Number One Boy, as well as the rest of the staff, huddled there, watchful and suspicious.

"Where's the dog?" Jane asked.

No one answered. Jane raised her voice. "Where's Lizzie?"

One of the young amahs crept out of the room and came back in a moment, carrying Pearl.

Jane shook her head in exasperation. "Not that dog." She felt her voice going out of control. Now she was almost crying. "Doesn't anybody care?" She looked around at the circle of faces studying hers. None of them replied. Jane turned and ran out of the room.

She put on a coat, went outside, and combed the garden, calling for Lizzie. After a while, she went out into the street and walked over to Bubbling Well Road. Here, the traffic picked up and there were more people on the streets. She wandered down the street, avoiding both cars and rickshaws. The clubs that lined that section of road were shuttered on a Saturday morning. They'd still be recovering from the excesses of the night before, when the street was alight with neon and packed with pedestrians and automobiles.

Jane called Lizzie's name and endured the stares of Chinese she saw along the way. For the first time in her life, she found herself resenting anyone with a Chinese face. They don't care. They don't care, she told herself over and over again.

A poorly dressed woman with two small, ragged children pushed the youngsters to get them out of Jane's way. Impassive eyes met hers. They hate me, Jane thought, amazed. All they can see is my white face, my good clothes.

She realized she didn't even know that many Chinese people in Shanghai. Electra's only friends—and these didn't seem to be close—appeared to be other Westerners—American and English women. Donald, to be sure, knew a great number of Chinese, but they were all businessmen and politicians, with whom he met in mysterious places downtown where Jane never went. Donald sometimes took Will to meet these men, but Jane and Electra joined them only when and where there were other women present, such as at the club or the racetrack or some of the fashionable restaurants. Sometimes, Donald brought prosperous-looking Chinese at these places over to be presented to Electra. Jane was always very much in the background on such occasions, a young "missy" who nodded and smiled, but said little.

These Chinese never came to the small dinner parties Donald and Electra gave—Jane assumed they were never invited—though Electra told her they met Chinese "of all stripes," as well as Japanese, at large receptions. Will told Jane that one of the men Donald seemed to know well and whom he, Will, had met, was Du Yuesheng, a great triad leader who had power over many important people, including Chiang Kai-shek. Du had risen from abject poverty in boyhood to membership in Shanghai's notorious Green Gang, then on to wealth and influence over all of Shanghai's underworld. He also had strong ties with the business community—both Chinese and foreign—and with Chiang Kai-shek and the Kuomintang. China's underground had been closely intertwined with the revolutionary movement in the first decades of the century. Now, it represented a force for conservatism and order, while maintaining its old ways of sworn brotherhood, total obedience, and summary justice if the brotherhood was betrayed.

Still combing the streets for Lizzie, Jane found herself on Nanking Road, caught up in one of those great, surging, noisy throngs that brought traffic to a halt and caused drivers exasperation. She felt frightened, strange, and not herself. She had never before felt out of place in a Chinese crowd; now she did. She stared at the strange faces, and they either stared back at her or looked away.

Jane's feet found the curb on the other side of Nanking Road. She jostled people on the sidewalk to make her way to the Cathay Hotel, where she telephoned Donald's office and asked if he would give her a ride home. That was when she lied and told him she had come downtown to shop.

The people in the Baumans' circles most often talked politics, particularly the encroachment of the Japanese, and the possibility of a war that could threaten them all. The Japanese were waiting, menacingly, just north of Peking, and everyone feared they were getting impatient. Jane had heard Donald and several of his business associates talking at the club one night about China's inability to fight Japan. One of the men, a lanky Englishman, had twisted his mouth as if he smelled something bad and waved his hand dismissively as he talked about Chiang Kai-shek and the Kuomintang. He said Chiang was more interested in defeating the communists than he was in warding off Japan. "The Chinese are fighting furiously among themselves, like tomcats, and will tip up off the table and tumble into Japan's lap."

Donald had watched the Englishman, not saying much, just keeping a small polite smile at the ready. Jane watched Donald, knowing he strongly supported Chiang Kai-shek because he believed the communists were bad for business. Still, he protested when the Englishman and others railed too much about "communist bandits."

"You underestimate the Chinese," Donald said. "Chiang needs the communists just now, and they'll work something out. You'll see."

The news had relieved some of the tension in Jane's mind. She had felt increasingly disloyal to the memory of her father if she sympathized too much with the communists—which she did sometimes when she remembered the things Han had told her—and to Han, when she wanted Chiang Kai-shek to prevail and things to stay the same in China. She knew, of course, that nothing would stay the same; Japan would see to that. Nonetheless, it made her feel infinitely better for the opposing sides in China to have united. When she first heard the news about the events in Xi'an, she wondered if somehow this could mean she would see Han again before long. Meanwhile, she watched and listened, trying to absorb all she could of what was going on around her.

"I feel like a teeny pawn on a great big chessboard," she told Will. "All these things happening and I can't do anything about it."

"You are a pawn," said Will. "We all are."

Both Jane and Will felt a great deal older than they had the day their parents had died, though it had been less than a year. Will was seventeen and in his final year of high school; Jane was sixteen, would be seventeen in June. They both felt Shanghai had made them much more mature. At Donald's insistence, Will had decided not to board at the school. Now Donald was putting more and more pressure on him to delay college and stay in China awhile, and make some money before the United States or England was drawn into fighting Japan, which would ruin any chances at quick wealth. Will was seriously considering this, although he knew—and admitted only to Jane, in whom he was beginning to confide for the first time since Cyrus and Della's deaths—that their parents would have deeply disapproved.

"They wouldn't have approved of any of this," Jane said, meaning Shanghai. "Ma must never have meant for that agreement to take effect—that agreement that the Baumans be our guardians."

"Would you rather have gone to some dour old second cousin in the States?" Will asked.

"I'm not saying what I would have wanted. I'm saying what Ma would have wanted."

Talk about his mother always put Will in a bad mood and he would talk about the coming war instead. He worried, he told Jane, because he saw the adults around him worry, but he also found it exciting.

He was the one who told Jane about conversations between Donald and his business contacts. Will told Jane that Donald talked to Kuomintang, communists, and Japanese alike. "He won't be caught out when the balloon goes up," Will told Jane.

"You sound more like an Englishman every day," Jane said. She meant it disparagingly, but Will admired the English and took it as a compliment.

Jane finally reached the Bund. Feeling exhausted, defeated, her feet aching, she sank down on a bench and stared at the river. "Big Ching," the fond nickname Shanghai residents had given the clock in the Customs House tower, had just struck one o'clock.

Donald was going to meet her at the corner of the Bund and Nanking Road at half past one to give her a ride home. All she could think about was Lizzie. Poor little thing. How many Jack Russell terriers would be loose on the streets of Shanghai? If the dog had run away, if someone had stolen her, there was always a slight chance Jane might spot her. Now, she finally had to admit to herself the futility of looking for one little dog in such a large city.

Sometimes it seemed as if all of Shanghai was out to defeat Jane. As usual, the tree-lined Bund was crowded, but the people were vastly different from the friendly and curious throngs of Peking. Here there were clerks and shopkeepers on lunch breaks, foreign women resting from rounds of shopping, lovers strolling along the water. A group of Chinese amahs congregated not far from Jane, their charges in baby carriages, resting their sore feet, all the time chattering away to each other.

Since Jane didn't understand much Shanghainese, she couldn't make out what they were saying. She had tried, in the months since arriving in Shanghai, to learn as much of the language as she could. It had not been easy. She had spoken Mandarin from birth, and had been truly bilingual. Now, she had to struggle with this unfamiliar tongue. She had learned a number of stock phrases, could hold her own when shopping in the old Chinese city, and of course she could read the newspapers, as Chinese characters were universal to all Chinese languages and dialects, but she couldn't converse in the easy way she had in Peking.

What particularly baffled her was the refusal of the Baumans' servants to speak to her in anything other than Pidgin English. This, as much as anything, made her feel distant from the Chinese in Shanghai. She was now acutely aware that she was a foreigner in China, something she had so often managed to put out of her mind in Peking.

There were other Westerners in Shanghai—people Jane sometimes saw, often heard about, but never socialized with: journalists and other members of the intelligentsia, who hung out at the Astor Hotel or the Chocolate Shop, talking about free love and popular Chinese opera singers, as well as all those topics of the day Jane heard discussed at home. There were also the White Russians, refugees from the Bolshevist Revolution in Russia. Jane heard people say they were pathetic, waiting on tables, even pulling rickshaws or begging like the poor Chinese. "White men!" people whispered, "Laboring like coolies!" Worst of all were some of their women. Jane had seen Russian girls overdressed and haggard, soliciting men on Nanking Road and in the French Concession. Donald and Electra had clucked their tongues in pity when the Packard passed them one night and Will had thrown Jane a significant-looking glance.

Still sitting on the bench on the Bund, Jane looked up and saw a White Russian girl, probably not much older than herself, hurry forward to meet a young man—a Westerner, though Jane couldn't tell much else about him. They clasped hands and kissed lightly, then turned and walked off arm in arm. Jane caught a glimpse of the girl's pretty face, glowing and happy, despite the heavy make-up. She felt an unexpected envy, a desolation. Those few boys at the Shanghai American School whom she found attractive—and they were few; most seemed immature — seemed more interested in hearing about her parents' murders than in getting to know her. There were one or two others, mishkids like her and Will, who were intent and serious, and might have interested Jane, only they seemed to have no interest in her. In any event, she had never found anyone remotely like Han — a friend and a powerfully attractive young man at the same time.

She reached in her coat pocket and drew out a folded piece of paper. She smoothed her hand over it but didn't open it. She had already memorized the words. It had been the only good part of the message Ambrose Varley had brought last night.

Jane had been up in her room, thinking she should wash for dinner soon, when she heard a horn toot on the drive, and the purr of an engine, followed by a light patter in the front hall, and the dogs barking as the Number One Boy ran to open the door.

Jane went out into the upper hall and listened to the murmur of voices from below. She inched forward and peered over the balcony just in time to see Ambrose Varley step through the front door, bundled up in Western-style warm clothing — a hat and a woolen coat.

"Mr. Varley!" she called out before she could stop herself. Below her, Varley's tall, stooped figure, foreshortened by her view almost directly over him, stopped abruptly. He had just stepped forward to hand his hat to the boy. Now he paused and looked up, still clutching his hat. "Jane?"

"Oh, Mr. Varley." Something both painful and pleasurable moved in Jane's chest. She was so glad to see him, yet he reminded her of her parents and her lost-forever home in Peking. She hurried around to the head of the stairs and started down, nearly stumbling in her eagerness.

"Careful," said Varley. He put out his arms as if to catch her. The boy grabbed at Varley's hat with great skill and cupped it in his small hands. Jane, seeing Varley's outstretched hands, ran down the remaining steps and threw her arms around his neck. "I'm so glad to see you," she whispered. He smelled of garlic, the cold, and coal smoke.

His arms tightened around her, then he quickly let her go. He grabbed her arms and held her back so he could study her. "You've grown up! What do you mean by running down and hugging me as if you were a small child? If you were Chinese, they'd have you married off by now."

He straightened up and studied her some more. "Yes, you look much better. They must be taking good care of you. That haunted look is gone from your eyes. You've gained some weight. You look pretty."

"You saw me in those awful days just after…"

He nodded.

Just then the library door opened and Donald came into the entrance hall. His eyebrows rose when he saw his visitor. "Varley," he said, using the name as a greeting. His small mouth twitched downward in his characteristic half-amused smile. "This is a surprise. I don't think you've ever come here before."

"I'm sorry for dropping in like this. I won't disturb you for long. I must talk to you."

"Certainly. Can I offer you something? Whiskey? Tea? Coffee? What are you doing in Shanghai?"

"Chinese tea, please." Varley towered over Donald. "I've been coming from time to time to oversee shipping out some of my antiques."

"A pragmatic man, eh?"

"I don't see any sense in letting the Japanese do what they want with my things."

Donald turned to Jane. "Jane, if you will excuse us, please—"

Varley intervened before he could finish. "Let her listen too. It concerns her parents. Find young Will, if he's here. Both children should hear this."

Jane's heart started beating fast. She stood by the staircase and didn't move, while Donald sent the Number One Boy to find Will and to tell Electra that Varley was here. She heard Donald say, "Tea, in the library. Chop-chop."

The Number One Boy nodded and hurried out of the room. "Notice how their expressions never change?" Donald said to Varley. "Spooks me sometimes. I've been in China twenty years and I still don't understand them."

Varley watched the retreating figure of the Number One Boy and didn't reply.

"But then you speak the lingo, don't you?" Donald said. "I never really bothered to learn. Wonder now if that wasn't a mistake?"

Will came out into the hall then and greeted Varley. Electra appeared at the head of the stairs, peered over the railing, then came down, hesitantly, dragging the train of a green silk, feather-trimmed housecoat from step to step, eyeing Varley as if not sure this was a visitor she would welcome in her home. By the time she reached the bottom of the stairs, she had summoned up some dignity, and put out a white arm and hand to greet Varley with some of her former style.

He bowed over her hand, formally and unsmilingly.

Electra took Jane's arm as they all moved into the library. "What is all this?" she whispered. Jane could feel her trembling.

Jane patted her hand. "Shhh. It's all right." She laid her other hand on her own breast. Her heart still pounded. She glanced at Will, who was sending Varley curious glances.

Jane whispered to Electra, "He says he wants to tell us something."

It hadn't taken either Jane or Will long to discover that Electra was addicted to opium. She took long naps in the afternoons, then appeared at dinner, often febrile. As the months passed, she napped for longer periods. She had aged visibly in a short time; her face had pouched and sagged. Once, Jane heard Donald scolding her, saying the opium would kill her. This wasn't the woman he had married. Electra had cried, and Donald had stomped off in exasperation. Jane felt terribly sorry for her. Having inadvertently peeped in Electra's bedroom that night and found her dancing with a fantasy partner and talking of a dead child, Jane now saw her benefactor in a whole new light. It made her feel protective. Ma would have tried to help her, if she'd known, Jane often told herself.

They settled themselves in the library. The Number One Boy brought in a tea tray, poured and passed it around, then lingered, drawing the curtains and switching on lamps until Donald asked him to leave.

As soon as the boy had closed the door behind him, Donald said, "Well, Varley?"

Varley sat perfectly still, his hands folded on his lap. "You remember the day you came to my house to pick up Jane?" he said to Donald.

Donald nodded. He pulled a cigarette case out of his breast pocket, offered one to Varley, who shook his head, and to Will, who took one. Electra slipped her own case out of the folds of her robe. There was a short silence, broken by soft clicking sounds as they all lit their cigarettes — Will somewhat inexpertly. Donald exhaled smoke and said, "I remember well. What about it?"

Varley's smooth face looked ageless in the lamplight. For the first time, Jane noticed he had the same kind of round-faced handsomeness Will had, and realized suddenly just how grown up Will had become. Now, here Will was, trying to smoke a cigarette.

Jane wondered how it was Varley could take opium and seem none the worse for wear, while Electra was falling apart. It wasn't fair, Jane thought. He must have been about the same age as Donald and Electra. She looked at Varley, waiting for him to speak. Her stomach churned. She clenched her fists and crossed her legs. Will, Donald, and Electra dragged on their cigarettes, inhaled, blew out smoke, and leaned forward to knock the ashes against the ashtray.

Only Varley sat still. Without shifting position, he said, "We spoke a little then about the police report and how little real information there had been."

Donald said, "I remember thinking it was a damned shame. Case stunk to high heaven, and the police seemed so eager to close it up. It was politics, I know. I understand. But these were my friends, damn it."

Varley nodded. "I remember your saying so at the time. Now, I've heard something new. There was more, after all."

Everyone stirred. Electra leaned forward to put out her cigarette. Donald lit another. Will smashed out his half-smoked cigarette and stared at Varley. His face, partly in the shadows, had taken on its sulky uncommunicative look, as if he resented Varley's presence and whatever it was the man was going to say.

Varley said, "I make no pretense, no apologies, for my habits. You all must know I sometimes go to opium dens. I find it soothing to lie back on a couch in a hazy room and know there are others present who might be sharing my dreams."

Donald moved his shoulders impatiently. "Yes, yes, man, get on with it. You know there's a young girl present."

Varley's expression didn't change. His calm glance took in Jane, as well as Electra and Will. "It was in one of these opium dens that I heard the information I'm talking about. One of the policemen who worked the McPherson case stops in there from time to time. We had quite an interesting conversation the last time I was there."

No one said a word, and Varley went on. "You could see the man had fallen on hard times. He no longer worked for the police. But I won't go into that now. It isn't relevant. And I can't stay long, so I need to pass on this bit of information and be on my way."

They all waited. Will crossed his legs again. Jane heard the click of Donald's lighter as he lit yet another cigarette. He got up and lit one for Electra too. He showed the lighter to Will and Varley and raised his eyebrows. Both shook their heads and he sat down again.

As if he had been waiting for Donald to settle himself, Varley said, "This was one of the two policemen who first showed up at the house that morning after Cyrus and Della were murdered." For the first time since they had gone into the library, Varley looked directly at Jane. "You were there, Jane. You probably remember him, a tall man, thin, kind of knobby."

"His ears stuck out," Jane said, her lips barely moving. She thought, Oh, tell us and get it over with.

Varley nodded. "The man said it had been so easy, tracing Little Gao to his house. Then, of course, Little Gao hanged himself."

Jane had imagined Little Gao's hanging body too many times to want to think about it now.

"The policeman fellow let me know that they'd had a chance to rough up Little Gao a bit first." Electra made a convulsive movement and Varley said, "I doubt they did much to him. He apparently was very frightened." Varley held out his hands as if beseeching the silent group that sat listening to him.

"So Little Gao talked after all," Donald said. He held his cigarette close to his lips and stared out across the room.

No one spoke or moved. Varley said, "A little. He was hysterical, sobbing and pleading. He said the murders hadn't been his idea, not his fault. Then he said something very strange—and I'm quoting the ex-policeman here—that it was the baby's fault."

Jane jerked her head up. Electra gasped. Donald said, "Baby? What baby?"

"I don't know what baby," Varley said. "I'm only repeating what the policeman told me."

There was another silence, deeper this time, more shocked.

The afternoon wind had picked up. Jane stuck the piece of paper back in her pocket and stood up. She glanced up at Big Ching, the clock tower on the Bund. Donald should be here any minute. "Are you sure that's enough time to shop?" he had asked on the telephone, not really caring, Jane knew, just wanting to be nice. He always made it impatiently clear that men's issues—business, trade, and war—were paramount, while women's issues were to be tolerated. He would be indulgent about shopping and clothes, he seemed to say, but wouldn't go so far as to actually take any interest himself.

"I'm only getting exactly what I need," Jane told him. "I can be earlier if you want."

"No, you go ahead. Get more things, if you want. Pretty things you might not be able to get if this war heats up too much more."

Jane felt badly about lying to him, but hadn't wanted to go into the problem of Lizzie over the telephone.

Now, Donald's Packard came into view. Jane could see Donald in the backseat. He held up a newspaper, obviously reading from it. Jane stood up and waved and caught the driver's eye. He slowed down along the curb, and Jane ran over to the car just as Donald looked up and saw her. He folded his newspaper and leaned forward to open the back door. "Get in," he called. "We can't stop here."

Jane stepped onto the running board and into the roomy back seat. She sank down, grateful to be riding home in comfort. Donald pulled the door shut. The driver glanced over his shoulder to make sure Jane was seated, then carefully pulled out again into the stream of traffic.

"Where're your packages?" Donald asked.

"I didn't find anything," Jane mumbled. She wondered why she hadn't told Donald the truth from the beginning. Maybe it was because he so obviously didn't care about Electra's dogs, she thought. He wouldn't understand walking all the way downtown, getting blisters on your feet, just to look for a missing dog. She stared out the window into the crowds and traffic and felt sick again, thinking of Lizzie somewhere out in an unfamiliar world.

She turned back to Donald. "Where's Will? I thought he came downtown this morning?"

"He stayed on awhile." Will had been working in Donald's office on weekends, serving as a kind of glorified office boy, a cut above the Chinese clerks, an apprentice, really. "He's going out with some friends later. Said to tell Electra he wouldn't be home for dinner."

"Then he'll be nightclubbing," Jane said. Will's closest friends were the sons and daughters of businessmen, not other mishkids. There was a rich and sophisticated crowd at the school—Jane didn't know any of them well—and Will had gravitated into it. He bragged to Jane about going to popular nightspots like Del Monte's and Ciro's. On several Sunday mornings, Jane had heard Will coming home at dawn. On such days, he pleaded a bad headache and stayed home from church. Usually, Jane and Will attended church with Donald and Electra, going as a family. It was a fun outing, not at all the solemn occasion it had been in Peking. They mingled with the Baumans' smartly dressed friends after the services, then went to their club for lunch.

"Of course he's going to a nightclub," Donald said. "You're only young once." He didn't ask her why she didn't go too, for which she was thankful. He had once asked why she didn't have a boyfriend, and Electra had protested and shushed him.

Jane leaned back against the Packard's comfortable backseat and said to Donald, "There was some trouble after you left this morning."

He threw her a quick glance, instantly alert. "Trouble? What? Was it Electra?"

"No. It's Lizzie. No one can find her. I've been looking and looking."

"The dog?"

Jane nodded, mortified to feel tears rising in her eyes. She gave a huge sniff and swiped at her nose. "I haven't really been shopping. I've been out looking for Lizzie," she said. She wiped the corner of her eye.

"Now calm down," Donald said, reaching out and patting her arm. "The dog'll be all right. I suppose Electra is beside herself."

"She's had her pipe; she's passed out."

Donald grimaced. He knocked on the glass partition and called out for the driver to hurry straight home.

"Do you think we could offer a reward?" Jane asked.

"What? I don't know. We'll have to see."

"Do they eat dogs in Shanghai?" Jane found herself voicing her worst fear.

"Now, now. The dog'll show up, you'll see." Donald looked around as if looking for a way to escape from what he would consider the minor household turmoil Jane was forcing on him. She knew he had enough to worry about — Electra's health, business, the approaching war. Even Varley's visit last night was far more important than a lost dog. Poor little Lizzie.

Varley had taken out his pocket watch and glanced at it. "I really do have to hurry," he said. "But let me finish."

They waited. Varley said the policeman had also spoken about the broken Ming bowl. It was one he had given Della, he said, his voice and eyes grave as he told them this. It was a rare and beautiful bowl.

Donald nodded impatiently and tapped his foot. He opened his mouth to say something, but Varley forestalled him. "We all thought the bowl had been broken in the struggle." He glanced at Jane and then Will. "Excuse me. This is painful. The bodies were at one end of the room. There was an overturned chair, other signs of struggle."

"We know all that," Donald said.

Varley went on as if Donald hadn't spoken. "We assumed the bowl was broken accidentally, but it wasn't. It was deliberately smashed."

Electra put her hand up to her mouth. "Why?" she asked.

Varley said, "I can't begin to imagine the kind of mind that would deliberately smash a rare and valuable object."

Jane's mind reeled. What about Pa and Ma? she wondered silently. You can imagine them being killed? The bowl was rare and valuable and they weren't? For the first time, she doubted Varley's judgment and good intentions. She stared down, not wanting to catch his glance. Then she remembered his obvious distress after the murders and felt ashamed.

"I don't understand," said Donald. He looked around at the rest. "What is this supposed to mean?"

Varley said, "The ex-policeman told me the bowl had been on a table at one end of the room."

"It was!" Jane said, then put her hand over her mouth to shut herself up.

Varley barely glanced at her. "That end of the room wasn't affected by the struggle. The table wasn't even overturned. But the bowl was badly broken. I tried to have it mended and couldn't. The policeman believes someone picked it up and threw it down deliberately."

Jane shut her eyes, remembering the pieces of blue-and-white porcelain on the sitting room floor. When she had seen the pieces again, they had been spread out across Varley's desk. She could still picture his long fingers pushing and arranging them. She shivered, remembering he had offered her the mended vase.

"There was a piece missing," Varley said. "I remember telling Jane about it. I thought it had just been misplaced, perhaps mistakenly thrown out, but it seems this wasn't the case. You remember Little Gao stepped on the broken pieces of the bowl and cut his foot? That's how the police found him? When they asked him about his cut foot, he said—and again I quote the policeman who was quoting Little Gao, a very frightened and not very coherent young man—he said, 'Wanted the bowl but couldn't have it. So broke it and took a piece of it."

Donald stared at him, open-mouthed. "I'm absolutely in the dark. What was he talking about?"

"Either he smashed the bowl and picked up the extra piece or someone else did."

"Who? The other murderer?"

Varley said, "I would assume so."

"But why?" Again, Donald looked at the others as if for confirmation. No one else said anything. "Why does this mean anything at all? You said yourself the bowl wasn't broken in the struggle. Why couldn't it just have broken on its own?"

"Then where's the extra piece?" Varley spoke calmly. "I asked and asked again when I talked to the McPherson servants. They all claimed no one had touched anything in that room. And why would anyone deliberately steal a small piece of broken porcelain—especially when all the rest of it was left lying there?"

"I think you're making too much of this," Donald said.

Varley stared at him. "But this particular bowl—"

Donald sat up straighter. "My dear Varley, most people wouldn't know about a bowl like this."

Varley frowned slightly.

"You're making much too much out of this," Donald repeated.

There was another silence. No street sounds, no sounds from within the household. Jane looked around the room, trying to avoid the others' faces. Books in glass cases lined the walls; their surfaces reflected the lamplight. Her eyes came to rest on Varley's face once more; it looked as smooth and unlined as ever. He caught Jane's eye and nodded almost imperceptibly. She nodded stiffly in return. She wasn't sure why.

Both Donald and Electra had asked Varley to stay for dinner, but it was a perfunctory invitation and Varley had treated it as such. All of them, except maybe Donald who still acted as if he heard such tales every day—and maybe he did, Jane thought—were silenced by what Varley had had to say.

They had seen him to the door, all of them crowding out onto the front steps, where the taxi Varley had hired waited under the branches of a pine tree. The driver sprawled on the front seat, dozing, the doors closed against the chilly weather. The Number One Boy knocked on the taxi window and laughed. The driver stirred, then sat up, looking dazed and stupid because he had just awakened. He shook his head as if to clear it and hurriedly started the engine. Varley said good night to each of them in turn.

When he turned to Jane, he put his hand in his coat pocket and drew out a small parcel. "I wouldn't have forgotten this," he said. He smiled down at her, but his eyes were grave.

She took it in her hand.

"You'll understand when you unwrap it," Varley said.

Jane looked up at him. "Thank you," she said. She felt the parcel. It was lightweight and round, about the size of a teacup.

As soon as Varley's taxi pulled away, Donald, herding everyone back into the house, said, "What a strange fellow. Was he always like this?" No one answered and he went on. "Makes me wonder why he bothered to come here. And then making such a fuss over that smashed bowl."

Will said, "You don't think what he had to say was important, sir?"

Donald shook his head. "None of what he said made any sense. None of it."

Dinner was quiet: the servants tiptoed around them with platters of food, which nobody much wanted. Silverware clinked against plates. Donald made a few commonplace remarks about the cold weather. Will coughed, then suppressed it. Electra sat silent, not even pretending to eat. As soon as she could, Jane slipped upstairs to her room to open the parcel Varley had given her.

Before she could unwrap it someone knocked on her door; a moment later Will entered her room. Although she resented the intrusion, since she wanted to open the parcel, Will so seldom confided in her these days that she didn't want to discourage him.

He came over and sat on her bed, slouched, elbows on his knees, mouth turned down, gazing at her in silence.

"What is it?" Jane asked. She put Varley's gift on the nightstand and went over to sit on her desk chair.

"How can you ask that?" Will said. "Did you really listen to what Mr. Varley said?"

"Yes. But I don't quite understand—"

Will's head shot up. "There's something you don't know." He ran his hands through his thick, auburn hair. "If that policeman was telling the truth—"

Jane's hand jerked out convulsively. "What are you talking about?"

Will leaned forward again and gave her an intent look. "Who has people killed on a regular basis?"

"How would I possibly know?"

"The triad. Du Yuesheng."

"What are you trying to say?"

"Think about it."

"But... why would the triad want to hurt Ma and Pa? That doesn't make any sense."

Will bit his lip. "There's got to be a connection." He stood up and looked down at her.

"Why on earth would you think that?"

He still wouldn't meet her eyes. "There's a man here in Shanghai. One of Du's henchmen. You could say he's an important triad member. Tough?" Will shook his head, emphasizing the man's toughness. "His name's Baby."

"What? Whoever heard of a Chinese called Baby?"

"It's his English nickname. I think he got it from some Hollywood film."

"You know this man?"

Again, Will averted his gaze. "I've met him."

Jane asked, "Did Varley's policeman say "Baby" in English or Chinese?"

Will bit his lip again, still staring at the floor. "I don't know. We should have asked him."

"Why didn't you?"

"I just remembered. After he left."

"How do you know all this?"

"Donald and I know Du Yuesheng." He pulled his shoulders back a little when he said this, a young man proud of his connections.

"Are you going to talk to Donald about this?"

"I don't know."

He left the room, and Jane sank down on the bed. It had been a hateful evening. Normally, she would have wanted to see Varley, but tonight his demeanor and, most of all, what he had to tell them, were disturbing. Donald was right. Varley was strange. It had never bothered her before.

She shook herself and reached for the parcel Varley had brought her. It was wrapped in Chinese paper, which she unwound carefully, both wanting to save the paper—the old missionary habit of frugality—and feeling an odd reluctance to see what Varley had given her.

It was a cricket cage, fashioned from a dried gourd, with delicate etched designs on the sides, and an ivory top with grid work to keep the cricket from escaping. There was something inside; it looked like a piece of paper. Jane unscrewed the ivory top and drew out the paper.

Varley had written her a short note. In Chinese characters, he had penned, "This cage is about fifty years old. No one knows how many crickets have slept here. When you look at it, think of the cricket, caged, yet singing. He is a powerful beast, despite his size. When he is angry, his jaws are like iron. There is another little cricket, not so powerful, but happy to be with those of his kind. He is not in a cage. He is safe and he asks about you. He will always be your friend. He wants you to know this."

The unexpected surge of happiness made Jane close her eyes. She opened them and smoothed her hands over the cage, then held it up to examine the carvings—warriors with wings on horseback. How meticulous the artist had been, she thought, making sure that every detail on the small object was a work of beauty and perfection.

She remembered a pet cricket she had once owned, a gift from her parents' gatekeeper. She had bought a cheap cage in the market—nothing like this beauty, though Jane had thought it lovely—and put the little creature inside, where he huddled in the darkness. Jane had hung the cage next to her bed and let the little beast sing her to sleep at night. After a while, the cricket's songs lessened and became almost too soft to hear, as if he had lost the passion for singing. Jane began to feel sorry for him, knowing the workmanship of the cage meant nothing to the little creature. Finally, she had set him free in the courtyard, where, she imagined, he could sing under the stars and make his home in the grass.

Now, she picked up Varley's note again and reread it. So, Han was safe, and he thought about her. She wondered how he had managed to get the message to Varley. Had he returned to Peking? If so, Wutang and Ailian must have been so happy.

She went to sleep with the cricket cage in her hand. It kept her from worrying too much, at least for that night, over the news Varley had brought them.

The Packard brought Jane and Donald to the front of the Baumans' house. The driver tooted the horn, and the Number Two Boy, frightened eyes on Donald, met them at the door. "Master," he said. He tried to say something, but stammered and had trouble getting it out.

"Calm down," Donald told him. "The whole household is upset because of a missing dog."

"It is Missus—"

"What about her?"

The man again stammered badly, barely able to say the words. Donald and Jane both had to cock their ears and watch the man's lips as they tried to understand his Pidgin English. "Wantchee wake up Missus," the servant said. "No can do. Call doctor man. He quick-quick come this side. Muchee trouble. She eat all her medicine."

"What?" Donald pushed past the man and ran for the stairs, calling Electra's name.

"She not here," the manservant told Jane. "Doctor say she belong hospital."

"Donald, Donald!" Jane shouted, trying to tell him Electra had been taken to the hospital. Her cries mingled with his as he ran through the upper hall, calling out to his wife.

CHAPTER 15

PRESENT-DAY CHINA

The train stopped and then started forward again in a village on the plain southwest of Beijing. Despite the small size of the town, and the desolation of the dusty landscape, there were vendors on the station platform. Mei was hungry and bought a container of meat and vegetables, but Jane and I didn't want to eat.

"You're excited, aren't you?" I said to Jane. "Returning to Beijing?"

"How come you're not eating?" Jane asked, taking the offensive, refusing to answer my question. Jane had become increasingly irritable as we approached Beijing.

"I guess I'm just not hungry," I said, pushing down my own irritation. My notebook was on my lap. From time to time I glanced at it. When I took the time to read over the notes by myself, I was excited about the documentary I envisioned. Or thought I envisioned; I still wasn't sure. There were aspects that would be difficult, if not impossible, to tape. I asked Jane again, as gently as I could, "How do you feel, getting so close to your old home?" I was at least feeling optimistic again, even though Jane seemed to be pulling away.

Jane shrugged. By now, I knew this was a characteristic gesture that hid a multitude of emotions. Jane glanced out the window, her face and her white hair dimly reflected in the glass. "I see Mao didn't do anything about the dust," she grumbled.

"If anything, he made it worse," I said, recalling something I had read about Mao Zedong instructing people to pull up grass and plants because they were "bourgeois." I pictured millions of people across the land, on their hands and knees, pulling up blades of grass. What had motivated them? It surely wasn't only fear. They had loved Mao with a burning intensity, even when his policies caused death and destruction to millions.

Mao had led the Chinese on a grisly, exhausting chase throughout the fifties, sixties, and early seventies, until he died, and then Deng Xiaoping had led the country out of Mao's ideological wilderness. Yet even today, I saw icons of young Mao and old Mao—the thin romantic, the full-faced dictator—on buttons fastened to backpacks, or laminated in plastic and dangling like charms from the rearview mirrors of taxis. Had he been reduced to a good-luck charm or did people still venerate him? None of the Chinese I had talked to had been able to give me a straight answer.

A man carrying a briefcase made his way through the car. He put down the briefcase and stared out the window, arms folded, rocking with the swaying movement of the train. He wore a white shirt, open at the collar, and a dark Western-style suit. He was slim-hipped and haggard of face: in all, so much China's everyman that I felt I had seen him at every stage of my journey. He was far too young to have known the China Jane and Will had known, but I was beginning to realize his kind had existed then, too. He might have worked among the minions who manned Donald's office.

A Westerner—perhaps an American—came into the car and went up to the Chinese man and spoke to him. The two obviously were traveling together; there was no greeting, no introduction. They conferred for a moment, then the Chinese man picked up his briefcase, and the two men hurried out together.

"I wonder what their working relationship is?" I said. I turned and looked at Jane. "It would have been different in your day, wouldn't it?"

"In my day, that Chinese would have bowed and scraped," Jane said, "and secretly regarded the white man with contempt." She thought about this a moment, then added, "Who knows? Maybe it's still the same."

By this time, dusk was falling. The train rolled through open farmland. We passed a man on a tractor pulling a flatbed wagon loaded with what looked like wood. Small rough buildings and small villages flashed by.

The evening outside looked cold and fresh. The land stretched toward the setting sun and the outlines of mountains in the distance. Inside the lighted train car, we were warm and cozy.

I began to panic, thinking of how my time was running out. I seemed to be nowhere near the end of Jane or Mei's stories.

"When did you meet your husband? You said he worked in a factory?" I asked Mei, which Jane interpreted.

"It was in the late sixties, when she worked in a radio parts factory on the outskirts of Chengdu. They met in the market. It seemed they always went to the same vegetable stand at the same time. At first it was just a coincidence, but later it became more calculated. Her husband loved to cook, you see, and said he had always dreamed of being a chef. While the government had assigned him to work as a steamfitter in a locomotive factory, he seemed to know all there was to know about cooking. He showed Mei how to choose the best vegetables and fruits, and gave her tips on how to prepare them. This impressed Mei very much. She figured that any man that would take such care when cooking a dish had to have a special kind of heart—one that is nurturing and gentle.

They were married a year later in a very simple civil ceremony, the only kind then allowed in China. Mei became pregnant right away, and gave birth to a son—the one who is now an engineer."

"Were times still hard?" I asked.

"In a way, yes. It was still the Cultural Revolution, and the country was still in chaos, but they were poor, and the Red Guards didn't bother them much. Mei couldn't think of any time after she met her husband as being particularly bad. Sure, there were times when they struggled for food and watched injustices happening all around them, but her husband was a good man, she had a son, she had her health, and they were happy."

"When did your husband die?"

"Her husband died fifteen years ago in a horrible accident at the factory. Facing the fact that he would no longer be there was one of the hardest things she had to go through. But by this time she had come to the conclusion that she was only allowed a certain amount of happiness, because it always seemed to be rudely taken away."

As the train picked up speed, Mei leaned forward to adjust something in the bag at her feet. The movement set her ceramic pendant swinging, and, as she had before, she clasped it to her breast to stop it. Both Jane and I watched this, the pendant swinging back and forth like life: one moment good, one moment bad; you go forward, then fall backward; you have hope, you have disappointment; you're healthy, you're ill; until one day it all suddenly stops.

I turned to Jane. "When we first started out, you said Mei's necklace, that piece of pottery, was something special, that it came out of your parents' house. This couldn't by any chance be from the Ming bowl Ambrose Varley talked about?"

"It is," said Jane.

I stared at her. "Not the missing piece? Don't tell me that."

Jane nodded.

"But how in the world did you get it?"

Jane gave me a half smile. "What are you trying to tell me?" I asked.

"That there's a story here," she said.

It struck me that I needed to hear the end of this tale in any case, even if it didn't lead to a film. I turned and asked Mei if I could see the pendant. Mei glanced quickly at Jane, then lifted the chain, drew it up over her head, and handed it to me.

I smoothed my hand over the cold ceramic surface. The blue of the leafy tendril was slightly blurred around the edges, the white background faintly tinged with blue. I held it up to the window to examine it more closely in the setting sun. The glaze seemed to absorb the rays, rather than reflect them. It glowed as if lit from within.

I turned it over. The back was set in silver. I handed the pendant back to Mei, who slipped the chain over her head, looking relieved to have it back on her neck. Without it she probably felt empty, I thought, as if something very important was missing—like her mother, or knowing where she came from. I wondered if the pendant was a reminder of what could have been. As the miles to Beijing clacked away, I had a faint perception, which I'd been feeling all along. Mei liked me, wanted to talk to me, tell me things about herself. Jane often threw puzzled glances at Mei, made comments about not really understanding the Chinese.

Could it be that Jane saw me—a young American woman—as a bridge to communication with her Chinese daughter?

At the same time, I realized something else: I liked Mei, too—an awful lot. I no longer saw her as a strange foreign woman. She was Mei, an individual, someone I knew and respected. I reached out again to her pendant and said, "Do you remember when your mother gave this to you?"

Mei tried but failed to understand my question. Jane answered for her. "I tried to hang it around Mei's neck when she was a baby, but she grabbed it and tried to yank it off. I knew she'd either break it or hurt herself, so I put it away, telling myself I would give it to her later when she was old enough to understand its significance. Somehow, it didn't strike me then that I wouldn't be able to tell her the full story until she was much older."

I said, "Tell me about it."

"After I got hold of this shard, after I realized its significance," Jane said, "I had two options: throw it away, or keep it as a reminder."

I stared at the pendent. "A reminder?"

"A reminder. It meant both death and love."

So she had had it set in silver and given it to her baby daughter.

I looked at her. "So you had it made for Mei?"

"I gave it to Mei," Jane said. "I didn't know it would take over fifty years to get it back."

Chapter 16

Shanghai, January 1937

The doctor told Donald and Jane that Electra would recover, but that it had been touch and go for a while. "She took a deliberate overdose of sleeping pills," he said. "That, mixed with the opium, just about killed her off. Why would she go and do a thing like that?"

Neither Donald nor Jane could provide answers. Donald's face was paper white, the corners of his mouth twitching. "May I see her now?" he asked the doctor.

"Go ahead. The woman is out of danger."

Donald slipped into Electra's hospital room, while Jane glared at the doctor's back for calling Electra "the woman" in such irritated tones. She became even angrier a few seconds later, when she heard him say something about "these spoiled, silly society women."

He doesn't know her, Jane thought, staring down the hall at him and biting her lips. He doesn't know what kind of problems she has.

Donald came to the doorway and beckoned. "Come in and see her, Jane. She can talk now."

Jane followed Donald into the strange white room, which smelled of disinfectant that seemed to be masking more unpleasant odors. Electra lay in the bed, a white cover tucked up under her arms. Her face was pale and drawn. Jane realized that she had seldom seen Electra entirely without makeup. Her eyebrows, which had been plucked into a fashionably thin line, looked almost nonexistent.

Electra saw her and tried to smile. "Darling Jane," she said. Her voice was cracked and weak. Jane went up to the bed and took her hand. It felt cold and flaccid. Jane gave it a gentle squeeze. "Are you all right now?" she asked.

Electra smiled again and moved her head forward, as if to nod. "Silly me," she said in that strange cracked voice. "They had to pump my stomach."

"Ugh!" Jane made a face.

"Silly me won't do that again."

Donald spoke from the other side of the bed. "Damn right, you won't." His face was still white, whiter than Electra's.

Jane looked at Donald, not sure what she should say. His eyes were all for his wife. While Jane watched, he tucked one of her arms under the blanket. "Cold. You mustn't let yourself get cold," he said. He looked up at Jane. "Jane, tuck in the other hand. She mustn't catch cold." Jane hurriedly complied. Electra lay still, letting Jane and Donald tuck her arms under the blanket.

When they finished, she smiled weakly again and said, "My darlings." She closed her eyes, then opened them again and said, "Where is Will?"

Donald said, "He's still downtown. We didn't have a chance to call him."

"I want to see him."

"We'll get him for you," Jane promised.

Electra smiled and closed her eyes. She opened them suddenly, as if a thought had just struck her, and asked, "What about poor Lizzie?"

Jane looked quickly at Donald, who shook his head with a quick jerking motion. Electra saw him do this and tried to raise her head. "Then it's true? Lizzie's gone?"

"The dog'll come back," Donald said, while at the same time, Jane said, "We'll find her." They both stopped talking, and Electra looked from one to the other. She closed her eyes and a tear rolled out from under her lid. "The dogs love me, you see," she whispered.

"We love you too," Jane said. Donald patted Electra's shoulder, his eyebrows drawn together.

"We all love you," Jane said, wishing Donald would say something. "Donald and Will and me."

Electra shook her head from side to side, keeping her eyes closed.

"Not true," she whispered. Shortly after that, she dozed off.

After a long silence, the nurse came in and told them they would have to leave, so Mrs. Bauman could get her rest.

On the way home, Donald spoke little, except to ask Jane if she thought Electra really had taken the pills because of "that damned silly dog."

Jane said she didn't know.

When they reached the house, Jane went straight up to her bedroom. She disliked the thought of going down to dinner and sitting through what was likely to be a silent meal with Donald. It wasn't that she didn't like Donald, she thought, but that she felt uncomfortable around him and certainly didn't understand him. Why, for instance, couldn't he have told Electra he loved her? Jane sighed and sank down on her bed. Maybe Donald didn't love Electra. But then why would he have been so frightened for her sake at the hospital? She tried to recall if Cyrus and Della had been demonstrative with each other, but couldn't remember either of them speaking words of love or caressing the other. Maybe old people lost their love when they got older. How sad, Jane thought, then thought of Donald ducking quickly into Electra's hospital room before anybody else, and thought again, he must care for her.

Depressed, she opened the bedside stand to take out her journal, and communicate some of these thoughts in another of her imaginary letters to Han. She reached for it without looking, her thoughts still on the bewildering habits of the older generation.

A second later, when her hand didn't touch the notebook, she bent down and peered into the drawer. There was the note from Mr. Varley, and a letter from the Li family, as well as some packets of headache medicine Electra had given her the last time Jane had had her period. But she couldn't see the notebook.

Jane got down on her knees and pulled the drawer out into her lap. She felt around in the empty space. The journal definitely was missing. Jane sat up and pushed the drawer off her lap. She was certain she had put her journal in the drawer, because she always kept it there when she wasn't writing in it. Thanks to Della's training, Jane had never been untidy or careless of her few possessions. She wouldn't have left it out in any case — the journal was private.

Her cheeks burned as she remembered how she started each entry as a letter to Han. No one had been meant to see this; she had written in English so the servants who cleaned her room would not start reading it out of curiosity. Surely, no one else in the household would have come to her room and gone through her things. But the journal was missing. Like Lizzie. Like Han.

She shut her eyes tightly, concentrating, trying to reconstruct some of the things she had confided to "Han" in the journal in recent weeks: loneliness, bewilderment at the way things worked in Shanghai, homesickness for Peking, feelings about China, Will, Donald, Electra.

Jane's eyes flew open. She had written of Will's sometimes-rude behavior to the Baumans, and how Electra's efforts to act motherly weren't working with him. He missed Della too much. It was too late for him to have a second mother. Electra mustn't try so hard. She had also written that she, Jane, loved Electra, but was losing respect because of the opium, and the silliness of her talk, and the strangeness of her behavior. Jane ran the back of her hand over her forehead. She thought, if what I wrote made her take the pills—

"Oh, no," she said out loud. She ran to the door of her room, pulled it open and raced down the hall to Electra's room. She pushed open the door, surveyed the room—tidied by the maid in Electra's absence—and then ran over to the dressing table and opened drawer after drawer. She opened the wardrobe and rooted around among the shoes that peeped out from beneath the skirts and dresses that were massed into the wardrobe. Here, too, the maid had tidied up.

The room had been especially untidy the night before, when Electra had taken too much medicine. Jane, who had not noticed much at the time, now remembered upturned medicine bottles and empty packets of powders. She also remembered wadded-up pieces of paper with writing on them, as if Electra had tried to write a letter and then, in frustration, tossed the rejected pages on the floor. What if those pages hadn't been a letter after all? What if they were the pieces of Jane's notebook? In any case, the maid would have picked them up and taken them away. It was as if anything left on the floor was to be thrown away—even Cyrus and Della.

Electra's maid. Jane sat down on the floor and remembered the young

amah who had run out of the kitchen and returned clutching Pearl
the dog the night before, when Jane had yelled at them all about the
missing Lizzie. This was the girl Electra used as a private maid. She
straightened Electra's things, picked dresses up off the floor, mended
hems, and created order among the jumble of boxes and bottles on
Electra's dressing table.

Jane shut the wardrobe doors and hurried out of the room and down
the stairs. She ran through the dining room and pushed open the swinging door to the kitchen, a vast, high-ceilinged room with a huge cooking
range and a number of smaller rooms and pantries.

The warm scent of scorched laundry assailed her nostrils. Jane
knew it meant that someone was ironing. She stuck her head into the
laundry room and saw that two maids—Electra's amah and a young
girl who helped in the kitchen—were talking there, heads together,
voices low.

Seeing them, Jane felt the same wave of irritation that had hit her the
night before, when none of them had seemed to comprehend or even
care how serious it was that Lizzie was missing. Jane remembered suddenly her parents' home in Peking and the cheerful turmoil of the house
where Li Wutang and Li Ailian had raised their family. There, in those
two houses—the McPhersons' and the Li family's—the servants had
been part of the family, as was the Chinese custom. They had laughed
and cried and scolded and been at home. Della had known better than
to try to exclude Amah from any important proceedings, such as the
day Ailian had come over to complain about her new daughter-in-law.
Jane remembered not only Amah being present—and freely airing
her opinion—but also the Number One Boy, the cook, and even the
gatekeeper.

Tears stung Jane's eyes and she blinked. The two maidservants stared
at her. Why were things so different in Shanghai, Jane wondered? Or was
it just the Bauman household? Here, the servants kept their distance;
there was distrust between servant and master, between Chinese and
foreigner. Here, she didn't feel at all close to the servants, either. This
was not the way she had grown up. This was an alien household.

Electra's amah spoke up. "Yes, missy? What thing can do? You likee
me iron dress?"

Jane realized suddenly that the amah might think she was being accused of stealing the notebook. She tried to frame her words carefully. "There was a little book, a notebook." Jane sketched the shape of the notebook in the air.

"Little book. You wantchee book?" the amah asked.

Jane shook her head, feeling tears again, this time of frustration. "No, no. I think Mrs. Bauman was reading the book when she got sick last night." Jane enunciated her words carefully, but she refused to speak the Pidgin English used by Chinese and foreigners alike in Shanghai. It made everybody sound half-witted, she thought. "The book had English writing in it. My writing. Mine. Not Mrs. Bauman's." Even as she said this, she realized the futility of trying to make the girl, who didn't read English, distinguish between her handwriting and Electra's. Again, she felt the wave of temper and knew she was being unfair. "The book was in Mrs. Bauman's room," Jane said. "Have you seen this book? Did you put it somewhere when you cleaned the room?"

By this time, she had despaired of finding the book, or of the girl's giving her any information, so it was a surprise when the girl said, "Book belong floor. Velly bad. Many piecee. I wantchee burn."

"You burned it?" Jane thought of all the hours she had spent writing in the notebook, pouring out her frustrations, her grief, her bewilderment, in imaginary letters to Han. Then she thought, just as well if it's burned.

But the girl was saying something else. She had not yet burned it. "You come. Look." she said, and led Jane to another room in the warren of pantries off the kitchen. Here, the servants kept the trash collected from the rest of the house each day. Here, they went meticulously through the things the Baumans didn't want, to salvage what they could for friends and families. There were many bitter quarrels over the contents of wastebaskets.

Jane knelt down beside the girl, who was rifling the contents of a large basket of refuse. "Here, let me help you," Jane said. She picked up the basket and upended it on the floor. Together, the two picked through the trash.

It didn't take long to find pieces of the notebook. The empty cardboard covers dangled uselessly in Jane's hand when she held them up.

She felt a surge of anger at Electra. This had been hers and hers only. What right did anyone, even Electra, have, not only to read it but also to destroy it like this?

Jane looked up and met the eyes of the young amah. "This is the book," Jane said. "We must find the pages. They will be torn and wadded up, like this." Jane picked up a wad of paper and unfolded it. It was a list of charges from a dress company.

The girl nodded and began unfolding other pieces of wadded-up paper. She held up one, her eyebrows raised inquiringly. Jane caught it and skimmed the handwriting. "No, this is a note from some woman to Electra. But you're on the right track." Jane nodded encouragingly and smiled. The girl smiled back and rooted again in the pile of trash.

A moment later, she handed Jane another wadded piece of paper. Jane recognized her own handwriting even before she unfolded the page. She nodded at the girl. "This is the paper. Find more." She unfolded the paper and began to read: "…and so I worry about it, as we live such strange, separate lives here. Donald goes to his office, and I don't even know what he does, but he takes Will with him. I don't even understand Will anymore. He's changed so much he's not even the same person. I don't know if Ma and Pa would have approved. Is this what growing up is like? Will's not always kind to Electra, but then he knows and I know she's not Ma. She never could be. She is loving and giving, but I must tell you she is a little mad. I will not put down in writing what I saw, but…" Here the page ended, the writing broke off. Jane looked up and saw that the girl had carefully lined up a row of crumpled paper from her notebook and was looking for more. "Oh, thank you," Jane said.

She grabbed another piece, unfolded and smoothed it, and began to read: "…understand, I know, how much I miss my parents and my home in Peking. This big mansion, all this luxury, could not ever make up for what Will and I lost. This is nothing compared to the warmth and love in our home with Ma and Pa, or to my beloved city. I hate Shanghai. I don't understand this place. I don't understand these people. I don't want to be ungrateful. I truly do love Electra, but she is not our mother. She…" Here, the page broke off again.

Jane wadded the paper in her hand. She thought, oh, she shouldn't have read this. The girl tossed several more pieces into the growing pile by their feet. Jane's anger at Electra began to burn steadily. She thought, it served her right. She deserved to be hurt.

Then she thought of Electra's white face in the hospital bed and felt a pang of love and pity. She's half-mad, Jane thought. She can't help it. Oh, I shouldn't have written those things. It was ungrateful of me. To write those things, here in this very house.

Jane gathered up the torn pages and put them in her lap. The maid watched her. "Are there any more?" Jane asked. The maid shook her head. Just to make sure, Jane rummaged again through the pile of trash. The girl had been right; there were no more of the incriminating, hurtful little pages.

Jane folded her skirt around the pages in her lap and stood up, carefully sheltering the pieces of the torn notebook. The maid remained hunkered down among the piles of trash strewn on the floor. She looked up at Jane, but said nothing.

"Thank you," Jane said. "I will take these now."

Upstairs in her room, Jane shredded the pages into tiny pieces — a task that took her a long time — then carried them to the bathroom and flushed them down the toilet, feeding them into the bowl little by little, listening to the thundering of the water in the pipes over and over again.

Then she went outside and looked again for Lizzie. As she had the night before, she called the dog's name repeatedly. She walked down the drive and out onto the street, walking up and down, searching for signs of Lizzie, but was reluctant to ask any of the Chinese she saw if they had seen a small black-and-white dog. She didn't want to see that indifferent look in their eyes that she had noticed yesterday for the first time.

Electra came home the next day and remained up in her room, crying and refusing to eat. After urging her repeatedly to take some nourishment, the bewildered servants began leaving the trays by the bed and going downstairs to deal with tasks they understood.

It wasn't just the Chinese. Donald, too, was puzzled and angry, unable to understand Electra. He called the doctor, who was unsympathetic. "She'll eat when she's on the verge of starvation," he said.

Jane took to slipping into Electra's room and persuading her to swallow bits of food. Will too came in from time to time. He backed up quickly when Jane motioned that he should spoon-feed Electra, but he came and sat on her bed and gave her bits of gossip about people they all knew. Electra loved his stories. She lay back on the pillow and watched him, her eyes shining. Once, she lifted her hand and touched his. "You bring in the whole lively world out there when you come to see me," she told him in her new, weak voice.

Another time, after Will had left the room, Electra said to Jane, "The servants have given up on me."

Jane said, "They don't understand why you don't eat."

"I could have died."

"You're fine now. Everyone is fine."

"Lizzie has died."

"You don't know that. I'm still looking for her."

Electra pushed herself up a little and obediently opened her mouth to allow Jane to feed her a spoonful of soup. "I suppose poor people like these Chinese just cannot understand such grief for a little dog." When Jane didn't reply, Electra said, "Why should they? They have to worry about feeding their families, their children. Children are more important than dogs."

Surprised, Jane looked at Electra. "I said I'll find Lizzie for you." In reality, she didn't feel very confident about finding the dog. As the days passed, it became more and more unlikely Electra would ever see her pet again.

Electra said, "I truly do mourn for Lizzie. And don't be kind and tell me I'll get her back. I know I won't." She turned away from Jane. "No more soup, please. That's enough to keep me alive for one more day." She gave a short, weak laugh. "What a worthless woman I am." She closed her eyes.

"No, no," Jane said automatically, smoothing the blankets around Electra's shoulders.

Electra opened her eyes again. "You see, I know exactly what you think about all this." Her voice was unexpectedly strong and clear.

About to pick up the tray, Jane stopped, and averted her eyes from the woman on the bed. Was Electra going to confess she had read the journal, she wondered? Oh, please don't say anything, she thought. I don't want to have to apologize for Will's coldness or for my being so ungrateful. "I only know that I love you," Jane told her. "No matter what you believe, you have tried to be a mother to me. You have tried to make me feel at home. I really am grateful to you. You must believe that." In her thoughts, she added, I need to love you. I need people to love.

"Darling Jane." Electra closed her eyes again, and Jane crept out of the room, carrying the tray.

She met Will in the hall. He took the tray from her and laid it down on a table. "The servants'll take care of that," he said. He peered closer at her face. "What's the matter, Baby Doll?" Since they had moved to Shanghai, Will had taken to calling her pet names such as "Baby" or "Baby Doll." He said to her, "You're looking tired and sad."

"Good heavens, Will. Why shouldn't I be tired and sad."

"You need to get out, think about new things. Electra was right about there being a whole lively world out there."

Jane averted her eyes. "I can't just go out there looking for excitement."

"Of course you can't. Nobody's asking you anywhere, are they?"

"It doesn't matter." She turned her back on him and stared at the tray he had set down on the table. "Should we ring for someone to pick this up? I can easily take it out there—"

"Jane, what do you think servants are for?" He put his hands on her shoulders and turned her around again, forcing her to face him. "Listen, I'm going to take you out with me. Want to go this Saturday?"

In spite of herself, Jane felt a slight easing inside her chest. "Where?" she asked.

"Del Monte's? Ciro's? You name it. I'll take you out on the town."

She felt herself smile. Will smiled back. "That's better."

"But those places are wicked," she said.

"Who said so?"

"Lots of people."

"That missionary crowd." He grabbed her shoulder again. "Listen. You should see what it's like at night here." When she didn't answer, he stared down at her again. "What do you have to say to that?"

"Can we go to a really wicked one?"

Will laughed, and Jane cursed herself for her ignorance. "They're all wicked," he said. "But you'll be all right. Don't tell Donald and Electra. Just say you're going out with me and get all dolled up. Wear your glad rags." He stopped and shot her a worried look. "You do have some dressy clothes, don't you?"

"I have a party dress Electra bought me."

"Good. Electra knows how to dress." He glanced at his shiny new wristwatch. "Now, I've got to run. We'll do this on Saturday."

Jane stopped him. "Will?"

He turned, his face excited. She said, "Did you think some more about what Mr. Varley said?"

His face hardened. "You let me worry about that," he said. He whirled around again and headed for the front door.

She yelled after him, "I worry anyway."

At ten o'clock on the following Saturday night, Jane was ready to go out with Will. He had arranged a taxi because Donald had a dinner engagement and needed the Packard. Electra was not yet well enough to go out. Now, Donald was long gone, and Electra had been upstairs all evening. Jane had entered her room once to say she and Will were going to a party and would Electra look over her dress and advise her on her makeup? Electra pulled herself up at once, eyes glittering with interest, and made Jane turn around several times.

"You look lovely, darling. So grown up. Come closer. I want to see."

Jane moved over to the bed. She was wearing a long, slender dress of flowered silk that hugged her knees and flared out around her ankles. When she had gazed at her reflection in her own mirror, she could tell she looked nice. Still, it pleased her to hear Electra say so. She had combed her hair the way Electra had taught her to wear it, pulled back on either side and curling over her shoulders. Then she had applied lipstick and a little powder.

"I thought maybe you could help me put on more make-up," Jane said, but Electra had raised an admonitory finger and said, no, she was perfect the way she was. There was no use gilding the lily, Electra said.

"I used to look like that too," she sighed.

"You're still pretty," Jane said, and went up and kissed her cheek. Electra looked anything but pretty, having removed her make-up and just woken up from a sound sleep. Her eyes were swollen, her curls stood on end. But never mind, Jane thought. She still looked better than the other women her age when she got all dressed up.

"Go get Will," Electra said. "I want to see the two of you standing here together, all dressed up."

So Jane had gone to find her brother and convince him to come to Electra's room. They stood at the foot of the bed, self-conscious, while Electra gazed at them. "Such beautiful children," she said finally.

"Hardly children," Will murmured.

"No, no. You're right, darling. You're almost a grown man now." Her eyes seemed to measure his height.

They put off Electra's eager questions about the party they were supposed to be attending, then rushed out together, waving and blowing kisses, when the Number One Boy came up to tell them the taxi had arrived. "You look wonderful," Will told her on the stairs. Jane smiled. She had to hold up her dress with both hands to keep from tripping. She could smell the expensive perfume Electra had insisted she use. Then they were rushing out into the cold night air, and the Number One Boy was holding open the taxi door. He slammed it shut and Jane felt enclosed in a bubble of perfume, cigarette smoke, and anticipation. Will leaned forward and spoke to the driver: "Lone Lane, please." The taxi jerked forward and they were off.

Nighttime Shanghai was a different world: red and green neon lights, crowds of Chinese and Westerners, voices, music, clinking glasses, a miasma of cigarette smoke. They had gone first for highballs—Jane's first—with some of Will's friends, then on to a series of bars and casinos. In what seemed like an endless whirl of bright lights and taxi rides, Jane, who hardly ever drank, felt giggly and lightheaded. She tried smoking and decided she liked it; one of Will's friends gallantly handed her his case and bought himself some more. Once, she waved to a long line of Chinese on a sidewalk just outside one of the cabarets. "Darlings!" she cried, trying to imitate Electra, but stumbling over the hem of her dress. "What are they doing?" she asked the young man next to her, trying to recapture her dignity.

"I don't know and I don't care," he said. He hadn't seemed to see her stumble. "As long as you're here with me."

"Sounds like a song," Jane said, and giggled again.

At three in the morning, Will insisted they go to the Nightingale Club. Some of his friends had begged off, saying they were tired or wanted to go somewhere else. "Why? What's the matter?" Jane asked, stumbling over her dress again. One of the young men had laughed and grabbed her arm. "Hey, beautiful, come with us."

But Will told them his sister would stay with him. "Anybody else coming along?" he asked. One boy, whose tie had ended up at a funny angle on the side of his neck, and a yawning girl agreed to go with Will and Jane. They all four piled into a taxi and ended up, hushed and disheveled, at the brightly lit entrance to the Nightingale Club. They scrambled out of the taxi and stood on the pavement. Well-dressed people, many of them Chinese, pushed in and out of the door. The small side street was packed with shiny black automobiles, most with drivers who waited inside the cars or congregated in two or three places on the running boards, smoking and chatting.

The boy with the crooked tie bent his neck back to take in the whole building. "Who owns this joint?"

"Du Yuesheng. The triad boss."

The boy raised his eyebrows. "He probably owns half of Shanghai."

Du's name and the word "triad" seemed to clear Jane's head all at once. She stared at the entrance to the club. People still came and went. A huge Chinese man pushed through the door, clapped a hat on his head, and looked around. One of the drivers saw him and jumped up and ran over to a waiting car.

"Come on," said Will. "Let's go inside."

The others hung back a little, but Will prodded them forward. Jane, uneasy, followed. She'd had her night on the town; now, she wanted to go home.

Inside, the club was glittering and noisy. Couples moved on a dance floor ringed by tables. A man stood on a stage, speaking Chinese into a microphone. Some of the well-dressed Chinese near the entrance turned and stared at the four young people.

Jane touched Will's arm. "Why don't we go home?" she said.

He shook his head and scanned the room, as if he were looking for someone. Jane and the other two stood just behind him. Jane heard the other boy say, "Should we get a table?"

After a confused few minutes — Will signaling, someone pulling out chairs, inviting them to sit down — they were at a table at the back of the room. A moment later, a waiter passed with drinks on a tray. Will raised his hand, and the waiter bowed his head. Soon, Jane found herself with an unwanted drink in front of her. She pushed it aside. Her head ached and she longed for a glass of cold, clear water.

Will had disappeared. He had got up suddenly, saying he would be right back. Then the other two got up to dance and Jane was left alone. She opened the cigarette case Will's friend had left with her. It was empty. She didn't really want another one — it would have worsened her headache — but it would have made her feel better, more grown-up, to lean on one elbow, a cigarette poised between her fingers.

There were tables of Chinese men on either side of her. From time to time, they all laughed uproariously, as if someone had told a joke. A waiter leaned deferentially over one. The men laughed again, a tide of sound that rose and fell.

The music changed, its tempo increased. A single instrument sounded a fanfare, then galloped into a running beat. A line of Chinese girls, arms around each other's shoulders, snaked from behind a curtain, kicking in unison. They were all bright smiles, lacquered hair, bare kicking legs. The couples on the dance floor, confused by the change of music, began to applaud. Some returned to their tables.

A voice spoke in Jane's ear. "Is this wicked enough?"

Jane turned. "Will! Where were you?"

A beautiful Chinese girl stood just behind him. She wore a long white gown. Her black hair was cut short and curled, and her red lipstick reminded Jane of Miss Ding. The girl pouted up at Will, after barely glancing at Jane. Even when Will said Jane was his sister, the girl barely smiled. Jane forced a tight smile in return.

The girl excused herself, and Will sank down into the chair next to Jane's. "Is she your girlfriend?" Jane asked.

Will leaned close and whispered, "No, she's Baby's girlfriend. I told you about Baby, remember?"

"The triad man?"

Will nodded, then poked among the glasses littering the table top, obviously looking for his own drink. Jane said, "Oh, Will, be careful." He smiled, his eyes raking the room. Jane persisted. "You don't tell me much about your life anymore."

"You're always with Electra. You probably tell her everything."

"I do not. You don't know how much I keep to myself." Jane thought of the destroyed journal. She had stopped keeping any record of her thoughts.

Will stared at the stage for a while and tapped his foot to the music. Finally, he said, "I've got a lot to think about."

"You mean about what you're going to do next year?"

"That and other things." His studied insouciant air was beginning to infuriate her.

"Are you applying to colleges in the United States?"

He gazed over her head, feet still tapping to the music. "I don't know. No. I want to wait awhile."

"That's not what Ma and Pa would have wanted."

"I know that. You don't have to tell me." His face took on a sudden bleak look. Jane reached out and touched his arm. "I'm sorry. I don't want to interfere."

He gave her a brief smile and looked down at his hands.

"Will? Don't you wonder sometimes at how funny life is? How we ended up like this?" She looked at the scene around her and raised her voice to be heard over the noise. "When we lived the way we did with Ma and Pa?"

He shrugged. "Nothing stays the same. You have to live for the present."

"You don't miss Ma and Pa?"

He whipped around to look at her. "You keep accusing me! I miss them every day of my life, especially Ma." He gazed at the stage again, where the line of chorus girls was still singing and kicking. "Look at those dolls," he said.

"You don't fool me," she said. "You haven't changed all that much.

You're still the same inside."

"That's what you want me to be." He turned one elegant shoulder and again gazed fixedly at the stage.

She spoke to the back of his head. "We shouldn't be coming here, should we? Should you even be talking to that woman? These people are dangerous. Even I know that."

He glanced at her, but said nothing and turned his attention back to the stage. Jane rubbed her forehead. The noise seemed to intensify. The chorus girls danced across the stage and disappeared behind the curtain. People applauded. The men at the next table laughed louder. Now, even the smell of cigarette smoke was making her queasy. She gazed at the profile of her handsome brother and suddenly blurted out her need to be taken home.

"Sorry, Baby Doll," Will finally said about her headache, remorseful for having shown her "Shanghai's underbelly." He bundled her into a taxi and sneaked her into the Baumans' house just as the sound of the birds in the trees intensified, signaling that the sky would soon be light.

Jane sat alone in her room, wide-awake, and watched the dawn breaking over the treetops. She thought about Will and Varley and the Nightingale Club. She got out pictures of her parents and studied them closely. She was exhausted. Her head ached and her emotions felt out of control. Tears coursed down her face; she reached up over and over, impatiently smearing them away, unwilling to let them blur her vision.

She held up two of the pictures—one each of Cyrus and Della—and was surprised by the anger that swept over her. How could you leave us? she thought. What did you do to get yourselves killed like that? You're not watching over us the way you should be. She stared at the pictures. Cyrus sat at his desk in the study in Peking, looking up as if surprised by his visitor, his half-smile showing he welcomed the photographer.

Della's picture was less formal—a dog-eared snapshot that Electra had given Jane soon after Jane's arrival in Shanghai. In the photo, Della was a slender young woman who grinned and shielded her eyes from the glaring sunlight. In the background, uniformed band members held aloft the Stars and Stripes. Jane turned the photo over, as she had so many times, and read: "Della. The Glorious Fourth. San Francisco. July 1919." She stared at Della's face for a while, then tried to make out the features of the people in the band behind her. There was a tall man, but his face was averted. A woman standing beside him was grinning and squinting in the sunshine.

She dozed off and dreamed about her parents. It was as if the people in the photographs had come to life. Lanky, awkward Cyrus sprawled in the worn chair at his desk, scribbling furiously. Della waved at her through the ranks of a marching band. Jane stood on the pavement and tried to see her mother better. Next to Jane, a heavily pregnant woman rubbed her belly as if comforting her unborn child.

The dream shifted and Della wandered through the streets of Peking. A Chinese funeral came by. Again, Della peered at Jane from the ranks of the marchers, then ran to join Jane on the sidewalk. The white-robed mourners wept while the people on the street cheered. Della sadly watched the the catafalque and casket pass. Tears ran down her cheeks, while all around her people cheered. While Jane watched, Della walked into the street, joined the marchers, and disappeared.

Jane woke suddenly from her dreams and lay in the dark feeling sad and frightened. She wished she had taken Pearl to bed with her. The little dog would have been a warm presence and a comfort.

Jane rolled over and buried her face in her pillow. Her headache was worse than ever, and now she felt slightly sick to her stomach. She didn't know whether to blame it on the drinks and the cigarettes or whether she was getting sick.

After a while, she fell asleep again. If she dreamed, she didn't know it.

CHAPTER 17

PRESENT-DAY CHINA

The train rolled steadily along the tracks, an open plain now between us and Beijing. Was it my imagination or had the train picked up speed? I glanced over at Jane. She now sat almost constantly by the window. She seemed to be looking at something. At what, I couldn't tell, for it was dark outside. No one spoke for a long time.

Finally, I broke the silence. "Time is getting short. We'll be in Beijing soon."

"Yes, you're right," Jane said quickly.

I had so many questions. I held up my hand and ticked them off on my fingers. "Who was behind your parents' murders? If you must know, you have the pendant. Also, what about Mei's birth? What were the circumstances? Why were you separated from her?"

Jane glanced at Mei and then watched me as I opened my notebook and smoothed it out on my knee. Jane hesitated, then she said, "Are you going to ask Mei more questions?"

"I can. Sure." I'd like to have had my questions answered, but didn't want to push it.

"Mei enjoys telling you about herself. She likes you," Jane said.

This gave me an unexpected surge of warm feeling. "You learn something new about Mei every time I question her," I said.

Jane leaned back and closed her eyes. "Exactly."

This time, Mei told her story starting with the most recent events and working back. Her friends and neighbors were now prospering, or trying to prosper—there was hope—under the new regime of "economic reform and opening up" to the outside world; she told me this phrase translated directly from the Chinese. Mei personally had no business plans: she was too old, she said, but her son's generation was different; these young people were smart and they were given opportunities no one else had had, Mei said.

"Tell me more about your childhood," I said.

Mei's childhood was fairly dull, despite the turbulent nature of the country she lived in. But she and her foster parents were classified as poor peasants, lived in a commune just outside of Chengdu, and were generally left alone. Commune children, especially girls, had little opportunity to go to school. She remembers mostly working in the fields with her foster father and uncle. Her foster mother had come from the northern part of the province and had been born to "rich peasants." Although she had received a basic education, she kept her background secret from her fellow commune members, as it was politically dangerous. In the evenings her foster mother would secretly teach her to read and write, thinking that her mother would be pleased to have an educated daughter when she found her. That was her childhood, basically a blur, having little order or reason.

Mei stopped talking for a moment. She looked at both Jane and me and hesitated. Jane said something to her in Chinese. Mei looked down and didn't say anything for a while and then continued.

Mei remembers very clearly when she became an adult. Her entry into womanhood was as difficult and uncertain as her entry into her Chinese peasant life. At the age of twenty-two, in the early 1960s, her foster parents decided that she should marry. A young man in their commune had taken notice of her and had told his parents he wanted Mei for his wife.

"This isn't the man who worked at the factory?" I asked. Mei held her hands up as if saying be patient, let me explain.

At that time, twenty-two was still too young to be getting married. Although the Communist Party forbade arranged marriages, they were still widespread, especially in the countryside. Peasants liked to hold on to the old ways of doing things as much as they could. Mei's foster parents thought this marriage would be a blessing; they were worried she would never find a husband, since she looked slightly different and rumors had always surrounded her. Mei was sure her grandmother was the one who couldn't hold her tongue and told people about her background, or at least told what she knew.

Mei took her parents' advice, and she and the young man were married. As was custom, Mei moved into the home of her in-laws, and right away she regretted her decision. As it turned out, Mei's husband was very sick with liver disease, and his family had wanted him married so they could have grandchildren by him before he died. He died a year later, his death hastened by Mao's disastrous economic policies. Mei found herself a widow and a mother.

Jane looked bewildered. "You were married before? The child you speak of is not my grandson?"

Mei shook her head. "Before I met my second husband and had a son, I gave birth to a baby girl." Jane translated this as well.

Jane and I glanced at each other and then looked back at Mei. She continued, ignoring the bewildered expressions that stared at her.

Mei's in-laws were disappointed that their grandchild was not a boy, but they loved the baby nonetheless. Their granddaughter was all they had left of their son. But Mei's daughter was born at a very difficult time: it was just after Mao's Great Leap Forward, which descended upon them as if the sky had fallen.

I had heard about the great famine after Mao Zedong had decreed rapid development of China's agriculture and industry. Everyone had to search through their belongings for bits and pieces of metal, pots and pans, everything that the Party could melt down to feed the backyard furnaces that were supposed to make steel. There was no time to grow food. Food production took a distant second place to a hurry-up steel production plan. Officials throughout the country covered up the disastrous harvest in those years, afraid of Mao's retribution if they told the truth.

There were moments when Mei wondered if they would starve to death. Many times she wouldn't eat so her daughter would have food. The people were starving even more in the countryside than in the cities, because it was government policy to provide food for city residents first. Mei heard of some peasants who had been arrested during this time, because they had tried to hide food from the commune officials. She knew many people who died, including her foster grandmother, and Mei came very close to joining her. The only thing that kept her alive was her desire to be there for her daughter. She was the only thing that mattered.

After that, Mei's in-laws turned on her. Mei still doesn't quite know why. Maybe it was because her daughter, as a baby, had loved her so much that no one else could hold her or even make her smile. This made her in-laws jealous. They told everyone that Mei had been adopted and that her parents had not even wanted her. They said she was cursed, and that was why their son had died and why they had almost starved—never mind that many people were starving at the time. They told her they could not afford to have such bad luck in their home. Mei was sent back to her parent's house without her daughter, no matter how much she pleaded with them. She was not even allowed to see her baby girl. Once, when her daughter was about seven, Mei had followed her home from school. She approached her daughter and told her who she was, but her daughter would have nothing to do with her.

The three of us were silent for a long time. Finally Jane said slowly, "What happened to your daughter?"

"Nothing happened to her," Mei said to Jane in Chinese. "She's still living."

"Where?"

Mei shook her head. "I don't know. I wish I did. The last time I saw her was in 1990. She was about Pippa's age. But even though she was married by that time and had a baby girl of her own, she did not want to speak to me. Believe me, not seeing her has never been my choice." Mei said this without looking at Jane. I glanced at the two women and thought how hard their lives had been. I wanted to say something, but couldn't find the words.

After a long while, Jane turned to me and said, "I don't know if I can talk about Shanghai after all."

"Why not?"

"For many reasons. In any case, some very terrible things happened. I don't know if I want such things put in a film."

"But..." I let the word hang there and tried to control my fear that

I was losing the story after all. I realized that it must have been very hard for Jane to have heard about Mei's little girl. I could only imagine what Jane must be feeling, but this was too good of a story to let go. Finally, I repeated, "You agreed to talk to me."

"I didn't agree to the film."

"You agreed to tell me the whole story and then we'd decide whether to air it. This is just a preliminary: I'd need to get a go-ahead from my boss; we'd have to come back with a camera crew—that sort of thing. All you need to do now is tell me what happened. Let me be the judge."

"No, I should be the judge. You said you wouldn't make a film if I didn't want you to."

"Right. I won't. But you can't just leave me dangling here, nothing to work with, no end to the story."

Jane narrowed her eyes at me. "So it's natural human curiosity now, is it?"

"Yes! I admit it, I'm curious." I said. My head was spinning from all the stories I had heard on this train that were tragic and unfinished. "Why not?" I wanted to know.

Jane raised her voice a notch. "I'm not sure I should. Besides, there is something so terrible I just don't want to talk about it."

"What could be more terrible than finding your parents murdered?"

Jane didn't answer. She tightened her lips and looked out the window again.

Through all this, Mei had watched Jane and me with fascination and dismay. She then said, "It's okay, Mama."

"Oh, all right," Jane said, a scowl on her face. "Mei and I were separated in Shanghai because I left the country and then couldn't get back. But Mei thinks I left her on purpose somehow, and I didn't," she added.

I glanced at the two women, who suddenly looked like mother and daughter. "Can you tell me about this?"

In the long months leading up to Mei's birth, friends had taken responsibility for Electra, convincing her to leave China, while Jane stayed on. Jane didn't say or do much during those days: she was too busy staring at her growing belly and waiting for each day to end.

This was after the Japanese invaded Shanghai. The city was falling apart around them. Chinese were tortured and shot for failing to bow deeply enough to the Japanese sentries at the Garden Bridge. Journalists were threatened. Newspapers were closed. People went out of business. Both the Japanese and Chinese nationalists were bleeding Shanghai's economy dry—the Japanese siphoned off resources for their own uses; Chiang Kai-shek ordered the dismantling of vital factories, their components to be slipped secretly onto boats at night and shipped downriver to end up in Free China.

At last the baby was born. By this time, Jane had hired the new amah, who assisted at the birth. When Amah asked Jane if she were afraid, she shook her head. She had been through so much, she didn't see how childbirth could be any worse.

She had been right. Labor had been short—perhaps hastened by random gunfire in the streets below—and when the amah had caught the child in her work-roughened hands and announced it was a girl, Jane took one look at the baby and fell in love. At first, she didn't know it was love; she recognized only a strong desire to clasp the child to her breast and bare her teeth at the others.

It wasn't until a few weeks later that Jane, rocking the baby and singing an English nursery rhyme, had thought of a name for the infant. "Meihua," she said. "Little Plum Blossom. As filled with fortitude and survivability as the Chinese themselves."

Jane had had the pendant made and was saving it for her baby daughter. By this time, it was the late thirties, and Shanghai was dying: the Japanese had mortally injured it and were now squeezing the life out of what remained.

Still, life went on "to some extent," Jane said. She began to speak faster, as if to get the story over with. She found a job as a receptionist in the Shanghai-British bank building. She was unimportant, the job paid poorly, and most people ignored her. She went to work, and then raced home, so she could snatch Meihua away from the baby amah she had hired especially for her daughter, and cherish her baby herself.

"The amah was a good soul, who understood," Jane said. "We raised Mei between the two of us." She stopped suddenly and thought about this. "No, I mean the three of us."

The three of you, I thought? But kept my mouth shut, vowing to let Jane tell it in her own way.

Jane went on to say that, although she might have been unimportant, her boss asked her one day to deliver some documents to someone in Hong Kong. The coming war made these documents especially important, he said. He knew he could trust Jane and would see that she got down there and back as quickly as possible—no expenses spared.

So Jane experienced the first plane ride of her life. She left the baby and some money in Shanghai, along with the silver pendant, for safekeeping. The amah knew the story of the pendant; Jane had confided in her. Jane knew by now that the amah could be trusted with her baby's life. Jane remembered holding Mei in her arms before she left, promising that Mama would be back. "Don't worry, my little Plum Blossom," she had said. "There is nowhere you can go that I can't find you."

She made the arrangements to fly to Hong Kong. Her adventurous spirit enjoyed the unfamiliar sensation of slowly lifting off the ground, rocking in the wind, seeing the objects below get smaller and smaller. Jane didn't even think about the danger—she was too excited.

Someone on the plane told her she was lucky. There would not be many more planes to Hong Kong; in fact, there would be very few planes leaving Shanghai at all.

"Is the end coming so fast?" Jane asked.

"Faster than you think," the other passenger told her. He was carrying as much luggage as the airline allowed, and did not intend to return.

By now, Jane had begun to worry. She regretted agreeing to come to Hong Kong, but she had no choice but to deplane in Hong Kong and deliver the documents to their destination. She hardly saw Victoria Peak rising dramatically out of the mist, or the beautiful harbor. All she could think about was finding a way back to Shanghai.

Hong Kong was a worried city and Jane quickly picked up on the tension, the fear. She stood in a long queue at the ticket office, and was told there were no flights back into Shanghai at this time, no matter that she had a return ticket. Check back tomorrow, they said. She walked the streets, cursing her boss who had sent her there, wondering if she could travel overland along the coast.

The boat companies also refused to make a run into coastal China.

She knew some boats were slipping in and out of China, but couldn't find out whom to contact about this. She knew no one and had no money to pay bribes.

Out on the street, she saw a news placard. The headlines screamed that Japanese forces were building up in the Pacific. The placards were dated December 7, 1941.

The next day, she heard the news about Pearl Harbor.

Jane's voice ran out and she began to cough. She then took a sip of cold tea.

"So what happened?" I asked.

She looked up from the teacup. "I couldn't get back," she said.

"And..."

She buried her face in the cup again. Finally, she said, "I was lucky to get out of Hong Kong in time. They put me on a boat for refugees. By then I was almost crazy with my need to get back into China. Some kind missionaries took charge of me then. They knew I'd left my baby in Shanghai, and they tried everything they could to get me back there. But I was an enemy alien by that time. We all were. They finally convinced me I would do no one any good if I were interned, either in Shanghai or Hong Kong. They asked if I trusted my amah, and I said I trusted her with my life. Well, Mei was my life, wasn't she? They said they firmly believed my good amah would take good care of my baby. So, I went to the United States, a true refugee."

There was a long silence. Mei was looking away, unable to look into Jane's face. The three of us sat for a while with our own thoughts.

Finally, I spoke. "And the loose ends of the story?" I asked. "Are you going to tell me those too?"

"I'll tell you what happened in Shanghai, leading up to the war. There were some awful tragedies, both in our home and in the city. The tragedies just wouldn't stop."

Chapter 18
Shanghai, June 1937

As Will's graduating class snaked across the grounds of the Shanghai American School, Jane shot glances at Donald and Electra on either side of her. Both stared straight ahead, watching the line of students move forward, the girls in white, full-skirted dresses, the boys in dark suits.

The Baumans stared only at Will, who was a full head taller than the boy at his side. He had slicked down his hair, as the other boys had done; yet now, it had dried and was breaking free—rich-colored and full—lifting in the warm breeze that played across the grounds. His face, his expression, didn't look like a young graduate's. He stared down, brows drawn together.

Jane kept her eye on her brother as the line moved forward. The breeze picked up. Band members grabbed at sheets of music that flapped suddenly in the breeze. As the wind shifted, the music sounded louder, then farther away. Some of the girls clamped their hands over their hairdos and squealed when the wind hit their faces.

Outside the school grounds, personal bodyguards scanned the faces of late arrivals. Jane knew that scores of ordinary Chinese had gathered outside, attracted as always by curiosity. They had stared with frank interest as a succession of foreigners swept forward in imported automobiles. Each paused at the gate to discharge passengers before the drivers took the cars past the gate to a temporary car park set up for the special day. Drivers, waiting there, could exchange gossip and cigarettes with other drivers and casual onlookers. The drivers were interspersed with the private bodyguards and a clutch of policemen.

After the diplomas had been awarded and the graduates and their guests began to mingle—parents hugging offspring, people snapping pictures—Jane, at Electra's urging, went to find Will, who seemed to have disappeared into the crowd. "He's very popular," Jane said, "I'm sure lots of people are crowding around, trying to congratulate him."

"Of course," said Electra. "But we should find him, darling." She balanced herself in the grass on her high heels and put her hand on her hat to keep it from flapping in the wind. She darted glances at some of the other women—proud mothers who posed for pictures with their children. Donald said nothing. He had maintained an uncharacteristically stony silence all morning and now stood almost immobile, his face half shadowed by his hat brim. A steady stream of friends and business acquaintances had approached the Baumans ever since they had arrived at the school. Donald had spoken politely to each in turn, but had not grabbed their arms or patted their shoulders as he usually did, nor did he take up a few offers to "come over here for a bit and let's talk."

Jane knew that Electra was uneasy because of Donald's silence. All morning, she had stolen glances at her husband, and chatted nervously about the servants and about what she knew of the families of the other graduating seniors. Many of them were returning to the United States, either going to college or leaving Shanghai altogether because of the unsettled political conditions.

"We're not going anywhere," was one of Donald's few voluntary comments that morning.

In her nervousness, Electra uncharacteristically scolded Pearl for jumping up on Electra's dress. "Pearl, get down. Naughty, naughty," Electra said quite sharply, swiping at her skirt with a carefully manicured hand, while Jane surreptitiously patted the lonely little dog who still roamed the house whining and looking for Lizzie, her lost sister and litter mate.

On the school grounds, Electra had not clung to Donald's arm as she usually did. She stood somewhat at a distance and studied him dispassionately. Jane thought, she notices how he's acting. I wonder what she thinks is the matter? Jane also wondered if Electra had smoked any opium that morning. The more Electra retired to her room, the harder it was for Jane to tell.

Jane wondered if Donald was angry with Will for some reason. He had been very short with her brother at breakfast, hiding behind his paper and barely bothering to answer when Will asked questions. If so, Jane wondered, would this affect Donald's offer of a job in Shanghai, which, earlier, Will had decided to take in lieu of trying for a scholarship to Harvard? Jane had not approved of Will's decision to postpone college, and knew her parents would not have approved either, but Will was adamant about remaining in China.

Jane shivered suddenly, causing Electra to put a hand on her arm and say, "Jane, darling, are you all right?" Jane nodded, and Electra said, "Mustn't get sick. Who would take care of me?" She laughed to show this was a joke, and Jane tried to laugh in return. She didn't like it when Electra said things like that. A part of her, deep inside, feared it might be true. As in the hospital after Electra had taken the overdose, there was the fleeting, scary thought: Whom else have I to love? While she waited for the graduation ceremony to end, she ticked off on her fingers the people she loved: Will, Han, Electra, Mr. Varley, Donald—though sometimes Jane was unsure about her feelings for the taciturn business-man. And, of course, there were Amah, and Li Wutong, and Li Ailian, maybe even Mr. Chen, the eunuch, all back in Peking. She supposed that was quite a few people, after all. She wondered if some of the classmates she saw around her would have longer lists.

There were two interesting things about her list, she thought: one, Ma and Pa weren't on it, couldn't be on it, because they were dead; and two, everybody she loved was in China. She was an American and had no ties to the United States.

Out of all those people I love, she thought, I see only Will, Electra, and Donald anymore. Even Mr. Varley has practically disappeared.

And whom do I hate? Jane wondered. Was there anybody? It wasn't Christian to hate people. She thought about people she disliked—Mrs. Appleton of course, several girls at school—and knew that emotion wasn't hatred. No, she thought, I don't even hate Little Gao; I don't know why, I just don't.

Jane's thoughts were interrupted as the people around her broke into applause—a soft, muted clapping; most of the women wore gloves. Shortly after that, the ceremony had ended and Electra had urged Jane to run and find Will. Electra had wanted to hold a small reception at home in honor of Will, but he had flatly refused. Hurt, she had insisted he come back to the house for a family luncheon, and he had agreed to that.

The luncheon, served in the Baumans' huge, polished dining room, had been too silent for a congratulatory affair. No one said much as the servants padded back and forth in their cloth shoes, serving dishes and removing empty plates from the table. The clinking of silverware on plates sounded louder than ever in the silent, cavernous room. Jane, Will, Electra, and Donald each sat on one side of the table, with large, polished spaces in between.

Electra, obviously in one of her feverish moods, tried to make small talk. "You looked so handsome out there today, Will."

Will nodded and threw Electra a slight smile. Jane wished she were sitting closer, so she could kick him. He glanced at her, saw her frown, and thanked Electra. Jane noticed that he studiously avoided looking at Donald, who was sitting at his end of the table, eating little and toying with his wineglass.

"You know you have a brilliant future ahead of you," Electra said.

Will put down his knife and fork, stared at his plate, and didn't say anything. Donald speared a piece of food with his fork and thrust it into his mouth. He chewed vigorously and studied Will, his face brick red, his expression unreadable. He swallowed, drained his wineglass, and then slammed it back down on the table. The sound rang out like a shot.

Jane jumped. Electra cried out, "Donald, what is the matter? You'll break the glass."

Donald stared at Will and didn't reply. Will tried to outstare Donald, but was forced to lower his eyes to his plate.

The servants brought in the dessert, a cake especially baked and decorated in honor of Will's graduation. Electra watched Will as the Number One Boy placed the cake down in front of him. A wash of red flushed Will's cheekbones. He wiped his hands over his face, then looked up at Electra and said, "Thank you. That's a beautiful cake." He immediately dropped his eyes to his plate again.

The Number One Boy, smiling and bowing, handed Will a knife. "Go on, Will," said Jane, "you're supposed to cut it." Even to her own ears, her voice sounded artificial. The atmosphere was so strained, she was almost afraid to move.

Will took the knife, clenched it in his fist, and drove it into the heart of the cake. Donald looked up, and Jane and Electra cried out together. "Will, such violence," said Electra. She laughed—such an artificial sound that Donald shot her a look of disgust, and Jane winced and looked away.

They all watched as Will carved four pieces out of the cake. After that first violent thrust, he now wielded the knife fastidiously, trying not to get icing on his fingers. When he finished, he handed the cake to the Number One Boy, who took it to the sideboard and put the slices on four dessert plates. He opened a drawer and got out four silver dessert forks. The rattling of the china and silver echoed in the otherwise silent room.

The Number One Boy came back to the table and set a piece of cake in front of each of them. Another servant brought a tray of glasses, and a third poured champagne.

Electra touched her glass. "Well," she said, forcing another smile. "This is an event. Donald, you must propose a toast."

Without looking at any of them, Donald pushed back his chair, stood up, and lifted his glass. "To Will and to his future. May he make the wisest choices." They all sipped from their glasses. "Hear, hear," Electra murmured.

Without prompting, Will pushed back his chair and also stood up. "To the Baumans. Thank you for my education and for providing us with a home." He took a sip from his glass, and the others raised their glasses and also took a sip. Jane looked at Electra through her eyelashes. Electra's face was white with strain.

Will remained standing. He raised his glass again. "To my parents. They should have been here today."

Electra looked down suddenly, tears in her eyes. Donald raised his glass again. "Here, here," he said. "To Cyrus, your father, my lifelong friend." Donald tipped up his glass and drained it. He set the glass down on the table, suddenly looking haggard. Electra didn't even try to raise her glass.

Will held up his glass again. A shaft of sunlight from the window behind him struck the cut glass bowl of the glass and dazzled their eyes. Will blinked and said, "To my mother, Della McPherson. I will never, ever forget you." His voice was overly loud, forceful, without a trace of tenderness.

There was a long silence. No one touched the cake. Finally, Electra picked up her fork and tried to smile. She held the fork suspended over her plate and Jane saw that her hand trembled. Electra said, "Will, you're a grown man now. In a little over a month, you'll be eighteen."

Will nodded. "Yes, Ma'am."

Electra dropped her fork. "Why do you keep calling me 'Ma'am?'" she cried out. She clutched the table. While the others watched, she loosened her grip on the edge of the table and looked around at them all. She drew up the corners of her mouth in a vain attempt at a smile. "Silly me," she said, her voice shaking. "Pretend I didn't say that." She focused her eyes on Will. "We must have a birthday party for you."

Donald put down his fork and swiped his napkin across his mouth. "If he makes it to his eighteenth birthday," he said harshly.

Electra gasped and Will said quickly, "Is that a threat, sir?"

Donald turned red. He pushed back his chair, but didn't rise.

Will also pushed back his chair, looking feverish and excited. "I'd like to know what you're talking about. What do you mean, if I make it to my birthday?"

Donald slumped in his chair, shaking his head. "You poor dumb kid. You want me to talk about this in front of my wife and your sister? You really want me to bring this up now? I was going to wait till we left the table."

Will's eyes fluttered. "I don't understand. Bring what up?"

Donald signaled the Number One Boy, who hurried over to his side. Donald whispered to the Number One Boy, who smiled and nodded, then sidled out of the room, grinning broadly and pushing the other servants in front of him as if he were a mother hen. Still smiling and bowing, he pulled the door shut behind him.

"They'll listen at the door," said Donald, "but at least I'll make them work at it."

The other three sat perfectly still, watching him. Donald pulled his chair back to the table, leaned on his elbows, and looked directly at Will. "I called you a poor dumb kid because you don't seem to realize the danger you're in."

There was another silence. Jane pictured the servants gathered on the other side of the door, pushing at each other to get close enough to hear. She knew that, in her home in Peking, her parents would have bowed to the inevitable and allowed the servants to stay in the room. But then, the atmosphere had never been so strained in her parents' home, the problems so insurmountable. As soon as this thought formed, a small voice in her head said, How do you know this?

Donald broke the silence. He looked at Electra and Jane in turn and said, "This young man, supposedly one of the brightest young stars in Shanghai, has been frequenting the Nightingale Club owned by Du Yuesheng—I don't need to tell you who he is—and paying court to the mistress of one of Du's right-hand men."

Jane remembered the beautiful Chinese girl in the white dress, whom Will had brought back to their table at the club.

Electra's face went paper white. "Oh, my God," she said. She put her hand to her mouth. "Donald, can't you stop it? Let's send him to the United States."

Donald snorted. "You don't think the damage has been done?"

Will said, "I've been very careful, sir. And I'm not courting her, as you call it."

"Then what the hell do you think you're doing?" Donald's harsh voice rang out.

Will pushed hard at the table with both hands, and his chair shot back, scraping across the wooden floor. "We're friends!" He rose halfway, then sank down again. He didn't take his eyes off Donald.

Jane thought wildly, they might as well let the servants in. Everybody in the house must be hearing the argument by now. She was horribly afraid for Will, and, at the same time, afraid of what more Donald might say.

Donald raised his eyebrows. He glanced at Electra, then at Jane;

finally he turned his eyes back to Will. "I have to confess I'm absolutely puzzled by your behavior, Will." Donald spoke now in normal tones.

"I don't understand what you're objecting to. You knew I went out to clubs." Will's voice was bitter.

"I didn't know you were consorting with triad members. I especially didn't know you were trying to steal their women."

If they ever found out I was there too ..., Jane thought. She gripped the sides of her chair and forced herself to sit very still.

"I'm not trying to steal anybody's woman."

"That's what it looks like," Donald said. "How do you think I know about this? Du himself told me. He came to me this morning. He said it very gently, which I'm smart enough — unlike some people I know — to take as a serious warning. This girl's boyfriend is extremely upset."

Jane heard Electra's voice and turned to look at her. Electra's eyes were shut and she was murmuring something to herself, as if praying. She opened her eyes. "Oh, help him, Donald," Electra pleaded.

Donald ignored her and kept his eyes on Will. "What are you doing there, going all the time as Du says you are, if you're not after this girl?"

"You should know."

"I? What should I know?"

"You're so close to Du Yuesheng. You've smuggled opium together. You even talk to the Japanese. And the Kuomintang. And the communists."

Donald threw up his hands. "What? Am I on trial here? What right have you to question whom I talk to?"

Will remained silent and Donald said, "There's a situation brewing out there, in case you haven't noticed. Don't you think it expedient of me to keep on good terms with all the parties in Shanghai?"

Will still didn't say anything. Donald shook his head. "But no," he said, not taking his eyes off Will. "You wouldn't think so. You're not mature enough to be realistic."

"Isn't it realistic to wonder what happened to my parents?" Will's voice was so low that at first Jane wasn't sure she had heard the words.

Jane heard Electra draw in a hissing breath. Donald slumped in his chair, his eyes boring into Will's. "Is that what this is all about?" he said.

Will nodded. "Mr. Varley thought it was important enough to come here and tell us what he knew."

Donald snorted. "He didn't say anything that made any sense."

Will flushed. "It makes lots of sense. That girl, the one you've been talking about, her boyfriend's nickname is 'Baby.' Remember, Varley said—"

"I remember perfectly what Varley said."

"Little Gao said it was the baby's fault. Baby, you see? I knew about this man called 'Baby.' The triad has people killed, doesn't it?"

Donald stared at him. "Why on earth—"

Will interrupted. "Because Pa was preaching so much about the communists. He couldn't be shut up. So I figured the Kuomintang, backed by Du and the triad, would have decided to use him. Kill him off and blame it on the communists. That's what really happened, isn't it? They did blame it on the communists."

Donald slumped back in his chair. "So you added up two and two and got five." He spoke slowly, his voice icy. "You really believe your father was so important to Chiang Kai-shek that Chiang would even notice him? You believe that your father, out of all the missionaries in China who are speaking out about the communists, would have been singled out? Is that what you've been thinking?"

Will's face was so white Jane was afraid he was going to faint. His mouth trembled and he clutched the side of the table. "People listened to my father, sir," he whispered.

Donald glanced at Electra, then bored his eyes once more into Will's face. "Electra says you're about to become a man. You need to grow up a little bit first. Look at the world a little more realistically."

Will burst out, "I might have known you'd stick up for Du. You'd cover up anything, wouldn't you? Just to make money."

Donald's head jerked back. "What are you accusing me of? What have you been thinking of me while you've accepted my money and my home? My wife, who has tried to be a mother to you?" Here, Electra made a choked sound and began to cry. For a long moment, there was no sound in the room except her sobs. Donald and Will stared at each other, neither looking away. Jane looked down at her piece of cake. The thought of actually raising her fork and putting a piece in her mouth nauseated her. She didn't dare look at Electra, so she looked up again at Donald and Will.

"My father was so naive," Will whispered. His mouth trembled again.

Jane put a hand on her stomach. She really thought she was going to throw up, but she didn't dare make a movement to leave the room. On the other side of the table, Electra sobbed quietly.

Donald carefully folded his napkin and laid it down by his untouched dessert plate. He spoke quietly: "I'm mainly concerned right now with protecting you, and let me tell you," He punctuated each word with a stab at the air, "you are in grave danger, young man. I take it you've been hanging around that club, trying to find out if someone there paid to have your parents killed."

"I have to find out!" Will's cry was hoarse.

"I've always assumed it was that unfortunate young man who had a grudge against your father. Little Gao, or whatever his name was." Donald waved his hand impatiently. He went on, speaking directly to Will. "You think I didn't look into these murders when I was in Peking, when I came there to attend the funeral and to get you and your sister? I talked to the police. I talked to your parents' servants. It was a terrible time, but it was obvious what had happened."

"So you don't believe Mr. Varley's story? All this about 'Baby' and the smashed bowl?" Will's voice was quiet, almost matter-of-fact.

"I curse the day Varley came and told us this drivel."

"And it's just a coincidence that Du's right-hand man is called 'Baby?'

Donald snorted again, repeated his dismissive wave of the hand. Will was silent a moment, his eyes darting back and forth. Then he pounced again. "Why did you threaten me just now?"

"I didn't threaten you, you stupid kid."

"You told me I wouldn't make it to my eighteenth birthday."

"Good Christ!" Donald looked first at Electra, who was still sobbing quietly, then at Jane, as if searching for someone who understood just how stupid Will could be. His voice rose. "I was talking about your taking up with the mistress of a prominent triad member. Going to the Nightingale Club and consorting with her there, for all to see." He lowered his voice again and ran his hand over his mouth. "I agree with Electra. We need to get you out of the country."

Will stared, open-mouthed. "They won't hurt me. You won't let them."

"Stupid, stupid kid," Donald murmured. He pushed back his chair and stood up. "Let in the servants," he said. "Let them clear away the remains of this disaster."

Will pushed himself up from the table. He glanced at Electra, who had stopped crying, but held her handkerchief in front of her mouth as if waiting to catch more tears. "I'm sorry," Will said to Electra. "I know you tried to make this a nice day for me."

Donald said, "Where are you going right now, Will?"

Will gave a snorting sound and started to walk out of the room. Jane ran after him and grabbed his sleeve. "Will, listen to him." She knew her voice sounded shrill and that this would irritate Will, but she couldn't help herself. She looked at Donald. "Stop him," she told Donald. "He'll go right back there. He doesn't believe you. He'll go back to that woman."

Donald sighed. "Why would you do that, Will?"

Jane said, "Because he believes she has information about what happened to our parents. That's right, isn't it, Will?"

Donald said to Will, "If you go back to the club, you're a dead man. They're waiting for you. I might just be able to stop them from harming you if you promise never to see her again, never to even go there again."

Will made a choking sound; his eyes were wild. "And never, ever find out what happened to my parents?" Jane still had her hand on his sleeve. He shook it off. His face crumpled and he started crying, huge, rasping sobs. He turned and rushed out of the room. They heard his footsteps cross the hall. The front door opened and closed, a banging sound.

They froze for a moment, then Donald shouted, "Boy! Go after Master Will!"

A moment later, the Number One Boy came back inside. "No catchee. Run too fast."

Jane whirled around and called out. "Stop him, Donald." She began to cry. "I can't lose him, Donald. Please stop him."

Electra had wandered into the front hall behind them. Now she sank into a chair and began to sob loudly.

Donald spoke quietly to the Number One Boy. Over Electra's sobs, Jane heard the Number One Boy say, "He say takee rickshaw. Packard no good."

Donald's eyes hardened. "Packard no good indeed!" He turned to the Number One Boy again. "I don't suppose he had time to tell you where he was going?"

The Chinese man shook his head.

"All right," said Donald. "The young fool might be going straight to that gangster club." He turned to Jane. "Do you believe this crap he's spouting?"

Jane shook her head, and Donald let it go at that. She was thankful. Right now, she didn't know what she believed. "Are you going to help him, sir?" she asked.

Donald looked at his wife, who was still sobbing. Electra looked up and wiped her eyes. "If it were the last time I'd ever ask you anything," she told Donald, "I'd ask you this. Go after him, please. He doesn't know what he's doing. He mustn't come to any harm. Not now."

Donald asked the Number One Boy to have the Packard brought around, and to get him his hat. They all waited in the hall, saying little to each other beyond mutual assurances that surely it would be all right. After a few minutes, they heard the Packard outside the door. The Number One Boy handed Donald his hat. Donald shot back his cuff and looked at his wristwatch. "I'll swing by the Nightingale Club and look for Will," he said. "Even if he's not there, I'll go find Du. Have a word with him. We'll get the young fool out of the country if we have to." He gave Electra a hard stare. "Will that satisfy you?"

She nodded slowly then began to cry again.

Jane went over and put her hands on Electra's shoulders. The Number One Boy held the door open for Donald. Jane heard the motor idling, then the heavy door slammed and the car pulled away from the house. She and Electra waited in the hall for a long time.

Of course, they didn't witness what happened outside the Nightingale

Club. They only heard about it later, as the few frightened witnesses tried to piece together the train of events. Even Du Yuesheng himself came to the house to pay condolences and assure them he had never meant for it to happen.

CHAPTER 19

PRESENT-DAY CHINA

"**D**onald was killed?" I stared at Jane with as much horror as if I had known him personally.

"He shouldn't have taken the Packard to the Nightingale Club. The girl's boyfriend was expecting Will, you see," Jane told me. "The man was jealous. Will was tall and handsome, and the girl was in love with him."

"I wish I could see what is out there." Jane interrupted her own story to search for signs of the capital city. "In my day, we would have seen the city walls from a great distance, but Mao tore them down."

I forced her back to the past. "So Donald went to the club—"

"Will had been in the habit of asking the Baumans' driver to take him to the Nightingale Club." Jane said. "He was a seventeen-year-old boy, after all. It was much more impressive to arrive in a big car than in a rickshaw. He had been trying to look like a man of the world when he walked into that place."

"And the killer thought it was Will who arrived in the Packard?"

Jane nodded. "When the Packard pulled up to the door of the club, the girl rushed out to warn him that her boyfriend was looking for him, but the boyfriend was waiting in the shadows. She cried out when she saw Donald, but by then it was too late. The boyfriend, crazed with jealousy, jumped out and sprayed the car with bullets. He killed everyone—Donald, the girl, and the Baumans' driver."

The scene was too vivid in my mind—the girl falling in the hail of bullets, Donald and the driver slumped inside the car. "But what about

Will?" I asked Jane. "Where was Will when this happened?"

"He hadn't even arrived yet. He was traveling by rickshaw, remember? He got there to find such a hullabaloo. You can imagine what he must have seen. Not that he told me much. He was stricken. He blamed himself."

"Donald took the bullets meant for him."

"Not only that. Two other people—innocent people—died in Will's place: the girl and the driver."

"That must have torn him up."

"I walked into Donald's study one day right after that and found Will bent over, as if he were in pain. He cried out for me to shut the door, that he had caused it all, he was to blame for everything, and didn't want anyone to look at him. The rest of the time, when he was with Electra, for instance, he covered up pretty well—pale, but in control of himself."

"And Electra? How did she take all this? Did it send her over the edge?" I pictured a ravaged woman in a straitjacket.

"Like Will, pale, but calm. But I could see her tightening up inside, as if someone were winding her up and her spring was about to break. I was more afraid for her than ever. She got through the funeral, however. She cried, of course, but then so did we all." Jane chuckled softly. "I bet we had representatives of every warring group in China at that funeral."

"Even the communists?"

Jane shrugged. "I suppose so. How would we know? Oh, and Ambrose Varley was there."

"Varley was at the funeral? Wasn't that a little strange?"

"He happened to be in Shanghai again. He was shipping more of his antiques out of the country, to get them out before the war began. He called at the house to offer condolences to Electra. She took him off to talk to him in private. They talked for a long time, and when he left, his face looked haggard."

"And what was the truth? I mean, about your parents? I bet it wasn't the triad."

"The truth is far more complicated than you think," Jane looked exhausted. "One should never relive the past," she said, shaking her head. "One should always look forward. I'm looking forward now to going to Peking."

I stared at her. "But the main questions," I said. "They haven't been answered."

"I told you, it's too terrible to talk about." She leaned back and closed her eyes. "So much emotion," she said, with a ghost of her previous grin, "can't be good for a woman my age."

"Your age, my foot!" I stormed at her. "You and Mei are stronger than any two women I have ever known. Just look at what you two have been through." I looked at Jane, who stared back at me in surprise. "Are you trying to tell me that you can't handle the emotions of your past?"

"Maybe I am!" Jane said.

"But you were completely innocent."

Jane shook her head. "Ha! Not completely. Look at what's happened to my poor Mei. It's hard to admit that you could have made a difference if you had done something differently."

I looked away. I thought about how I was always hiding behind my work, always afraid to take chances when it came to my personal life. I was tired of always wishing I had done something differently. I was tired of being lonely. I forced myself to concentrate on the present and the two women in front of me. "I wish you both knew what you have. Maybe you do. I don't know. Maybe for some reason it was supposed to happen the way it did, no matter how painful it might have been."

Jane's expression changed and she reached over and gave me a pat on the hand. "Perhaps you're right, dear," she said. Despite myself, I couldn't stop the sting of tears, and I had to quickly wipe them away. I then shook myself and grabbed my notebook again.

"We're almost to Beijing," I said, waving to the women to get their attention. "You won't be able to tell me anything there. Jane, you'll be too busy introducing Mei to her father."

"Her father?" Jane struggled to sit up straighter.

"Li Han. Didn't you say you're going to see Li Han? Aren't you taking Mei to see him?"

Jane blinked. "Yes, I'm taking her to see him. I want to show her everything about my Chinese childhood."

Jane turned to Mei. She put up her hand and whispered into Mei's ear like a rude child. They both laughed, Jane out loud and Mei in a gentler way, raising her hand to cover her bad teeth. I chuckled despite myself, glad to see the two women found something mutually amusing, but I was confused about what was so funny. Yet, the more I insisted they tell me the joke, the more they laughed; it seemed they would never stop. They had even attracted the attention of the other passengers. Finally, Jane managed to say, "Li Han isn't Mei's father."

I stared at her. "Then who is?"

This created another laughing fit and I started to get frustrated. Jane, especially, seemed to enjoy the joke as tears rolled down her face. Mei, as if trying to hold it in, put both hands to her mouth and covered her face. I wasn't sure I liked this emotional roller coaster I was on, or being the brunt of the joke.

"That's the part that's so hard to tell," Jane said after she had regained control.

I had to know. "This has to do with the murder, doesn't it?"

Jane bowed her head in assent. The two women suddenly stopped laughing. "I don't know why we think this is so funny," Jane said. "Maybe because it's so tragic, there's nothing left to do but laugh."

"Then just tell me. You've told me so many terrible things already. How can this be worse?"

"It can be worse," Jane whispered. At that, mother and daughter grabbed hold of each other's hands.

CHAPTER 20
SHANGHAI, AUGUST 1937

T he distant thudding made the house shake and the windows rattle. The sound came in waves: a distant booming, a pause, then a booming again. The servants gathered at the windows or stepped out into the garden, shielding their eyes to gaze off in the direction of downtown. They winced every time they heard the thudding, but couldn't stop watching and listening. Jane and Will too had been outside. Now, they sat in Donald's library, heads bent, listening intently to a radio broadcast announcing the Japanese attack on Shanghai.

The Japanese had attacked Peking a little over a month earlier, and now occupied Northern China, including Peking itself. On August 11, the Japanese Third Fleet steamed up the river and positioned itself directly opposite the Bund—and the International Settlement. On August 12, Chinese troops lined up facing the Japanese fleet. By Saturday, August 14—on what would become known as "Bloody Saturday"—tensions were unbearably high.

Bombs rained down on the International Settlement, hitting the areas where the white people reigned supreme. They sheered off the front of the grand Palace Hotel at the corner of Nanking Road and the Bund. They exploded in the great emporiums where the rich white women shopped—Wing On and Sincere. White corpses lay among the Chinese. Nearly all the people who tried to sum it up afterward said this attack had been the beginning of the end of legendary Shanghai.

Will had matured in the two months since his graduation and Donald's sudden, violent death. He watched over his sister and Electra, and accepted a job with one of Donald's business counterparts. He told them he would attend college in the United States "someday," but not for a while. "China is in my blood," he said. "It's all I know. Let me get my start here."

He had lost his schoolboy demeanor, was quieter, more watchful. He refused to confide in Jane, or, as far as she knew, in anyone else. He went to work every day—eerily like Donald—in a car Electra had bought to replace the Packard.

Electra now openly took opium, sometimes asking Jane to fetch her pipe. Jane knew that one of the servants was buying it for her. Electra lay on her bed most of the day, lost in dreams, only coming to life on occasional evenings and sometimes on Sunday, when Will joined them for dinner or took them to the racetrack or to join friends at the Shanghai Club. On these occasions, Electra was a ghost of her former self. She was too thin; she seemed propped up on stick legs, large eyes peering out from her furs. She said little and depended on Will to make decisions for her.

Will told Jane that, because he blamed himself for Donald's death, he had vowed to be more loving to Electra. His intentions were good, but it was as if she had retreated too far away to come back. She watched him constantly, but—probably because of the opium—she seemed in a kind of daze, and seemed content to listen to the conversation around her, rather than joining in as she had done in the past.

The day the Japanese attacked, Electra had made an effort to come down to lunch. It had rained heavily the night before, and the morning was windy and overcast. Will had gone out early, and had come back and told Jane and Electra over lunch that he was uneasy. He had heard the Chinese troops were on full alert, and the Japanese flagship *Idzumo* had moved closer in to shore and rode at anchor within full sight of the crowds of people on the Bund.

"Something's about to happen," Will said. He sat across the long, polished table from Electra and Jane. He had refused to sit in Donald's old place at the head of the table, though Electra had wanted him to.

Electra, propped up in her chair, barely nibbling at her food, stared at him out of hot, burning eyes. "They'll go away again," she said, speaking in the new, slow way she had adopted since hearing of Donald's death.

"You know how it is. They'll kill some of the Chinese in the native city, just to prove a point, then they'll leave us alone."

"This time it's different," Will said.

"It's not different," said Electra, her voice unexpectedly stronger. "Things like that never change."

A few minutes later, they heard the first sounds of the bombing—a distant thunder. Planes flew by overhead.

Will tossed his napkin on the table and pushed back his chair.

"Where are you going?" Electra asked.

"Outside. I want to see what's going on." Will's face was flushed with excitement.

"Don't go," said Electra. She struggled to get up, then sank back down on her chair.

Will gave a short laugh. "Don't worry," he said as he rushed out the door. "You said they can't hurt me."

Barely glancing at Electra, Jane too threw down her napkin, pushed back her chair, and raced outside to join Will, who stood at the foot of the garden and strained to see in the direction of the Bund and the downtown buildings. Another spate of booming sounded from the direction of the harbor. More planes roared by.

"What are they?" Jane shouted over the noise. "What's happening?"

Will whirled around to follow the flight of the planes. "They're Chinese," he yelled. "Go to it!" he shouted at the planes, raising his fist in salute. It was the most animated Jane had seen him since Donald had been killed.

Boom. Boom. Boom. The guns shook the ground. Jane could actually feel it tremble under her feet. Across the treetops, she could hear a wailing sound and didn't know if she was hearing sirens or human voices. Despite the oppressive heat of the day, she shivered suddenly and hugged herself.

Will saw her shiver and said, "Go back inside."

Jane shook her head. "Not till you do."

He put his hand on her shoulder. "Come on, we'll both go." Brother and sister raced back across the lawn. Inside, they found Electra still at the table. Pearl, shivering with fear, had climbed into her lap. Electra clutched the little dog and stared at Will and Jane, but didn't say anything.

Will went up to her and put his hands on the back of her chair. "Come on, Electra. We're going into the library to listen to the radio. We're safe enough in there."

Electra stretched her neck to look up at the tall young man. "No, I'm going upstairs. Jane…" She pushed at Pearl, who clung to her lap. Jane leaned down and took the dog in her arms. "Will Electra be all right upstairs?" she asked Will.

"I don't know." He stared at Electra with a worried frown. "I'm not sure what we should do."

Another booming sound shook the house. "If they don't come any closer than that, we're all right," Electra said. She pushed herself up from the chair. "Where are the servants?" she asked, looking around at the cluttered table.

Jane shook her head. "Maybe they're frightened too."

"I'm not frightened," said Electra. "A bomb would be a blessing." She held out a hand to Jane. "Help me upstairs, please. I don't know why I'm so weak. If you could get someone to fetch me my pipe…"

Jane flashed a look at Will. "Don't say anything," she told him. "Electra'll be fine. Let her have what she wants."

Will shrugged. "She's probably as safe there as anywhere in this house. If a bomb falls directly on us, we're all dead."

Again, Jane saw his face was flushed, his eyes excited. It was as if he welcomed the changes the attack must bring, as if he had been waiting for something to happen.

Still carrying the dog, Jane followed Will into the library, where they switched on the radio and listened to Radio Shanghai broadcasting news of the attack.

Japanese and Chinese forces tangled in Shanghai in the days that followed. Jane and Will learned that they had lost friends and acquaintances in the initial bombing. They also learned that the bombs that exploded at the corner of Nanking Road and the Bund had been accidentally dropped by Chinese pilots flying out toward the harbor to attack the Japanese fleet.

After days of fighting, Jane felt worn out but no longer afraid. Instead, she felt numb. After hearing of the death of a school friend and her mother, who had been in the Wing On department store when a bomb exploded there, Jane wondered why she couldn't feel any emotion. There have been too many deaths, she thought. Then, this is wartime, she realized. Cyrus and Della's deaths seemed long ago.

As the days passed, Electra seemed to withdraw further inside herself. Jane summoned the doctor who said this was what you could expect from someone who was addicted to opium. "She's in a dream world," he said. "Maybe it's better to leave her there."

"What will happen to her?" Jane asked.

"She'll fade away. She reminds me of the wives of some of the rich Chinese in town. They're disappointed ladies, some of them. Maybe they can't bear sons, maybe their husbands have taken concubines; whatever's happened, they escape into a dream world and eventually succumb."

"Isn't there anything we can do?" Jane asked.

The doctor walked over to the window on the upper landing—they had been standing just outside Electra's bedroom door—and looked out at the garden below. "This world here isn't going to exist much longer," he said. "I'm getting my family out of China. Why don't you and your brother take Mrs. Bauman and go back to the States?"

Go back? Jane didn't say the words out loud. Go back to what? I don't belong there. She stared at the doctor. In all their discussions about where to go and what to do now that their parents and their benefactor were dead, Jane and Will had never entertained the thought that Jane should leave China. Will had known he would go eventually to college in America. Jane had always assumed she would find a job, maybe help with the missions, and probably marry—someone like her, who knew China better than anywhere else. The face of this unknown man had always remained cloudy in her mind, but she had supposed he existed somewhere. He would give her children and a reason for staying in China.

The doctor turned from the window. "Don't you think that's what you should do? You won't want to be here when things get worse, believe me. I'll speak to your brother about it."

Jane felt frozen and unable to answer. She wanted to say, don't speak to Will, but knew it made no sense.

"Why are you looking at me with such big eyes?" said the doctor, who seemed to be trying to make a joke of it. He turned back to the window again, dropping the pretense that all was well. "Yes, you should all get out of here. My missus is going." He nodded his head at whatever it was he saw outside.

Will came to Jane later that day and said the doctor had talked to him too. "I've been thinking about this, myself," he told Jane. "Lots of people are leaving. They're saying we should get out. This show's over. Shanghai, China, all that. It's going fast."

"Oh, don't say that."

"Funny, I thought you always faced the truth. I've admired you for that."

"You admired me?" Jane thought of tall, handsome Will, a star at school, the adored of his parents and his foster parents. "I admired you, not the other way round."

Will laughed. "Don't believe me, then. Good lord." He ran his fingers through his hair. "We're talking like it's the end of the world."

"You make it sound like it is. What about the people we knew in Peking? Mr. Varley?"

"He's been shipping his antiques out like mad. He'll probably be going out himself before long."

"And the Li family?" Jane could barely form her lips around their name. She didn't dare ask about Li Han — she was afraid she would cry.

Will stared at her. "Jane, they're Chinese. They can't go anywhere else."

"But the war —"

"We can't do anything about it."

Jane looked at Will a long time, then said, "I bet you're staying here, aren't you?"

He shrugged. "It's different for me. I have work to do here. You need to leave. You need to pick up your life somewhere else."

Afterward, Jane went up to her room and found the cricket cage Ambrose Varley had brought her. She pulled off the lid and pried out the piece of paper inside. She read it once again, though she had memorized the words long ago. She held the paper to her breast and closed her eyes. "There is another little cricket," she whispered Ambrose Varley's words. "He will always be your friend."

I am only seventeen, she thought. There are too many forces against me and I'm not sure I know how to fight back.

She gently slid the paper back into the cricket cage and replaced the lid.

In the midst of the chaos in that August of 1937, Electra insisted on celebrating Will's eighteenth birthday. She telephoned their friends, including some of Will's best friends from school and from the office where he now worked, and asked them to come to dinner. She rallied the servants to prepare the foods Will seemed to love most. "A Shanghai dinner," she announced, clapping her thin hands together. "With dripping sauces and savories." She thought about it for a moment, then added, "and a big, beautiful birthday cake."

Jane wondered if anyone else noticed the effort Electra was making. She seemed to be staying away from the opium. Food sickened her and she ate practically nothing. She grew even thinner, complained of terrible headaches, and was restless and irritable, yet, she pushed herself to complete the preparations for the party.

Jane had the new driver take her downtown to Sincere's department store, now open again for business, though some of the windows were still boarded up. There, she bought a small silver picture frame. She took it home, dragged out her box of photographs, and inserted the formal picture taken of her family in 1932, in Peking. Then she wrapped it carefully in some wrapping paper Electra had given her, and slid it into her bedside drawer.

On the morning of Will's birthday, while the servants pushed the furniture around and cooked the food for the party, Jane found Will alone in the library and presented him with the framed picture.

Will unwrapped it slowly, dropping the wrappings on the floor, then held it and looked at it for a long time without speaking. Finally, he looked up with tears in his eyes. "Thank you," he said. "I didn't have a copy of this." He ran his finger lightly over the photograph, as if stroking his parents' faces.

"You think they would have left China now?" Jane couldn't help asking.

"I don't know," Will said. "I only know we have to make the best decisions we can. They aren't here to guide us anymore."

That afternoon, Jane found Electra in a tizzy, throwing clothes around her room, trying them on and rejecting them. She had tried to make up her face, put on too much makeup, and now stared at Jane through a kind of clown's mask of smeared mascara and powder.

Jane couldn't bear it. "I'll help you," she said. "Don't worry about how you're going to look. Just calm down. Try to rest."

"I can't calm down." Electra paced the floor.

"I'll help you dress," said Jane. She ran her hand through the soft silk and crisp linen of the dresses lined up in Electra's wardrobe. She pulled out a green silk dress and held it up. "Wear this," she said. "You'll look beautiful."

"What are you wearing?" Electra asked.

Jane smiled. "I've decided to wear a Chinese dress today. A *cheong-sam* with a high collar—"

"And a long slit up the legs!" For a moment, Electra almost was her old self. "You'll look lovely, darling."

"I hope so. Right now, let's get you ready."

Electra hurried over to her dressing table. "Look, look. I have a birthday present for Will." She swept her hand across the assortment of bottles and boxes on the table. "Where is it?" She dropped to her knees and began searching the floor.

Jane dropped down beside her. "I'll find it." She patted her hands around on the floor, not knowing what she was looking for. She saw a small box under the dressing table and scooped it up. "Is this it?" she asked, holding it up.

Electra grabbed the box out of Jane's hand and rocked back on her heels. She cradled the box against her and began to rock back and forth. "This is my present. Oh, this is my present."

Jane crawled over and sat down beside her. She tried to take Electra's hand, but Electra snatched it away. "Electra," Jane said gently, "I gave Will my present for him earlier today. It's better to do this before the guests arrive. These are private, family gifts."

Electra clutched the little box tighter still. "Oh, don't worry. I would never, never allow others to see this."

Jane scrambled to her feet and smoothed out her skirt. "Come on, get up now. We're going to make you beautiful for this party." She led Electra to her dressing table, feeling sad because it wasn't that long ago that Electra had energetically taken charge of her and taught her how to dress and wear makeup.

Jane needn't have worried about the party. Electra rallied and, if not her old self—she was much too thin—she looked stylish and managed to greet the guests with some of her old verve. There was no need for concern about keeping the conversation going; the current situation provided the grist for that. The servants prepared and served the food as well as they ever had in the days when Donald held dinner parties in the vast dining room, and Electra had entertained what she called "tout Shanghai" in the large rooms that still seemed to echo with the beat of past jazz bands and the clinking of glasses.

Late in the evening, after the guests left, Electra called for her opium pipe and asked Will to come to her room after she had prepared for bed. She asked that Jane come too. Jane and Will waited in the library until the little amah summoned them, then climbed the stairs together, not saying a word to each other.

Electra's room was dim, lit only by a single lamp, and full of the sickly sweet smell of opium. She lay back on her pillows, resplendent in her lace-trimmed gown, her face scrubbed clean of makeup and her hair smoothed down. Her eyelids looked heavy and she smiled faintly. Jane, still in her Chinese dress, took Electra's hand, which lay limply on top of the covers, and squeezed it. "It was a beautiful party, darling," she told Electra. "You did such a wonderful job."

Will moved in close to the bed. "Yes," he said. "Thank you for my party."

Electra raised her other hand—the one Jane wasn't holding—and held it out as if waiting for a gentleman of the old school to kiss it. Will awkwardly took her hand and held on to it. A few minutes later, when he tried to reclaim it, she clung to it, her eyes huge and feverish. She stared into his eyes. Embarrassed, he looked down.

There was a long silence, then Jane, believing she should say something to relieve the tension, asked, "Aren't you going to give Will his birthday gift?"

Electra turned her burning eyes to Jane. "Gift?" she whispered.

"The one you showed me this afternoon."

"I didn't show it to you." Electra's voice was so faint that Jane and Will had to lean close to hear. "I only showed you the box."

"Where is the gift?" Jane asked.

Electra turned her head to the bedside table. Jane turned to look and saw a small, gaily-wrapped present. "Do you want me to hand it to him?" she asked Electra.

Electra nodded. Tears rolled out of each eye and ran down her cheeks.

"Oh, don't cry," said Jane. She took a handkerchief from her pocket and dabbed at Electra's cheeks. "Take the present," she told Will. "The one on the table. Open it. She's been wanting to give it to you. Can't you see she doesn't have any strength left after that party?"

Will picked up the gift and clumsily untied the ribbon while Electra and Jane watched. He pulled off the wrapping paper and, as he had with Jane's gift earlier that day, dropped the paper onto the floor. He held up the small box in his hand.

"Open it," Electra whispered.

Will pulled the top off the box.

There was a silence, so long, so deep, that Jane looked up. Will stared into the box. His lips moved, but he made no sound.

"Will? What is it?" Jane asked. She looked at Electra, who lay back with her eyes closed.

Will, white-faced, handed the box to Jane. He looked over at Electra. "Was it you or Donald?" he asked, his voice rough and cracked.

Jane looked into the box and felt a jolt hit her stomach. Inside, nestled in cotton, lay a blue-and-white shard of porcelain. It was a small triangular piece, roughly one inch across at its widest spot. There was just enough room to see the trailing end of a blue tea leaf vine on a white background.

Jane put her hand on her throat; her pulse was pounding. Her vision blurred, then righted itself. As from a distance, she heard Electra say,

"Donald? Never. It's mine. Always mine!" She tried to sit up, then dropped back on the pillow. "Now it's yours," she said to Will. "It belonged to your father."

Jane heard herself ask, "To Pa? But—"

Electra's thin voice cut across Jane's protest. "Not your father, Jane. Will's father."

Jane swallowed. Will was just behind her and she couldn't see his reaction. Hardly realizing what she was doing, she lifted the shard out of the box and held it in her palm. It felt cold and smooth.

Then Will spoke. "Jane and I have the same father."

"No, you don't." Electra barely spoke above a whisper. "Jane's father was Cyrus McPherson. Your father is Ambrose Varley."

"No!" It took Jane a moment to realize Will had spoken. For a moment, she thought she had said it too.

Will's next words came out in a rush. "You don't know what you're saying."

"But I do, darling. You had to know. It's your eighteenth birthday. You're a man now. Time for the secrets to stop."

Will put his hands over his ears. It was Jane who asked, "How do you know this, Electra?"

Electra lifted her head again and shifted, so she was partially sitting up. Normally, in the past, Jane would have gone to help her, but not now. "Della was with me in San Francisco in 1919," Electra said. "So was Ambrose Varley. He was on his way back to China after one of his periodic trips back to the U.S."

Will shouted, "Not my ma! Not my ma and Ambrose Varley!"

Electra made a half-crying, half-laughing sound. "Oh, darling. Della McPherson was as pure as the driven snow."

Jane's fist closed over the shard. She held it up for Electra to see. "Did this come from the Ming bowl? The one Mr. Varley gave my ma?"

Electra tore her gaze away from Will and looked at Jane. Before she could speak, Will shouted, "She's a liar, Jane. Don't listen to her."

Electra fell back on the pillows. "I'm not lying. It's Della who's lied all these years. She happened to be there in San Francisco that summer—"

Jane interrupted. "That picture you gave me. Ma in San Francisco.

It was the Fourth of July."

Electra nodded. "Yes, darling. It was the Fourth of July.

Jane squeezed her palm shut again. The shard bit into it. Electra said, "Darlings, listen to what I'm saying."

Will said again, this time in a lower tone, "Don't listen to her."

Electra spoke gently. "It was eighteen years ago. Count back from 1937. Your birthday, Will. Do you see it now?"

Jane reached out blindly with her left hand, keeping the shard in her right. Without looking at Will, she grabbed his arm. She didn't think she would be able to take her eyes off Electra. She felt Will's hand fumble for hers. He bore down on it, pressing it against his side.

They couldn't stop Electra from saying the words. She said, "Will, you're my son, not Della's. Della was so slender in that picture taken in July, 1919. You were born scarcely a month later."

Jane made a whimpering sound, and Electra stretched out her hand. "Darling, am I frightening you?"

Jane nodded. Will pressed harder on her hand. Electra said, "Jane, you are your mother's child, but Will is mine. He's always been mine. Della would never have admitted this. She loved you so much, Will. Everyone did."

Jane managed to choke out a few words. "How did this happen?"

At the same time, Will said again, "She's a liar."

Electra said, "No, I'm not lying, Will. I was waiting in San Francisco for Donald to send for me. We were to be married in Shanghai. I was so excited. I didn't know Donald well, but I had accepted him to get away from home." She gave a short laugh. "Young girls are always the same, aren't they, Jane? Can't you understand the way I was then? I really didn't know Donald and then I met this young man, Ambrose." Electra closed her eyes. "He was like no one else. He took me for a ride in the cable car, up, up into the hills till we could look out over the bay. He kissed me and told me about China—his China, not Donald's."

Jane cried out, "But where was my mother?"

Will made a convulsive movement.

Electra opened her eyes. "Della and Cyrus were on furlough in the States. Just as they were leaving to go back to China, Della found out she was expecting a baby. She'd had several miscarriages, you see,

during their early years in China. This time they didn't want to risk
it. Cyrus knew I was in San Francisco, waiting to join Donald, so he
asked if I would let Della stay with me until she and the baby could
travel. He had to get back to China and he didn't want Della traveling
in her condition." Electra lifted her hand, waved it dismissively. "I don't
remember now exactly why Donald couldn't have sent for me sooner.
If only he had. But no, things had to be just right..." She paused.

"What about my mother's baby?" Jane jerked her hand away from Will
and tugged at the collar of her Chinese dress. The high collar pressed
on her windpipe. She felt it would choke her.

"She lost the baby. She rebelled mightily against all the instructions
Cyrus had left with her: don't do this, don't do that. He was too per-
snickety. I think he bored her."

"Don't say that." Will's words seemed to echo in the room. Jane put
up a hand as if to ward off Electra's words.

"I'm sorry, darlings. I forget sometimes how young you are." She
went on. "Della rebelled. She wanted to have a good time. We went
out one morning and stayed out all day. We were with friends. We
ate strange things in Chinatown, rode the cable cars, laughed till our
sides hurt. After we returned to my home, Della began to complain of
a stomachache."

Electra looked away, blinking her eyes rapidly. "Oh, you can imagine
how Della felt. Your father had told her she must stay quiet. She hadn't
done this and she lost the baby. She told me she couldn't face it. Couldn't
face him. 'Lie,' I told her. 'You don't have to tell him the truth.' 'But
I've never yet lied to him,' Della said. Even then, I knew better about
relationships between men and women than she did.

"So I told her my great secret. Now I was going to have a baby. What
was I going to do? Donald would never have me now. If only I could
have gone straight out to Shanghai, married him right away. He would
always have thought Will was his. Will looks like me, the same hair,
the same nose—haven't you seen it?"

Jane shook her head violently, all the while realizing that Will did
look like Electra and dazedly wondering why they hadn't seen it all
these years?

Electra went on. "I was desperate. I had written to Donald, begging to come out right away, but he wouldn't hear of it. Everything had to be just right." Electra rolled her head from side to side again. "If only, if only—"

"My mother took your baby?" Jane asked.

"It solved both our problems, don't you see? There were other ways, doctors who operated secretly if you paid enough and knew who to go to, but I was afraid. Even more, I couldn't have harmed his baby. So Della and I swore on a Bible—it was very solemn—never to reveal the truth. I didn't know then how I would feel."

"I gradually found out I couldn't have any more children. It wasn't Donald's fault. I took lovers here too, but never again did I become pregnant. And there was my beautiful son, growing up in Peking, absolutely devoted to his adopted mother, whom he thought was his own." Electra tried to sit up again. "Aagh, I'm dizzy." She sank back down on the pillow. "Della hated me, you see. She loved you, Will, with all her heart. She was horribly afraid of me. Always. She tried to poison your mind against me, didn't she? She tried to keep you away from me. If it hadn't been for Cyrus..." Electra broke off and then cried out, "She not only had my baby, she had two children. And I had nothing."

Will moved up close to the bed. "I don't believe you." He pressed his lips into a thin line and stared at Electra. "You're crazy."

"Look at the picture," Electra said. "How could she be so slender shortly before your birth? The picture proves she wasn't your mother. It proves the date, the place."

Jane asked, accepting Electra's words, "Does Mr. Varley know?"

Electra nodded, tears running down her cheeks.

Jane drew her clenched fist up again, opened it, and shoved it under Electra's nose. "Why do you have this?" she whispered. "How did you get it?"

Electra stared down at the shard. She raised her eyes to Jane. "He gave her that bowl; it probably meant nothing, but it should have belonged to me. He gave me nothing. She had everything."

Electra's face crumpled and she began to sob. She made no attempt to hide it or to cover her face. "I didn't mean to hurt them, but they were trying to take Will away from me."

Behind her, Jane heard Will make a choked sound. Electra raised her hand and wiped it across her eyes. "Little Gao came with me that night. He followed me everywhere. I told him Della had stolen my baby." She made a half-laughing sound. "Little Gao was my knight in shining armor."

Again, she passed a hand over her eyes. "I told Della I would let everyone know, starting with Cyrus, the mission, everybody, if she didn't let Will go on visiting us as he did before. Was that so much to ask?" She addressed this question to Jane.

Jane opened her mouth to reply, but no sound emerged.

"Della was so stubborn," Electra said, "so self-righteous! One of us struck out at the other. I think it was me." She wiped her hand over her forehead. "I don't really remember. I honestly didn't mean to hurt her." She shot a pleading look at Will. "It's not in me to hurt people, you must know that. But then Cyrus burst in from the other room and saw what I had done, and Little Gao brought out his knife." She put her hand over her eyes, then said, her eyes still covered, "I didn't want to watch! I went over to the Ming bowl at the far end of the room. There it stood. He gave it to her and it should have been mine. It seemed a symbol of all that had gone wrong." She looked up at Will again, pleadingly, "there was no mystery about that smashed bowl. I smashed it. Afterward, I kept one little piece. It was the only thing I ever had of his." Her gaze grew more intense. "I gave it to you on your birthday. Don't you see what that means? Can't you understand?"

"You're insane," he said.

Electra didn't take her eyes off his. "You're my life."

Will turned to Jane, his face ashen, his mouth drawn into a tight line. "Jane, get out of here. You shouldn't hear anymore of this."

Jane's lips were so numb she could hardly speak. "But I must stay with you."

"No. I need to talk to her alone. Wait for me downstairs." When she hesitated, he shouted, "Do this for me!" His voice was full of pain.

Jane hardly remembered leaving the room. She saw the floorboards of the upper hall rush by under her feet. From inside Electra's room, she heard Will say, "Liar, liar." She opened her hand once again. The shard had cut into her palm, streaking it with blood. She transferred the shard to her other hand and wiped the blood on the skirt of the

Chinese dress. She thought, funny, it doesn't hurt.

Behind her, she heard a high-pitched wail. The sound seemed to propel her faster down the stairs. She put her fists over her ears to drown out the continuing sounds from upstairs — Will shouting, Electra sobbing loudly. These contrasted sharply with the clinking of silver and plates coming from the dining room; she realized the servants were cleaning up the remains of the party. She knew she had to get outside the house. She couldn't face the servants. Holding on to her long skirt, she ran across the front hall, pulled open the door, and stepped outside. The door fell shut behind her.

Hot, humid air hit her face. She could hear the sound of insects in the garden and see the lights of the neighbors' house through the trees. She glanced at the Bauman house over her shoulder, then hurried down the steps, her feet crunching on the gravel drive.

Just outside the gate, a rickshaw driver waited, the shafts of his rickshaw resting and pointed at the sky. He was trying to read a news-paper in the dim light from a streetlight. When he saw Jane, he stood up. "Missy wantchee ride?"

"Yes," Jane decided suddenly. "Missy wantchee ride." The man righted the vehicle and Jane climbed inside. She felt the familiar rock-ing motion as she settled herself and the man bent to pick up the shafts. "Where Missy go?" he asked. His voice sounded unnaturally loud on the silent street.

"I don't care." When he persisted, not moving until she gave him directions, she said, "Go toward the town. That way." She pointed in the direction of the Bund and the city lights. "Just go."

The man began to trot.

It must have been an hour or two later that Jane found herself in a night market in the old Chinese city. She felt dazed and sick as she wandered from lighted stall to lighted stall. A smell of roasting meat wafted by, and she felt, for a moment, transported back to the scenes of her childhood.

The people in the market stared at her curiously but didn't bother her, and she realized she must look strange — a white girl in a Chinese dress wandering around by herself. A thought struck her: they'll think I'm a White Russian prostitute. She backed up against a wall as a group of children raced by; one bumped into her. Jolted, she tightened her fist and again felt the sharp edges of the ceramic shard. She looked down, surprised. Why am I trying to hang on to this? she wondered. Still, she didn't let go.

Jane looked around, thinking she should find a rickshaw and go home. She saw a narrow alleyway between a bookshop and a medicine store. Both stores were lit by dangling electric bulbs, and people moved inside. She moved toward the alley, wondering if it was a way out of the market.

The group of children raced by again, and she ducked into the alley to get out of their way. Was that a dim light on the other side of the alley? she wondered. She moved farther down the narrow space between the buildings, but discovered she was afraid to go on.

Jane had just turned to go back to the lighted market area when two dark figures blocked the entrance to the alley. She felt a pang of fear, and struggled to make out their shapes in the dim light. One of them called out to the other, softly in the dark, and Jane realized they were speaking Japanese.

The figures moved toward her. One called out in Chinese, a high-pitched sound, as if he were coaxing an animal. *"Lai, lai, lai,"* he called. Even that one word he couldn't pronounce quite right. She panicked and began to back up. "No, no, no," she heard herself saying. One of the men laughed. Again, they spoke in Japanese. She heard the man again trying to speak in Chinese, just as a hand closed on her arm. Another hand clamped roughly across her mouth. Belatedly, her mind numb, she realized they thought she was Chinese because of her dress. It was too dark in the alley to see her features or the color of her hair.

She felt the rough material of their uniforms against her mouth. She heard the rustle of their clothing and their laughter. She felt them tug at her clothes. Suddenly, she was flat on her back, the wind knocked out of her. After a terror-filled moment or two, while she fought to keep her legs together, she felt bare flesh against her own, and a sudden agonizing pain. She jerked her head from side to side to escape from the rough hand across her mouth. A pain stabbed her hand and she realized she was still clinging to the shard. Suddenly, in her panicked and befuddled mind, it became important not to let go of it.

As the second shadow moved in on her, blocking out what little light there was in the alley, she closed her eyes and wondered if, somehow, she was being punished for sins of which she wasn't even aware.

Chapter 21

Present-day China

There is a park in Beijing, east of the vanished city wall, called the Park of the Temple of the Sun, otherwise know as Ritan Park. The Temple of the Moon is at the opposite end of the city, far to the west. The Temples of Heaven and Earth lie north and south. They remain despite the burgeoning city that grows around them. The whining and the pounding of the construction that seems never to cease—a sound like the heartbeat of the changing city—are muted in these temples. The noises there are those that have existed for centuries: Chinese people talking, laughing, spitting, and arguing; Chinese children shrieking at their games. To those of us raised in the West, the Chinese are not and have never been a quiet people.

Jane tried to make me see more than the vanished splendors. She laughed and called me a romantic. I agreed that she was a consummate realist. Jane pointed out the vigor, the eagerness, the Chinese-ness of today's China. Jane said all this was better than in her day, when only a few had enough to eat and the foreigners were encroaching from every direction. I asked, "Aren't there still a whole lot of foreigners around here? Are you sure this is so Chinese?"

She chuckled and said, "It's not the same."

Only once more did we refer to what had happened to Jane all those years ago. It was while we were still on the train, in the last moments before it pulled into the Beijing station. I had been shocked by the denouement of her story—not just Electra's guilt, her forcing her story on those two vulnerable young people, but that Jane had been raped by Japanese soldiers. The unfairness of it rankled me; Jane's stoicism, even now, I found inexplicable.

"And yet it happened all the time," Jane told me. "Mostly to Chinese women, of course. And those soldiers thought I was Chinese." She had told her story with quiet dignity. "And think of the great good that arose from such evil." She glanced at Mei, who had wandered over to the window to stare out.

I was sure Mei felt her scars were deep, but I was also sure she realized that she did have happiness and that life wasn't always unfair. She had a son, a son who had always been by her side. Knowing that, if she had a chance to have a different life, would she want it, I wondered? So many horrible things had happened in her past, as with her mother, but there were good things, too, things she never would have known if the bad things hadn't happened. But it was time to put the past behind them.

Jane looked at me, defiant.

"What?" I asked.

"Your documentary film?"

"Forget it. I could never ask you to try to relive that again. I'm finding out I have to draw a line somewhere in this business. Maybe I haven't got the stomach for it, I don't know, but without the whole story..." I broke off and raised my shoulders. Let Tim get his drug story, I thought. I suddenly wanted to help and encourage him on this idea. The thought of working together brought warmth and a feeling of certainty.

After a while, I asked, "Are you so sure Electra told the truth that night?" I spoke quickly, afraid I wouldn't hear the last vital details. Already, Jane was drawn back into the present, darting her glances from side to side as the train slowed, jerked forward, then slowed again. A man's voice blared over the loudspeaker, speaking quickly in the rising and falling tones of Mandarin Chinese.

Jane looked away from the window and spoke almost impatiently. "She was always chatting with Little Gao in the kitchen. He loved her dogs and wanted to play with them. He used to stare at her like she was the most beautiful woman in the world. He probably would have gone with her anywhere, wanted to protect her. Besides, there's the 1919 picture."

"And you don't think she got the shard from Donald?"

Jane shrugged. "That wouldn't make sense to me," she said. "I think Electra's story is the best we're going to get. It's what I believed happened."

"And why were your parents beheaded?"

Jane closed her eyes. "I don't know. I suppose it was some misguided attempt to look like the Boxers. Maybe it really was revenge. Little Gao might have thought of that, mightn't he? Well, he paid for it, whatever he did. As for Electra, whether or not she survived the trip to the States, she had lost everything. Her life must not have been worth living."

"What happened to Will?"

"He was always my brother, no matter what. He stuck by me through all of it, when I was having Mei, afterward. He was interned by the Japanese, survived that, went to the States, got married, had kids. He died in 1979."

"What about Varley? The Li family?"

"I never heard another word about Varley. On one of my first trips back here, I found out that Wutang and Ailian didn't survive the war." Jane sighed. "Miss Ding remarried. So did Han. Like I predicted, it was someone he met in the mountains, back when it took guts and dedication to be a communist. Any other questions? We're almost there."

I grinned. "I have to know. Did you ever find out what happened to that little dog?"

"Lizzie? No. Poor little thing. I suppose one of the servants got careless and let her out that day. There was a market for such valuable dogs."

Jane got up to go over to Mei and I called her back. "Jane?"

She turned around and waited. I said, "Just one more thing. The shard. Why did you keep it?"

Jane looked down, evidently thinking about this. She looked up and said, "I really don't know. There were so many lies. Maybe it was the only thing that told the truth?"

When the train stopped, we gathered up our bags—I insisted on carrying Jane's burgundy bag—and stepped down into Beijing's polluted air. We walked through the station and out into the city. Noise and traffic were all around us despite the early morning hour. Jane stopped and stared. "Good Lord, is there anything left?" she asked.

"Not very attractive, is it?" I said.

"Well…" Jane took a deep breath. "I suppose they've done what they have to do."

Just ahead, Mei had found a taxi driver. They held a rapid exchange; she was obviously haggling with him over the fare. When she saw Jane and me look at her, she held up her thumb. "She's got a good price," Jane said, smiling proudly.

"How did Mei first react to the fact that she is part Japanese?"

"With very little emotion. I felt like I couldn't get through to her, couldn't get past her Chinese-ness. I, who was born here." Again, Jane looked around at the crowded city street.

"I suppose since she's been through so much…"

Jane nodded, then chuckled. "I say she's Chinese, then I remember."

"She seems all Chinese to me."

"She's international. She'll come to realize it in time, I hope. Half-American, half-Japanese, raised as a Chinese." Jane turned suddenly to me. "You know, I think she now has a better understanding of what happened and why it happened. You actually helped me out, do you know that? When I felt I couldn't get through to Mei and she seemed to like you so much, I thought, we'll go over these things again, in your presence. You brought out something in her."

"The story about the nursery song."

Jane nodded. "And other things too, I think."

"Then why did you almost refuse to tell me the ending?"

"It was too much. Besides, I suddenly feared that retelling the story was only going to make things worse. What happened, happened. But I wanted to make it clear that I always loved her, that I might have done some foolish things, but haven't we all?"

Mei signaled us then, drawing us forward with a wave of her arm, laughing in her impatience to get going.

Jane straightened her shoulders. "Peking," she said, looking around. "Now I have come full circle. Now the story is complete."

"It's not quite complete," I said. "Not until we see Han."

"We?" She had her old sarcastic expression on her face again.

As the three of us climbed into the taxi, I said, "You think I'm going to bail out now, before I've heard the complete story?"

"It's all right. I'm content right now, without seeing him."

But I didn't believe her. Jane's cheeks were flushed, her eyes excited. She darted glances from one window to the other, looking out at the city that she swore she didn't recognize.

Later, we were again in a taxi, moving slowly through the congested city center, made famous by all the photographs: Tiananmen Square on the one side, the Forbidden City on the other, Mao's huge features staring down at us from the famous portrait on Tiananmen Gate. Tian An Men, the gate of heavenly peace.

"Behind those walls," Jane said. "That's where the emperor used to live."

"And your house?"

"You go up that street... not that one. It's all so changed." The taxi moved forward again, the driver jerking the wheel suddenly and moving us into another lane.

"That street," Jane said, pointing. "It's up north of there. We'll go there soon. Mei has to see all this. She has to see everything."

The apartment building Li Han lived in was not tall—six or seven stories—and was dwarfed by several much newer buildings around it. Water and pollution stained its outside walls. The balconies were crowded with drying clothes and what looked like bedding.

A boy was waiting for us. He was about twelve, had short, spiky hair, and wore a bright-red pullover and cotton trousers. His face lit up when he saw us climb out of the taxi, and, while I paid the driver, he ran up to Jane, smiling broadly. I didn't hear their first exchange, but I saw Jane's face, which worked with emotion. She gestured toward Mei and said something to the boy in Chinese. Mei grinned and bowed.

"Pippa," said Jane, her voice cracking, "I want you to meet Li Guang-guo, Li Han's grandson. I think I'd know him anywhere just by looking at him."

"How do you do?" the boy said in English, pumping my arm in a strong, eager handshake. Jane's emotion was catching, and I felt a shiver, a rising of the scalp.

The boy led us up two flights of stairs. Two small children crouched on the stairs and stared at us. The youngest began to wail, and a plump young woman darted out of an apartment and picked him up. She watched us as we climbed, absently slapping the child's hand from his nose as she watched. Jane, pausing for breath, nodded to her and greeted her in Chinese. The young woman smiled and replied. Li Han's grandson called out to her, and I caught the Chinese word for America.

"We are relatives come home," Jane said to me.

On the second floor, a door flung open, and a pretty woman in a sweater and slacks grinned widely and greeted us in English. She took Jane's arm and led her through the door. Mei and I followed.

The small room seemed filled with people. I caught glimpses of inexpensive, new-looking furniture: a Formica-covered kitchen table and metal chairs, a sofa covered with a bright quilt, a coffee table, a largish television set on a metal stand. Light from a single set of windows illuminated the room.

Right away, the three of us were surrounded by warmth and curiosity. People grinned at us and nodded. I heard murmurs and exclamations, indrawn breath, and a curiously drawn-out "ahhhhh." It was a friendly sound.

The group parted to reveal an old man sitting in a chair by the window. Now he struggled to stand up. A young woman gripped his arm, helping propel him to his feet. He straightened his shoulders and searched the faces around him, his eyes coming to rest on Jane.

"Li Han," she said, in Mandarin. "You are well?"

"Ah, little sister," he said. "I am well. And you?"

She moved forward and took his hand. He gripped it and put his other hand over hers. Someone rushed to push a chair next to Li Han's and, with gestures, invited Jane to sit. Li Han sank back into his chair and turned to her with a graceful sideways movement. Jane gestured to Mei and me, and we came forward to be introduced. I saw him up close then. His eyes were bright. He stared at me with curiosity.

Later, someone led me to the sofa and I sank down. Li Guang-guo, the grandson, perched at my feet, telling me he spoke English, though many of the others didn't. Never mind, he said, he would be my interpreter.

I smiled and nodded my thanks, and watched the old couple by the window. Li Han was tallish—like many northern Chinese—and thin, as if he had been ill. His shock of still mostly black hair was combed directly back from his forehead. Its color contrasted with the lines on his face. He wore a white shirt with open collar and dark trousers. While he talked to Jane, he kept one hand on his knee and gestured gracefully with the other.

In her chair by his side, Jane leaned toward him, saying little, letting him speak.

A woman brought me food and urged me to eat. Someone else handed me a glass of clear liquid that turned out to be a too-sweet soft drink. I ate and drank, and answered questions put to me in a range of English proficiency. The grandson stayed by my side. Once, toward the end of the visit, he told me Li Han was telling Jane about the day in 1949 when the communists marched into Beijing—Peking, as Jane always called it—Li Han among them.

Li Guangguo laughed. "I don't remember, of course. I was born much later. But there was a siege and hardship and then the communists marched in. The people of Beijing—how do you say it in English?—they take things with a grain of salt. There were songs and floodlights and banners that wished long life to Chairman Mao, but most people knew this was just a good show by the victors. 'Ten thousand years, ten thousand years,' the people who lined the streets shouted. I suppose they had been told how to behave, what to say." The boy lifted his thin shoulders. "And of course some were very happy." He glanced at his grandfather. "But most just wanted to live and eat."

"And now?" I asked.

He looked at me. There was a moment's silence. In my mind, the cheering suddenly stopped.

Then he grinned and waved at the television set. "Now we have a chance to get rich. That's the best of all."

I started laughing. Li Guangguo tilted his head to one side and looked puzzled. "You Chinese," I said. "Money, money, money."

His face split in a broad smile, and he laughed too.

Jane and Mei encouraged me to stay with them for the next several days, so I could learn more about China. I had a few days to kill, anyway, until I was to meet up with Tim. We saw a lot of Li Han. He tended to ask the same questions I did about modern China, though his point of view was 180 degrees from mine. He argued with Jane in a pedantic way that irritated me, though I gradually got used to it. He agreed, nodding vigorously, that China was better off than it had been, but he couldn't accept that conditions now were so desirable. "What did we fight for?" he asked, in his quite good English. "Why did we have a revolution? So we could be like the West? This new economy is causing all kinds of problems. Most of the country is still backward."

His words shocked his children and grandchildren, mainly because he was saying them in front of a foreigner. "China is better, stronger than ever," they argued, keeping their eyes on me as they talked. "Everyone agrees that China will rule the world in the twenty-first century," an older grandson said. "The Americans don't understand this because they don't understand China at all." The grandson began to take on his grandfather's insufferable, pedantic air, and I wanted to laugh at him and burst his balloon.

Li Han laughed. "You don't want these Americans to hear what I say? Is that it?" He said it in English, which irritated the grandson further.

"No one agrees with you, Grandfather," the young man said. "And I still say the Americans don't understand us, don't know who we are."

Jane wasn't afraid to try to puncture his young pomposity. She liked him, because he was Li Han's and because his grandfather also took himself so seriously once, as young people do. She laughed to take the sting out of her words as she asked, "And so? Who are you?" No one answered her.

Li Han stubbornly maintained that China had a lot to learn, but so did America. He reminded Jane that she had missed the most significant period of China's history, and for that reason she was a poor judge of what the grandson called "the modern miracle of present-day China."

Jane was tart in her reply to her old friend: "I'm supposed to wish I'd been here during Mao's time? I suppose you enjoyed yourself during the Cultural Revolution?"

The grandson told her all that mattered to him was the present. Why did she and his grandfather need continuously to wrangle over the past?

Then Li Han's face broke up into that warm, dimpled smile that made me like him again, and he said something nice like, "Dear Jane, you have not changed. You are still my little sister."

They looked at each other, seeing the young Han and Jane of long ago.

On the last day I was with them, we went to Ritan Park: Jane, Li Han, Mei, the older grandson, the twelve-year-old, and me. There was a restaurant in Ritan Park, decorated in an Old-China way, where streams of tourists crowded in to eat the so-so food and stare at the fountains and the rock garden. The main dining hall was chock full of round tables, so close together that waiters and patrons had trouble edging their way among them. The din was terrible; voices rose in many languages—foreign emissaries liked to lunch there—but mostly in English and Chinese.

Beyond the restaurant was the park, a spot of greenery in the midst of the encroaching city, now surrounded mainly by embassies and foreigners' apartments, since this was Beijing's "embassy row." Markets catering mostly to foreigners lined two sides of the park.

But the center of Ritan Park remained Chinese, and prosperous-looking Chinese people crowded into it and strolled across its lawns. Chinese children scrambled up the decorative rocks and called out to each other and to their parents. They scooted across the broad expanse where their distant ancestors used to worship the sun. Fond parents watched or chased after them. Most were single children, as city residents took the government's one-child policy seriously.

We strolled through the park to look at the remains of the ancient temple. There wasn't much to see, so we stood awhile, and then looked for a place to sit. Han's young grandson spotted a bench not far away. "Let's go here, Grandfather," he said, and took Han's arm and led him to the bench. Mei came hurrying up behind Jane and took her arm as Jane settled herself on the bench next to Li Han. Another old man, already sitting on the bench, nodded politely, then settled down, folded his hands, closed his eyes, and prepared to sleep in the sun.

Mei, the two grandsons, and I settled ourselves on the grass a few feet from the bench. The scene was unexpectedly peaceful, and I half-closed my eyes too, enjoying the spring sun on my face and dreaming of doing a documentary on former Red Guards—where were they now? Nearby, a Chinese father helped his daughter launch a kite. The girl was about five years old, dressed in bright-red slacks and sweater. She laughed excitedly while her father unraveled the long string and the kite began its ascent into the blue sky.

At that moment, an old woman wandered by, walking somewhat un-steadily. Through my half-closed eyes, I watched. Her gray hair was pulled back in an untidy bun, her face was creased with wrinkles, and she wore the faded blue jacket and trousers of the Maoist era. Shielding her eyes against the sun, she studied all of us.

"See that old woman?" the older grandson whispered to me. "She must be from the country, wearing clothes like that." He sounded embarrassed. I realized I had seen few people dressed in the Maoist clothes that were ubiquitous in pictures of Communist China even just a few years earlier.

Unexpectedly, the old woman began to sing. Her voice, sharp and cracked, but strong, split the air, rising above the calls and shrieks of the children in the park. People turned and stared at her. Some glanced at each other and giggled, a few looked annoyed. Seated beside me on the grass, Han's older grandson shuffled a little and stared at his Nike-clad feet. He shot a glance at his grandfather, who was watching the woman, his face impassive. The old man on the bench next to him kept his eyes shut.

"What is she saying?" I whispered to the grandson.

"It is nothing. An old song."

"What are the words?"

He looked uncomfortable, glanced at his grandfather again, then chanted:

"Without the Communist Party,
There is no new China."

He frowned at the old woman and twirled his fingers beside his head. "She is crazy, of course. Look at her."

"Poor thing," I said.

The woman wandered into the crowd and disappeared. The father went back to unraveling the kite string. The little red-clad girl turned her face to the sky to watch, her fat little face split in a delighted smile.

I glanced at Jane and Li Han, both looking at the place in the crowd where the old woman had disappeared. Then Han turned back and looked at Jane. When their eyes met, they both smiled. True friendship endures all, I thought.

The grandson shuffled uncomfortably on the grass and darted a look at his watch. Mei had taken some of Jane's family photos out of her handbag and was showing them to twelve-year-old Li Guangguo. A bevy of well-dressed Chinese children raced by, shrieking. The old man next to Han smiled in his sleep but didn't wake up.

"Han, look," I heard Jane say. I didn't see what Jane pointed at, but Han did. He replied in Chinese.

I remembered Jane saying to me on the train, "Life comes round in cycles, doesn't it?"

I pulled the Tang Dynasty poetry book out of my bag and rubbed my hand over the cover. I flipped through the pages, smelling the newness of the paper, then reached the back of the book where I discovered that Tim had written something. "I hope you enjoy the book," he wrote, "Can't wait to see you in Beijing, where you can show me which poems you liked the best." My heart raced as I looked up from the book, thinking we would see each other the very next day.

I watched as the little girl's father finally got the kite into the air. It turned and twisted as it rose high above the park, where it could see both the tall, new buildings going up all over town and the geometric grid that was the old Peking.

TRANSLATION SOURCES

Cover: Tony Barnstone, Willis Barnstone, and Xu Haixin, trans.,
Laughing Lost in the Mountains: Poems by Wang Wei
(Hanover, NH: University Press of New England, 1991), 86.

xiii: Barnstone, Barnstone, and Xu Haixin, *Laughing Lost*, 76.